Praise F

"Sometimes you begin rea... exact book you always wished someone would write. *The Gospel of Salome* instantly rang all those bells for me, giving us full, complicated, flawed people who also happen to be central characters of the gospels. In just-barely-CE Alexandria, Salome — a fierce survivor and healer — begins to tell the story of how she gave up her infant son, a boy named Yeshua, to a couple from Nazareth. From there the mess of humanity rolls on. Brilliantly written on all levels (psychological, dramatic, lyrical), this is a phenomenal novel."

— Rebecca Makkai, author of *The Great Believers* and *I Have Some Questions For You*

"I loved the dark beauty of Kaethe Schwehn's *The Gospel of Salome*. It has all the scope and depth of vast history, and all the intimacy and emotion of detailed imagination. Schwehn's language brings an incredible range of characters and places to life, pairing poetic force and narrative suspense for a story that will have you torn between flying through the pages and lingering over every word. An astonishing achievement."

— V.V. Ganeshananthan, author of *Brotherless Night* and *Love Marriage*

"Kaethe Schwehn utterly transported me to a different time and place. The hypnotic quality of her writing and the compelling story of Salome created the perfect storm in this propulsive narrative that speaks to both modern and ancient sensibilities. Salome touched my soul as a character."

— Renée Ahdieh, *New York Times* Bestselling Author of *The Wrath & The Dawn* trilogy

"*The Gospel of Salome* startles readers with an alternative story of Jesus' birth, ministry, and death. Carefully crafted and meticulously researched, Schwehn's novel explores a range of spiritual questions some may fear to ask. But Salome's tale haunts -- and you will be mulling over her account of the Good News long after you close the book. This one is powerful and original. Take up and read."

— Diana Butler Bass, author of *Freeing Jesus* and *A Beautiful Year*

"The narrative moves like a metronome through time. Salome's memories are a warm window into her formative years learning medicine. Indeed, the prose shimmers thanks to her organic details about the biology of the human body... *The Gospel of Salome* is an enthralling biblical novel in which a woman reckons with her past, helping a man choose what story he should tell the world."

— *Foreword Reviews*

"An extraordinary novel shaped by the kind of rare imagination that brooks no limits. Inside the outlines of a story familiar to many of us, Schwehn has conjured an utterly original and vivid tale of agency, of callings, of self-definition, of suffering and love and devotion— so that reading this novel feels like digging up a well-trod path to discover, beneath, a whole subterranean ocean. This is a gorgeous, daring book, and I loved it." — Clare Beams, author of *The Garden* and *The Illness Lesson*

"*The Gospel of Salome* is a bold and beautiful reimagining... In this richly rendered tale, Kaethe Schwehn breathes life into Salome, a complex figure with her own compelling voice and vision."

— Rebecca Kanner, author of *Sinners and the Sea* and *The Last One Seen: A Thriller*

"*The Gospel of Salome* is not a canonical book; you will not find it in your Bible. What you will find in Kaethe Schwehn's novel is the depth of sensory detail and rich emotion that are lacking in the gospels written by Mark and other early Christians. Evocative, intricate, and poetically crafted prose draws Schwehn's readers into first century Mediterranean life and into Salome's story."

— L. DeAne Lagerquist, Emerita Professor of Religion at St. Olaf College

◈ The Gospel of ◈
SALOME

Kaethe Schwehn

Copyright © 2025 Kaethe Schwehn

Design by Melody Stanford Martin

Map artwork by Christopher Coffey

Published by Wildhouse Fiction, an imprint of Wildhouse Publishing (www.wildhousepublishing.com). No part of this book may be reproduced in any manner without the written permission from the publisher, except in brief quotations embodied in critical articles or reviews. Contact info@wildhousepublishing.com.

Printed in the USA

All Rights Reserved

Print ISBN: 978-1-961741-22-5
eBook ISBN: 978-1-961741-24-9

For Thisbe and Matteus

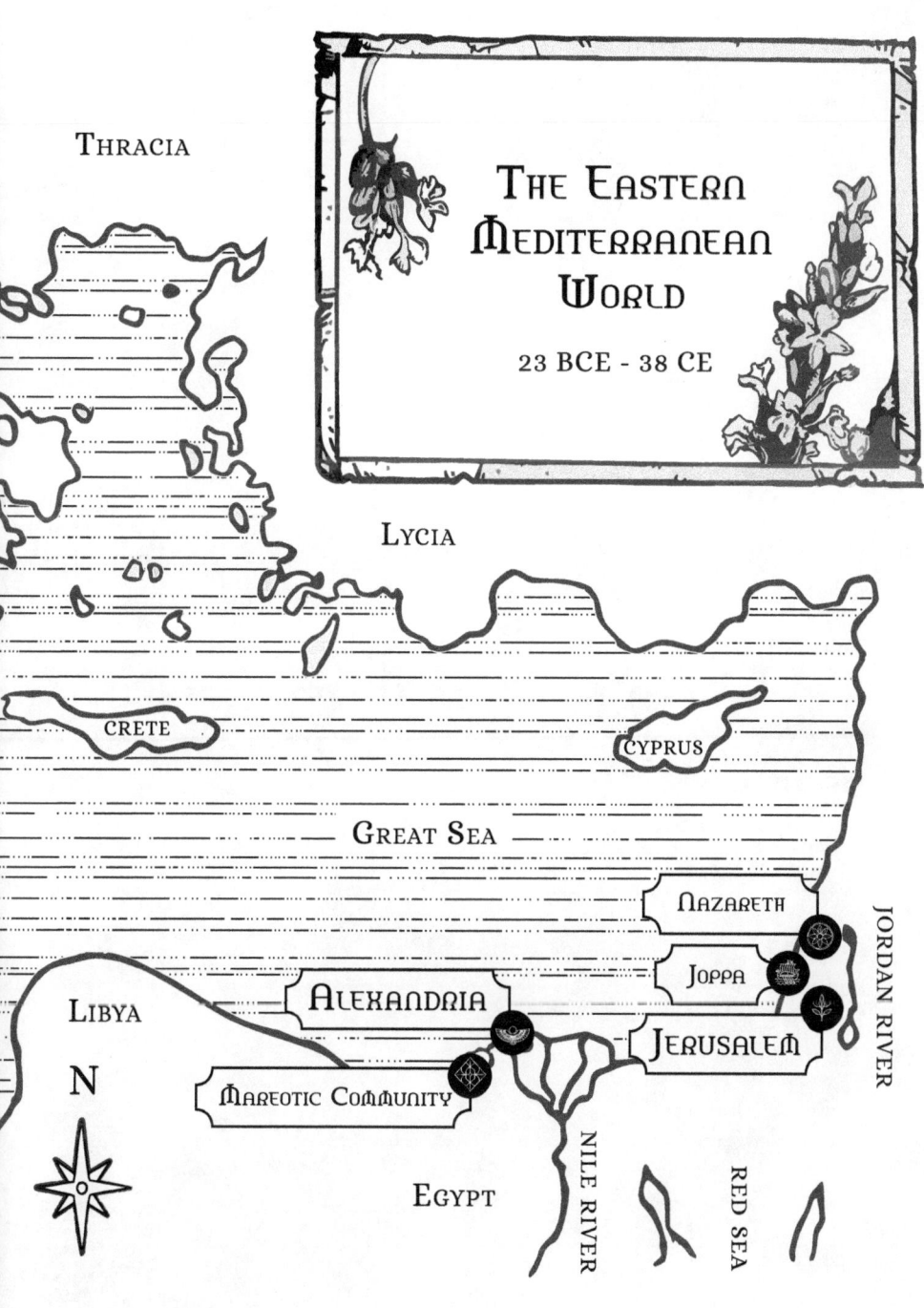

Characters

Greece
Aria, Lyra's mother
Lyra's father
Anatolis Manatos, a wealthy landowner

Alexandria
Flaccus, Roman governor of Alexandria
Herod Agrippa, Jewish king of Judea
Gaius Caligula, emperor of Rome

John Mark, a First Follower
Asha, a wig maker
Lilo, a caller
Milos, a student physician
Nicodemus, a fish seller
Carabbas, a beggar
Alexander, a clinic owner
Nadjem, a physician
Albion, a physician
Castor, a physician
Sarah, a Jewish woman

Philo, a Jewish philosopher
Broom Boy, Philo's servant
The Jewish elders: Levi, Judah, Elisha, Benjamin, Eleazar, and Zeloph
Trypho, a merchant
Xenia, a hermit
Hamish, a cart driver

Nazareth
Mari
Josef
Yeshua
Abraham, a rabbi and Mari's father (deceased)
Simon, Mari's stillborn child
Ezra, Josef's cousin from Alexandria

Nathan, a shepherd
Aaron, a baker
Judah, owner of blind chickens
Caleb, a man with a withered arm
Asa, a man with a cough (and cheese!)
Asaph, a man with an aching tooth and walking pains
Anna, a widow with a twisted spine
Eden, the goat

Rome
Augustus, emperor of Rome
Livia, Augustus's wife and Julia's stepmother

Julia, Augustus's daughter
Marcus Vipsanius Agrippa, Julia's first husband (deceased)
The children of Julia and Agrippa: Lucius, Gaius, Little Julia, Agrippa
    Postumus, Agrippina
Tiberius, Julia's second husband, Livia's son, and future emperor
Vipsania, Tiberius's first wife

Julia's slaves: Maia, Nona, Juba, Abel, Pulco, Cassia, Luca
Julia's lovers: Iullus Antonius and Cornelius Scipio

Rufus, a physician
Phillipos, a surgery owner

"Jesus said: No prophet is accepted in his or her own village.
No physician heals those who know him."
— *The Gospel of Thomas*, 31

"Jesus said: Blessed is the one who is disturbed by her discovery.
That one has found life."
— *The Gospel of Thomas*, 58

"Then Jesus gave a loud cry and breathed his last. And the curtain of the temple was torn in two, from top to bottom ... There were also women looking on from a distance; among them were Mary Magdalene, and Mary the mother of James the younger and of Joses, and Salome."
— *The Gospel of Mark*, 15:37–40

Many historians believe that the historical Jesus
was born sometime between 6 and 4 BCE.
This novel reflects that assumption.

GREECE

23 BCE - 10 BCE

I was born on a cliff overlooking the Ionian Sea, birthed to the sound of gulls dropping mussels from great heights to salvage the meat inside. My mother loved me with stories and songs; my father loved me by not escaping on a sea that could have taken him anywhere.

I learned to count watching our sixty sheep cross from pasture to pen, touching each fuzzed back with a stick. We had a pasture and a stream of fresh water and a path that switched back and forth down the side of our promontory to the sea. We paid for these good things with our distance from others. A one-and-a-half-hour walk to Elis, the next town, and forty-five minutes to the nearest neighbor. So I grew up knowing only my mother and father.

I have been obsessed with bodies as long as I can remember. I rubbed salve into my mother's sunburned face so I could feel the knobs of her cheekbones; I pressed the silver stems of her earrings through her lobes over and over again and licked the perspiration along my mother's hairline like a kitten. Had we lived near others I'm sure my mother would have taught me how to be a proper woman sooner. Instead I pissed on rocks and shells and sand to see if the texture changed the scent; I rubbed honey on my shins and let different insects sting me just to see how big the welts would bloom.

When I turned ten and my mother and I began to accompany my father to Elis more frequently, I was finally presented with rules: cover up, look away, lips closed, limbs in. But a body can go in so many directions. I stared in amazement at the people of Elis, who seemed to try, everywhere they went, to turn their bodies into pillars.

Because there were only three of us, we had to make good use of everything: the daylight hours, the strength in our muscles, each tangle of wool, each spoonful of oil. Work wasn't a burden to me: it was simply the way my parents raised my body to be in the world. When we had a long, slow task before us, my mother told stories: Persephone and the ruby seeds, Medusa and her coiling hair, Actaeon and his ravenous dogs. The gods explained the way the world worked—why the rain fell like a soft curtain one day and spit pellets of ice the next, why my father's left leg ached with the bloom of each new moon, why one of the new sparrows had fallen from the nest before its wing feathers grew in. While she spoke, we picked out blackened lentils or carded the wool. My mother was gentle; she chastised me with the content of her tales rather than the sharpness of her voice. My father didn't speak much to me at all, at least not in Greek. He had a complicated collection of mouth sounds he used with the sheep—clicks and tsks, kissing noises and whistles. When I was born, he used these to communicate with me as well.

My father spoke more to my mother than he did to me, but almost always it was simply her name coupled with *please* or *thank you*.

"Aria, thank you" after porridge.

"Aria, please" when he had a sheep settled and it was her turn to do the work with the shears.

He used the same phrases at night in our cottage when I had my back to them. "Aria, please," he said first, his voice coming out stretched and thin. And then, a few minutes later, "Aria, thank you," his voice slow and soft.

He was always kind to her; only once I saw him beat her. She and I were down on the beach scouring the cooking pots with sand. She was telling me the story of Arachne and I was acting out all of the parts. I stood on a piece of driftwood as Athena, arms first crossed over my chest in consternation and then swirling in the air as I changed Arachne from expert weaver into tiny spider. My father spotted us before we spotted him. He grabbed me by the arm and pulled me out into the sea; the cold water made me cry out more than his tight grip. When the water reached my thighs, he took both of my ears in his hands and said, "You're not a god," then pushed me backward, off-balance. A wave broke across my face, and I took in a breath of saltwater. He held me down, though I don't know whether he meant to drown me or to hide my face to save me from immortal wrath. But before another wave could break, my mother attacked, biting his arm until he released me and I sank, terrified and thrashing, certain I would die.

Then I remembered the water was shallow; I could stand. When my mother saw me upright, coughing, only then did she release her jaws. There was a moment when my parents stood facing each other, blood thinned by water slipping down my father's forearm. My mother's nipples pressed defiantly against the wet fabric of her stola. Then a wave scooted me forward so that I was closer to shore and my parents became mere shadows, dark cutouts of a man and woman. The sun on the horizon was a thing they held between them. He slapped her then, his arm a dark slash through the light. Afterward she turned to face me, her body blocking the sun, and I could see her features: long lashes, small chin, cheeks browned and toughened by the sun. She reached out her arms to me. She was my mother again.

My father blamed me for everything that happened afterward. Traced it to that moment. He never said so, but I knew. His violence at the edge of the sea was his way of trying to erase my hubris, to put me in my place, to flood me with humility. His actions had the opposite effect. I'd assumed the gods wouldn't care about a girl's actions on a lonely beach, the press of her feet into a softened log, the way she lifted her chin to meet the clouds. But my father's reaction meant I had more power than I thought. I could disturb the world.

I didn't know my parents beyond age twelve, so I never got to see them as complex, never heard much about their pasts. Never thought to ask. I am not so nostalgic as to pronounce my childhood one of happiness. It was one of rightness, which is different than happiness, and stronger.

My father believed everything that went wrong began, as I have said, on the day I imitated the gods on the beach. But it began with my mother's first sick cough. That first cough happened when I was still inside her. You don't believe me. That's fair. But I remember the slosh and roll of her womb interrupted by an abrupt rise and fall, like a wagon wheel catching on a rock. It was a tic, a jolt, a catch. Then I was returned to gentleness.

Her coughs became a background to my childhood, like the gulls and the sea and the snorting of the sheep. I listened to my mother's chest each morning. Sometimes the cough was cloudy, sometimes it was clear; sometimes the passage of the air into her lungs was full, and at other times it was thin and wheezing. At night I added mint leaves to white willow and hot water, soaked a rag in the concoction, and laid it in the rift between her breasts. She tolerated this, but her main defense against the creeping illness was her libations to the gods. She bought amulets and rocks, tiny pewter jars with heroic stories carved into their flanks. It wasn't just the famous gods she knew but smaller deities too, Aceso and Aegle and Epione and even ones said to linger on our isthmus alone. When a relapse came, she didn't forget the gods but doubled her enthusiasms, proclaiming her gratitude in whispered prayers at intervals throughout the day. The inside of our house was simple, spare. Two stuffed mattresses. A brazier and soot-stained walls. Dried herbs hung from rafters, and a few amphoras and a trunk held our other belongings. But our household altar swelled with the residue of incense; the stain of fallen petals; hard, tiny moons of wax. The altar was a living thing, its surface overstuffed, so that in the darkness it felt inhabited by all of the ones to whom she prayed. I was a child then, and one who loved her mother. And so, of course, I matched my own belief to hers.

Once we started going to the market in Elis, my mother made a habit of offering me a coin if I was good so I could buy an apricot or sweet or pin for my unruly hair. To stymie thieves, my father taught me how to curl my hand around the coin with fingers straight. He said, "The greatest men hold on to things in such a way that common men don't realize they are holding anything at all." And I'd head off obediently and return, pleased to show the way I'd navigated all the people and returned with a prize to share, like Jason with his golden fleece.

But one day when my mother's cough had increased to the point where she could barely catch a breath, she sent me off with a larger sum of money. The largest I had ever held at once. "I need a single pearl," she said. "When I talked to the ancient last month, she said to bury a pearl below a nest of kindling and sage. The burning will attract the eye of Panacea, who will see the pearl and vest it secretly with what I need to heal. When all is ash, I am to place the pearl in wine and drink it. When the pearl passes through my body, the cough will be inside it." And so I went to find the pearl to make my mother well.

But on the way, I passed a clinic for the sick. I didn't know it by the sign (snake curled around a staff crudely carved into a plank of wood): I knew it by the open door and the line of people outside of it. Everyone else in Elis was doing their best, as I have said, to walk like pillars, straight and narrow. I noticed the people in this line because they hunched and sprawled, held their limbs at odd angles, bent backwards as though their eyes might roll from their sockets if they stood. At the end of the line, a woman on all fours coughed and coughed until she expelled a glob of blood, and then she used a stick to poke at it as though the tinted phlegm could divine her certain future. I didn't know the woman, but I knew the cough. It matched my mother's perfectly.

Remember, I wasn't proper then but feral and didn't understand that people line their bodies up to wait, just one way humans try to show that they are civilized. I passed into the clinic house and no one caught me, but I paused upon the threshold to let my eyes adjust. A dirty groaning man lay upon a couch. Beside him, sitting upright with both feet squarely on the floor, a balding man placed a cup upside down upon the sick man's abdomen. Another man stood at the ill man's head, passing more cups to the balding sitting one. The standing man had thick black hair upon his head, along his lip, high up his cheekbones; I could even see hairs springing from his ears. His hand and forearms, though, were hairless, and I wondered whether he shaved them and whether clean-shaven hands could better heal the creep of a disease. Once he'd handed all the cups, he took a sponge on a long pole and started blotting at the floor.

"Get out," the sitting one said evenly. The hairy one looked up and for the first time noticed me. He pushed the sponge in my direction.

"You have to wait like all the rest," he said.

"There's nothing to be done about your face," the physician said, though I was certain he hadn't looked at me.

I didn't move. I watched the way the sick man's body responded to the presence of the cups. His groaning eased, his breathing quieted. He let his tightened eyelids flutter open. "There," he said, "that does it." It was lovely, I thought, the way the attempt to heal was followed so closely by the healing. With prayer you never knew. Always a lag of time between the supplication and the effect inside the body. My mother always said she knew, could feel the press of Hygieia's generosity around her lungs, the scraps of Iaso's mercy in her throat. I wasn't sure. But I knew I liked this place immediately, the way it offered a result. Or maybe no result at all, but then at least you knew to try a different course or fetch the burial wrap. Either way, you no longer lived inside the waiting.

"I'm here to help my mother's cough," I said abruptly, "and I can pay." I flipped my hand and was proud of the way the light caught the coin and flicked it at their eyes.

"You'll have to bring her here," the hairy one said, though not unkindly. Then he placed one clean white hand on my bare neck and sent me on my way.

Remember, I was only ten and so the disappointment lasted briefly. I knew I'd never coax my mother here. That much was certain. And so I blinked and sniffed, then made my way between the stalls in search of her single pearl; I passed barley and lentils, lamps and herbs, cups of clay and cups of stone. A hill of olives that dripped thick rainbows of oil. I let the beast scents stick to me: brine of oyster and the thicker scent of butchered lamb, sea monsters scaled with eyes still gleaming. I watched the human bodies, too: how far whiskers grew down the necks of the men, which leg a woman favored. Some children followed me and called me *cur* and *cunt* and *dirty*, but their teeth were rotten and so their curses grew no legs. Then I entered the area of adornments: body jewels and flax tunics and stolas swaying from old wooden bars so that wind could fill their figures. A woman sold sandals beside a man who could fit you with a wooden leg or finger; I touched the calfskin leather braces, but he growled me away. At the end of the aisle a woman dipped her necklaces in water to magnify the shimmer.

"Ah, ah, ah," she said as I tried not to catch her eye, "I have a necklace that will make sense of that face."

I wondered what face it was that she could mean, thought it strange that two people in one day had made mention of the strangeness of a face to me. She drew me to her with a finger and laid the necklace over me so that it bit into my skin. Then the woman raised a sheet of polished metal, and for the first time in my life I saw myself.

My eyes were gold, my lips were thin. My nose was long and cut me evenly in half. My chin did not observe the gentle tuck my mother's chin possessed but pressed down to a jutting point. The children who had called me names, the physician and the jeweler—it was the spots they noticed when they saw me. Twelve in all, I counted, each no bigger than a fig seed, as though a god had dipped his hand in shit and flicked his wrist my way. Or perhaps the spots were portents, like a scattering of dice or the sprinkled clots of entrails. Some truth, I knew, was written on my skin.

I wasn't civilized, but I was smart enough to know a girl with marks across her face would get no dowry. This was a relief to me; I had no interest in living in a house beyond our hilltop, no warm thought of sweeping my own floor, a mewling babe upon my hip. Hestia, my mother's favorite goddess, was dull to me, the way she spent the day scraping Zeus's hearth and gathering up the pleas of women whose babes refused to suck. I saved my murmurings for Artemis, and sometimes when life got cold and dull and the days droned on, I even prayed to Ares for a skirmish, just something to disrupt banality. But my longing never lasted. The pull of sea, the needs of sheep were enough most times to keep my mind in check.

But now I understood my father's gruffness, my mother's worry at the lowering cost of wool. A son could build a house nearby and slowly shoulder the running of our enterprise. A daughter's marriage could bring prestige or wealth. With me there'd be no wedding and no labor; I was just a never-ending mouth to feed. And still my parents had been kind to me.

I looped the necklace off my head and asked her for a pearl, so distracted by the sight of my own face that I forgot and showed the money before the woman showed the wares. And so the pearl I got was tiny, not round and full of light but just a small white seed.

Sobbing, I made my slow way back to our stall. My father wouldn't look. My mother, worried, set her loom aside and pulled me onto her lap. "Did someone put their hands on you?" she asked.

What could I say? That I had failed to be a child that would be of any use? I showed the pearl instead, tiny white scar at the center of my palm. "It's too small," I said. "The gods won't even see it."

My mother smoothed my hair and kissed my cheeks. "Never presume to know what gods can see," she said. She held on to me. And that made me cry harder.

I will not draw the next part of my story out. How I turned from ten into eleven into twelve and my mother's cough got worse and worse until she couldn't walk beyond the outskirts of our house. How she lay upon her cot and tried to help until the end: sorting lentils, twisting her spindle, carving letters into dirt so I could learn a little, her soft voice echoing the movement of the stick:

"Delta is a house for a nymph to live inside
Psi is for our own two hands, reaching towards the sky
Omega makes a shoe for a fancy horse to wear
and Sigma is the broken back of—"

And there she would stop, feigning lack of breath, though I was certain it was the words themselves she wanted to hide from me, some truth she thought I couldn't shoulder.

It is still hard to say the words *my mother died*. No matter how you age, there is a part of you that's unbelieving. The sound of your first heartbeat disappears and the world, I swear, is quieter thereafter.

I'd never seen a body robbed of pneuma. All the bodies I had known had been alive. My father put a coin below my mother's tongue to buy her passage over the Styx, and then he brought a long flax sheet to wind her in. I screamed and kicked and pummeled at his thighs until he lit a candle on our household altar and said, "I will give you one night with your grief, and after that it's back to work." Then he plucked a pinch of lavender from the rafters just above his hand and rubbed it down to dust between his fingers. I didn't know the rituals the dead deserve, and so I made my own. I ground mint and white willow with fresh lavender, added oil, and smeared it on her chest so her cough would not go with her. I lifted her shoulders from the cot and propped her up so I could do her hair: two parallel parts and one long plait wound tight around itself. Clean, I felt that she should be, so I hauled fresh water from our spring and swished rosemary between my palms to release its fragrant oil. And I washed her: feet and calves and thighs and hips, belly and ribs and breast and armpits and all the swatches of skin in between. Each part stiffened as my fingers left it. Now, of course, I know the way a body goes rigid just on the heels of death, but then I thought it was my hands' own doing. I couldn't believe they'd betray me in this way. If I was possessed with power, why couldn't I push life back into her instead of pulling all the softness, all the gentleness right out?

You will think me heartless, but even as I honored her, I paid attention to the parts of her I'd never seen so still so long. The wrinkled, puckered skin below her navel, the tiny hairline cuts along her cuticles, the fruity scent inside her mouth. I touched her crotch-wool and the cool, dry wedges of skin between her toes. And when it was time to sleep, I took my tunic off and pressed my skin to hers. I knew that she was dead, but I also knew, from the stories that she told, that sometimes death could be undone; I hoped that somehow in my dreams my breath would fill her and revive her. Or perhaps the gods would see us as one body, place us in the heavens as a star, just like Orion, so my father could look up and see us, grinning out of reach.

I woke in time to watch my father carry her wrapped body to the starkest edge of the promontory, the place where, as a child, I was forbidden to go since an unruly gust of wind could push a child over. There was no beach below, only the waves angry with the rocks for not letting them farther in.

He dropped her.

Without ceremony. Without waking me. Without letting me tuck dried hibiscus in the sheet. By the time I reached my father's side there was only sea again. When he turned to look at me, I realized I was naked.

"Shame on you," he said. "Cover up and do the chores."

Those are the last words he spoke that I let pass into me; I made myself that day a kind of shell. We lived together two years more, but the other phrases that he uttered I took as bunch grass: wild but harmless, they offered little sustenance.

My mother and I did not become a constellation. She did not breathe again or stroke my hair. The tiny pearl and all her other offerings did nothing except pave her way to death with interesting baubles. And so the first chore I undertook was to erase every bit of all that dumb, false hope. The candles and the incense bowls, the tiny terra-cotta statues, the amulets and gems and sticks of half-burnt herbs: I took all these to the edge of the promontory and let them fall. Maybe they could do for her in Hades what they could never do on earth. If my father noticed, he didn't say a word; his belief in all the gods was grounded in his fear of unbelief.

We made our way through my mother's absence without stories, without song. For the first time in my life, I began to see the world as untainted with the fingertips of the divine. Maybe the sea was just the sea. Maybe nymphs did not laze amid the streamers of the willows. Maybe no one sent the wind that thumbed our cheeks and screamed through every open crevice of our house. My mother's death had lifted off divinity's grimy residue. What remained was raw-boned but true.

After my mother died, work was no longer coupled to her stories, no longer simply a thing my body did to fill the daylight hours. Now each duty contained her absence: stacking wood beside the fire grate, boiling the grains for porridge, cleaning the wool in tubs of heated water. Each day I took the finest rug my mother had woven and beat it with a broom, then placed it neatly on the floor so it would cover up the last few figures that she had taught me, those letters carved in dirt.

I learned to tame my hair, and when my monthly bleeding started, I pressed the rags into a broken pot and hid it underneath the corner of a mat until I could find a time to wash them. Each night my father turned his back to me and made a tsk-tsk sound to acknowledge I was there. I said good night, but more and more I felt that I lived only with myself.

The sheep did provide some comfort, Ajax with his jaunty prance and Isis who chewed only if she stood within spitting distance of Apollo. Dite was my favorite. My father had found her, right after birth, having climbed the wrong side of her mother in search of teat. The spent ewe lay on her side, eyes flickering, but Aphrodite sat primly on her mother's flank, "like she'd come into the world that way, all frothy on a bed of foam, just like the goddess," whispered my father in the darkness of our cottage. And then he scooped me up from my own bed and carried me through the night to see the newborn lamb. Dite gave me my father's tenderness that once. But also, if I laid flat my palm for her, she set her chin upon it, not to nose for food or scent as did the other sheep but, I let myself believe when I was loneliest, out of love for me.

A few weeks after my mother's death, Anatolis Manatos, a wealthy Greek from Elis, began to erect a country villa upon our land. Well, not our land. The pasture where we grazed our sheep wasn't ours exactly, but because we lived so far from Elis, the wealthy Manatos had never paid us any mind. Now he wanted a summer escape, and so the space was his to claim. Although it was Manatos's fault that our sheep were squeezed into a smaller space, my father also blamed the Romans, who he claimed lived only to press us into oily oblivion. Our true parcel of land was rocky and modest; there wasn't nearly enough vegetation to feed the sheep year-round.

So we watched the villa slowly rise, the pale arm of a column, the ribbed crest of a portico, like a man rising out of the sea to devour us. We watched. My father was certain our path to destitution would be slow but sure. I didn't disagree.

The gods must roll with laughter when humans believe they know which tragedy will choose them. Summer turned to fall, and fall slipped into winter. But winter refused to budge, held on with sharpened claws. I wore my child's stola underneath my mother's, and my father brought raw wool into our cottage so we could stuff it into every crack that leaked the frigid air. The wool needed to be spun but the house was either too smoky or too cold, and if I tried to spin beside the sea, my fingers hardened into points. So I took to warming stones in the brazier, then settling myself on the aft side of the house where the wind was less but there was no view of the water. I'd cup the stones until my fingers softened enough to feel the thickness of the wool, then I'd spin until the chill had rendered my hands stiff and white again.

During the brief pauses to warm, I observed the sheep. They moved cloudlike through the green, never fast enough to truly catch the eye, but while my head was turned to work, they drifted so that by the time I looked again, they were configured in a slightly different pattern. It was a comfort knowing time was passing but not speeding downhill like a cart untethered from a horse.

One day when the temperatures had risen and I'd just begun to melt the coldness from my joints, I noticed that Isis and Apollo moved strangely, at an odd angle, snouts tipped to earth and rears rising high. I kept turning the rod and letting the wool ease through my fingers, but I did not look down, and soon it snagged. I set my work aside. Perhaps the sheep were simply feeling the first smudge of warmer weather, the cheekiness that comes with springtime. I walked toward them.

They were not teasing me or playing coy with one another. They were sick. Thick saliva coated the corners of their mouths and dangled in ropy strands. I was afraid to touch them and equally afraid to leave them while I ran to tell my father, lest they contaminate the herd. I shrieked to my father from the shed (where he'd been bundling the wool for sale) and he came, storming curses, drawing his shearing knife from his belt. He straddled one sheep and then the other, slitting each throat and then dropping each body to the ground.

When it was done, he sat back on his heels. His panting had replaced my primal shriek. Behind us the rest of the sheep dotted the field like Circe's pigs, and beyond them a few young pines trembled as the workers eased them into pockets of earth near the villa. It wasn't the blood or the newly dead bodies that frightened me so much as his lack of hesitation. He knew these sheep would not get better.

My father traced a circle around the bodies and then carried each carcass to the cliff edge and dropped it into the depths. He didn't let me shear them first. Although I knew my mother's spirit had passed on, I couldn't fight the image of her lying at the bottom of the sea, Isis and Apollo floating down to her like cottonwood but stained with blood.

We built rough mounds of stones above the places where their bodies had bled to keep the other sheep from licking the clotted earth, but it didn't work. By summer's end we had lost all but seven of our sheep. We went on drawing circles in the earth and piling mounds of stones to mark them, but after the death of the first two sheep, my father let me shear them before we rolled their stubbled bodies to the sea. The water I used to wash the wool turned pink and pink again, and still when I laid the fleeces out to dry the ghost of rust remained.

"We'll have to dye it, then, before we sell," my father said, though where we'd get the money for the color or who'd teach me amounts and times and the temperatures, he didn't say.

Instead he went to Elis more and more. He said it was to hear from others what they knew about this sickness in our sheep, if we could somehow stop its spread. Then it was to look for buyers for our herd. He fancied for a week that he could pick up another trade. How difficult could it be to work some leather into belts or make a dovecote so the rich could have their offerings? Those were the earlier days of spring when only a handful of the sheep had been lost. His musings offered hope: perhaps not all was lost.

But often just at waking, I mistook the sound of sea waves for my mother's rheumy breath, and despair settled into me again.

As summer nestled its hot white days upon us, my father left for days on end. He didn't bother to explain his trips to me. I knew his motives were now more desperate: wine and dice and women. When fall arrived, we'd have to pay our tax to Rome. Something in me knew he was determined we'd have nothing left to give them.

The work he left to me. Our days had been full with three of us working, and exhausting when my mother died and we were only two. With only one of me it was impossible, although our dwindling flock eased my labors some. Still, they needed to be watered, let out to graze, and gathered in again. The pen and shed needed cleaning, or else the stench settled thickly over our whole hill. And because my father was gone so often, I learned the work of how to slaughter, though the first time I straddled a sick ewe and felt her fearful breath between my knees I forgot my shunning of the gods and said a prayer to Ares, for bravery in a skirmish. Most wars are fought this way, not with swords and spears and men slit nave to nose but hungry people squaring up against the light of each new day, simply trying to make it to the other side. You know this. Then there was wood to gather and porridge to make and pots to scrub and floors to sweep. Our supply of barley dwindled. The lamp oil I had to thin. The few times that I caught a fish I ate it raw because it seemed a waste of time to cook it.

At that time of the year most of my daylight hours should have been spent carding the wool, but, as I have said, much of it was stained. Instead of returning from Elis with dye, my father had returned with nits and alcohol-soaked skin and rage that coiled in his belly and made him strike out abruptly at the door frame, at the fence post, once even at a sickened ram before he slit its throat. I gave him a wide berth and pushed the edges of our property to find what I might use to craft a dye myself. Crumbling red stone I tried and boiled olive skins, the rind of pomegranate, and the leaves of almond trees. Even lavender. Although I knew it had no potent color, it gave me an afternoon with the scent my mother had loved.

There was, just on the other side of the almost-completed villa, a patch of wild violet. I knew it bloomed this time of year because when I was little, I'd rip the petals off and adhere them to my forehead with sweat. So one afternoon, with my father off at Elis and all the workers resting in the shade the columns of the portico now lent them, I ventured down to find the flowers. On the way I checked the seven remaining sheep, all still free and clear of the disease. Well, I checked six of them—Dite I couldn't bear to lose just yet, though if I am honest with my memory, it's possible that as I passed her I could hear the churning gravel sound that traveled from her throat. I didn't let it register; my mind was on the violets.

They were there, just where I thought they'd be. I used my shearing knife to cut them at the root and filled a small amphora, pleased to see the way the tint of purple stained my fingertips a little. Of course, I should have turned on my heel and trotted obediently back toward home. But the violets grew near the stream that had been mine for fourteen years. Ever since the villa work had begun, we'd had to follow a sickly winding trail from our cottage to a single spot to fill our buckets and to bathe. The spot was rocky, wide, and shallow (it barely rose above my ankles in the summer), and so to bathe or fill took far more time than those tasks should.

Clutching my amphora, I followed the stream the opposite direction to my favorite place, a deep pool with a rock just close enough for jumping and for sunning. I shimmied off my stola and set the amphora and knife gently in the folds, and then I leaped. The bottom silt was soft. The water skimmed the heat and sweat right off me, and when I surfaced, I felt like a crescent moon. I pulled myself onto the rock and stretched my body long. I didn't even make the choice to sleep; I was so exhausted that oblivion came immediately and closed its fist around me. Now I see how vulnerable I was, but then, the water and my nakedness made me feel stronger, certain in my skin.

I woke to the sound of footsteps. When I opened my eyes, I saw Dite first. She was quite a few yards farther down the bank, nosing at the flat, wet grass, but when she raised her snout I could see the way she kept opening her lips around a tongue too swollen for her mouth. Tears pricked my eyes.

I heard another footfall behind me; she hadn't been the sound that stirred me from my sleep. I turned and stood, my stola still a pool of tawny wool. The worker who stood before me was my height, although a frail moustache and some whiskers on his jawline suggested he was of marrying age. His tongue lifted over his top lip as though directing my attention there. He'd folded the lower half of his tunic neatly over one arm; he held his penis with the other. It was pink and brown in color, and his face quaked when he slid his hand across its length.

I was stunned but also fascinated. I'd seen my father's genitals while he dressed, hanging like a satchel of herbs between his legs; they looked of little use. But the worker's member looked enflamed with purpose. Then I saw his eyes, like sheep shit hardened and glazed over by the sun. And the way his gaze made my naked body raw and ugly, a tentacle the sea-meat vendor would hold and flick to show its freshness.

The astonishment dissolved; fear took its place. I grabbed my things and pressed them to my chest, began to back away, still facing him.

When a wild animal confronts you, turning your back invites a pounce, invites its teeth marks in your neck.

"Stay there," he said, and he took a few steps forward, his mouth opening wider, his hand still on his cock. I took a few more steps away, the grass below my feet slick and wet, and I could hear the sound of Dite's breath, sand swirling around the bottom of a cooking pot.

"I said stay put," the worker growled, and then he took a few quick steps and grabbed hold of my elbow. I sent a kick that landed at his knee and he released me, but the strain of pulling backwards sent me toppling, belongings scattered, tailbone pressed to mud, but he kept coming as I crab-walked backward until a rope of Dite's saliva slithered down my neck. I froze against her.

His face filled with satisfaction; he knew he had me cornered. Now he took his time, narrowing his sheep-shit eyes, tucking his tunic into his belt to leave both hands free. His thighs were pale, with tiny red bumps pricking them. "With that face of yours, I'm doing you a favor," he said, and while he took his time to laugh, I inched my fingers toward the fallen shearing knife. Then I grabbed it and stood.

"Don't be feisty now," he said.

I looked him in his dung-glazed eyes, curled my fingers into Dite's wool, pressed her to the ground, straddled her, and slit her throat. The precision of my movements was good and kind to her—at least as good and kind as death can ever be. She deflated, expelling shit and piss and blood and breath, but I didn't think about the loss of her, not then. I kept my eyes on the worker and held out the shears in front of me.

His face crumpled in disgust. Now that I know more of men, I know that I was lucky. There are those who would have been excited by the sight of blood, the act of violence. But this worker was a rapist, not a sadist. He undid his tunic so it could veil his wilting cock, and then he turned and trudged back toward the villa, but not before he said, "You'll die alone, you stupid whore."

I put my stola on before I washed. I didn't duck my head below the surface of the stream but kept my face, alert, turned toward the creekside path, the villa. The coldness of the water burned my skin. The silt wasn't soft but oozing slime. When I drew myself back out again, the fabric made me heavy. Sunning on a rock, naked and stretched long, seemed absurd, a thing a very stupid girl would do.

Look. Look what a man can do without hurting. He'd changed the way the world felt rubbing up against my skin. He took away the way my creek felt. My rock. The very sun.

My fear is what made me slaughter Dite; it's what would have pressed the knife between his ribs if he'd kept coming. But should that scene unfold again I knew it would be rage, not fear, that would make me hurt another. What's more, a part of me would like it. The worker did that, too.

It took the rest of the day to fashion a stretcher that I could use to carry Dite from the stream's edge to the cliff. Dragging her took twice as long because instead of going straight across the pasture by the villa, I took the long route down along the stream and then the frail, scuffed path that wound back to our home. Even so, part of my trek took me along the far corner of the villa property. Night had begun its descent, but I could see the row of newly planted pines and the fire that licked its chops almost as high. A few workers wandered my way and threw handfuls of gravel toward me as I passed, too distant to do much hurt, but two pebbles left pockmarks on my skull deep enough for blood. They called out curses, too. I gripped the handles of my stretcher and pulled harder.

Before I rolled Aphrodite's body into the sea, I wiped the green pus from her eyes and tucked her tongue back in her mouth. I made a salve of milk and tender grass shoots and spread it on my hands so she would meet her herd-mates with the scent of good life still upon her.

Her form disappeared into the maw of night before it hit the sea.

I missed my mother: her stories, her kind fingers, even the clotted sound of her breath filling the cottage at night. I missed the presence of my father, whose bulk might have tempered the ribald songs the workers sang around the fire. I missed Dite, whose nose in my palm offered a moment of comfort, at least. And I missed the person I had been that very morning. It seemed that life, if you survived it, was simply a process of hardening. Against loss, against harsh words, against the gazes of those who tried to own you. What humans did was take the freedom of the world away from one another bit by bit.

If the workers filled themselves with enough wine and boasting language, I knew they might come to find me, to follow through on what the worker by the stream had given up on. And so I went out to the shed and pulled all the unscoured wool into the house and laid it out around me. Tainted wool, unsellable, knit through with rust and seeds and burrs and brambles. I spread it over the entire room. At fourteen years, of course I knew the wool possessed no camouflaging charm, but still it eased the nakedness I felt even with the layers of my stola and my cloak. I built a small fire just outside the doorway (a paltry obstacle, but I'd at least see them if they came for me) and then I covered myself: wool a cape around my shoulders, wool a blanket over legs and belly. I slept upright with the shearing knife in my left hand; with my right hand I found, below the rug, the written figures from my mother. I fell asleep tracing those outlines with my fingers.

My memory is this: that I wake in the middle of the night, still covered in the wool, still with the knife in my hand. My father stands in the doorway. I cannot see his features, but the dark outline cast by the fire contains his wide shoulders, his slight left-sided slump, the bristle of his thinning hair. "Oh Lyra," my father says, and the sound is strange, both the "oh" that contains grief (instead of rage) within it and the contours of my name, which he utters as though he loves the thing he calls. I'd stopped letting his words touch me two years ago, but fuzzed with the in-between of sleep and waking, I forget I shouldn't listen. I let his kindness in. "Oh Lyra," he says again, "this is no way to live." And then he takes a glowing stick from the fire, and he touches it to the broom that hangs beside the door, to the tip of each stuffed mattress, to the herbs along the rafters. He does it as if he is blessing the space the way my mother would, but as the flames crawl up the walls, he vanishes.

I see him out our single window as the heat draws close. His body is a shadow once again, but this time lit behind by the gray glow of the moon through clouds. He stands at the cliff edge where we have let so many bodies go. And then he goes himself.

It is possible this memory is only a dream. Perhaps the blaze began because I built the simple fire ring too hastily or added, in my exhaustion, too much wood. Perhaps my father simply abandoned me.

The story I hear the workers tell the slave trader two days later is full of bravado and rescue: how they heard my calls, how they dampened their tunics and crashed through falling embers, how honorable they were with my charred and weakened body.

And that last part is true. They didn't touch my body. Drawn by the flames and deep groans a fire makes, they did climb up our promontory. And when I emerged, wrapped head to toe in wool, they got down on their knees before the creature who had walked through fire in that strange cocoon.

I was born on a cliff overlooking the Ionian Sea, birthed from a womb of fire, and I survived.

ALEXANDRIA

DAY ONE

38 CE

It is morning and Salome believes this day will be like any other. It is morning and Salome is ignoring the cacophony of Alexandria to focus on the patient before her. She dismisses the acrid scent of palm-leaf fires and the heavy roll of the fuller's urine barrel, erases the bickering of widows and the scrape of the baker's paddle. Gone is the sound of sandal on mosaic tile, of hoof on stone, of merchant voices extoling the freshness of cabbages already wilting in the sun. When everything is quiet in her mind, she begins.

The Egyptian girl on the examining couch before her has been blind for three days. Perhaps more. The girl's mistress, a rich Greek woman, stands against the wall patting her own eyelids protectively.

"Keep still." Salome says the words in Egyptian, but they are clunky and ill-formed. Egyptian is her fourth language, and learning it so late in life means that words she knows perfectly in her mind often come out strange and garbled on her tongue.

Milos braces the girl's head between his knees. Her body is wrapped tightly in a sheet to keep her arms and legs from moving, but she wriggles like a fish anyway.

"Be still," Salome says again, this time more sternly.

"She's scared," Milos observes in Greek.

"I know that. But she's old enough to understand that her fear must be put aside for healing."

"She can't see what's coming."

"Then tell her what's coming."

"I don't speak Egyptian."

"That's hardly my fault."

Milos leans towards the girl and hums a little. Her body quiets. Salome readjusts her position so that the light from the window will fall most brightly across the girl's face. In the center courtyard of the clinic, a number of the student physicians are harvesting herbs in the garden. On the table beside her are her smallest forceps, the cauterizing needle, the candle, the copper ointment, and a few of their softest blotting rags.

Salome braces her left hand against the girl's cheek. The girl doesn't wiggle, but her breath comes faster, and tears leak out the corners of eyes that are already puffed and red. Pus lines the lower lids.

"I can't work if she's crying. Distract her," she says. Milos is in his third year and should know this without having to be told.

Milos hums more loudly. Most of the time he can swallow being taught by a woman, but there are moments, like this one, when he wields his halfhearted obedience as a form of insolence. Salome grunts at Milos because she both understands his behavior and has no time for it. She stands and moves swiftly to her medicine case, where she takes out six other vials. The rich Greek woman presses herself against the wall and wraps her arms around her waist as though Salome might ask her to assist. Salome hands five of the vials to Milos and opens the sixth, holding it below the girl's nose.

"What do you smell?" Salome asks the girl in Egyptian. Then Salome watches as the tiny divot below her nose quivers slightly.

The girl's brow wrinkles slightly in concentration. Then she shakes her head. Salome dabs a bit of the ointment from the jar below the girl's nostrils.

"Mint?"

"Yes."

Salome wipes away the scent and then gives the rag to Milos. "Continue." He nods, opens a different jar, and dabs a new scent below the girl's nose, then murmurs assent when she makes a guess, although he cannot understand what she says.

Salome focuses on the face of the girl; likely the blindness is caused by an eyelash grown inward. She blots the right eye clean and uses her thumb to peel the eyelid back so the pink underside is revealed.

"Trachoma?" asks Milos quietly in Greek.

Salome nods. "There are only a few nodules, though, and still translucent. The copper should help."

Salome reaches for the smallest forceps, using it to pluck out three offending lashes that have grown inward and begun to scratch the cornea. The girl's body tightens, but she does not move her head. In the candle flame Salome heats a needle and uses it to cauterize the places where she's plucked. The girl tries to buck her head backward, but Milos's grip is firm. When Salome is done, she dabs copper ointment along the exposed eyelid and folds it gently over the eye again. As she moves to the other side of the examining couch to repeat the process, her right hip constricts, sending painful surges down the outside of her thigh, but she doesn't grimace or let her gait betray her. Instead, she pulls the candle closer and lifts the needle to the flame.

When she is finished, she tells the Greek woman to keep the girl's eyes bandaged until dinner tomorrow, to wash them gently with clean water, to apply more ointment as needed. The woman sighs and nods. The girl reaches out and grabs Salome's wrist.

"Then I will see?" she asks.

Perhaps is the word Salome wants to offer the girl, but she cannot find the Egyptian version of the word. "Wait and see," she says instead. She touches the top of the girl's hand gently, and when the girl does not release her grip, Salome unwinds the fingers from her wrist and stands. "Bandage both eyes and make sure she has a good supply of ointment," she says to Milos.

When she is around the corner and out of Milos's eyesight, Salome pauses to rub her thumb into the flesh of her right hip until the spasm there relaxes. When her breathing has steadied, she continues down the hall to the large examining room.

Even today, ten years after Salome laid eyes on it for the first time, the room is still beautiful. Five examining couches repose in the light that falls through the open windows. The white and black mosaic tile floors are scrubbed clean; low shelves below the courtyard windows hold cups and scales, and the large cabinets on either end of the room contain limewood boxes and clay pots and glass vials filled with medicinal herbs and decoctions and pastes.

It is time for the midday meal, and already Salome has tended to earache, menstrual cramps, wasting gums. Already the examining couches in the main room are free of her patients. She will return home to eat with Asha, then work at the clinic until dusk. Meat pies for dinner, perhaps. Or Nile perch steamed in papyrus. Sleep will walk its tender feet across her bed. Yes, there is the pain in her hip and sometimes the forgetting, moments when it feels like moths have worried through parts of her brain. But this is what it means to grow older. Today, she can bear it. Today is the thing that matters.

Salome exits Clinica Philoxenus and turns right on the Water Way. Two minutes later and she can see the breeze lifting and settling the hair of the four wigs always on display in front of her house. The hairpieces are bolted to dowels embedded in the surface of a table. Every evening, Asha brings in the display rug with its pins and clasps, jeweled crowns and ivory clips, and every morning, Asha reshapes the hair of her Girls, as she calls them, before she touches anything else. And shockingly, no one destroys the wigs in the night, no one cuts the hair or saws the dowels; perhaps the Alexandrians believe, in this city where gods outnumber the people, that the wigs are sacred, or perhaps it is just a comfort to watch wigs disheveled by the elements at night become smoothed and beautiful each morning. Anyway: Salome is home.

In the front courtyard, Asha is nose-deep into a bag of horsehair, haggling with a vendor about price. As she passes, Salome watches Asha take a single hair from the bag and pass it over her tongue, a gesture that offers no insight to the quality of the hair but always convinces vendors of Asha's knowledge.

The front room contains the wig workshop and is built in the style of a Roman villa atrium. In the back are two rooms, one meant for dining and one for sleeping, but Salome and Asha have each taken a room for their own because neither of them stops long enough to recline to eat anyway. They do not entertain, although potential customers and neighbors often sit for hours with Asha at the shaded table in front, fingering pins and watching Asha's quick fingers braiding and twisting and shaping the wigs. In back is a tiny courtyard with a simple brazier, a shed for storing food, a rudimentary oven, a grooved wooden table, and two footstools. Salome makes the porridge every morning; Asha sends one of the wig workers to the market at midday for fruit or bread or cheese for their midday meal. At night they sleep on separate cots in separate rooms. Their love for one another is a basket, a mikveh, a dormouse, a bruise.

Today, on the table, Salome finds a bowl of yogurt and a handful of figs. Asha joins her a few moments later and their actions become predictable and easy: Asha spoons oil over the bread and Salome slices the figs; Salome brings two foot-washing bowls and Asha brings water warmed on the brazier to fill them; Salome raises her tunic and Asha rubs balm of narcissus into her hip; Salome removes Asha's wig and blots the accumulated sweat from her hairless skull. They sit on the stools, the plates of food on their laps, their aching feet in the water, the sound of carts and the voices of vendors filling their ears.

Except that, instead of crumbling rosemary into the water to scent it, Asha crumbles between her thumb and forefinger tiny petals of fresh lavender.

It is only when Asha asks Salome why she is not eating that Salome realizes she is not eating. It is such a small thing, that scent. But suddenly her mother is here in the courtyard, and there is wool curled in her fingers and heat singeing her eyebrows. Salome closes her eyes against the memory.

And Asha, dear Asha of the wide brow and kohled eyes and bald head and earlobes pulled long by heavy earrings, sets down her plate, kneels before Salome, lifts her foot out of the water, and tenderly, so tenderly, kisses her ankle.

And Salome jerks her foot away, back to the bowl, splashing the water and leaving Asha's stola damp and her face stricken.

"There is nothing I want to tell," says Salome defensively.

But for the first time in ten years, Asha has not asked or cajoled or demanded or invited Salome to tell her anything at all. In fact, Asha has risen quickly and is already gone.

By the time Salome leaves the courtyard to return to the clinic, the figs are covered with flies.

It is 38 CE in Alexandria, and the scent of lavender has begun to change everything.

Salome returns to the clinic hungry and rubbing her nose to rid it of the clinging scent. In front of the clinic Carabbas, the mad beggar, sits in the middle of the Canopic Way, holding his right foot and screaming. A line of patients stands below the turquoise awning in front of the clinic, and Lilo, the caller, stands ready to usher the next patient inside. Carabbas licks the wound or kisses it, then tries to offer the foot to a vendor pushing a cart piled high with three kinds of olives. The vendor does not look at him. Some of the patients in line stare, and some turn away. The woman at the front of the line raises her mantle over her lips as though madness and foot wounds are contagious.

When Salome kneels next to Carabbas, Lilo, who has a neatly trimmed beard and well-oiled hair but whose eyes are red and tired, says loudly: "This woman is next." He opens his hand rather limply toward the woman covering her face.

Salome ignores Lilo and takes the foot Carabbas offers. In the middle of the thick yellowed skin of his heel is the base of a tiny nail. Around it the skin is red and inflamed. "Come," she says, and wraps an arm around the leathery skin of Carabbas's back and helps him to his feet. Salome does not look at the caller or at the woman, who puts her hand against her abdomen as though to show that she, too, is wounded.

Once she has Carabbas settled on the examining couch, she finds the nail is fairly easy to remove, but Salome calls the first-year students over so that she can show them how to clean a deep wound with a mix of turpentine and vinegar and then how to press comfrey paste into the wound using the end of a probe. When she's finished, she tells Milos to wrap the foot with bandages and then to find a piece of leather to wrap over it, too. "This is not a man who can stay off his feet," she says.

"Should we treat him for sunburn as well?" asks one of the students eagerly.

"Yes," says Salome, "and make sure he's given food and drink before he leaves."

Before Lilo can call her a new patient, Salome goes to scavenge in the small triclinium for food for herself. Her hip aches again and she cannot seem to rid herself of Asha's expression when the water splashed her face. But hunger is a thing she can fix.

But she cannot fix it, because the scent of lavender has begun to change everything, and there in the triclinium is Philo's broom boy rolling the last two grapes back and forth across a silver tray. "Fruit races," he says, smiling.

Salome does not smile. Philo of Alexandria is a Jewish scholar and orator who publishes soporific religious treatises. He is impatient, obstinate, and prone to terrifyingly long tangents. He also fed, housed, and blessed Salome at a moment in her life when she was without home or family or future. She owes Philo a great deal and resents this debt immensely. "Why are you here?" She takes both grapes off the tray and pops them into her mouth. Their flavor is too sweet, on the verge of turning to rot.

"Philo is in need of you."

"My patients are in need of me."

The Broom Boy shrugs. He is eleven or twelve and much taller than the last time Salome saw him. He has long limbs and a harelip and a cap that used to be crimson but which sun and oil and sweat have softened to a dusky rose. "He says I am to bring you. I will wait until you are done."

"No," says Salome, but as she turns away from him the ache in her hip careens across her belly and into the space between her ribs. The pain fastens her to the ground, so she asks, "Why does Philo want me?"

"The quarantine. People are dying at his gates. He says to tell you he has Balsam of Mecca and a traveler with fresh word from Jerusalem."

Salome does not turn. The pain pulls her ribs together so that she can draw only very thin breaths in and out.

"I was supposed to say the last things as a way of tempting you. He told me to use charm."

Salome smiles slightly and her ribs loosen. She gulps a deeper breath. "I will say that you have."

"So you will come?"

Asha's face blinks back at Salome. Shame and guilt begin to claw at her, two emotions Salome does not tolerate. She wants to be as far away from Asha's disappointment as she can. "Yes," says Salome.

The Broom Boy smiles and takes off his cap to wipe the sweat from his forehead. "And Philo says you are to bring an extra physician's tunic as well." And the Broom Boy smiles, widely and generously, for no reason Salome understands.

Salome and the Broom Boy walk from the clinic down the Canopic Way, pausing first at the crossroads fountain to submerge their wrists and to splash water on their faces. Each breath one takes in the Alexandrian summer is full of light and heat. There is no rain and clouds scuttle southwards as soon as they form. If people were sensible, they would be resting during the heat of the day, but instead the Alexandrians grin and preen and shout through the blare. The Canopic Way is wide enough to fit six chariots abreast, enough for narrow troughs in the center where thick orange fish barely have the space to make their languid rotations. To proceed down the Canopic Way is to walk through the greasy haze of sizzling meat pies, it is to feel the spray of the onion vendor as he bites the skin to prove its freshness, it is to see the way the Greek Alexandrian women are styling their hair (half piled on top of the head, a few curled tendrils resting on the shoulders) and to note that a striped mantle is now preferred over a solid-colored one. It is to be jostled by the boys with handcarts who race each other, to be almost run over by the litters with drawn curtains that sway and pay no heed to who stands before them. It is to beware of ill-fitted stones on the ground beneath you, it is to be able to thin your hips through the line of people waiting to buy barley beer.

Alexandrians fill the streets: the Greeks and the Romans and the Egyptians. Each with their own quarter and language and customs. Each with their own gods, though sometimes, like recipes, these are traded among the people. But this summer, the people of Israel, the Jews whose ancestors helped to build the city three hundred years before, they are missing from the streets.

Three weeks ago, Flaccus, the Roman governor of Alexandria, issued a *mandatum* that the rights of the Hebrew people are rescinded; they are designated as aliens and foreigners. And so an entire people have been pressed together into the New Jewish Quarter, their tiny territory marked by stones and guarded by members of the Greek *gymnasia*, mostly big dumb men who have a thirst for power. The houses of the Jewish people, stripped before their eyes, now stand empty.

Were you to look just now, you would see a Greek woman with a cat slung around her neck opening the door of one such home, testing a stone bowl against her teeth, sniffing a linen wrap, moving a slow finger through the olive oil. The oven is better than hers; no stains on the back wall from smoke. And she likes the smell here. Plus, this side of the street is shady in the morning; she can sell her porridge from the front window of this house without customers going sunstruck. Her father had a Hebrew woman on the side; she knows a little of their love of purity. "Nubis," she calls, and the cat pricks its ears. The woman takes out a papyrus packet filled with animal entrails meant for making offerings. She finds the Hebrew household's best bowl and smears the scent around the inner sweep of stone. Then she shrugs the cat off her shoulders and watches with satisfaction as its rough tongue grates the vessel.

But more importantly, here are Salome and the Broom Boy, arriving at the marked stone border of the New Jewish Quarter. What is spoken between Salome and the gymnasia man who sits on an overturned crate, thick legs splayed, is not important. Her medicine case and her physician's tunic, indigo with red embroidered at the throat, permit her entrance. And anyway, little attention is paid to who goes into the New Jewish Quarter. What matters is who comes out.

On this same day, a man named John Mark sits on a bench in a synagogue in the New Jewish Quarter. John Mark does not know a single person in Alexandria. The tiled floors of the synagogue and the Lebanon cedar benches are covered by the bodies of men who sit and squat and stand and hunch, who cover their faces with their hands, who follow the watery light and dust motes drifting downward from the circular hole cut into the center of the roof down into the muddy dank of the room below. The aroma of sage rises from an offering bowl and does nothing to mask the scent of this many sweating, pressed bodies. Instead the cloying sweetness of the herb mixes with the body odor and coats the insides of nostrils, throats, and tender eyelids.

The rabbi reads from the Book of Daniel. The part where lions circle the prophet with snapping jaws. The interpretation that follows is not fussy or complicated, how Daniel sees the danger but does not submit to it; instead he submits to the will of Yahweh. And so he is delivered.

Someone coughs. Another man moans. The man beside John Mark grips John Mark's knee as though it were his own. The rabbi offers prayers. Then he leans back in his chair and raises the index finger on his right hand, which is the sign that those who have been chosen may now come forward to speak.

John Mark stands and moves to the circle of dim light in the center of the room. He is careful not to stand in front of the rabbi but beside him, in the position of deference. This close, he notices all the ways that this chair is different than the chair in which his father sat. The one in his father's synagogue was wooden, all hard angles, so heavy that it took four men to lift it. This one has a metal frame with purple linen for the seat and backing. "Begin," says the rabbi.

John Mark makes the mistake of looking at the gathered men. They have been six hours in this space. Some bounce on their toes to keep from fainting. A few rise, and a few sink to the floor in exhaustion. Others blot their foreheads, their necks, or try to fan themselves with their hands. But to John Mark the bodies seem to boil like the first large bubbles that rise and break in a vat of lentil stew. It is unsettling. Now a minute has passed and he has not spoken, and already he is losing their patience.

"Greetings from Jerusalem," he says into the dim heat, but his words are thin, not loud enough. There is a brief flash of light and sound as someone opens the heavy doors at the back of the synagogue and departs. Tiny black dots swim before his eyes when the doors close. His heart pounds and the room rocks gently, like the ship that took him here from Joppa four days earlier.

"I bring you news of a savior. A messiah. *The* Messiah," he corrects himself. Now the men quiet a little. John Mark sees them leaning toward him. Some are tired of being lectured about submission. A few have had Roman soldiers or Greek gymnasia men inside their homes, confiscating not just weapons but also small treasures: fine lamp oil, alabaster vases, red glass bowls. A man who sits in the front row had to watch as his wife was stripped of her favorite tunic. He had to see his wife, fully naked, as he had never seen her before. This man had always made love to his wife below a coverlet or mantle, her body a soft, mysterious darkness that moved and pleasured him. In the bright light of the Alexandrian summer she looked like a sea creature. Her nipples were strange and dark; one breast hung larger than the other, and around her midsection the flesh dimpled and sagged. The thatch of dark hair between her legs looked rough, a thing you would use to sand wood. Her humanness was unbearable to him. And so this man is tired of being told to submit to the will of Yahweh; he is ready for a story that is not about waiting but about acting instead.

In the room, there are fifty more like him. John Mark feels each of them acutely. If Peter the First were here, he would raise two open palms to the sky in thanksgiving for this room, for these devout people who are so ready for salvation. John Mark tries to raise his own palms but finds that he cannot stop clutching the sides of his robe.

His words continue without him: "The Messiah was crucified by the Romans. In Jerusalem. Eight years ago, after the feast of unleavened bread. Before he died, he shared a meal with his closest followers. And there were miracles. He fed the living with bread; many people, I mean, with very little bread. And at a wedding in Cana he provided wine, he made the water into wine when there wasn't enough. Then there was enough. He cast demons out from between the chattering teeth of lunatics. He promises to return, but we must prepare the way. Our lamps must be lit. We must be in the practice of burning."

John Mark can hear the way his sentences scatter like grouse roused from hawthorn shrubs. The way the men who had leaned forward settle back into their seats and darken the walls with the sweat of their hair.

John Mark's unstrung speech is not for lack of practice. In Jerusalem he recited the message over and over again, alone on the rooftop or carving tent pegs, but each time he testified before the Followers, the words became cross-legged inside his mouth.

Peter the First had found this significant. "Think of Moses," he said, "slow of speech and slow of tongue. What did Adonai say to him?" And John Mark had dutifully replied: "I will be with your mouth and teach you what you are to speak." For this he had received Peter the First's warm hand on his shoulder. And a few weeks later a commission to Alexandria. Alone. To share the good news of Yeshua, the Messiah.

John Mark realizes he has stopped speaking and also that he is not sure what else he has said, only that another man is standing now, edging him away, speaking in a voice that rises to the cut hole in the roof: "Grace and peace to you from your brothers and sisters in Syria."

John Mark makes his way to the back of the room, swings open the door, and steps into the street. Narrower by far than the Canopic Way, this street is filled with people who teeter between exhaustion and despair. No one moves on the street because there is nowhere to go. A woman dumps a chamber pot into the gutter; six men crowd a table, bickering over a scale one claims is weighted. Vendors sit on their carts, shading wrinkled produce from the sun. Another synagogue breathes out the murmured unison of prayers. In a storefront, a few linen mantles and tablecloths dangle limply in the heat. He has failed at his task and there is nowhere to go. He must find the woman instead.

Philo and Salome regard one another.

Salome notices Philo has more gray in his beard and that his shoulders climb more easily toward his ears. Philo notices that the skin at Salome's neck has slackened, that although she stands perfectly straight, the lower right corner of her lip tenses slightly, as though she is trying to contain something.

They stand in Philo's study in the middle of the New Jewish Quarter, and while they speak a servant girl wipes the baseboards, the window slats, the scroll cupboards with vinegar water. Salome is glad to finally rid herself of the scent of lavender, and Philo is glad for the way he can almost see the vinegar clear away any disease from the air.

Down the hall, in the large triclinium, the Jewish elders are gathered. They are talking about sending a delegation to Rome to plead their case. They are talking about how to make sure clean food enters the Quarter so the people do not turn on one another. They are talking about the rumor of Herod Agrippa, newly appointed king of three Judean territories, sailing to Alexandria on a ship from Rome. Agrippa is Jewish, but the rumor goes that now he is the pet of the emperor. If he arrives in Alexandria, will it be to strip away the dirt of the words *foreigner* and *alien*? Will it be to give them back their homes, their right to argue in front of a court? Or will he come as the puppet of Emperor Gaius Caligula?

The elders fill the rooms of Philo's house, but unlike the men in the synagogue and on the street, these men are washed and perfumed with oils. They recline on couches and eat bowls of simple porridge while they talk about whether Flaccus, the Roman governor of Alexandria, will allow the Jewish vendors to go to the harbor and the fields to restock their supplies.

There is one servant whose only job this afternoon is to make sure the men are not bothered by flies while they talk. He carries a small palm leaf to waft them away and a stick with a bit of leather attached to kill the insects once they're slow and fat with food.

Philo is an elder like these elders except that he prefers to write instead of talk. But he cannot write because of the sick and infirm who think, because he is wealthy, he hoards medicines here and spend all day banging at his gates. He decided, this afternoon, that perhaps quiet and healing could arrive hand in hand.

"I want you to make a clinic in my upstairs room," says Philo to Salome, "just for a week. Maybe two. Until the Quarter is opened again."

The serving girl steps near Philo, and he stands so that she can wash the chair.

"I serve at a clinic already."

"I know that, Salome," Philo snaps. "My people are not allowed at your clinic. My people are dying."

"There are clinics in the New Jewish Quarter."

"They have been stripped of supplies. It has been two weeks since anyone has eaten a decent meal."

Salome keeps herself from sniffing in the direction of the door, where the scent of bread and garlic drifting from the kitchen has begun to fight the vinegar for purchase in the room. She does not sniff, because Philo fed her from his kitchen when she had nowhere else to go.

"I have some supplies. And you can bring more. You can lead the patients up the outside stairs, through the side entrance. There's an alley where they can line up."

"You've given this some thought," Salome says drily.

Philo holds up a finger in warning. "No more than seven patients at a time," he says, as though Salome has already agreed and argued for larger numbers. "Seven planets, seven stars in the constellation of the bear, seven motions of the body, seven secretions of the body, seven vowels, seven tones of the—"

"I understand. And I will do this so that, what? You will have enough quiet to finish your treatise on—"

"Cherubim," Philo finishes. "But no, Salome, you will do it because you are a competent physician. Because these people need you more than the wealthy Greeks. Your people need you."

Salome pulls her head backward. "They are not my people."

Philo regards her and lets silence settle between them. "Perhaps they are not your people, but you do belong to them." And he says it in such a way that Salome wonders how much he knows. Of Rome. Of Nazareth. Of Jerusalem.

Philo places his fist above the desk and opens his fingers to reveal an empty palm. It is only when Salome looks at his eyes that she realizes he is gazing over her shoulder and using his fingertips to guide her attention behind her, to a man with large, close-set eyes who hugs a leather satchel to his chest. "This is John Mark." When Salome turns back to Philo, he has set a large ointment jar on the desk. Under the lid she finds the hardened red gum of Balsam of Mecca inside. "He preached today at the synagogue and seeks shelter and rest and, strangely, you."

"Me?" Salome is rarely surprised, but this is a turn she was not expecting. She looks back at the man. He does not look familiar, and he does not speak. He only looks at her with those wide eyes.

Philo touches his chair to be sure the vinegar solution has dried, and then he sits. "John Mark does not deserve this quarantine. I've told him you will find him shelter in the Greek Quarter—dress him in a doctor's tunic. You can ask your questions, and he can ask his. And tomorrow morning he can sail on a ship to Tarsus or Joppa and preach about his messiah, and you can return here and help my people."

And then Philo bends his head to his desk and smooths out a scroll. Salome and John Mark stand idly for a minute until they realize he does not mean to bid them goodbye or dismiss them. He has stuffed his head back in with the cherubim.

"Come," says Salome, and John Mark follows her out the door and into the atrium. At the gate, John Mark slips the physician's tunic over his head.

The ill who gather at the gate are too weak to make enough noise to bother Philo. It's their presence that weighs on him, Salome realizes, the way they list their heads against his wall in an exhausted half-sleep or hold their darkened bandages out to those who pass the threshold. Many are only sick with hunger, dehydration, summer fevers, ailments she could remedy quite quickly. "Peace be with you," she wants to say to them in Aramaic (her third language) but the words retreat, burrow away. Most of the Jews in Alexandria speak Greek anyway. When a small girl reaches out and grabs her tunic, Salome uncurls the small fingers and hears herself promising she will return tomorrow, although she has decided no such thing.

"Don't speak to me," Salome says to John Mark, "until we have crossed out of the Jewish Quarter. You must look like a physician who is tired and eager to be home to your wife and a honey cake. Keep your gaze ahead of you. The Greeks will likely be dumb with wine by now, but they can smell fear like street dogs."

Feigning confidence is difficult for John Mark, but he grits his teeth and lifts his shoulders. He is glad to have an excuse not to look down any longer, a reason not to notice again and again the filth and the open palms of beggars.

And so neither John Mark nor Salome notices the woman who nurses an infant and wets tiny pieces of bread to feed to the baby who sits on the blanket beside her. They do not see the man trying to boil a handful of lentils in a chipped bowl above an insubstantial fire. In an hour the man will eat the lentils anyway, although they are too hard and his back teeth will crack and infection will come, not then, not for six days, but when it does come, he will go to the clinic in Philo's house and Salome will turn him away because by then there will be men who are bleeding from their noses and their eyes, men who bleed inside their bodies and women who curl up like fiddlehead ferns to cover their shame. But the infection will kill the man a few days later. This is how poverty works: first you cannot make a big enough fire, and two weeks later you are dead.

The guards are too drunk to give either Salome or John Mark much of a hard time when they reach the border of the Jewish Quarter. One reaches out in the twilight as though to paw Salome and the other slaps his friend's hand away. "She's ancient. Save yourself." They laugh.

The Canopic Way is a relief to both Salome and John Mark. The wide boulevard has begun to empty, though there are groups of men around the carts that sell barley beer and meat pies. Egyptian boys climb the lamps with burning torches clenched between their teeth. A small breeze skims coolness off the sea and wreathes their faces and necks; the scents of the day dim enough that they can smell the brine. Salome pushes her knuckles into her hip to urge it onward.

"So," she says finally, her eyes still locked ahead of her, "who are you?"

It is 38 CE in Alexandria, and the lighthouse rages its welcome to ships that fleck the dark trouble of the sea. On one of these ships stands Herod Agrippa, newly appointed king of the northeast territories of Judea. Just a year ago, Herod Agrippa was wasting in a prison cell, only roaches and rats and excrement for company, punished for wishing too loudly for Emperor Tiberius's death. When Tiberius's heart finally gave out, Agrippa was pulled from prison by his friend and the new emperor,

Gaius Caligula. Now Agrippa has fine new sandals in the Roman style. A diadem, an entourage, a ship. But he also carries signs of those years in darkness: thin frame, darkened gums, thinning hair, and a perpetual fear that at any moment his fate could turn again.

Below Agrippa, in the hold of the ship, are sixteen statues of Emperor Gaius Caligula, his face smoothed into white marble and pink granite. Here is Caligula's bust, here is his face pressing out of a column, here is his arm laced through a shield, the other with a sword raised to strike. Agrippa is here to deliver the statues to Flaccus. They are to be placed in sites of honor around the city, to remind the people that Rome is always watching, that the emperor deserves their awe as much as any god. Agrippa knows the Jewish elders will not approve, but surely Yahweh understands. As long as the images do not infect the synagogues, the Jewish people need not fuss. Agrippa will visit the Jewish elders, smooth down any concerns and listen to their complaints (there have been rumors of unrest). He will bring a hand of peace. Quickly. Exhaustion gnaws at his bones.

All of the faces of Gaius Caligula have the same wide brow, the same pressed lips. All of the faces of Gaius Caligula know what happens next.

"Pardon?" says John Mark, who feels like a small child trying to keep up with Salome's long strides, even though she is perhaps thirty years his elder and seems to possess some sort of limp.

"Who are you?" she asks again, still without turning her head to look at him.

Mercifully, they arrive at a fountain before he finds his words. Though the day has cooled considerably, it feels lovely to wash the scrim of salt from his face. Salome pulls a cup from her bag, and after nudging a few young boys away from the filling spout, they both drink in long gulps. The city is beautiful in its gloaming, thinks John Mark. Or rather, the city is beautiful without the scent of urine and unwashed bodies, without the desperate songs wafting out of synagogues and children who chew the ends of their mothers' braids for something to fill their mouths.

"I am John Mark from Jerusalem." He pauses to study her face: the scatter of small brown spots, her long sharp nose, two golden eyes. Where her head scarf pushes back, wrinkles strafe her forehead; more line her mouth. "I have come to talk to you about Yeshua."

"Yeshua?" Salome lowers the drinking cup she had just pulled to her lips. It feels, for a moment, that perhaps they have conjured him by saying his name, that perhaps he, too, could step out of the shadows and Salome would take both of his hands in hers and say, "There you are. Finally, you are arrived."

But there is no Yeshua, and already this man is talking, in a voice that is deep but somehow not loud enough, as though he is afraid that the actual heft of it will break things. And he seems unable to speak in a straight line. His thoughts jump around like a rabbit. Finally Salome gathers that he has been sent from Jerusalem to proclaim the story of Yeshua to those in need of salvation. He has failed at this. Also, his father was a rabbi. He carries many questions with him, questions that eat at him, and he would like to hear what she knows.

He is better at writing than speaking. It came to him today, in a flash, he says (though that part feels like a dramatic flourish), that if he could write the story down in its entirety, then he could read it.

"Read it," he says again, this time with the full, round timbre of his voice behind the words. Salome feels an odd shiver, as though his voice has struck her bones. "And then the words would come out as I wanted instead of—"

And at this point Salome says, "Instead of like this."

"Well, yes," he says.

"How do you know my name?"

"Mari, Yeshua's mother, said you were here."

"Mari is still in Jerusalem?"

"Yes."

Salome pauses then, fits the cup back in her satchel so she will not have to gaze on his face when she asks, "What did she say I had to do with Yeshua?"

John Mark sighs and wipes perspiration from his upper lip. "When Mari found out I was being sent to Alexandria, she said I should find Salome. I asked her if she meant Salome the Jewish princess who danced for King Herod. She said no, no, I must find Salome the physician. She said so after one of my bouts of questioning. It was late at night, and I asked who was there when Yeshua died, not at the moment of the crucifixion, but who took Yeshua's body down, who put him in the grave, who came the next morning."

"And what did she say?"

"Well, Peter the First said it was the women. He wasn't sure which women exactly. If anyone asked, he said I could use the names of any of the women in the settlement. We were all part of the story now, he said."

"And what did Mari say?"

John Mark pinches the top of his nose and closes his eyes. "She said"—and Salome can see he is reciting, that he has an extraordinary memory—"Salome will have some of the answers you want and some that you do not want." He opens his eyes again. "It was rather cagey. Truthfully, I wasn't going to find you. But I hadn't expected this." John Mark waves his hand at all of it, at the press of bodies, at the sky that looks so enormously empty, at the heat which has thinned only slightly. In the circling of his wrist is the impossibility of preaching to a crowd of two hundred men, the words *alien* and *foreigner*, the parts of the Jewish Quarter that are now silent, stripped of bodies to fill the houses, and the cramped streets of the New Jewish Quarter, thick with bodies and hunger.

Salome's hip has started to throb.

"Mari is the one who sent the Balsam of Mecca to you," he adds.

Salome pulls her gaze away from him and begins to walk, even more quickly than before. "Come," John Mark thinks she says or pretends she has said as he follows the line of her shoulders into the growing dark.

John Mark follows Salome as she turns left on a boulevard that runs north to south, from the harbor to Lake Mareotis, but he does not ask her the name of the street. When the masts of the ships come into sight she turns right, up a sweeping set of marble steps, and he does not ask excitedly whether this is the Library of Alexandria, does not ask whether the small amphitheaters at the top of the stairs are still used for teaching. They pass by iron doors pressed with a diptych of the Muses, and John Mark does not ask whether they guard the scroll room.

They enter a building and walk down a hallway painted scarlet to a vibrant purple room bisected with a golden frieze of lotuses and crocodiles. The room contains a few dining couches and one low table; scuff marks on the tile show where other furniture legs once rested, and scorch marks along the walls show this was once a room well lit. On the low table sits a plate of fresh figs. John Mark does not ask to whom the figs belong or why the room looks so abandoned. At the end of the scarlet hallway there is a courtyard with a simple kitchen and a staircase that leads to a small upper room. When they enter the upper room, Salome answers his question before he can think it: "This is my study."

In Alexandria there are many sacred spaces. There are temples and synagogues, there are household altars and prayer rooms, there are alcoves on side streets where you can make a small offering for a small fee and sit in that space you made and feel your desire or your gratitude slide up to the sky on thin ropes of black smoke. And what makes those spaces sacred, of course, is the presence (fleeting or furious, coy or benevolent) of the god or gods who find favor in that place. Salome's room is not a space shaped to a god or for a god or by a god: it is shaped only to her.

She immediately lights two lamps that sit on stands framing the windows. The first thing the light catches is the rug. It fills the center of the room and dazzles. John Mark has never been dazzled by a rug before. It makes him feel stupid; in fact, everything about this woman makes him feel dumbfounded and off-balance. The rug itself is wool, woven in the tight weave of the Grecian countryside, the border of the rug bucolic: multiple shades of green flaunt sheep and shepherds, nymphs and dryads. In the center on the rug a woman falls from a cliff, the length of her body almost entirely filling the frame, but she is pulled at the bottom by Hades, his arm curved around her ankles. At the top she grips the arm of a younger woman (a daughter? a sister?), at whom the falling woman gazes. It is the story of Persephone and Demeter, except not quite. It is the older woman being taken below, and, stepping closer, John Mark sees it is not Hades but Poseidon who claims the falling woman. A fish wriggles through the god's hair, and scales fan his shoulder blades.

"Don't ask me about the rug," says Salome, so John Mark lifts his eyes and takes in the rest of the room. Salome is busy clearing a large desk that sits below a window framing the sea, a portion of the harbor, a few warehouses, a domed roof speckled with bird shit. The scrolls and pieces of parchment from the desk Salome moves to a large cabinet that contains writing supplies, a variety of medical tools, and, at the bottom, a bed roll and a few chests and small amphoras.

The walls of the room are papered with pages, plant after plant drawn in absurdly specific detail with notes around the leaves and tendrils that describe habitats and preparations and side effects. "I got tired of hefting open the pharmacopeia," says Salome, "so I put all the pages where I could find them."

John Mark has never seen a book desecrated before; they are too rare, too precious. But the pages soften the walls, and the plants are their own kind of strange and beautiful design. Below the pages, around the perimeter of the room, real plants struggle upward in slim planter boxes filled with dark earth. Salome removes one of the boxes from the windowsill and replaces it with another from further back in the room.

John Mark leans his face toward the green leaves and sniffs. "Mint?"

"Yes." Salome hands him one of the small amphoras from inside the cabinet. "Not too much water," she says. And he finds himself obediently moving from planter to planter, drizzling the shoots and sloshing the hardier stems. As he moves over the rug John Mark thinks of Moses, trembling before the flaming bush as a voice told him he was standing on holy ground. *Absurd*, thinks John Mark. *There is nothing sacred about this space.* It is only that after the cramped New Jewish Quarter—after the scent of so much body odor and fear, after the moans of sick patients and the constant chatter of the street—that this room, with its clean scent of growing things, with the softness of the rug and the papered walls, with the breeze from the sea and gape of its possible futures, feels both cozy and warm and wide enough to think and to breathe. It feels like a miracle.

"I trust you have enough money to pay your passage on a ship tomorrow?"

John Mark nods.

"Peace go with you," Salome says, and then, without telling John Mark anything, she is gone.

The distance from her study to her home is less than a mile, and though she is exhausted, though her hip aches and her belly growls, Salome wishes the distance were longer. Yeshua and Philo and the lavender scent of her mother—it is as though her past has conspired today to beat her into some kind of submission. Salome despises people who wallow in the past, who dig up old grievances and humorous anecdotes alike and make these things into their present. And Salome has kept the past at bay so long. Eight years. Ten years, really. She has made a life. Work that she loves. Dear Asha.

She wants to lay these things at Asha's feet, to bury her face in the scent of Asha's hands, the scent of water lily and wig paste. A few months ago, Asha climbed into Salome's cot in the middle of the night, traced the outline of Salome's face, rested her hand on Salome's belly, her breastbone, her hip. And Salome lay unmoving as a corpse, eyes closed, measuring her breath as carefully as she measures tears of poppy until

Asha sighed and left the room. Asha's touch is what she wants and what she cannot stand.

Asha has fed Salome her own past in little lozenges, one story and then another over the years, as they play their nightly game of latrunculi or sit with their morning porridge in the beginning of the sun. Salome doesn't mind it. She loves the way Asha's voice fills a space, and she likes the way the telling relieves something in Asha.

But Salome will not put the burden of her story on Asha. And yet somehow the not-telling of the story is curdling them both.

Now Salome is home. The hair of one of Asha's wigs has already come undone. It blows across the imagined face of the dowel and then settles, revealing the thickened paste that holds the upper crown of hair in place.

Asha sits on a low stool in her room, laying out the ivory and onyx latrunculi pieces. "It is late," she says when Salome enters, and though Asha's face is watchful, it is not accusatory; her eyes do not carry the hurt of earlier in the day. Salome nods and sets down her medicine case.

Asha stands and moves to the center of the room while Salome takes a small jar of ointment off the chest beside the door. Asha is small—the top of her head comes to Salome's sternum—and so it is easy for Salome to remove Asha's wig, to place it gently onto the waiting dowel, to rub the ointment into Asha's scalp. The fine bristle of gray hair above the ears, the brown spots of age, the red, irritated skin where the placement of pins makes the wig chafe more deeply: Salome knows each bit of Asha's head intimately, better than she knows any portion of her own skin. This evening, as she rubs in the ointment, bile stings the back of her throat. She swallows.

"What did you have today?" asks Asha, closing her eyes and leaning into the fingers that press gently against the bones of her skull.

"An eyelash inversion, menstrual cramps, earache, wasting gums."

"Anything interesting?"

"Nail embedded in Carabbas's foot."

"All the way?"

"Yes."

"Hm."

Salome finishes with the ointment and Asha turns to face her. Salome unfastens the clip that holds the deep-orange mantle in place. Asha unknots her belt and rests one hand on Salome's shoulder while she steps out of her tunic. Then she turns again so Salome can unwrap the extra padding from her hips and her chest.

Asha's nipples are wide and wine-colored against the flat, barley-colored skin of her torso. Hairs bristle there, too; Asha will go to the baths tomorrow to be shaved and oiled and perfumed. Asha has a small belly that protrudes only slightly over genitals that hang like a leather pouch between spindly legs.

Asha wears the clothes of a woman but has the body of a man, and though Asha is neither Jew nor Greek, neither Roman nor Egyptian, she has made her home here, in the city of Alexandria, because this is a city that is voracious in its appetites for more: more learning, more finery, more gods. This is a city unashamed to fill a temple with both Ra and Zeus, a city that worships a woman with the head of a crocodile and hindquarters of a hippo, a city that has no trouble taking two gods and bashing them together to make a stronger one.

Salome pulls the linen sleeping tunic over Asha's head and they sit down to their game. "I went to the New Jewish Quarter."

Asha raises her eyes but does not speak.

"Philo wants me to hold a clinic in his house."

"And you told him you will not."

Now it is Salome's turn to be silent.

"He is a fine man who took you in when you arrived in Alexandria with little. But you have paid back his generosity."

"It will only be for a week. Maybe two. Philo says Herod Agrippa will arrive soon and this will be settled."

"You think this will be settled easily, handily, when a rich Jew arrives on our shores?"

Salome focuses on the board, sliding her onyx piece forward and collecting three of Asha's ivory discs.

Asha moves a white disc backward, lets her question settle.

Unlike Asha, Salome does not carry the worlds of both man and woman within her, but she has been many versions of herself over the course of her lifetime: a daughter and a slave, a pariah and a physician. She was a girl in Greece named Lyra once, for instance, and now she is a 60-year-old woman named Salome in Alexandria. And so she understands Asha as much as anyone ever understands anyone else.

"What did you forget today?" asks Asha finally. It is the question they have both come to dread even as they understand it is as necessary as the ointment Asha will rub into Salome's hip to heal the ache.

Salome lists the items methodically: "I forgot the name for the third-smallest cutting knife. For a word that is close to *maybe* in Egyptian. I forgot the name of the vendor who sells cabbage outside the clinic. And when I entered the home of Philo, I forgot the Aramaic greeting."

"Your illness is eating up the past now."

Salome does not correct her.

"A man came to see me today from Jerusalem." Salome is going to tell Asha about his questions, about how she'd guided him to her study to sleep. Somehow the day is not ended until she has told Asha what has been inside it.

But Asha is collecting her pieces, though the game isn't finished, though they have only just begun to drink their beer. And when Salome looks up, Asha is crying. Tears drip over cheeks furrowed by the breadth of her easy smile.

Salome knows she should reach out and take Asha's hand. Or stand and rub the ache out of Asha's shoulders. "What?" she says.

"You will die without letting me love you," says Asha.

Night falls, and the history of the world pirouettes on its axis. Agrippa's ship slides into the harbor. In Salome's study, John Mark uses his traveling cloak for a pillow and burrows his head deep into the pocket where his mother stitched a tiny packet of cardamom because it is good to carry with you the scent of home. In Philo's house, the elders continue to talk, but now they have had enough wine that their conversation meanders into the past. They are full of nostalgia for the world as it was, so they bring it into the room and let the smoke of the lamps circle around it, let their eyes grow wet with it. The old men breathe it in and hold it in their lungs. Meanwhile, Salome dreams of a basket of asps. She picks up one of the snakes with two hands and holds it before her face, opening her lips to speak to it. It strikes quickly, pushing into the softness of her mouth to sink its venom into her tongue.

Salome wakes with a start. The moon is not yet fully risen. She dresses and takes bread and barley beer. A solution has come to her in her dreaming: she will give her story to this young man, this First Follower from Jerusalem. She will run Philo's clinic. And in doing so she will feed the past what it needs; in so doing she will ease the pain in her hip, pause the tremors of forgetting in her brain. And when Asha reaches out to her, Salome, free of the burden of her past, will finally be able to lean back into Asha's touch.

Minutes later, Salome is standing above John Mark, toeing his sleeping body awake.

"I will tell you about Yeshua," she says. "Where would you like to begin?"

DAY TWO

38 CE

In the darkness of waking, John Mark imagines it is his father who hovers over him, his face wrapped in a purple robe. Even through the darkness John Mark can see the sadness and disappointment in his eyes.

Then Salome toes him in the ribs again, and he is fully awake. The lamps beside the windows are burning brightly again, although it feels like he extinguished them only minutes before. He pushes himself onto one elbow, and Salome sets a cup of barley beer before him.

"What is it that you want to know, exactly?" She squats in front of him. Her voice is clipped, impatient.

"Is it still night?"

"It will be day soon enough. Do you want my answers or not?"

"I want the story of Yeshua," he says finally, rising to a seated position and rubbing the grit from his eyes. "Your story of Yeshua."

Her eyes narrow. "I thought you already had the story of Yeshua."

"I do. But there are details missing. I have talked to a number of First Followers who knew him at the end of his ministry but few who knew him before it began. And I have spoken to no one who actually took his body to the grave. Mari said you lived beside Yeshua for 28 years in Nazareth."

Salome rises and presses her thumb into her right hip. "Did she say that?"

"Yes."

"Surely then Mari told you what you needed to know about Yeshua's childhood."

"She doesn't talk about him. It is rare for her to open her lips at all. The First Followers told me to consider the few words she spoke to me a small miracle."

"Does she still have moods?"

"Moods?"

"Is she filled with grief, is she unable to rouse herself from her cot?" Salome's voice is impatient. John Mark cannot tell whether she is irritated with him or with Mari.

"She is thought to be the one to carry our grief. She and a few of the other women carry the burden of Yeshua's loss so that the rest of us can proclaim the good news."

"How convenient." Salome does not look at him. He can feel rage lifting off her like perfume, but he doesn't know how to stop it or from where it originates.

"I want to know if Yeshua died," John Mark says abruptly. The words surprise him.

Salome turns to face him, eyebrows raised, and laughs a single, low-pitched bark. "Didn't you come all this way to preach the good news of the resurrection?"

A blush spreads up John Mark's neck. "I did." He is horrified to feel his sight blurring.

Salome's face changes then. The skin loosens and her features widen. "Ah," she says, nodding, "I see you now."

"I have some conditions," she says, and her voice is matter-of-fact. From the cabinet she fetches a papyrus, a metal inkwell, and a reed pen. "I will tell you the story of Yeshua, but I will tell you my story, the whole story." John Mark nods. "Not only the parts that titillate you or that serve to stuff cloth into the windy cracks of your theories of resurrection." John Mark nods again. "I will not have one or two of my actions singled out as strange or deplorable simply because you have not taken the time to understand." John Mark does not understand, but he nods anyway.

Salome leans her weight against the desk slightly as she speaks to take the weight off her right hip. Her voice is louder than it needs to be, the voice of an instructor, not the quieter, warmer voice of seconds earlier. "I am not asking you to favor me in your story. But if you want to understand a patient's illness, it is not enough to ask only about the symptoms, about onset and so forth. You must—" she says, and here she touches her temple gently. "Never mind. You understand?"

"I do." Mostly what John Mark understands is that this is not the task of a single hour.

"I will come in the mornings and I will tell you the story, and then you will spend a few hours writing it down." Salome nods toward the writing tools. "At midday you will come to Philo's house and show me what you have written."

"So I am to be like a chained woman in a tower," John Mark says.

"No. You are to be like a man who has a job," says Salome. "That tunic allows you the ability to wander freely in this city. I will make sure you have enough food and water. In the afternoons, you will assist me at Philo's house. Or you can return to the synagogue to continue your preaching." Salome looks down at him. They both know this is what he should do; he should return to his people who are suffering; he should find a way to convey to them how belief in the Messiah offers comfort and salvation. But the city is a pregnant woman about to enter her birthing pangs. The city is going to writhe and suffer and pull its hair from its roots. John Mark understands this, at some level, already.

"I accept," he says. "Where would you like to begin?"

Salome stares back at him, and for the first time John Mark sees trepidation in her eyes. He leans toward her. "How did you come to live in Nazareth?" he asks.

And then it is not Yeshua who comes into Salome's mind but a different man, balding, a runty lamb slung over his shoulders. "Nathan," says Salome. "My life in Nazareth began with Nathan."

5 BCE

I arrived in Nazareth when I was eighteen years old. I'd come by way of Greece and Rome and finally, with Mari and Josef, by way of Alexandria. I was introduced in Nazareth as a cousin of Josef And, because newcomers to Nazareth were rare and mostly inspired suspicion, I was watched.

At the time I arrived, Nathan was a shepherd who could graze his sheep only on the dusty slope below Nazareth; the pain in his feet prevented him from walking farther. He had warts, dozens of them on each sole, tiny stabs of pain. His mother tried rubbing them down with a file, but these went deep, below the skin's surface. He needed henbane, Balsam of Mecca, and someone who knew how to use a scalpel. But there was no one in Nazareth. So he had gone to Sepphoris, the nearest city, where a healer had given him a salve made of plantain and donkey dung. The plantain didn't actually help much, but the dung made a thick enough crust to ease the pain a little. So that's what he was doing when I arrived: hobbling around on donkey dung.

I only possessed a handful of Aramaic words then and no knowledge of the customs of Galilee. A few weeks after I arrived, I was fetching water at the cistern (one of the few tasks Mari trusted me to accomplish) when I saw Nathan hobble over, ladle water into his cup, and sit on the low wall that framed the place. Other people also sat along the wall or chatted quietly while they waited to fill their jugs or pots or cups.

Though I didn't understand any of the words, I noted that people relaxed their bodies in this place. Standing close to water made the Nazarenes forget, momentarily, the charring blaze of the summer sun and the endless series of tasks in front of them. It reminded me a little of the water fountains in Rome, the way women leaned against the cool walls as they waited, tracing the painted graffiti or picking nits from their children's hair. I ached to be elsewhere—or at least to be some version of myself in this place, not simply the strange Alexandrian cousin of

Mari and Josef who did not seem recognizably Jewish in any way. At the very least, I thought, I could be a doctor here. Even if these people couldn't pay me, even if I lacked almost all of the necessary supplies. I approached Nathan, bent down, tapped gently on the top of the right foot and, when he nodded, lifted under the heel so that I could examine whatever was causing him pain.

I barely had time to note the raised bumps when a hand grabbed a fistful of my hair and yanked me backward, onto the ground. The woman who'd grabbed me let loose a stream of Aramaic and then spit on me. Or she tried to spit, but her mouth was so dry that she conjured only the sound and a few flecks of moisture. Then she pinched Nathan on the back of the neck and hurried him away. And the rest of them went with her, scattering with their dry, empty pots back to their homes and fields. Better to be thirsty than to be with whatever I was. A Gentile. Or a prostitute. I'm still not certain which was worse.

I stood and wiped the spittle off my cheek. I took my time filling the cooking pot, using the ladle instead of the larger bucket. I knew they were watching from afar, waiting for me to leave so that they could make the space their own again. Before I left, I raised the ladle to my lips, drank the cold water directly from it. Then I dropped the ladle, fastened with a rope to a ring at the top of the cistern, back into the water. I didn't know most of the customs then, but I'd watched Mari and Josef wash their hands enough to know that touching, however briefly, dung salve on a man's feet had made me unclean. By touching the ladle, drinking directly from it, I had made the water unclean, too.

Now I know enough not to bring hatred purposefully upon myself. But at that moment I was lonely, exhausted, ragged. Sometimes an act of defiance is the thing that keeps you alive, even if it brings you closer to your death.

And so they shunned me. The Nazarenes drew back, averted their eyes. Their gazes snarled. You have to understand Nazareth was and still is a tiny town—seventy, eighty people at the most. Even Mari and Josef, who had traveled with me so very far, did their best to distance themselves. We'd been living together, sort of, in the house of Mari's dead father, Abraham. Mari, Josef, and Yeshua in the right-side room with the stores of wine and barley and oil and me sleeping on the left side with the mule and the goat and the mice. But after the incident at the cistern, Mari insisted on separate dwellings, and Josef, of course, obliged. We could have been two dwellings in a single compound, as many families were, but Mari insisted on a wall. Two houses, two courtyards, two entrances, two lives.

Josef was never an expert builder, but he was smart enough, I know, not to leave cracks big enough to poke a finger through. But he did, and so I watched Yeshua grow up with my forehead pressed to stone: Yeshua sanding wood with Josef, Yeshua sorting beans with Mari, Yeshua drawing circles in the dirt. When he stepped inside the ring he'd say, "The demons cannot touch me." Instead of turning away, or tsking the idea, or giving the child a chore, Mari would nod and ask him if he'd protect her, too. I clawed my fingers into the fieldstone wall but couldn't bring myself to look away.

But I have skipped ahead. A few weeks after the moment at the cistern, I found Nathan as he grazed the sheep, close to Nazareth and away from prying eyes. This time he offered me his feet and seemed to understand I meant to help. The next day I brought my medicine case, numbed a portion of his right heel with an anodyne of white mandrake, and offered him a stick to bite upon. I cut the skin around the wart and eased it back with my smallest hook until I could see the thin, smooth tissue below. I cleaned the area with Balsam of Mecca and fenugreek and dressed it. After about two weeks it had healed well enough that I could remove another wart. And then another. It took almost a year to remove them all, but eventually Nathan could walk normally again. He took the sheep farther to graze, and they fattened on sweeter grasses.

By then I'd become an unwelcome but permanent fixture in the town. No one really spoke to me, but they no longer spit on the ground and muttered as I passed. My presence in distant fields with Nathan confirmed their view that I was a prostitute, and so I became a useful caution to their daughters. *Look at the woman who lives alone, who no one speaks to, look at her stippled face and listen to the way she can't form simple words on her dumb tongue. This is what happens when you lie down with men to whom you don't belong.*

They weren't so far from the truth. The man I had lain with was nowhere to be found. Though I didn't much care for being a pariah, I didn't mind the solitude. But I missed being a physician.

38 CE

Salome pauses and studies her hands in the flickering lamplight. They look foreign, unfamiliar. If someone replaced her hands in the night with a new pair, would she even notice the difference? Is it possible to forget your own body? She thinks of how the Jews have been declared foreign in Alexandria, made to seem as though they do not belong to the body of this city.

John Mark's low voice is droning. He has asked her something. "What?" she says.

"You say you were introduced in Nazareth as a cousin—but you were not?"

"I was not."

"You were born in Greece?"

Salome looks out the window; deep blue is beginning to replace the darkness. "I was."

"So who were you to Mari and Josef? Why would they take you all that way, from Alexandria to Nazareth? And why did you go with them?" John Mark has placed his elbows on his knees. He leans in with his close-set eyes as though he can divine out the truth in the tiny brown moles that strafe Salome's face.

Salome imitates his posture, leaning in until there are only six inches between them. Then she makes her voice slow and certain, enunciating the next four words as though John Mark is a deaf-mute: "He was my son."

"Who was?" John Mark's eyes remain fixed on Salome's face, but he turns his head slightly to the right so she will know he is regarding her with suspicion.

"Yeshua. Yeshua was my son."

"Mari was Yeshua's mother." Then, more gently: "This is a known fact."

"Mari was like a mother to Yeshua in many ways. But she did not birth him."

John Mark sits back and sighs. "You would like me to believe that you gave birth to Yeshua, gave him to Mari somehow, then followed him to Nazareth and lived beside him."

"For thirty-two years. He called me Salome. Or Auntie. I watched him through that wall."

Outside the window the sky is still dim enough that John Mark can see the fire burning in the lighthouse, a few stars pricking the west.

"You don't believe me. That's fair. Suspicion is a sign of intelligence. We have enough night left for me to tell you the beginning. You can decide if you believe—or believe enough to carry on."

John Mark nods. Yesterday, while walking to the synagogue in the New Jewish Quarter, he'd watched a grown man wrapping a piece of bread in three pieces of cloth and then binding it around his waist so no one could take it from him. And in an alleyway another man suckled at a woman's breast. He thought he was watching an act of lust and then saw that it was an act of hunger. The woman saw him staring and said simply "one tetradrachm" above the suckling man's head. Any story is better than the one his people are living on the other side of the city.

Salome settles herself against the wall and massages her upper thigh. She thinks of Asha. Of resting her own warm hand on Asha's thigh casually, easily, affection flowing through the tips of her fingers instead of curled like a frozen snake in her belly. She makes herself speak again.

5 BCE

When Yeshua was born, he wouldn't latch. I was living in the Mareotic community then, a handful of hovels cobbled together on a ridge outside of Alexandria, pressed between Lake Mareotis and the sea, Jewish mystics who'd shrugged off their inlays of alabaster and in-home mikvehs and unions of the flesh to allegorize all day inside prayer rooms in the dark. I saw the community members rarely, only at night, when they emerged like sea creatures, bleached and mouthing words they'd ridden in their minds over and over, while the rest of the world shat and fucked and complained of the catarrh.

I was not supposed to be there. I was supposed to be serving in a clinic of my choosing in Alexandria; I was supposed to be prowling the library, sucking in the words of those physicians I'd heard Rufus, my teacher, mouth on about so many times. But on the voyage from Ostia to Alexandria I realized I was with child. I had waited so long to have a life that was mine, I couldn't bear to share it with a baby. For days I held out hope the world would do away with the child of its own accord. A storm's violent rocking would smash the blue-veined thing to bits, perhaps, or my womb would surge and cramp and the being would expel itself of its own volition. I even tried the things Rufus claimed only the daft obstetrix did: I lifted heavy things, I pummeled at my belly, I asked an old widow from Syria for the hottest spice she had and then took a spoonful on my tongue. I could have filled a pessary with hellebore; that would have done the trick. But I'd likely have died with the baby, both our bodies sluiced into the sea and no one to tuck hibiscus in our shrouds, to balm our bodies with myrrh and musk. I didn't want to die uncertain that a single living soul would grieve my loss.

Luckily Trypho, a Jewish merchant who chatted up anyone with ears enough to listen, took note of my mealy stomach and my terrified face and was shrewd enough to guess at my predicament. He was not devout—he sold exotic animal skins as medicine—but his cousin, he explained, lived in a community a half day's cart ride from the city, a desperate place really, but maybe it would be good for me. I could fatten and give birth away from prying eyes and then pawn the baby off. There'd be an Egyptian family, surely, desperate for another brat to press papyrus, and maybe I could even make a little money in the end. And then, when all was said and done, Trypho declared, eyeing my medicine case, I could come and work for him. He'd buy a real silk awning and I could do a healing, and then he'd have his powders out for purchase. We could make a fortune.

I knew he was a bladder filled with air, knew I'd never peddle any of his cobra powders or his leopard dander, but I also knew I had nowhere to go. I'd left everything behind in Rome. So I consented. What choice did I have? I couldn't bring a squalling babe into the scroll room of the library, couldn't hold the cauterizing iron with one hand and wipe its tiny bottom with the other. And so, bereft of choices, I consented.

I spent seven months ripening alone, knifed by dusty winds, wiping the long Lebanon cedar tables down after the hermits had eaten their fill, mostly bread and hyssop, fruit already fallen, an egg boiled and divided into servings so small they disappeared.

Xenia, Trypho's cousin and the community member appointed to speak to me if I needed to be spoken to, found the requisite Egyptian couple who agreed they'd take the babe. She found a midwife, too, though I was wary of a witchy woman chanting false charms above my seizing abdomen, who'd catch the infant with bare hands instead of in papyrus or a beaten cloth. I worried over the wrong thing, of course. The birth was fine enough. But the baby boy refused to eat.

I had seen it four or five times before, in Rome, and so when the midwife brought a tiny cup, I expelled and tipped the clay to his thin and howling lips. He refused. I held his head to each breast at every angle I could think of, and he refused. I tickled the roof of his mouth with my pinky and let a little milk slide in beside, and he was satiated for an instant, but my nipple he refused. I let my breast dangle over him like swinging fruit; I took him to the sea and to the lake, let him rest on my still-swollen belly as I washed away the blood that gummed my hairs together. And still he wouldn't latch.

Xenia came to say the family wouldn't take the baby if he couldn't nurse. A dead baby at planting time was bad luck. So I tried goat's milk and cow's milk, wine and water, cold cabbage leaves laid across my breasts. Sometimes he stilled and sometimes he howled, all his limbs pulled up and in as though he wanted to be transported, slipped like a pessary back inside of me. I let the midwife make a tea from my placenta and I drank it on the third day because I knew that he was dying. His urine became thick and orange. His skin tented itself away from his bones. His indigo eyes were bottomless, night folded in on itself as he screamed the stars into being, and then he was quiet. I couldn't get his eyes to open, though I tickled his feet and lifted him into the dust-stung air and hummed inside his ear.

I won't draw this part out except to say that Mari saved him. The arrival of Mari and Josef at the Mareotic community is a different story. What is important to say is that my labor pains began when I saw them roll in on the cart, that I witnessed the way she wept and the way her own milk stained the front of her robe. I didn't know her name then, but I recognized her grief.

So when my son was almost dead I offered him to her. She offered her breast to him, and he lifted his chin and sniffed and a change came over his visage, a storm crossing the face of the waters, and he opened up his lips and found her. She bowed her head over him and I felt, I know Josef felt, a bond thickening between them, the two of us limp with love outside of it.

38 CE

Salome stands abruptly. John Mark knows better than to ask a question. "I don't mean it as poetry," she says, looking down at him.

"What?"

"Limp with love. I mean it as an admission of frailty." Salome gathers her medicine case, her satchel. The rising sun struck her face as she stood up, and now black spots startle in front of her eyes. When she looks down, she sees the face of a man she does not recognize; for an instant she doesn't know whether she loves him or hates him or fears him, if he owes her something or needs her help.

She closes her eyes again and finds the scent of lavender, her mother's scent. When she opens her eyes, she remembers again. John Mark. She nods toward the pen and papyrus. "You can find your way back to Philo's house?"

John Mark begins to nod and then stops. Truly, he was so busy staring at Salome as she led him across the city that he wasn't entirely sure of his directions.

"Then make your way to the crossroads fountain where we stopped to drink. I will send someone at midday."

Then she is gone.

John Mark bends over the desk. The sensation of writing is not the blank emptiness granted by Peter the First's hand upon his scalp, that cool water upon his forehead, but it is good nevertheless. It is the feeling of his questions rearing and kicking, skittish and foaming, finally bridled and reined, a dark force leading the chariot he rides. He writes Salome's answers as quickly as he can, his hand trembling as it gallops across the page.

And then it is morning, gray clouds thinning along the eastern horizon. The swollen Nile pushes farther over the fields, inundating all that she touches, while insects rise and spin along her marshy perimeters. Egyptian boys wearing only linen loincloths wade in the shallows, scooping red clay to dry in kilns along the bank. In the wide fields farther west men cut the thin papyrus stalks that rise over their heads in swaying green masses, and at the edge of the fields Egyptian women, many with babies slung across their chests, begin to finger the crosshatched sheets left in the sun the day before to see which are dried and ready to be joined and rolled.

Flaccus, governor of Alexandria, reclines upon a couch, warming his ankles in the sun. Attached to his wrist is a blue rope; the other end circles the neck of a kitten pawing the dirt of a potted marigold. Beside Flaccus, a goblet of wine and a small plate of cheese and sardines, mostly untouched.

Last night the leader of the Alexandrian Greeks came to tell Flaccus that Herod Agrippa had covertly arrived in the harbor. The Greek leader had leaned in close, stale barley beer on his breath, to say, "The rumor is that the King of the Jews will arrest you and bring you back to Rome in chains." He gripped Flaccus's shoulder to keep the drink from destroying his balance. "But there are things that we can do. Even with his crown he's still a Jew." Flaccus had nodded and then shaken the Greek away.

Now, Flaccus pulls on the leash and the cat stutters over to the couch. He picks it up by the scruff of the neck and offers it a bit of cheese. "What to do?" he says. The cat paws the air helplessly and extends its rough pink tongue for the morsel. Flaccus settles the cat on his chest and lets it feed. "Shall we let the Greeks have their way? Or offer our open arms to Agrippa?" He holds the cat firmly with his left hand and strokes it between the eyes with his thumb. It tries to squirm out of his grip. Then it purrs.

For five years, Flaccus ruled well. He was fair and just. He kept Rome stocked with corn and forbid promiscuous men to gather in public spaces. He made certain the soldiers were compensated and spoke eloquently at festivals in the theater. He was known to walk briskly at dawn along the colonnade, trailed by two bodyguards and a servant bearing a chair for his observance of the sunrise.

Then Emperor Tiberius died, and Caligula took his place and promptly killed off everyone he deemed a threat. All of Flaccus's alliances are now wrapped in shrouds, their bodies rich with poison. Flaccus no longer walks at sunrise. He beats the servants. He ignores affairs of state and spends his time collecting miniature glass elephants and scourges with decorative inlays. He satiates himself with wine and food and the bodies of Egyptian women. He's gained flesh around his face, a thickened waist, a propensity for flatulence. And now that his relationship to Rome is unsteady at best, he cloaks himself with the protection of the Alexandrian Greeks.

For five years, Flaccus didn't mind the Jews. They paid their taxes and didn't mar the streets with drunken revelry. But the Greeks helped him see the truth: the Jews were not to be trusted. They hid their hands behind their backs when they spoke and removed their women from the sight of men. They reviled certain foods and refused to worship any god as holy but their own. So he called them *aliens* and *foreigners*. Took away their legal rights. Pushed them to a corner of the city. Let them unroll their bedding by the seashore or among the graves. And now their king arrives on his shore, to offer gifts and greetings from Rome or to arrest him for his former loyalties. It is impossible to know yet which way Agrippa leans.

The kitten frees itself and goes scuttling away from him, the blue leash trailing behind her. Flaccus pulls the cat back to him, enjoys the sound of it clawing unsuccessfully against the stones. He is tired of obedience to Rome. He knows he hasn't lived a life worthy of Elysium, but if Agrippa comes to usher him to Tartarus, let the Jews make the journey with him.

He grabs the kitten by the tail and raises it until it blocks the sun, lets it yowl until its tiny throat goes hoarse. Then he smears fish oil from the breakfast plate across his face and pulls the cat close so it can lick him clean.

THE GOSPEL OF SALOME

On the deck of the ship, Herod Agrippa dips bits of bread into diluted wine so that chewing won't cause more pain to his rotten tooth. A servant oils his hair, trying to comb the strands to cover the white patches of scalp. The winds across the sea are patient, ready to fill sails safely, to deliver men to foreign shores unharmed. In a week or two the winds will quicken, drive sailors into the depths of the ocean, deaf to pleas of mercy. Soon Agrippa will meet with the Jewish elders. He will quell any concerns about the statues; he will see for himself if the whisperings of persecution are true.

Then he will go to Flaccus. Truly, this part unnerves him. If the rumors of unrest are true, then so too are the rumors that Flaccus has become a fat, unstable maniac. Agrippa's bladder squeezes for the ninth time this morning. He calls for the pot but cannot make any liquid.

In the New Jewish Quarter the people wake or the people no longer try to sleep. They are hungry, and the world is the same.

In the Greek Quarter, Asha brings out the rugs hitched with pins, rolls out the awning, begins to comb the hair of the blond wig. Asha waits for Salome to bring the porridge, and it is only when Nicodemus creaks by, sloshing water over the sides of his handcart, talking about the beauty of his perch, that Asha realizes Salome is already gone.

Inside the clinic, the light through the garden windows is thin and smells of rosemary. Salome is refilling her medicine case, packing a satchel with extra bandages, cups, a speculum, a few bronze tubes, a clyster, some abdominal forceps. Philo's house, she is certain, will have oil and milk and wine for mixing tinctures and salves. Beside her, Nadjem fills a bag as well, carefully moving items on the shelves so that the absence of the borrowed goods will not be missed.

Nadjem is almost as old as Salome, but her face remains mostly unwrinkled; age shows itself only in the wasting of her gums and the thinning of her lips. Nadjem has worked at the clinic for twenty years, tending the herb garden, mopping the blood off the floors, washing the instruments, hauling the soiled cloths to the fuller's. When Salome first arrived in Alexandria ten years earlier, she had her choice of which clinic she wanted to serve; many that she visited in Alexandria had callers whose breath reeked of beer or small rooms where dirty cloths teemed with flies in the corners. While the size of Clinica Philoxenus was nothing to scoff at, its true wonder was its cleanliness and tidiness and organization. This was Nadjem's doing.

These last ten years, Salome has managed to teach Nadjem in gulps and snatches. Often she calls Nadjem to mop a room while she is performing a procedure; Nadjem holds the clamps and Salome uses the tip of her pinky to point out the bladder and liver. And Nadjem has offered Salome teaching in kind. Squatting in the herb garden, it is Nadjem who instructs Salome on harvesting the marjoram when the leaves begin to flower, how to oil her hands before collecting the rue to keep her skin from reddening. Although she has not been able to lay her hands on many patients, Nadjem is an expert diagnostician. She can smell a rotten tooth from five feet away and feel a gallstone below the skin without the use of probes.

Nadjem has agreed to come with Salome to the New Jewish Quarter because Salome has agreed to let her treat patients and to pay her wages. Nadjem leaves a message for Alexander, the owner of the clinic (she has caught a fever, will keep her distance from the clinic until it ebbs) and then goes on ahead to Philo's house.

But Salome waits for Alexander. She lets him find her with the stuffed bags, the sunlight now fully bloomed and spinning motes of dust in high columns across the room. Alexander enters as he always does, panting. He is the rare Greek who possesses light Roman coloring, pale skin and thin blond hair. He seems to Salome always in the process of disappearing. Only his anger keeps him lit in this world. He eyes her two packed satchels and bunches his lips. "Where do you suppose you are going?"

"To the New Jewish Quarter."

"You are needed here."

"I am needed more there."

"Your job is here." Alexander tries to make his voice steely, but every word must squeeze through his thin nasal passages, so he sounds like he is wheedling with her instead.

"I will return in a week. You will have plenty of students here today. And"—she smiles thinly—"they have such an able teacher." She holds out her open palm toward him, and it takes all of Alexander's strength not to swat the wrinkled and liver-spotted thing away from him.

Alexander despises Salome. She is old but endlessly exacting; she is demanding of the students, and they love her for this, most of them even forgiving her for being a woman. But she views the clinic as a catch-all for injured animals and not as a business. She's always creeping Egyptians to the front of the line, and she refuses to visit the homes of rich women who feign illness because they want talking companions.

Alexander was born with a voice that sounds shrewd and whiny, even when he expresses gratitude or concern. This is not his fault. But because of it, he can tell the other physicians do not respect him in the way they respected his father. And because Salome once saved his father (and apparently half the city; the number always grows with each retelling) from an epidemic a decade ago, he owes her a personal debt as well. And so he has to wait for her to die or become brain-addled enough that the students can see she's become a liability.

Until then, his only recourse is to issue small dumb punishments: no, she cannot give the madman food and water; no, she cannot treat the Egyptian girl for free; no, she cannot perform that surgery until she has scrubbed the baseboards in the red examining room and helped to harvest the peppermint.

"I won't pay you," Alexander manages finally.

"Fine," says Salome, and she turns and disappears before Alexander can think of another small humiliation to pile upon her.

At midday the city is pierced by hoofbeats. The sound does not immediately reach Nadjem in Philo's upper room, where one of his couches has been positioned near the window, where supplies are arranged on low serving tables, where seven patients (no more than seven!) wait against the walls, their heads framed by lotuses and gold and scarlet bands of color.

The sound will never reach Asha as she places a blond wig on the head of a woman who complains about the cheap mantles her mother buys, how the dye rubs off on her upper arms.

It is John Mark who hears the hoofbeats first, as he waits at the fountain, holding his recently written pages away from his body so they will not be splattered by the water he scoops over his head and dribbles down the back of his neck. Alexandrians do not rest in the heat of the day as Judeans do. Boys with buckets and amphoras and pitchers jostle at the water-filling station. Outside the clinic, a line of people wilt under the long turquoise awning. From the theater on the northwest corner come the shouts of a military ceremony, while from the southeast corner men emerge from a door to the baths with their dark hair clean and wet. Vendors with handcarts try to outshout the vendors with large wagons, and two Egyptian boys with a few dark hairs sprouting from their chests point up toward one of the lamps, arguing about how best to refill it.

What do the pages in John Mark's fingers make him, exactly? A failure? A traitor? How long ago was it that he stood before the men in the synagogue? He should be there now, he knows. Or squatting with those who sit on street corners, filling the hungry with the good news that they are redeemed and forgiven. Why can't what he already knows be enough? Why, when he tells the story, does it feel insufficient and flimsy? He tries to push the questions away, but they keep flocking: who is this woman, really? Did Mari and Josef actually come to Alexandria? Did Peter the First know this and simply believe it didn't matter?

But there is the clatter of hooves again, not the steady clop-clop of the vendor carts but a rush of pounding. Around him, the activity of the crossroads quiets, and then here is the Broom Boy, at his elbow, sweat soaking the rim of his ridiculous pink hat and reeking of vinegar.

There are thirteen horses in all, though neither the Broom Boy nor John Mark nor anyone else on the streets of Alexandria actually counts the horses. It is enough to see that there are many. It is enough to see the bronze helmets and cuirasses, the red tunics and high-laced sandals, the oval shields and swords nestled into leather scabbards. It is enough to see that these matching men surround another, this one cloaked in a purple mantle and bright white tunic, a gold diadem glinting in the thinning hair on the rider's head.

"Behold," says the Broom Boy, "Herod Agrippa." And as the last bodyguard passes, the Broom Boy hustles afterward, close enough so that John Mark wonders if he plans to collect the brown turds that drop from beneath the horse's tail. "Come," he says, and John Mark follows.

The sound of the hoofbeats reaches Salome last, in a pharmacy just outside of the New Jewish Quarter. John Mark has not yet arrived—the Broom Boy has gone to fetch him—and one of the patients needs oil of myrtle. So here she is, holding a small clay pot in one hand and pressing her thumb into her hip with the other as the procession clops by. She sees what John Mark and the Broom Boy saw only minutes earlier, but she is the only one who notices what happens next.

There is stillness for a few seconds, even after the noise of the horses has dimmed. The Alexandrians in this area of the city are Greek and Egyptian and have only recently adjusted to the chafe of Roman rule upon them. And now comes a Jewish ruler who likely thinks they belong to him as well. Hands rise to cover whispered words, one man touches reflectively the short dagger at his waist, another crosses his arms and lifts his chin toward the place where Agrippa disappeared from sight. Even the street sweeper digs his broom forward with such force that the end of the broomstick kicks back into his ribs, leaving a bruise that will last for weeks. The street sweeper will touch that bruise and consider it a wound from Agrippa himself.

Salome sees all this and understands that Agrippa will not be able to help the Jewish people.

A few minutes later, Agrippa arrives at the house of Philo, the wealthy Jewish philosopher, to hear the petitions of the Jewish elders. Within minutes of Agrippa's arrival, everyone in the New Jewish Quarter knows that he is listening to the elders, that his diadem is gold, and that he has a pink scar on his knee. These things are true. But quick talk also spreads untruths: Agrippa bathes in the scent of myrrh, Agrippa speaks with a stutter, the panniers of Agrippa's horses are filled with gold to save his people, Agrippa will arrest Flaccus and take him back to Rome to be crucified.

And so, as the afternoon wends on, the people of the New Jewish Quarter let themselves think about what they will buy with Agrippa's money; the streets and alleyways thicken with the visions of yogurt and dates, lentil stew with coriander, warm bread rounds with clotted cheese, honeyed sweets, and Nile perch falling in slivers from the bone. They are hoping, for the first time in twenty-two days, that someone has come to redeem them.

The Broom Boy stares at the bodyguards who rest in the courtyard, the curves of muscle pressed into their breastplates, the rows of leather strips that hang from their waists to protect their massive thighs. In the lower room Agrippa reclines and listens, and the elders try to keep the desperation from their words.

Above the elders, Salome and Nadjem creak back and forth across the floorboards of the upper room. By the window, Salome tends to the burnt flesh of a man who tried to steal a loaf from a hot oven; in the corner, Nadjem monitors those who retch and ache from eating what they should not: hay, moss, handfuls of spices, fruit riddled with worms, vegetables gone slimy. One man has taken to eating the dirt of graves and had to be carried into the clinic by three of his sons.

John Mark's tunic smells of garlic and onion; it is wrinkled and stained and in its previous life belonged to a much taller man. In spite of the smell, in spite of feeling like a child playing dress-up, John Mark is grateful to have small, manageable tasks to do. He helps the infirm up the stairs and repeats Nadjem's instructions to men who turn their faces when she comes to help them. He recites each of the sixteen herbs Salome requires to the pharmacist without needing to write a single word down. He retrieves water from the cistern in Philo's house with help from a beautiful servant who shows him which ladle to use. She winces when she smiles, some kind of toothache or jaw pain, and John Mark thinks how good it would be to reach out and apply a compress to ease the pain, how sweet it would be to have a job that relieves suffering almost instantaneously.

His job *does* relieve suffering. News of the Resurrection is a compress. Well, a compress and a whip. If spoken well, the story of Yeshua forgives sins and brings the kingdom of Yahweh closer. The first time John Mark heard the gospel of Yeshua it was like this.

Two years ago, John Mark left his family home. At that time, the infirm lined the streets of Jerusalem in the hopes that they might touch Peter the First's shadow and be healed. You could spot a crowd of First Followers by the way they crossed their arms over their chests as they listened, ready always to receive the Word. Young boys liked to go crashing into the devout to see how many they could topple, all pressed together like that without their arms out for balance.

John Mark went directly to the compound of ramshackle buildings where the First Followers stayed, turned out his satchel and his pockets and gave his few earthly belongings over to them for a flea-infested bedroll in a room dank with the scent of other men, for monotonous meals ladled into chipped stone bowls, for dull labor in the city itself, drawing water or hauling stone or setting scaffolds for men who knew how to hold a chisel properly. There were perhaps a hundred followers who lived in the compound at the time, and unlike the silent home in which John Mark had been raised, the place of the First Followers was filled with bickering and laughing and boasting and humming, everything spilling out of everyone like a hundred overturned garbage bins. John Mark delighted in the stench.

It was Peter the First himself who told John Mark the whole story of Yeshua, start to finish, while they sorted lentils on the roof. John Mark remembers not so much the words Peter used (and this is strange because John Mark remembers everything) but the physical sensations of hearing: the ache in his thighs because they squatted on their haunches, the rattle of the palm leaves, the way that as Peter spoke the shadow of the rooftop awning crept up John Mark's back until he could feel the sun begin to heat him slowly, so by the time Peter finished John Mark was panting and dripping sweat. Peter dipped his fingers into a bowl of water for washing the lentils and baptized John Mark without asking his permission, using the washing water to clear the sweat from John Mark's brow. And in that moment, all of the questions, all of the words, all of the wondering that had filled his head like a plague his entire life disappeared. A sweet quiet settled over his mind, and he became a smooth, blank page, waiting to be inscribed.

So that was his baptism. He never described the sensation to Peter or any of the other followers; it felt profound but also incorrect somehow. Nevertheless, it was an act which fastened John Mark to these followers. And his devotion was solidified when they welcomed his questions. In his father's home, in his father's synagogue, questions had been John Mark's flaw and his undoing. While his father invited the questions of other believers and answered them patiently, he chastised John Mark for his questions. They were impertinent and displayed his ignorance for all to see. Besides, they indicated weakness, a flaw in his faith.

What sweetness to come to a place where his greatest shame was welcomed as a strength, as a gift. And so he asked and asked: Which Jewish laws did they keep and which did they disregard? Which holy days were still observed? How many mouths did Yeshua feed on the day the loaves were transformed? Why did Yeshua wait for Lazarus to die instead of

going right away, when he was first called? What kind of ang
who came to Mary? How was an angel different from the Holy

John Mark's questions became famous in the compound, and soon, instead of doing dull labor in the city, he was charged with training the Followers so they would be ready to go out, to Sidon and Tarsus and Lystra, and preach the good news. It was important, said Peter the First, never to fear a question. A question was a knock upon a door. Keep the door closed, and the hearer will believe you have something to hide; but if you offer an answer, even if the answer is imperfect or incomplete, then you have invited that person in. So John Mark knocked and knocked and knocked. And his life, for two years, was filled with the bliss of opening doors.

But now John Mark is in Alexandria, alone, baptized into a story he can't speak properly and still filled with questions. As he hauls water and fills his satchel with pouches from the pharmacy he thinks of the sensation of cool water on his forehead, trickling down his scalp, how when Peter's hand was upon him the questions, somehow, were not. He knows it is foolish, but the moment of baptism is the place to which John Mark longs to return. When he thinks of the return of Yeshua the Messiah it is a clearing he thinks of, a soft space where doubt does not itch at you, curiosity does not hound you. Where somehow you are known and without knowing.

He sounds like a cheap sage in the marketplace when he thinks these things. He knows this. And yet, John Mark also believes that if all of his questions are answered, he will arrive in that space again. A clearing from which he can finally tell a story that makes sense.

Hours pass. The Broom Boy brings Salome and John Mark and Nadjem clean rags and water and olive oil, but he also brings them news from the room below. How the elders repeat the same complaints over and over again, bolstered by words from different prophets. How Agrippa keeps mentioning statues of Caligula. How they eat Roman fish sauce and burn incense to dim the odor of body musk.

"But does he show compassion?" asks John Mark.

The Broom Boy shrugs. "He listens with a sad face and eats very little. He has called me seven times for the pot to empty himself, and each time he makes only a spoonful of piss."

Salome lifts the pestle from the mortar where she is grinding the myrtle for a balm. A few flecks of herb drift across the front of her dark tunic. "Go and tell Philo that Herod Agrippa should see a physician to make sure he is of sound body before he goes to Flaccus. Tell Philo to send for me."

When she is called for, Salome leads Agrippa down a narrow hall to a small bedroom where she used to sleep when she lived in Philo's home. Although it is used for servants, it is kept well: a clean purple coverlet on the couch, a stool, a lamp with fresh oil. The walls are decorated not with the usual lotuses and palm but with a series of animals that are two things at once: a dragon and a lion, a horse and a man, a cat and a bird. When Salome first met Asha, she thought of this room, what beauty and terror there was in refusing to be one thing or another.

Agrippa reclines on the couch and Salome lights the lamp; the brightness catches in his hair, the oily strands splayed against his scalp. His head will leave a stain on the mattress. Usually when Salome works her focus is intense and single-minded, but this whole day, ever since her confessions to John Mark, other thoughts kept snagging her: the way Yeshua pulled his arms and legs into his belly as an infant, the way she had to hold stolas open into wide circles so that Julia could step easily into them, the tug of her mother's hands pulling her hair into a tight plait. And if not the past interrupting her, it was the forgetting (asking Nadjem for "the clamp with long jaws" instead of the staphylagra because the word simply refused to come), and if not the forgetting, it was Asha, the way her jaw hung open after her melodramatic proclamation.

But now, in this room, Salome is entirely alert. She understands men of power, knows that Agrippa's presence in the city is more liability than hope. He gives Flaccus and the Greeks further reason to hate the Jews; his procession through the city, the flaunting of his wealth, his horses, his men—no good will come of it. He will incite violence instead of quelling it. She must shoo him from these shores before he can do more damage to the people who believe he will save them.

With her back to Agrippa, Salome asks about his condition. Many years ago, Rufus held her chin affectionately when he told her that she should turn away from patients initially because her face would not bring forth confessions. "You have a sharpness," he said. He did not mention the spots, but Salome knows people mistrust her for the brown flecks across her cheek and chin and forehead. Asha once said that gazing at her face was like gazing at the bottom of a soothsayer's bowl, waiting to see your future in the design of tiny bones or entrails, fearing the arrangement portends destruction. So Salome offers only her back to Agrippa as she asks about the timing of onset, about duration and diet, about the scent of the urine when it comes and his ease of defecation.

It is a straightforward case of strangury, she knows, and she has never lied about the treatment of a disease; but Salome knows this man needs to be on the next ship pulling from the harbor, his diadem and citrus scent climbing the dark waters up the coast. She takes a limewood box of butcher's-broom from her case and spreads the woody roots onto a small metal table beside the lamp. She calls the servant girl and asks for hot water, honey, and wine.

"Any animal bites or wounds?" she asks.

"No."

"Any unusual visions or dreams?" Salome hates this question, but Rufus insisted upon it; it was important, he claimed (though no other schools of medicine seemed to think so), to know why the patient himself thought he was ill.

When Agrippa doesn't answer, Salome looks over her shoulder. She is about to ask again when he speaks.

"I dream about rats." Agrippa has his eyes closed and is patting his beard gently. "In the dream my family, my bodyguards, my friends all believe me dead, but I am not. They wrap me in a burial shroud and place me in a tomb. The rats arrive with the chill of the night, and at first they are kind; they cover me like a blanket and sit motionless. The shroud protects me from their tiny claws, so I feel only the warmth of their bodies.

"But then one of them moves. I cannot see anything because it's dark, and this makes it worse. The one that moves takes my earlobe between its teeth." Agrippa touches his earlobe as he speaks, eyes still closed. "Even then, in the dream, I am not yet afraid."

"And then?"

"And then it bites. And the other rats come for my face. They all come for my face. And I want to open my mouth to shout, but I know that if I do, they will have my tongue. That is the terror that wakes me." Tears slip from the corners of his eyes.

Salome picks out her sharpest cutting knife and begins to peel away some of the dry skin from the roots. "The pain, you mean? Is the terror?"

"No. In the dream it is the not knowing whether to scream or hold my mouth closed. Which will prevent me from suffering."

The servant girl arrives then with the water and honey and wine. When Salome drops a handful of the roots into the hot water, the room is momentarily overcome with the steamed scent of a forest after a warm rain.

"Will you take the medicine in honey water or wine?"

"Wine."

Salome strains some of the hot liquid into the wine. "And will you help them? The Jews?"

Agrippa pushes himself into a seated position. "Physician, look at this."

When Salome turns with the cup of medicinal wine in her hand, she is certain he will be pulling back his cloak to reveal a wart or a birthmark, but he is holding out the gold chain he wears around his neck. Each link is large, the size of a small onion. "Caligula gave me this when he pulled me out of prison. A chain of gold to replace the chain of iron that held me. For how many years?"

Salome offers the cup and stares back at him steadily. "For how many years?"

Agrippa takes a sip of the drink, pulling it through his teeth to prevent both burning and bitterness. "For four years. Because I miscalculated my loyalties. I supported Caligula—in murmurs only, across dining tables after rounds and rounds of wine had been served—and Tiberius found out." Agrippa stands. "Where is the piss pot?" he yells toward the door, and the Broom Boy appears from the shadows. Now it is Agrippa who turns his back to Salome. "But then Tiberius died, and it turned out that my choice was the right one. Now I am free."

Salome listens for the sound of piss but hears nothing but a low grunt of air.

When he turns back to face her, Salome notices how thin he is, how the corners of his eyes turn downward slightly, how he winces slightly when he speaks.

He steps closer to her, hands at his sides, palms facing toward her. He does not need to explain himself to a physician, but he continues anyway, and the bergamot oil the servants use in his hair is a bright yellow field between them. "The elders are sometimes full of hot air, but they are good men. And I am not blind. The situation is dire. I am here to prove my loyalty to Caligula. I am to deliver statues in his honor to Flaccus. But I will also plead the case of the Jews. How can I not?" His whole body sways and he sits heavily down on the couch again. He picks up the cup again and takes the rest of the liquid down in one quick pull.

"Flaccus will not hear reason. He is unhinged. Ever since the death of Tiberius he's taken on the mantle of a Greek. They say he whips his servants with the scourges they have made for him. Braided leather inlaid with alabaster. He hates the Jews. He hates Caligula."

Salome turns and kneels, although her hip aches painfully as she does so. She fixes her gold eyes on Agrippa. "You want to be a hero to your people. That's admirable. But you'll do more harm than good if you take things up with Flaccus."

Agrippa leans closer to Salome. "You have a strange face, physician. I feel as though I have seen it before." Then he sighs. "I think you are right."

Salome nods, takes the empty cup, and returns to the table, where she sets about scraping the excess butcher's-broom into a papyrus packet. "Wouldn't it be best to leave now? Surely someone can deliver the statues. I would write a letter, if you desired. I would explain your ailment and how it was best for you to return home immediately."

Agrippa takes a long breath and lets his shoulders fall. "I have a necklace to give my wife," he says. As though the stone might spoil like fruit.

Salome turns and nods to encourage his strange reflection. "Your wife should see you sooner rather than later," she says. And she holds out the papyrus package of medicine.

Agrippa is slow to take the small package, and when he does, finally, he rests it lightly on his fingertips. "Do you have a hunch about this illness, physician?" Fear floats into his voice.

It would be easy to lie then. To say that she feels his death close at hand or that of late she's seen cases of strangury end with burial shrouds. She cannot. Instead she tells a story, the way that Rufus would. Or Yeshua. "My father once brought home a small bag of bergamots for my mother. She knifed the rind off in a single piece, showed me how you could press the rind together to make the bergamot look whole again, and then release the bottom and let the yellow skin uncurl into a long, unwinding spiral."

"My aunt did the same with pomegranates."

"And my mother said, each time I let the bergamot undo itself, 'That's how the gods come down to us.'"

Agrippa smiles a little, holds his index finger up and mimes the spiral in the air between them.

"I have thought since then that it also means the route from earth to immortality is just the same, not a ladder but a long and winding thing.

It requires turning your back on the place where you are in order to return to it again."

Agrippa nods.

"Perhaps you sail away from us so that you can sail back again."

"When I have enough power to assist the Jews," he muses.

"Yes," says Salome, although both of them know that he will never return, that further power breeds only a desire for further safety.

"If I leave, they will say I am a coward."

Salome shrugs. "You are not meant to be a hero in this story."

"Usually I don't listen to women." He says the words limply, without rancor.

"You have a simple case of strangury. The remedy you hold will be enough to bring you comfort on your journey."

Agrippa tucks the medicine packet into the folds of his tunic. "Be careful with that face," he says, as though he is offering her a benediction or a payment. "Tell the stable boy to ready my horse," he says to the Broom Boy without turning his face in the boy's direction.

When both the boy and man have gone, Salome sits down heavily on the small stool and retches a small pile of yellow bile into the empty chamber pot.

As the people of the New Jewish Quarter hope for gold-stuffed panniers, as grown men stuff grave dust onto their tongues to satiate their hunger, as vendors prepare to roll their carts back into the heart of the city, John Mark digs his knuckles into his eyes on Philo's rooftop as Salome tells him Agrippa's plan to depart without confronting Flaccus.

"Surely you could have poisoned him," croaks out John Mark.

"I could have. To what end?"

On a plate between the two of them, a pile of small, salted fish and a loaf of bread. Around them, dusk pulling its corners over the city. The patients have gone home, and Agrippa has returned to a boardinghouse by the docks. Some of the elders have retreated and some doze on the couches, satiated with their own efforts. Philo sits erect in the chair of his study, wreathed in the scent of vinegar, writing about the flaming sword and fixed stars in the outer circumference of heaven. Nadjem has returned home; she was invited to stay with John Mark and Salome, to sleep on bedrolls beside the dovecote on the roof, to share in the simple meal, but although Nadjem feels a strong affection for Salome, she can stomach only so much of the physician on a single day. Nadjem feels Salome's way with the world is sharp and unyielding; Salome is the kind of woman who would cut a linen tunic and then burn the leftover scraps. It is a Greek way of knowing: one thing being true makes another thing untrue. Egyptians find this kind of certainty tiring.

Across the city in the wig shop, Asha slides the latrunculi pieces back and forth on the board. Until Salome returns, she will play for both of them.

In the harbor, Agrippa watches the statues unloaded by Egyptian men who cover themselves with only loincloths. They do not grunt as Judeans would while they move the heavy crates; instead, they make a kind of hissing sound. It seems an ominous portent, the way the dark gobbles up the flesh of the men, leaving only scraps of floating white cloth and sizzling breath sounds. Agrippa clutches the paper packet of medicine more tightly and boards the ship.

"Why didn't you, then?" John Mark continues. "Poison him or tell the elders. You simply gave him butcher's-broom and kept your mouth shut?"

"Because his presence in the city is a fist in a beehive. He will make things worse."

"Not if he bargains for the Jews' release, for a rescinding of the mandate?"

"Do you think Flaccus will take orders from Caligula's pet? Do you think the Greeks will happily succumb to requests from a rich Jew who has set his toe in our city for only a moment?"

Salome takes another fish, savors the crack of tiny bones and the oil squeezed out by the pressure of her teeth. "It is a cowardly thing, perhaps, but not a reprehensible thing. I know what it is to be pulled two ways in this city. I know what it is to make a choice filled with shame. So I suppose I felt compassion for him."

John Mark stands and walks to the edge of the roof. In the alleyway they have made the entrance to the clinic, the ill have laid themselves around the side gate like a litter of dogs. Smoke rises from a small fire, but the scent is acrid, the smoke too dark. Two children gallop in some game, pelting each other with tiny pebbles. Just across the street a woman sits with a pile of rags in her lap, her head tilted back as though to sleep, but John Mark sees that her eyes are open and her jaw slightly slack; either she is dead, or she is waiting to be filled by some word of promise.

John Mark turns back to Salome. "The choice you made in this city. Was this a choice about Yeshua?"

"Sit down," says Salome.

5 BCE

I left the Mareotic community five days after Yeshua's birth in a cart pulled by a Jewish man named Hamish. Mari and Josef rode in the cart with me; the plan was for all of us to settle in the Jewish Quarter. That much Xenia, who spoke both Greek and Aramaic, had made clear to me before I left. I didn't believe I would see the baby often, but I thought occasionally I would catch a glimpse, looking up while tying a sandal strap or scooping water over my forearms at one of the fountains. Or maybe they'd bring him to whatever clinic I chose, and I'd press charred figs to the blue-veined skin of his chest when he had a cold. I'd mark his growth, a measured distance between us.

As we rode, Hamish's voice was a low drone of Aramaic gossip, Josef lobbing the occasional inquiry. Yeshua nursed, shaded by a portion of Mari's cloak. The sound of his suckling made my own milk let down, and I could feel it staining the cloth I'd used to bind my breasts. Every bump in the road jolted my tender birthing flesh, and I remember worrying, momentarily, about leaving a puddle of blood behind on the base of the cart.

When Yeshua finished nursing, Mari did not slide her pinky in between her flesh and his to release the seal that held them; instead, she let him sleep with his mouth fastened around her. This gesture prickled me a little, a low tingle at the base of my scalp, but I closed my eyes against it. He wasn't mine to mar or marvel over any longer. I focused instead on the scent of eucalyptus and the flickering of light and shadow on the backs of my eyelids. I followed, in my mind, the route that I would take to the house of Philo, Xenia's cousin in the Jewish Quarter.

Then Hamish's voice turned graver, slower. Josef asked another question and Hamish's response, whatever it was, caused Mari to rise up onto her knees and lean toward the running board where the two men sat. Josef began to stroke his beard violently, as if he wanted to wipe the skin off his face. He tried to ask another question, but Mari rose to a crouch and interrupted him, her voice high and thin, and as she did the arm that held Yeshua began to sag, and he fell away from her. Yeshua, pulled from the comfort of her nipple, began to scream, and she let him. She didn't even look at him, so I reached forward and took him in my arms, let him suck my pinky until he calmed. Mari was turned fully away from me now, pushing her questions at Hamish, and though I couldn't see her face, I could smell her panic.

Back then I couldn't understand a word of what was being said. Now I know they were learning that Herod, King of Judea, had died while they were away, and that Jews from Sepphoris and the crumbling towns surrounding it had gathered up their scythes and spears and pruning hooks and taken over the Roman armory. The uprising was put down eventually, of course, when more recruits from Rome arrived and burned the city to the ground. The rebels were slaughtered or sold into slavery. Mari was certain her father, a rabbi with zealous tendencies, had been a part of the revolt, and she was certain he was dead. As it turned out, she was right.

But then what I saw was a pantomime of feeling instead of a play that I could understand. I watched as Mari rode the rest of the way to Alexandria with both hands flat over her breastbone, drawing breath after breath into her lungs with great difficulty, as though her breathing tube had narrowed to a blade of grass. I eased my pinky from Yeshua's mouth and used that hand to open my medicine case and remove the vial of poppy. If her breathing became too labored, I could sedate her; sleep would return her body to its rightful rhythm. Mari, I learned that day and would be reminded of many days thereafter, rode emotions to the cliff edge of the abyss but never further. She could teeter at that edge for hours, days, or weeks; it was impossible to pull her back.

So Hamish didn't take us to the Jewish Quarter. He took us to the harbor. Josef took all of their belongings on his back, over his shoulders, and I could see, in the way he let the extra weight pull his body down, in the way he didn't try to fight the heaviness with his spine or shoulders or thighs, that he had lost something, too. His loss is another story altogether, of course.

"Nazareth," he said to me, gesturing toward the sea, and I understood that I would never see the baby while buying olives or testing a dab of expensive perfume against my wrist. They would get on a ship, and I would never see them again. Mari, made almost translucent by her worry, held out her arms for Yeshua and took him stiffly, like a young man who would rather be holding a grain sack or a chamber pot—anything besides a baby.

Josef placed a hand on his chest and said his name. Mari did the same. Then she put a thumb on Yeshua's forehead and whispered his.

I touched the divot at the base of my throat and said "Lyra," and they each repeated my name back to me, and I knew in that moment it was a name they'd never say again. I touched my thumb to the baby's forehead as Mari had done and said his name as best I could, and then I walked away.

Medicine case banging against my thigh, I trudged to the Canopic Way. Through the blare of the Alexandrian sun at its zenith I walked, past the gemstone inlays and droops of bougainvillea and silk awnings of the Royal Quarter, until I reached a side street paved with pink quartz. I followed the lighter stones. My whole body was leaking, sweat and blood and milk and tears now, too. And then my body turned around.

I hated it for turning. I hated myself with every step I took back toward the harbor. Hated that when I found Mari and Josef again, they did not look surprised. Hated how easily I handed over money and stepped on a ship bound for Joppa with them the next day. I hated myself all the way to Nazareth, and though the hatred dimmed a little, I kept at it every day I lived there. Each time someone spit at me or averted their gaze, each day my medicine case gathered dust in the corner of my room, each time I watched Mari bury her face in the crease of Yeshua's neck, I hated my choice.

So why did I leave Alexandria? And why did I stay in Nazareth for thirty-two years?

Maybe because I saw the way Mari's arm sagged on the cart ride, how quickly Yeshua disappeared when something else took over her vision. Maybe I was afraid for him because of the way she burrowed into a feeling, wore it like a cloak of camel hair. This is what I told myself for many years.

But the truth is that something pulled me back. Not a mother instinct. Not a physician's urge to protect a patient. It was a hand gripped around my ribs. A yank. I do not follow any gods, as I have said, but in that moment my own will felt like a clod of dirt, a crushed grape, a crumb, a crack, a mustard seed.

And so I betrayed myself. A self I had spent years making strong and swift and certain. I have not told you those parts yet. What I survived.

In that moment I became a quivering, boneless thing inside that grip. I followed Yeshua.

38 CE

By the time Salome finishes, night is fully upon them. John Mark stands and walks to the edge of the rooftop again to see if the rag woman is still there, but everything has been turned to lumps of shadow. John Mark can still taste the acidity of the smoke if he pulls a deep enough breath, but the fire, if there is one, gives no light. Besides the doves, there are no animal night sounds on the rooftop, only very human ones: a wailing baby, the splash of liquid turned out onto stones, voices raised into barks and then softened to whispers.

The Broom Boy arrives with three small cups and the dregs of the elders' wine. Its taste is Roman, watered, bitter, but it clears the stench from John Mark's nose and makes his stomach burn in a way that both satiates his hunger and feels like punishment.

"You said that you made a choice like Agrippa's. But his choice was selfish, and yours was selfless."

"I have just said that it was not a choice."

"But your decision arose from a sense of duty."

"I have just said it did not." Salome's voice is growing tight, but John Mark presses onward.

"Agrippa wants to save his own skin, but you sacrificed what you desired to do the rightful work of mothering."

"How many patients might I have saved if I had stayed in Alexandria? You forget, in your calculations of goodness, that I am a physician."

"But look who Yeshua became. He needed you. Perhaps a messiah needs two mothers." John Mark says this with the confidence of a man who has just found a sweet date in a loaf of bread he thought would be stale.

"I will tell you what kind of mother I was."

4-2 BCE

While Yeshua grew, I studied Mari and watched her mothering so my gestures and attention would not feel like an echo of hers, a flimsy shadow sliding over his skin. When I saw the way she let him eat his lentils in big globby handfuls, I offered him a spoon; when I saw the way she carried him until his legs dangled to her knees, I made him walk with his hand against the outside of my house, around and around again until he found his balance; when I saw the way she gave him dollops of honey just for the gift of sweetness, I taught him a letter of the Greek alphabet, then offered him a sesame sweet so he could see the way it tasted better when he accomplished something first.

In Nazareth, when a child turned two, he was weaned. Sometimes this meant a mother dabbed vinegar on her nipples or sent the child to live with a cousin for a week so he could forget the yeast-scent of her skin. Not Mari. Yeshua nursed and nursed and nursed. And she used it as a tool to keep my son away from me. If I entered their courtyard bearing lanolin or beeswax, water from the cistern or dates from the widow Anna's tree, Mari would see me before he did and make a cooing sound between her lips. Yeshua would come toddling over, pull down her tunic, and begin to suck. He'd see me, then. I'd watch his eyes grow slightly wider, watch his smile open slightly to reveal the dark skin of her areole. But he wouldn't come to me. Her milk fastened them together. It always had.

I struck Yeshua when he was a little over three years old, after Mari had grown large with another child who had then slipped into the birthing cloth I held when he was only in his sixth month—too early, dead. Simon, she named him. And though I think she had desired this new child mostly so her milk would not run dry for Yeshua, Simon's death demolished her. She lay naked on the rug inside their house, refused to wash the birth blood off herself. Black flies swarmed. When

Yeshua came and touched her breasts, now hot and full with milk, she batted him away. Whatever disdain I felt for Mari, I never questioned the depth of what she felt. I had known patients who feigned aches to earn a doctor's touch or who curled around their pain and made of it a pet, but Mari's grief always felt as though she'd taken the unuttered yearning of the world and let it swell below her skin. Her suffering felt holy. So though I tried to make her physical pain diminish, I did not try to sweep the other darkness away.

Three-year-old Yeshua, of course, turned sullen. Threw his food, kicked at Josef's shins, grabbed handfuls of my hair and tried to tear it from the roots. I calmed him firmly, without anger. But then one night, a few weeks after Simon's birth and death, Yeshua found his way to me in the middle of the night. I woke to him lifting up my sleeping shirt, pressing his small hand against the soft tissue of my breast to raise my nipple to his mouth. I grabbed his bony shoulders and flipped him on his back, and then I said *no* and *no* and *never*, and with the last word I lifted him and then pushed him back against the ground roughly so his skull thudded on the earthen floor.

I terrified him, of course. He didn't try to fight me, but his eyes swung from side to side and refused to gaze up at my face. I let him go, horrified by my violence and also by my impulse. Why had I pushed him away from me? Isn't this in fact what I'd wanted as I watched him cling to Mari, as I'd seen them seal themselves together again and again? The truth—that perhaps I didn't really want to bear his need—I couldn't face.

He covered his eyes with both his hands. I should have gathered him to me. Should have pressed his body to my chest and rocked him, smoothed my palm down the ridgeline of his spine. But I had seen Mari do this a thousand times. Those were her gestures, not mine.

So I rose, and for the first time since I left Rome, I took out my medicine case. I unpacked the limewood boxes and the small clay pots and glass vials. I laid out in a neat row the hooks and retractors and blades, the marble stone for rolling pills, the tiny scale for weighing herbs. I thought I did it then as a means of distraction, but I understand now that I was trying to show him what I was, who I was.

Eventually he uncovered his face and curiosity raised his head, drew his fingers to uncover the boxes, slide off lids. The scale engaged him most; he placed a pebble in the right-hand dish and a lentil in the other. He added a tuft of thread, then a fly mummied in spider web until the scale was balanced. Then he put his hand gently on my knee.

He returned to Mari and Josef when the dark began to blue toward dawn. In his sudden absence the scale looked precarious, and I wanted to protect its tender balance in a way I'd failed to protect my son from my own self. So I carried it gently to my window ledge to keep it safe, but when I set it down, something shifted. The pebble bounced away. As the sun reared over the horizon, I watched the right arm rise higher and higher until the gold dish caught the light; the left side, sunk in shadow, released itself to earth.

DAY THREE

38 CE

Salome wakes from a sleep that barely was, her tongue sucked dry from the salt of last night's fish and the scent of bergamot oil tart on her fingertips. She rises and regards the purpling clouds in the east as she reties her head scarf, as she walks unsteadily back and forth across the roof until the pain in her hip loosens. She does not allow herself thoughts of Asha or Yeshua; she does not allow herself to stop by the dovecote to listen to the comforting rumple of cooing. Once the light offers the outline of the side stairs, she climbs down them; the clinic needs to be readied.

Agrippa wakes in the berth of a ship halfway to Joppa. The waves ease his body side to side, and he thinks of the feast he will have prepared on his return: tender Judean lamb stippled with mint, curded cheese and honey, spiced almonds and fig cakes. Agrippa stands and pisses a healthy, steady stream of urine into a pot, so much urine that it sloshes over the edge and onto the sleeve of the servant who takes the pot away. From his satchel, Agrippa takes Salome's remedy and pours it into the dregs of last night's wine, sips it, and returns to sleep. And in this way, with wine-stained teeth and dreams crouching just behind his ears, Agrippa sails out of this story, toward omens awaiting him on a farther shore.

Back in Alexandria, Asha stands at the doorway of Salome's room, plucking tender grains of sleep from the corners of her eyes. The covers of both sleeping cots remain unwrinkled. Because it is the third day of the week, Asha removes the sheet that hangs above the cot on the right side of the room, the cot that is never used, the cot that waits, endlessly, for a visitor of whom Salome never speaks. But once a week, faithfully, Salome changes the cedar shavings inside the sheet, and because she is not here, Asha does this work, dumping the dried bits of wood beside the brazier to use as tinder and pulling from the burlap sack fresh shavings, slightly damp, full of the smell of a forest Asha has never entered and never will enter. Asha does all this before placing her own wig, before wrapping her padding, before kohling her eyes and plucking the hairs that thicken her brows. There are a million sacred spaces in Alexandria, and Asha knows to enter Salome's room unadorned—although, like so many things, this is something she would never say to Salome; this is a truth Salome would not understand.

By the time John Mark clomps down the stairs to the clinic, Salome and Nadjem are already busying themselves, Nadjem folding a basket of clean linen bandages and Salome organizing herbs and instruments on a low table along the east wall. The servant girl from Philo's study is also there, filling the room with the scent of vinegar.

"Porridge downstairs," says Salome curtly.

"Ah," says John Mark. He feels dumb and slow in the midst of this activity. "I will return to the roof and transcribe last night's words after eating."

Nadjem continues to roll a linen bandage but casts a glance toward Salome.

"No," says Salome, "we need a caller."

"But yesterday"—was it yesterday? he wonders—"you said I was to transcribe in the morning and assist you in the afternoon." Truthfully, until he writes the story it will hover—the scale, the sound of Yeshua's skull against the packed dirt floor, the jolt of the cart ride to Alexandria—but also the smell of vinegar nauseates him, and to be crouched near the companionable sound of the doves in the cool of the morning with parchment spread across his lap feels far superior to—

"That was yesterday," says Salome. "The world changes. We need a caller. Look at those stairs. Should Nadjem and I be up and down them a hundred times today? Look at your own thighs." All three of them turn their gazes to his thighs, which are completely covered by the tunic. "Like a mule," declares Salome. "Besides, right now the city is unsettled. Word will travel that Agrippa has departed, and by midday the Greeks will have swallowed a bit of the fierceness of their rage. Then I will walk you across the city myself, and you will have the afternoon in my study."

Before John Mark can answer, Salome has turned and addressed Nadjem in Egyptian, and soon the two are bickering about a packet of herbs in a mostly affectionate tone. So John Mark eats his porridge and then escorts the first seven patients from the alley to the clinic: a man with eyes leaking pus, a pregnant woman with puffed fingers and wrists, an elderly woman who cries silently, a mother holding a child flushed with fever, and three different men who can barely walk, whose beards and tunics are stained with vomit and bile.

Still, John Mark carries the stories of the night before like a veil between him and the patients. Back in Jerusalem, he asked so many questions about Yeshua—his ministry, his miracles, the kingdom he envisioned—and certainly, the answers to those questions were what mattered most, not whose nipple Yeshua preferred or how he learned to walk or whether a hand was ever raised against him. Those details feel private, like seeing the Messiah unclothed in a moment of prayer. And yet. John Mark wants more.

The sun shoves morning light down the alleyways and through the shuttered blinds of Alexandria. The vendors raise their tarps and Asha sets out her cacophony of sparkling pins and hairpieces while Nicodemus sloshes by with his cart of fish. Lamps are extinguished and plants are pulled from the shadows of atriums into the light of doorways and window boxes. Motes of flour from the bake shops and the dust of beaten rugs puff the air, eclipsing momentarily the faces of the rich Greek men who enter the baths with clean tunics tucked under their elbows. Carabbas, the beggar, limps along on his bandaged foot, singing an idle song to the sunlight. He begs the sun to be gentle, to be merciful; he pleads it not to strafe his back. "I will build a dwelling place for you," he sings to the sun, in the shadow of the date tree, below the rattle of the palm.

The Greek Quarter, the Roman Quarter, the Egyptian Quarter—all wake, but nowhere is there news of Agrippa's departure. Before the men from the docks can blurt the news to the barley beer vendors, before the vendors can whisper to the water runners, before the water runners can jostle the news into one another at the crossroads fountain, before the servant girl can overhear it and whisper it to her widowed mistress, before the mistress can tell it to her nephew, who comes in the morning for date cakes before he goes to the baths—before any of this can happen comes the procession.

The procession is so reminiscent of the one from the day before, when Agrippa rode in all his pomp and plumage to Philo's house, that no one notices that Agrippa is not, in fact, present. Instead what the Alexandrians see are seven carts carrying human-sized figures covered in burlap wrappings. On each cart stands one of Agrippa's bodyguards, positioned to keep the statues from teetering. It was Agrippa himself who thought the statues should be removed from their crates and processed, veiled, to Flaccus's doorway; the entrance would be more grand, more mysterious, the wraps could be whipped away to reveal the marble chests and heads of Caligula over and over again, shining and decadent in the famous Alexandrian sunlight. And Flaccus would be reminded of Caligula's power and his own precarious standing in the eyes of Rome.

Agrippa did not consider that veiled things heighten suspicion; he did not count on the fact that the presence of his bodyguards would be an assault. He did not understand that in a city where the gods outnumber the people, no one shrouds their beliefs. To hide a god is suspect. And surely that's what these shrouded figures must be, the Greeks whisper among themselves, images of the Jewish god, Yahweh, the god they keep separate from all other gods, a god they will not let into the sight of others.

Consider for instance this Greek, a tanner, his wares spread before him as the procession of carts rolls by, close enough that he could spit onto the soldiers' cuirasses. The sun-warmed scent of leather wrist guards, leather belts, leather ties, and leather sandals wreathes his palms, his knuckles, his forearms. This tanner thinks of a small beach down the coast at Pelusium. How his grandfather swam there as a boy, naked in the shallow waters, hair shaved and skin oiled, slippery as an eel, the water clear enough to count the ripples of the sand. How when the Romans came, they rutted the sand with their carts and let their horses shit along the jetty, how their animal sacrifices stained the rocks with blood and wedged tiny bones between the limestone rocks farther up the shore so that even after their conquest was complete, wild boars took up the space, rooting out the ghost scents of death. Then the tanner's grandfather would show the scar, a smooth white comet trail across his thigh, and say, "That's what you get from one of those," and he meant the boars and the Romans both. And if he still lived now, the tanner knows, he'd touch the scar and say, "The Jews are hungry like the Romans." He'd say, "Look after what you have."

The tanner uses one arm to slide his wares from the table into a sack. He ties leather guards onto his wrists and straps a leather belt and hilt around his waist. His grandfather said he turned his back on the boar and ran. "Should have kept my footing," he said. "Should have charged instead."

And so Salome's plan, well intended, has the opposite effect. Instead of the city settling, it roils: the Jews have not been humbled, they have not learned their place; saying *foreigner* and *alien* is not enough, collecting them into a rotting ball in the corner of the city is not enough. They must be made to listen. They must, somehow, succumb.

By midday the violence has begun. John Mark leads to the clinic a man whose face has been split open by fists and another who cradles his midsection and struggles to breathe. An hour later comes a man with rope burns around his neck, "Taken," he says hoarsely, "from the courtyard of my house, my own house, near the border of the New Jewish Quarter, but not outside it, not outside it," he says. "A sack thrown over my head. Bound," he says, "at my neck, at my wrists, but not at my knees. They spun me," he says, "like a child's game and said if I wandered the wrong way, if I blundered out of the Quarter, they would kill me. So I didn't move. They jeered at me. Maybe hours?"

"Fetch him a clean tunic," Salome says to John Mark.

The odor of vinegar in the clinic has been replaced by urine and vomit and the rancid curl of fear-sweat. John Mark is glad for a chance to tumble down the stairs and into Philo's study, where no one is moaning or bleeding or murmuring prayers. Glad for the clean window slats and the orderly arrangement of parchment on Philo's desk, glad for the sunlight that falls in even bars across the floor, glad for the neat, crisp folds of the tunic he is given by Philo, for its deep gray hue. He is even glad for the way Philo all but ignores him, does not ask about those suffering in the room above him, does not mention the elders who have gathered again in the large atrium outside, does not mention the way they slump together and moan and pull their beards. Philo simply nods at John Mark's request and then returns to his work.

"The elders know that Agrippa has gone," says John Mark when he returns to the upstairs clinic. Nadjem is winding a bandage around the tortured man's rope burn while Salome spoons salted broth into a man who opens his mouth like a bird and smiles each time he swallows.

Salome stands and gestures with her spoon. "The elders may know that Agrippa has left, but the Greeks do not. Look at his neck," she says, gesturing to the now-covered wound of the Tortured Man. "This is because a Jewish king paraded through their streets yesterday. We will have to spread the news of Agrippa's departure on our own."

"We? How? Do you plan to stand on the blocks and deliver proclamations?"

"I plan to deliver the news to the clinic, to the vendors at the crossroads, to the library. It will be enough."

"How?"

"It will be enough."

When John Mark arrives at the crossroads fountain with Salome, he no longer recognizes the place. A mass of people presses toward the theater, while another group gathers near the baths, shouting and laughing. Vendors are using the opportunity to send boys through the crowd with sweets and packets of fish and meat pies. The people press and sidle and elbow and rise up on their tiptoes. There is something wild on their faces, a panting excitement that makes his scalp tingle.

He and Salome tunnel their way into the smaller crowd near the baths to try to make sense of what is happening. In the middle of the crowd is a puppet booth. Two likenesses bob and weave and wave their tiny arms: a fat puppet dressed in red that must represent Flaccus and a skinnier one draped in purple with a golden crown so big that it has fallen around the puppet's neck to make a noose instead.

"But let me see if you are circumcised!" the Flaccus puppet says. The Agrippa puppet shrugs off his purple robes and there, on the bare, smooth forearm of the puppeteer, is painted a cock so small, John Mark thinks at first that it is a birthmark or a mole. The crowd roars.

"Ta-da!" says the Agrippa puppet.

"How am I supposed to tell if there is foreskin on *that*?" jeers the Flaccus puppet.

"Go to the library," says Salome to John Mark. "Tell who you can. I will come later with food. Go."

And though it is clear that it is far too late for their words to be of any use, John Mark turns up the Water Way toward the harbor. He will do as Salome asks, and then he will retreat to her study. He will study the smudge of sea he can observe from the window; he will burrow his nose in the cardamom scent of his traveling cloak; he will water the rosemary and the thyme. And then, like Philo, he will settle himself into writing to escape the chaos and misery that surrounds him.

Salome intends to go directly to the clinic, but instead she finds herself following the crowd of people surging into the theater. Suddenly aware of her exhaustion and the throbbing pain in her hip, Salome finds a seat to watch whatever spectacle is about to be performed.

She does not have long to wait. The crowd lifts a roar to the heavens as Carabbas, the beggar whose injured foot she treated only two days earlier, is led into the middle of the theater on a rope. She stares, unmoving, as one Greek man crowns him with a leaf of papyrus and another throws a door mat over his shoulders and another offers him a stick of papyrus to use as a scepter. A few young boys are pulled from the audience and offered bigger sticks and the opportunity to play his bodyguards. They grin with pride.

Carabbas strokes his graying beard and the crowd goes wild. He raises the stick, and they howl. He begins a slow march forward and the boys cluster around him, trying to walk in sync and failing miserably. Then the chant goes up. "King of the Jews! King of the Jews! King of the Jews!" they shout. And then, although Agrippa is no threat to them, although he has done nothing in their city that deserves mockery or shame, they shower Carabbas with pebbles and stale bits of bread, olive pits and the softened ends of cucumbers. The beggar's triumphant smile turns into a howl of surprise as his face and ribs and thighs are pummeled with detritus, as the crowd surges forward and raises Carabbas up on their shoulders, begins to pass him up and over them, each person desiring a touch. His crown and his cape and the scepter fall away, and he is naked and wriggling now, terrified and trying to scramble his way back to earth. But there is no purchase to be found in the bodies below him. They carry him out of the stadium, the dark shouting mob of them balancing his helpless body. "King of the Jews! King of the Jews! King of the Jews!"

And then the sound dissipates and the people are gone, and Salome stares at the empty expanse before her and wonders where she is. There is a tightness in her chest and her two hands sit limply on her lap like onion skins. She has wet herself, and also she knows that she has lost something, a something that is big and important, but she cannot remember what it is or where it has gone. In front of her, a man drags a half-rotting carcass of a deer into the center of the theater and leaves it there. Salome wonders if she is dead. She weeps because she is inside a loss that has no memory, that is only feeling.

Then there is a man beside her. He lifts her up like a baby into his arms and carries her home.

In the back courtyard of the wig shop, Asha lowers Salome's body into the tub of warm water. Asha adds lavender oil to the water and sponges Salome's neck.

For a long time, Salome sits limply, her eyes dull and her mouth open slightly. Asha wipes Salome's clavicle, her brow, her upper arms. It is when Asha takes Salome's chin in her hand, when she raises Salome's face and begins to wipe her forehead, that Salome's eyes turn sharp again.

"Your makeup is dripping," says Salome. "I told you not to buy kohl from that hussy down the street. She thickens her charcoal with barley flour."

Asha laughs and presses her nose into Salome's hair. "I knew you'd come back."

"Of course I came back. Where else would I go?"

After the bath they play latrunculi on the front patio. Against all odds, it is still not night yet; the day holds on with sharpened claws. Salome knows she should finally rest in these familiar sensations: the wet plait of hair on her shoulder, the citron laced into the barley beer rising up her nose, the gentle scrapes of their stones across the board, the tap of Asha's foot against her own ankle, a tiny pulse. She should go and lay down on her cot, have a good deep sleep before returning to Philo's tomorrow. But she is restless; she can feel John Mark waiting in her study, studying the pages of the pharmacopeia on the walls, putting pinches of her herbs upon his tongue, rubbing his dusty feet over her rug. Asha looks up from the game to find Salome gazing over her shoulder.

"I don't know what to ask you anymore, Salome. It feels like there is nothing you want to say to me."

Salome studies Asha's face, lashes thickened with charcoal paste, cheekbones rouged to lift them higher, brows plucked into thin arches, lips widened beyond their natural outline with wine lees. And then, always, Asha's eyes: large and green and always somehow able to hold two things at once: irritation and charm, impatience and curiosity, affection and loss. This is one of Asha's gifts—it's what life has given her—but still Salome would like to turn to Asha, to touch Asha, to speak to Asha in such a way that for a minute she feels only one thing: the rightness of the world, the feeling that Salome had in childhood, that she has longed to return to ever since.

"Give me the week," says Salome. And with the tip of her index finger she touches each of the knuckles on Asha's right hand.

Before Asha can move or speak, a woman approaches, shaking an ill-made wig above her head like a rat. "Look at this, Asha. Look at this monstrosity. Has my cousin listened even once?"

"Not that I can recall," says Asha, rising.

"I will be home in time to sleep," says Salome quietly.

Asha nods but does not look at her. Already she has taken the wig from the customer and flipped it over so that the woman can see the way craftsmen far inferior to Asha have glued together the hairs. "With piss and spit" is the last things Salome hears as she urges her aching hip down the Water Way.

John Mark is surprised that transcribing Salome's stories from the night before makes him dislike her. He has seen with his own eyes her wisdom in treating patients, her care for those who are suffering; he understood, he thought, her sharpness and impatience. But writing about the woman who was ready to put her infant on a boat and let him sail away from her, the woman who rammed her toddler's head into the earth, this builds a sticky bile in his stomach.

And so after she arrives, after they have eaten a simple meal of bread and figs and rosemary oil, after she has settled herself on the low stool, right leg outstretched in front of her, head resting against the wall, he says, "Tell me about a moment of tenderness."

"Tenderness."

"Yes, tenderness. Between you and Yeshua."

Salome thinks of the sponge on her neck, of Asha blotting her forehead and ears and cheeks. "Tenderness," she says again.

1 BCE-2 CE

When most people are sick, they open up to you and you can see them clearly. It is in health that we protect our bodies; we have the energy to hide what we don't want others to see. If someone truly wants to be healed, they must offer up their body to the physician fully, with trust.

Yeshua knew this instinctively. And so my most tender moments with my son were the times he was hurt or ill, in part because he so willingly offered his body to me and in part because he was so fascinated by what I did, so ready to learn.

The first time he truly understood what I did, what all those boxes and vials meant, he was four years old. A wasp listing over the last of Josef and Mari's meager grape harvest lit into his skin. Mari applied kisses and I applied plantain, and he felt in his own body the kind of comfort that worked. When the pain had eased a bit, he asked to pick the plant himself, and so we squatted in the yard together and I showed him all the places the plant grew wild along the ground, the oblong leaves that, when pulled up gently, contained a filament of ruby at the bottom of the stem. A few months later, when Elul dust kicked up along the plain and clogged our lungs, he came to me again with his dry cough, and together we placed figs on the brazier grates, thumbed them open, then placed the charred fruit upon his chest. He held my hand, and each time the dry cough wracked his lungs, I felt the way his tiny fingers jerked.

He began to come to me for even the smallest bodily concerns: thin skin peeling off around his fingernails, flea bites on his ankles, a thin splinter in his wrist. He narrated the size and quality of his excrement, picked at his own scabs so he could track the tiny rush of blood, made up his own words to describe the taste of sweat and nasal fluid and eye sand.

Yeshua was so busy with me he stopped returning to Mari to nurse during the day. Then he stopped altogether. And yes, I did feel some gladness about this. But mostly, at the time, I thought my joy was rooted in his love for medicine, his curiosity about the world. I didn't know that part of what I loved was seeing my own self alive in another person.

I am surprised Mari let us continue this way as long as she did. Perhaps it was because during that time she had two more stillbirths, two more bouts of the kind of rancid grief she had experienced when Simon was born. But then one day when Yeshua was six and Mari was finally recovered from her most recent loss, the two of them sat in the courtyard together, grinding barley down into a meal that we could use for bread. While they worked, Mari unspooled her stories and her songs. I was watching on my side of the wall.

Mari began to sing a song about the great escape, how the Israelites had packed up everything they had so quickly. It was a song for children, and at one point the singer was supposed to ask the little ones what they would pack. Usually Yeshua called out the names of his cousins, his favorite foods, sometimes even a part of the landscape he loved. "Issac!" "Fig jam!" "I would put Mount Horeb in my sack!" But this time, Yeshua held up a tiny pot he used to make poultices with me and said, "My medicine." Mari's face lurched and the song dwindled. Yeshua didn't seem to notice; instead, he stirred whatever concoction the pot held, and even from that distance I could hear him sniffing at it to see if the potency was right.

That night, I knew enough to keep my lamp lit, not to unroll my bedding. I dragged in two low stools from the courtyard and sat on one, tying up the rosemary I'd picked that day. Dread slid down my throat and pooled at the bottom of my belly. Mari came in the dark after Yeshua was asleep.

"Peace be with you," she said.

"Peace to you," I said. I offered her water and wine, dates and bread, but she refused. She wouldn't sit on the stool.

Mari and I rarely spoke. Never at length. Never alone. You have met her, so perhaps I need not describe her. Then again, age does its best to disguise our former selves. She was, back then, a beautiful woman in the way that a button is beautiful: round and sweet, perfect in its usefulness, easy to dismiss as decorative until you find the cold wind swaying over your frame because your cloak won't stay fastened shut. She was short but not heavy. Her eyes were brown and wide, her face round, the divot above her top lip pronounced. She had dark hair on her arms but no soft growth on her face; she smelled of fresh milk, and her gaze pressed at you from behind her skin, her head always pushed forward toward the hearer's face in a way that looked uncomfortable.

"You are making medicine," she said plainly.

"I am drying the plants so they can become medicine," I corrected.

There was the small scratching sound of my hands busy with the stems. I knew her cloak hid the dimpled, loose flesh at her abdomen. My cloak hid two hip bones jutting out of a flat span of flesh like the prow of a Germanic ship.

"Yeshua is impressionable right now," she said.

I waited for her to go on, but she did not go on.

"It's only a few plants," I lied. "A little play with a mortar and pestle."

Mari squatted down beside me. The muscles of her thighs trembled beneath her cloak, but her gaze was steady, her face pushing too close to my own. "Why do you cast me as the villain?"

I did not look at her. I began to weave the bunches of herbs I'd created into a longer braid for hanging. "I do not really think of you at all," I said.

She covered my hands with hers, stopped my work. I didn't try to shake them free but instead returned her gaze. You may have noticed my eyes are thin and hard and, in certain lights, a golden feline color. A patient once told me I had eyes that were man enough to make people listen. She squeezed my hands harder and harder until I was the one who spoke: "You keep him from me." My voice was petulant, a child stripped of a trinket.

"You *gave* him to me, Salome. Remember? I am now the guardian of the path Adonai intends for him. There are things Yeshua needs to know, right now, as he grows, stories of the prophets, the wisdom of the scrolls, the habits that honor Adonai's gifts. He is meant to know all of this."

"Meant to?"

"Meant to. Yes. You are a woman without a people, Salome. I do not expect you to understand. But I do expect you to abide by my wishes."

"To stop teaching him, you mean."

"Yes."

"It's Yeshua who comes to me, not me who seeks him out."

"Nathan is in search for someone to assist him with his sheep."

"You are instructing me to become a shepherd?"

"You are fond of Nathan," she reminded me. "I am requesting that you spend some time away, during the days at least, so that I can set Yeshua on his path. When he is ten or eleven you can teach him again if you want. By then the story of our people will be set in his bones. Now he is so young that the words swim through him. I must repeat them over and over again."

I laughed a little. It was not a kind laugh. My mother and father had kept sheep. After so many years of travel and learning I would be doing exactly what they had. A shepherd?

"Or you can come and listen." And this time it was the optimistic lilt of her voice that was false.

I removed my hands from her grip and pulled the bunches of rosemary toward me, as if she might taint them with her presence. The next words were hot coals I lined up in front of her: "You built a wall between us."

"Did you want to live with me, Salome? With Josef? Did you ever actually want to be a part of our family?"

"You built a wall."

"Nathan leaves at dawn. He expects you." Then she stood and blew out the lamp without asking, the scent of rosemary heavy and baleful in the dark.

I sat for a long time, then, running over all the things I did not say: I did not say that I was lonely. That every day I hated myself for following them here and then again for staying. I did not say that her mistrust of me was palpable. That I saw the way she used her breast all those years to turn Yeshua away from me. Never had she set her palm on the ground beside her to invite me close. Never had she offered to bind my hair or wash my feet or clip the loose threads from my tunic. And I did not say that I offered Yeshua medicine because I had nothing else to give: no easy tenderness, no honeyed sweets, no stories or songs. I was miserable at games like hide-and-find and bandits. Even after these years in Galilee, my Aramaic was awkward, halting. What interest did I hold for a six-year-old boy?

And it turned out I was right. I did my best to obey Mari's wishes: I shadowed Nathan and the sheep and let my medicine case gather dust. When Yeshua came to my house, I tried to interest him in drawing figures together in the dirt. He came less and less. I even ground a precious cup of grain, hired Josef to make a small wooden tray and filled it with the sandy powder so my son could learn his letters. He drew a spear, a sword, and three decapitated heads instead.

I am not proud of what I did next. As he wandered away from my yard after drawing those pictures, licking the tasteless powder from his fingertips, I said, "Yeshua, here." Then I let the fire from the brazier lick the inside of my forearm until the skin puckered and a pink blister formed.

"Auntie!" he yelled, excitement trumping concern.

"Get the case," I said.

He ran into the house, so full of importance to have a task. The pain rang and rang on my skin, but I took my time, patient with him when he reached for fenugreek first. Telling him to think again. What did we use for pain, what did we use for skin that was inflamed? Once he chose the proper herbs, I asked what kind of medicine we should make: a tincture or a poultice or a salve?

He said, "A tincture would take too long."

"Good."

"But the oil in a salve might infect the wound?"

"Yes," I said.

"Poultice, then. But fresh herbs would be best. I know where plantain is but not the comfrey."

"Get the plantain, then," I said, and I watched him pick it, did not hurry his gentle tugs, the slowness of his gathering, though the pain made me sit, made my eyes swim. He mashed the herbs, added a few drops of boiling water to achieve the right consistency, found a long, clean rag for wrapping. He was too tender applying the poultice, too gentle wrapping the bandage around my skin, his physician's flaws already appearing. But then I was only glad for his glee, his attention, his small body working next to mine.

Two days later, Yeshua cut himself, on purpose, with his father's double-headed axe. He tried for the forearm, where I'd made my burn, but he cut too close to the wrist. Yeshua almost bled to death. Then the wound became infected, and he almost died again.

The night when death was closest, when fever swept up and down his body, Mari and Josef let me sleep inside their house, so acute was their fear of losing him. Mari wept over him, rubbing her tears into his skin, crooning his favorite songs so close to his ear that the skin there turned a deeper shade of scarlet from the intensity of her breath. Finally she slept, heavy and deep, and that's when Josef picked up Yeshua and nodded for me to come with him. We walked down the lane, past Judah's blind chicken pecking aimlessly in the moonlight, past the singed bread scent of Aaron's courtyard, until we reached the mikveh. I had never been allowed to step into it, reserved as it was for ritual cleansing.

"Take him under his arms," said Josef, and I did. Josef lifted Yeshua's thighs over his hips and walked backward down the stone steps, the dark water erasing Josef's calves, his knees, his thighs. I followed, holding Yeshua's bandaged wrist out of the water. Yeshua did not open his eyes, but he shuddered slightly. Then we were only three heads, floating, and I thought of the heads Yeshua had drawn and wondered if it was this moment he had been drawing, if he had known. His cheek against my neck was so hot that a sheen of sweat formed between us. Josef sang, I think. I had never heard him sing, but I believe that is what the sound was. I do not believe in gods, as I have said, but this was the first time I felt what others must have: that I was a tube and the capacious universe could sail through me at its leisure. I could feel my mother, my father, my mentor, Rufus, press close from the past, and whatever was to come was not so far away. Sense became blurry. Days were vials, lichen a mist, the small sound of Yeshua's tongue unsticking was a dog who had haunted me when I first arrived in Rome, the curl of Yeshua's white fingers above the water was the sound my father made to call the sheep in. From my son's open mouth came the scents of dried lavender and Roman fish sauce, the oily tang of a body scraped clean at the baths, the boozy scent of Julia's neck, the iron-ocean smell of a patient laid open on the table. Josef's song turned into a choking sob and I felt Yeshua's body cool, his sweat go dry, and I saw him clearly in my mind's eye, riding beside Hades on a coal-black horse, and then I saw Yeshua slipping off the side, out of that god's grip, and as he tumbled he curled into a ball and, flecked with the horse's foam, rolled swiftly away and all the way back to me until he was inside me again, and then I rebirthed him into that pool and the sun was a single clarion note as it crested the hill and my son was alive again.

You asked for my most tender moment with my son, and I tell you it was this, when I held his head against my shoulder in the mikveh at the cusp of death. When my actions almost killed him.

I understand what kind of mother I am.

38 CE

Salome speaks the last line pragmatically, efficiently, in her physician's voice. She does not let shame or grief creep into the words. She holds them steady. But she does have to tilt her chin up slightly so that John Mark will not see the trembling around her lips.

But John Mark has barely heard the last few sentences anyway. His whole being snagged and caught on the phrase *alive again*. He sits up in the dusky light and rubs his palms against his knees until he feels them grow warm. "You are saying," he says excitedly, "that Yeshua died in that mikveh and was then returned to life."

Salome regards the man trembling before her. She thinks of her mentor, Rufus, of how he treated a man suffering with vomiting and nausea. How they offered him daphne and periwinkle, but his symptoms did not subside until Rufus found a beetle inside the man's ear. Once the beetle was removed, all of the other symptoms stopped. "Everything is connected," said Rufus. "One body. Sometimes one part will beg for the attention, but it's actually a different area causing the pain." Salome does not tell John Mark this story. Instead she takes a breath and remembers that he is young; of course he will pay attention to the dramatic height of the story and let the rest fall away. It's not his fault, exactly.

"No, I didn't say he died. I said his fever broke."

John Mark stops rubbing his knees and regards her steadily. "You said he died."

"I meant his fever died."

"This won't work if you won't tell me the truth."

Salome offers him her physician's face. They sit in quiet for a long time. "I need to go soon," says Salome finally. "Perhaps one more story."

John Mark leans back against the chair, crosses his arms over his chest. "And is that when you left, then? When you came to Alexandria?"

"You know I lived in Nazareth for thirty-two years. Remember your facts."

John Mark looks out the window and clenches his teeth to keep from saying something he will regret.

"It isn't a bad supposition to make," Salome allows more gently. "I wanted to leave then, more than ever."

"And why did you stay?" John Mark brings his eyes around to her as though they are very heavy and require a great deal of pushing.

"Because of Josef."

2-3 CE

After the night in the mikveh I fell into a kind of darkness. I had experienced grief before, despair that soured the inner pink of my cheeks. I was not a tender thing. I was an orphan, I had been a slave in Rome, I'd—well.

But this was different. This was shame. For the first time in my life I despised the company of myself. Mari wouldn't look at me, and I could barely look at Yeshua. I feared absurd things: that if I touched his face his jaw would erupt in boils, that if I embraced him I'd dissolve his ribs. I had mistrusted others before, had mistrusted the way the world wheeled forward, knew to doubt the intentions of a man with small teeth and the woman who drew me to her and called me by names that were not my own. I mistrusted the future and clouds pregnant with rain, and the vendor in Sepphoris who stuffed his trout with pebbles to fetch a better price. But this was the first time I had mistrusted myself.

I did not live inside my darkness the way Mari lived inside hers. I did not curl on the floor or sleep through an entire Sabbath or let my tears fall continually into water, into wine, into the hair of cousins and the fibers of the cedar courtyard table. I rose each morning and followed Nathan, clucked at sheep that curled in shadowed clefts and nibbled the tender shoots of clover. I fetched water from my cistern, slapped balls of dough into thin circles to cook on the brazier. When harvest time came I knotted my tunic with the rest of the women, bared my legs, and crushed the grapes in the stone tubs on the hillside.

Months went by. Yeshua's baby fat thinned, and the bones of his true face began to emerge. He had my high cheekbones but not my narrow, golden eyes. His were round and curious like his father's. Around the time he turned seven, he developed a stutter. Though it had been almost a year since he cut himself, the quick tisk of his tongue against the backs of his teeth felt like a rebuke, a continued punishment for what I'd done. And though, in the first weeks after his accident, he still came to me, with herbs he'd picked or insects he wanted to dissect, he soon lost interest in Auntie Salome, whose answers to every question were wooden, who kept her medicine case up and out of reach, who did not even set out the sanded tray for letter-making.

You asked me why I didn't leave then. I had no money. No chance of a traveling companion. But those things might have been overcome had I not lost all faith in myself. "You are a woman without a people," Mari had said. She was right. I was peopleless. My independence was no longer strength but weakness, a failure to belong to anyone, anywhere.

And then one day, almost a year after we held Yeshua together in the mikveh, soon after Yeshua developed his stutter, Josef woke me before dawn. He waited outside while I dressed, then led me to the wall that stood at the rear of the property, a structure that roughly ran the edge of the hillside, an attempt to offer the few domestic animals a little grazing room and a feeble attempt at keeping bandits who traveled the Great Road on the plain below from wandering into our dwellings. Josef was a stonemason, though not a particularly good one (his attention to detail too high, his propensity for telling others what to do too low), but he kept our portion of the wall neat and sturdy. I'd never paid it much mind, and I'd certainly never seen the other side of the wall, the part that faced the Valley of Jezreel. This is where Josef brought me.

We stood facing it without seeing more than its dark silhouette against the violet fabric of the sky. I didn't know what we were waiting for, but I didn't mind the long moment with Josef. Wind swept up the hill and stirred the light hairs at my ankles. The morning birds were just beginning their songs, and you could hear them waking each other, pleased by the gathering of their own tones. Josef dug his hand into his waist satchel.

"Fig?" he said.

"You keep figs in there?" I said.

"Why not?" he said. I held out my palm, and instead of just using his thumb and index finger to place the fruit, he took my wrist in one hand and then used his other to curl my fingers around the offering.

"Now my palm will be sticky," I said, trying to scold but failing, so glad for human touch that it was delight that filled my words instead. The dim of night thinned. I could see his lips curl and his two dark eyebrows rise.

This was the smile he first gave to me on that ridge above Alexandria, when he and Mari rolled in on that cart and my labor pains began. Mari had studied her hands, lost in her grief, but Josef had looked at me where I stood, and grinned. This was a rare thing for a Jewish man to do—look directly at a strange woman, offer her joy between his teeth—and it was a gesture completely extinct in the Mareotic community, where, if any smiles were given, they were given to the Existent One in prayer rooms in the dark. The smile was not flirtatious, nor was it mocking of his wife's distress. It was simply that his eyes found mine and there was a moment of understanding—that we both suffered and that what we suffered was somehow absurd, and yet, there we were. I think I smiled back, but perhaps I was too surprised. I know I noted his dark curls, his beard that needed trimming, his solid bearing. I couldn't have seen his hands then, but they are inside that memory: wide palms, long fingers, the nails almost perfect squares. The labor pains tightened my waist. The cart rolled on, and he was gone.

I will return to our moment at the wall—that is the important thing—but I should also explain how Mari and Josef found me a few hours later, that same day, hunched on all fours on a path beside the lake. The midwife had never arrived, you see, and so I went off to find her. It seems stupid, I know, a pregnant woman wandering around after dark, but I was strong and capable and overconfident. The pains came every few minutes, but I could pause for them, I thought, and then continue. The midwife's home wasn't far, Xenia had told me, a twenty-minute walk at most, the first small gathering of huts just up from a cluster of weathered fishing boats pulled up along the shore. But the pain doubled down on me, and I had to meet it braced fully on the earth. Legs were suddenly absurd, willowy and insubstantial. We are animals when we are in pain.

So there I was on the path in the darkness and along comes a bobbing lamp, held by one of the hermits, who was offering a tour of the place to Mari and Josef, saying, "Here are the small fields of barley, yellowed in the sun, here is the fallen-down kiln we don't know how to use, here are the chicken coops where the hens pull out their own feathers out of boredom."

They knew me by my gasping. They exchanged hurried words in an unfamiliar language. "Xenia," I said, though it felt like the word took a long time to travel from my thinking into the night air. The hermit scampered off, leaving Mari and Josef to tend to a complete stranger.

The lake frogs tremored the air with their song, and I was glad for the way the ground gave way slightly under the heels of my palms, my knees. Josef put his hand flat on my lower back, and it was warm. Mari squatted in front of me and prayed, and though I didn't understand her words I liked the way they seemed to mirror the pain, the rise and fall of her cadence, the way she'd stop for breath and begin again. The one time I looked up I saw that she was crying and also that a few small gnats had lit on her cheeks, eager to taste the salt, and she did not bother to brush them away.

This must have gone on for some time, but inside birthing pain, time does not exist. This is a thing you would not know, John Mark. An end to the pain is not conceivable, nor can you cast your mind back to a time before pain existed. Women go to a place without beginning or end and from there they can call a new life into being. If I believed a god created the world, I would believe it began like that: out of pain unbound by time.

Eventually they walked me to the water. We followed a fluttering road of moonlight into the lake. They held me the same way Josef and I held Yeshua in the mikveh: Mari supporting my shoulders and Josef my legs. The water made the pain stronger. I tucked my chin downward and Mari dug her chin into my shoulder, and I started up a low note of moaning. When my breath tired, she would take the note up while I rested so that when the pain came back, almost immediately, I could find the right note without having to look for it.

Only once I looked at Josef, and he wore the same smile: my suffering, all suffering, was absurd but not remarkable, and he was glad, I could see, to be in it with me.

At some point the midwife and Xenia found us and there was a flurry of shouts and commands. I was half dragged, half lifted back to the beach, and it was there I threw my head back and chinned the moon and cursed every god I'd ever been told existed as I pushed the one you call a savior out into this world.

I saw Josef one other time in the next three days, those terrible three days when I ached and bled and Yeshua wailed and would not latch. I had not expected to see my child, to touch my child at all. I was certain the midwife would whisk him away before the placenta had even been expelled. But here he was, in my hands and dying, hour by hour.

At the beginning of the third day, I left him alone in the hovel, swaddled and sleeping. I walked the switchbacked path down the front of the ridge to the sea. Gray clouds pushed each other in a rising wave across the horizon and spit flecks of rain. It was no day for swimming, but I stripped off my rough tunic and went in and under, deep enough that I could feel the waves paw me back and forth. The salt washed its way inside me, and I opened my eyes and everything stung.

When I returned to the hovel, Yeshua was gone. All that remained was the old linen tunic I'd wrapped him in, a small smear of deep-green excrement at the middle. The excrement was good, a sign that his tiny body was working, that maybe some of the liquid I'd offered him was moving through. I bent down and swiped my finger through it, just to make sure it was real. I was half out of my mind, half feral, my body wracked with chills from the ocean and the air; and it was in this state that I went out looking for my son.

It took only seconds to find him. Ten yards away, just beside the hovel across from mine, the man from the day before stood with his back to me, bouncing from his knees. I knew what he held in his arms, so I gathered up my righteousness and walked over and screamed at him in Greek and then in Latin that he was a thief and that he'd better give my baby back to me immediately (although I think my words were slightly rougher then). Josef turned to me, naked Yeshua nestled to his chest, a perfect red ball of flesh sleeping peacefully, and smiled and said something. When I continued to scream, he used his free hand to point to Yeshua and then he touched his own face, tracing two lines down from his eyes so I would understand that Yeshua had been crying, that Josef had found him alone, that he was trying to assist.

I didn't care. I hated this man, hated the way his helping seemed to expose all of my incompetencies, and I shook my finger at him and screamed some more and then I held out my arms for my baby. He smiled again, that stupid, knowing smile, but he raised his eyebrows at my finger as if to say, "Don't you want to perhaps wash the feces off your hands before I give you your beautiful naked baby back?" And so I reached up and wiped the shit down the length of Josef's cheek, and then I grabbed his tunic and smeared the rest there, and then I took my baby so violently that he woke and started to cry again. I stormed back to my own hovel anyway, still smelling of shit though I had just bathed, and by the time I reached my doorway I regretted it, wiping feces on the man, screaming at the only person who had offered me help these last few days. I looked over my shoulder.

Josef stood watching me, not just smiling but laughing. And it is so hard to make this clear: not mocking me—I knew that even then—but the laugh two people share inside a horrible thing. And then I laughed too, I laughed and I cried both at once. And we stood ten yards away from each other, shaking with raw incredulity, and I was, for a moment, seen.

I see you shifting, John Mark. You want to know what there was between us. Let me be clear: Josef's devotion to Mari was a pure thing. I have never seen a man so bound to a woman. He loved her but he didn't understand her; perhaps he loved her *because* he didn't understand her. He honored her moods as holy; he made space for them. He knew she had wanted to be a rabbi like her father, knew how the prophets lived under her skin. So he let her be a teacher to Yeshua while he boiled the porridge and split the kindling and restuffed the mattresses with hay; inside the walls of the courtyard he did the woman's work so she could live inside her stories, inside the strange waves of her emotion.

Once we arrived in Nazareth, Josef and I were polite to one another but nothing more. You want to know if I lusted after him, if he longed for me. These descriptions are too simple. Let me try to explain. (Then the wall: we will return to the wall where the sun is finally starting to rise.)

Men use the word "friend" easily; it is not hard to find a comrade, companion, buddy, chum. Men raise houses together, go to war together, travel together, plot together. They slap each other on the shoulders or they grip forearms. They sit on either side of a table filled with wine and dice and say little, their knees almost touching. Women, on the other hand, are allowed daughters and mothers and cousins and aunts.

And yes, they trade gossip with those they share blood, they comb one another's hair and share good olive oil for the feasts, and they will circle the one who has suffered loss, wrap their arms around her waist, match her grief breath for breath. But friends are rare in a woman's life. The person who understands you not because of blood or marriage but because you match in some strange way, because you choose each other's company. If the world worked differently, Josef and I could have been friends.

But our world does not work this way. You know this. Rufus was my friend in Rome only because he was also my mentor; we had a relationship we could wear in front of the rest of the world that permitted us to have friendship behind it. Josef and I had no such thing, and so yes—if we were alone the air became heavy between us, late summer heat filled with the drone of bees. I was only nineteen when I came to Nazareth, when I lived on the other side of their wall. When I touched my breasts to remember they were there, when I touched the wet place between my legs, did I think of him? Yes. We turned into the thing we were supposed to be to one another. We grew into the only relationship the world offered us.

He built a wall between us. He built in gaps for me to see. I watched Yeshua, but I watched him, too. Years passed and we did not touch. Then he came that morning and took me to the wall.

The sweetness from the fig dissolved on my tongue as the sun rose, and so the seeing of those stones is always knit together with taste, as though the fieldstones themselves were lozenges that could dissolve at the back of my throat. At first the wall simply looked aged. The surface was more wrinkled, more puckered somehow. Then I stepped closer, stared more closely at a single stone, and I saw that it was the holm tree that sits at the entrance to Nazareth, the one that has been pushed long enough by the wind that it stretches perpetually right. Out of the stone beside the tree, a pair of eyes gazed at me, Yeshua's eyes but from a time before, when he was three or four. I could see in the stone the tiny fleck of consternation he always wore between his brows as he asked us why, and why again. Those eyes, that expression, they were something I thought was gone forever, and here, in the stone, they were returned to me.

"Oh!" I must have said, like a dumb bride. Josef took my hand then, the sticky residue of the fig between us, and he led me slowly down the length of his creation. Here was the chipped amphora we used for lamp oil, here was Mari's head from the back, her naked neck and the rounded coil of her hair. Some images were less recognizable at first: a simple line meant to mark the vista of hills from where we stood, another that tried to offer the hovels of the Mareotic community in their bunch and sway along the ridge. And then there I was, my eyes on one stone, nose and lips on another. Josef had even captured the strafe of moles that covered my face: four on one side, eight on the other, twelve in all. The marks were there, but done gently, as though the wind might be enough, in a few years, to dissolve them altogether. And beside that stone, another that caught my chin and ear; others displayed my ankle, my neck, the crook of my elbow. Not arranged to make a body—there was no clear form—but Josef had made me just the same.

I let go of his hand and fell to my knees, and I touched those stones, and I sobbed because he had captured what I had felt since Yeshua's accident: broken and rearranged, unpieced and undone. But each stone was so perfectly done, so beautiful, that I could see that the woman who lived in the wall, all of her pieces were there. Her outline did not blur; each part of her was clear in its presence, necessary. The woman in the wall could not put herself together again, but the beauty of her parts suggested that I could.

"When did you do this?" I said when I could breathe again.

Josef leaned against the wall, half-watching the sunrise, half-watching my face. "Mostly since we returned from Alexandria, since Yeshua was born. You like it." He raised his eyebrows and smiled. This was the phrase Yeshua always used when he was three and offered us anything. Not a question but a command.

"I like it," I said.

"We were going to Alexandria for me," he said. He'd turned toward the wall now and was plucking out bits of vegetation.

"For you?"

"One of my cousins is a merchant in Alexandria who seems to have a finger in everything. He travels the Great Road sometimes, selling exotic medicines or rare spices or red glassware. He stopped in Nazareth with his whole caravan for a few days and wandered out here, to survey the scene, I suppose, or maybe it was just to take a piss away from everyone. I was working on a stone. I'd only done three by then. He motioned me toward the other end of the wall. 'Nehemiah, Moses, Zechariah,' he said, pointing to stones that were more crudely drawn but showed images from Mari's favorite prophetic stories. They were for Mari. They were going to be."

"Has she seen them?"

Josef shook his head. "Ezra saw them first. Said he had a synagogue in Alexandria, but the numbers were waning. There were a hundred gods to love in Alexandria, he claimed, not like here. Even the Jews could wash their hands of animal fat one day and make an offering to Anubis the next. The other religions weren't stingy with their images, and the Jews, he proclaimed to me, shouldn't be either."

"I thought images weren't allowed in synagogues."

"They're not. He wanted to change all that, and he wanted me to do it. A frieze that would wrap all the way around the prayer room, so the stories were right there in front of people. And he promised me the best limestone, a slew of workers, delicate tools. So I dragged my pregnant wife to Alexandria. I did. I did do that. There was unrest here, rumors of Herod's death."

"Had Abraham told you this? You knew he was in danger?"

"Everyone was in danger. But I was a coward, if that's what you mean. I didn't want to join the rebels. And so I convinced Mari to go to Alexandria instead—there was everything to be gained, I convinced myself. We'd leave behind this town; I would have good work, we'd make a better life for our family ..." He didn't finish his thought. Instead, Josef took a slim metal tool from his waist satchel, a small hook on one end, grip etched into the other. He began to clean the dirt from the fine cracks in the stone, wiping the collected detritus now and then on his tunic. He wouldn't look directly at me.

"And then," I prompted gently.

"And then Mari," he said. He worked the grit out from between the edges of a leaf. "Do you recognize this?"

"Palm?" I asked.

"Yes. Egyptian palm." He smoothed the stone fronds with his thumb. "Mari lost the baby along the way, and when we arrived she couldn't stop crying. Her moods, you know."

"I know."

"And so Ezra, the cousin who was housing us, thought it would be better to send us away until her grief had waned. Mari was frightening the servants, he said."

"That's when I met you."

Josef nodded his head. "I had one day with the limestone. In Alexandria, I mean. Just a piece, a sample of what I'd use. It was so soft compared to this. As though the curves of flesh were built into it. But"—he turned back to me, spun the thin tool around his thumb and then back into the satchel in an easy motion, raised his brows at me—"that's not why I brought you here. I wanted to show you—I have found a way. I think there is a way—for you to have a wall."

"I don't understand."

"You are so hard, Salome. Mari is soapstone and you're granite. Porous and impenetrable, a sponge and a—"

"Fine. Yes. That I understand." His words were a prickle inside my chest. "Thank you for showing me this. I should go." I tightened the knot at the back of my scarf, tucked in a few strands of hair that had not come untucked.

"I haven't shown you."

"This is enough. For a morning."

"Salome." His voice was gentle, wrapping around the name he'd given me when Lyra proved too sharp on his tongue. And then that smile. He turned and began walking quickly away along the goat path. I turned one more time for a glimpse of that woman, whole in pieces on the wall. Then I hurried to catch up, the sun bright against my cheek, watching birds sweep up from the shrubs as Josef worked his way through them, his hips switching the branches away.

It was a ten-minute walk. Down the goat path to a clump of jujube trees that yawned over a small clearing the size of a courtyard. In the middle of the clearing, a low wooden table and a stool framed by four lamp stands.

"What's this?"

"Your clinic." He lay down on the table, placing his head in a shallow divot at one end.

"You did this?"

"No one will see you in the daylight, but they'll come if they think they can't be seen."

"They won't."

"They will. I am bringing Anna tonight. I have promised her. You'll need to find your own lamps, bring your own oil." He sat up and swung his legs over the side, reached under the table, and pulled out a large wooden box with a latch that could swing shut. "You can keep supplies in here."

"I can't. Yeshua—"

"I won't bring Yeshua. I will bring the others. They will be made better, and you will be made better. It isn't difficult."

"Why would you do this?"

"One woman with moods is enough. Yeshua needs you."

"I have nothing to offer him."

"I will be here with Anna tonight. Her twisting spine is causing her pain."

"I know."

"Mari's moods have no escape but waiting them out. Your darkness has an end if you choose it."

"It isn't that simple."

"You choose, Salome."

That night I treated Anna. And Josef was right: it didn't take long for word to spread. After a few weeks, everyone knew the clinic was there. Within a year I'd treated almost everyone in the village for one thing or another. They came mostly at night, paid with the smallest coins or sometimes an offering of oil or food. Some paid with labor: rerolling the clay of my roof, watering the animals, mucking out the left-side room of my house. I never turned anyone away. Soon the clinic was a shared secret—everyone knew but no one spoke of it. Our allegiance to belief wavers in the face of pain and our fear of death. They came to me, and I treated them, then I sent them on their way.

And true to her word, when Yeshua was ten, when he knew the scriptures backward and forward, when he was drawing circles in the dirt to keep the demons out and practicing table prayers over the dry lentils, Mari sent him back to me. By then I had forgiven myself enough to begin his medical training in earnest.

DAY FOUR

38 CE

Salome wakes from a dream of a linen sack thrown over her head, of being bound and spun. In the dream the Greeks tell her she must find Yeshua by scent alone, but all she can smell is the dusty scent of the cloth. Awake now, she calms herself by finding the scent of cedar that drifts from the sheet above the empty cot, warm with a trickle of sweetness on the back of the tongue. She lets herself think of Yeshua in the stream among the cedars, damp hair cooling, tunic darkening in the water. Dreams offer power only if you give your power to them.

After dressing in the lamplight, Salome makes porridge for Asha and leaves it beside her sleeping form. It was only six hours ago that she left John Mark in the study, but this is not a time for sleep. The sky is still uniformly black and salted with stars. Salome knows that death is not far away, the death of her mind if not the death of her body. She knows that one day her knowledge and her memory will slide away from her, and neither will return. She quickens her pace.

Because it is still early, Salome turns down the side alley to enter Philo's house. She hasn't eaten herself and knows the cook will offer her warm bread and yogurt from the back kitchen before she climbs the stairs to the clinic. A few patients curl along the wall in cloaks and mantles, trying to sleep, but one figure stands at the closed gate, arms hanging limply at his sides, fingers uncurled. Carabbas.

It is not until he has eaten some warm bread, not until Salome has guided him up the stairs, not until she has lit the lamps beside the windows, not until daylight stains the sky that Salome sees what they have done to him.

His body is covered with bruises and scratches, too many to count, from the fingers that gripped and lifted his legs, from nails that carved into his ribs for purchase, from knuckles that dug into his back, his shoulders, his thighs to hold him aloft. They have blackened his groin with lit charcoal sticks. When Salome dabs at the area with a wet rag, Carabbas shrieks and lurches away from her.

So Salome prepares a dram of poppy for the pain, and Carabbas sips it mixed with milk while Salome uses mortar and pestle to mash fresh comfrey and plantain. Nadjem arrives, fetches boiling water to make the poultice, and then four men from the street to hold Carabbas down while the women wipe the charcoal from his burnt skin. Salome's pressure with the rag is firm and steady, and she couples it with questions in an even tone to distract the beggar: "How did you come to the New Jewish Quarter? Where did they take you after the theater? Where else do you feel pain?"

But Carabbas only wails, one long note again and again, his fists pounding the floorboards, his midsection lifting on the floor, twisting for release. The four men, though they are weak with hunger, manage to hold him fast. When the cleaning is done and the poppy has taken the edge from the pain, the men loosen their grip and Nadjem dabs myrtle paste on the burnt skin to protect it from infection. Carabbas cries with his eyes closed, stroking the hair of his chest to calm himself. "I was king," he says softly, over and over again. "I was king."

Salome steps back from Carabbas's tortured body as sunlight spills over the eastern edge of the harbor and into Philo's house. The servant girl brings in her bucket of vinegar water, and the Broom Boy enters and asks, before noticing Carabbas, if they are ready for their first patients. Most Alexandrians have not yet eaten their breakfast, and Salome already wants the day to be done. Nothing good will come today, thinks Salome, and mostly she is correct.

What Carabbas does not tell them, what he cannot find the words to say, is how the day before, the Greeks carried his body all the way from the theater to the house of Flaccus, governor of Egypt. How they presented Carabbas as the King of the Jews and made him demand the statues of his god, his weak and insubstantial god. How Flaccus himself came out in a scarlet robe, dragging a dusty kitten on a leash, how his smile in front of the mob was easy and unconcerned, how his brow remained dry. How he brought Agrippa's statues before the crowd and said, "Let them be disrobed," and how the people cheered so loudly that Nadjem's niece in the Egyptian Quarter asked if the goddess Ammit had opened her crocodile jaws and roared. How when Flaccus saw that the statues were not images of Yahweh but instead the Emperor Caligula, he turned his back and spit and ordered wine and drained two goblets before he faced the crown again. How he raised himself up on his toes and placed the kitten on one of Caligula's marble heads and said, "May I request that you, bold citizens of Alexandria, deliver these visages of our emperor to the New Jewish Quarter tomorrow? May I request that you place them in the synagogues? May I request that if the Jews forget how to drop to their knees in prayer, you remind them how to do so?"

The crowd roared again, and Nadjem's niece, shaking, went into the courtyard and smeared her face and arms and legs with mud so that Ammit, part crocodile, part water horse, and part lion, would not see her. The girl went to sleep in the middle of the afternoon, terrified that the whites of her eyes would give away her human form.

The Broom Boy helps Nadjem and Salome arrange Carabbas's body on the far side of the clinic room so that the burn salve can do its work, so that he won't worsen his internal injuries with unnecessary movement. Carabbas sleeps peacefully, and the eyelashes that fan his cheeks are long and delicate.

A stone's throw away, a cart with four of the statues wrapped inside it rolls down the main street of the New Jewish Quarter, accompanied by half a dozen Greek men who know that however they behave, their actions will have no legal consequence. Flaccus has finally called the Jewish people what they are: *foreigners* and *aliens*. The more the Greek men wash these words around their mouths, the more the words feel true. It is good to let the Jews know these spaces are no longer their spaces. Take the Egyptians: they are not citizens, but they know their place. They stay in their quarter. They fish and cut papyrus, and you can stand along the bank of the Nile and worship their gods along with them. Offer them a medallion of Mars on a string, and they'll gladly throw it around their necks. They cast their eyes down; they don't make trouble. But the Jewish people insist on their one dumb god, on the cleanliness of their bowls; they turn up their noses at good roast pork; they push their women into back rooms so you never even get a glimpse of their figures. They are a clean people, but there is a filth about them nonetheless, like white maggots, writhing.

This feeling grows like scales inside the mouths of the Greek men, coats their flesh until they cannot feel their own tongues, cannot taste their own saliva; they hate until all of their own tenderness is covered so that, when a half-blind, starving Jewish man reaches out and grabs the cloak of one Greek man, all of them turn, and all of them fall upon the beggar. They kick him in the belly and the ribs; they kick his face and his buttocks and his groin. They kick until he is dead and splayed flat instead of curled so there are no satisfying places left to kick.

When they enter the synagogue, their hands are still surprisingly clean.

Here is the same synagogue John Mark stood in just three days earlier, still pressed with the bodies of hundreds of men, hungry and tired. It takes all six of the Greek men to carry the statue inside. They center it below the wash of light that beams down from the hole in the roof, and oh how the marble takes the light, how Caligula's robes fall in creases like a waterfall, how his lips press together in certainty.

For the Jewish men who line the benches, watching the Greeks place this statue into the middle of the synagogue is like watching them shove spears between the legs of their women.

The rabbi stands and says, "You cannot" and then sits down again.

One Jewish man rushes forward with a cloak and tries to cover the statue; he is shoved to the ground. Another starts up the prayer of Moses and other voices join in, and for a moment the rhythmic cacophony unsettles the Greeks, a reminder of how heavily they are outnumbered.

But then one worshiper makes the mistake of rushing at one of the Greeks, of grabbing the thick neck with the last of his strength. The Greek tosses him off like a cat, smiling because now they will make an example of this Jew, this alien, this foreigner. They pull him into the street and they force him to his knees, and when he will not say that Caligula is his god before all other gods, they take one of the statues of Caligula and use it to hammer the man into the ground: his shoulder blades, then his buttocks, then the backs of his knees. Last is the head. The skull opens and death slides in between the split fragments of bone. The Greeks pick up the statue, make another Jew clean the blood from its base, and then move off toward the next synagogue.

With each statue placed, the chaos increases. Men stream out of the synagogues, some weeping and some praying and some retching and some holding on to one another's arms to keep themselves from revolting. Some are so hungry and tired that they lie down on the empty benches the other men have left behind. Women and children are pushed into the back rooms of the houses in the Quarter, more and more of them shoved in so that there is no room to sit, and the children weave through the jungle of legs and scents, losing and finding and losing their mothers again. Doors are locked and barred, and those who have not been able to find a hiding place roam the streets in mounting terror, the synagogues no longer a place of refuge. Some people, noting the absence of the guards, slink out of the Quarter under the hoods of cloaks far too warm for the season.

Philo has his own gates barred, and though the Broom Boy is still allowed out through the small side entrance to fetch patients, he returns, eventually, with torn clothing and scratches along his forearms, his face pale, tongue nervously touching his harelip.

"Well, who have you brought?" asks Salome.

"They took my cap," stammers the Broom Boy, and he touches the place where his hair has been shaped by the brim.

"What of it?" asks Salome sharply.

"How can I decide? They all want in. I can't tell who—I'm not an authority—I don't—" The Broom Boy raises his chin and pinches his lips together with his thumb and forefinger to keep away the tears.

Nadjem wags her head from side to side, sets down the bowl she has just wiped clean of the burn salve, and makes for the door herself.

"No, Nadjem. I will go with him," says Salome in Egyptian. "You have the oak gall powder to finish; we'll need it soon enough."

Nadjem raises her eyebrows. "I'd be of more use than that boy. He has the strength of an ibis."

"Better his bones break than mine," Salome answers with a smile.

"I'm not setting your bones or his; you can howl like cats for all I care."

"We will be back soon."

"Not too many new ones. We have our hands full enough." Nadjem nods toward the naked beggar who snores gently in one corner and a feverish elderly woman who lies like a corpse but blinks occasionally to show she is not one. Not yet. Then Nadjem stuffs bandages, ammonia salts, vinegar, and a small jar of Balsam of Mecca into a satchel and hands it to Salome. "May Horus the protector go with you." She smiles slightly. "If you'll have him."

The sun has finally inched past its apex, and John Mark is on his way to Philo's house with his finished pages. Before he reaches the New Jewish Quarter, he knows that something is wrong. Smoke billows up from one of the rooftops, and from far away he hears a sharp sound, a scream, he thinks, and he is suddenly pushed from behind and falls on his hands, the pages scattering.

"Take your tunic back into the real city, physician." A Greek man on a horse says the word *physician* as though it is a scorpion in his sandal. He has flour in his beard; his comrade, astride behind him, has leather wrist guards and an exquisitely tooled leather belt.

"Come on, then," says the belted one with a grin. "Something's burning." They tie the horse up at the house nearest the New Quarter and cross the boundary, nudging one another back and forth like schoolboys.

John Mark is unhurt besides his scraped palms, but he feels winded nonetheless. He gathers the papers and sits on a bench between two homes. In the balls of his feet he can feel a trembling, although here, just outside the New Quarter, it is relatively quiet.

Around him are the abandoned homes of the Jews, no alabaster inlays or arched trellis entries, but good wooden doors. Solid. Each fitted with a different handle in the center. John Mark does not know that this is a tradition of this street, that when a new family arrives or an old one changes shape, the people of this street choose a new handle (iron or red glass, ivory or stone) and affix it to the door with friends gathered around. A prayer of hospitality is uttered; the men intone it from the outside and the women murmur it from deeper within the home, their voices joining at the lintel, at the place of passing. Now the doors cannot decide whether to remain open or closed. A cat smooths out of the shadows of one slightly ajar, a doormat flattening itself against the closed face of another.

Whatever is happening inside the New Jewish Quarter, it is not his concern, not really. He can turn around; he can go back to Salome's study and sleep. He can eat a bowl of thin yogurt and watch the pigeons peck at the domed roof. He closes his eyes and lets himself be rinsed in the watery sunlight.

Back at Philo's house, the elders wait. Though the servant girl makes her rounds with vinegar and rags, the number of bodies in the space means that everything is filmed with a layer of use: the cloth of the couches, the mosaic floor tiles, the cornices, the painted plaster, the cups. The light from the courtyard is old bath water lapping into the wrinkles on their brows, the bowls of shadow underneath their eyes. The individual names of these men will slide off the books of history; their bodies will be tied together with the string of a single word: *elders*. But today they are six different men, each coping with the cramped room, the banging at the now-locked gates of Philo's house, in a different way. Levi sits beside the young man who came directly from the synagogue over three hours ago. Judah offers the man watered wine and presses his knee. "Please begin again."

Elisha and Benjamin have put on their tzitzits to pray, rather loudly, and Eleazar sits on the couch with his chin cocked and eyes closed as the barber-boy clips at his beard, flecks of gray snowing down across his deep-purple mantle. Zeloph is certain that Agrippa's bodyguards will protect them, but every time he moves to the doorway to peek into the courtyard, the bodyguards are gone, and he cannot bring himself to remark on this to the others. So he paces, pushing up his sleeves, cursing them when they fall loose again.

"We have done what we could," says Philo, who stands in the middle of it all, shaking out his hands as though blood rushing to his fingertips will be of use. "We told Agrippa, we showed him. The hunger of our people. How we have been cast down, cast out."

"Maccabees," says Zeloph suddenly, stopping in his pacing.

"We have no weapons," says Philo. "They have taken those, too."

"And we are old," says Eleazar, shaking the gray hairs off his mantle.

The banging on the gate reaches a crescendo. Zeloph goes again to check on the bodyguards and sees only a girl with dark hair washing the stone walls.

"Should we let them in?" asks Levi of the young man who brought news of the terror at the synagogue.

"We cannot let them in," sighs Philo. His throat is dry, but his thirst does not deserve to be quenched.

"Adonai has forgotten us," says Judah, and no one corrects him.

Before they have even shut the door to Philo's house, Salome and the Broom Boy are set upon by people pulling at their tunics, gripping their ankles, squeezing their forearms, begging to be allowed into his home. "Step back!" Salome bellows, and the people recede like the waters of the Red Sea, finding places along the wall to crouch or stand. Salome casts her eye up and down the line and then steps toward a man cradling his right arm to his chest. He is almost unconscious with pain.

"Hold his left arm," says Salome. The Broom Boy looks at her quizzically but obeys. Sure enough, as soon as Salome tries to pull the right arm gently from the man's chest, he jabs out fiercely with the left hand. The right arm is not just broken, it is mangled, the bone broken through the flesh in two places and the tissue swollen, one band of muscle partially torn. "Hold tightly," Salome instructs again, and this time the Broom Boy tucks the man's left arm gently between his knees. Salome quickly splashes vinegar onto the wound, using it to flush out as much of the dirt as possible. The man howls to life, but Salome holds his arm with surprising strength. "We will take care of you," she says, and the man permits the Broom Boy to help lift him to his feet, permits Salome to bind the wounded arm to his body.

By the time they get the man back to the room, Salome is sweating and her hip has begun to ache. She knows exhaustion is coming, knows her mind will slip again, but she beckons to the Broom Boy and they go out again, this time returning with a three-year-old boy with an infected head wound carried by a father whose cheeks have grown inward from hunger.

Footsteps startle John Mark out of a strange half-sleep. The two Greeks, the baker and the one with the leather belt, emerge from the New Jewish Quarter with a man struggling between them. They shove him toward the horse. The man with the flour in his beard holds the Jewish man's arms behind his back while the man with the leather belt straddles the victim's legs and ties a knot around his ankles so quickly and beautifully that John Mark wonders for a horrifying second if the man is a kind of magician. They attach the other end of the rope to the saddle of the horse, and then both Greek men pull themselves up, one facing forward and one backward so that they look almost festive, almost as though they will play a silly part in a play.

Then the one in the front digs his heels into the horse's haunches, and for one brave second the terrified man hops forward until his feet are pulled up and out in front of him. Because his arms are not bound he takes the fall mostly on his elbows and then tries to sit up, to undo the rope, to reach for his toes, but he cannot reach because the horse has picked up speed, and instead he tries to claw at the ground, tries to slow himself down, but there is nothing to grab. John Mark can see as they turn the corner how the man still keeps his head up off the stones, even as he leaves blood and torn pieces of his own skin behind, raises his chin enough to call, "Abba, Abba, I am coming."

Then the street is quiet again. John Mark still holds the pages. The light is the same, though it should be different. And it's only then that he realizes he has done nothing. It was not that he felt frozen as he watched: it was that the whole scene was happening elsewhere, and as with all of Salome's stories, his only choice was how to write it down. He bends his head between his legs and vomits onto the paving stones.

Then there is the clattering of horse hooves again. The flour on the face of the Greek baker is now cut by streams of sweat. The dragged man no longer lifts his head. The man with the leather belt unfastens the rope.

"There you are, physician," says the other before they canter away, still riding back to back, the one raising the bread paddle into the air, as though he is trying to poke holes in the very sky.

The dragged man is still alive, somehow. And so John Mark bends down and unties the rope from his ankles and heaves the man over his shoulder; John Mark is not a strong man, but the bloodied man is light, made of air and feather bones. John Mark walks the length of the street until he comes to the paltry border of stacked rocks and sacks filled with sand.

To his right, on the door where the horse was fastened, is fixed an alabaster handle in the shape of a bird, wings outstretched. It is impossible to tell from this distance, from under the weight of the man, whether the bird is ascending or descending. John Mark smells the warm-metal wet of the man's back, the urine that soaks his cloak, and he thinks of Noah on the ark all those years ago, the trembling white heart of the dove against his thumb. How quickly the dove dissolved into the white forgetting of the clouds. How there was no rainbow, yet.

There is no longer any certainty that this physician's tunic will protect him. The only protection is to turn away now, to say that he is something other than what he is.

John Mark tightens his grip around the Dragged Man's thighs and steps into the New Jewish Quarter.

The third time they leave the building, Salome uses the handrail to descend the stairs and stops at the cistern to drink. She takes a sprig of hyssop from her pocket and chews it to revive herself. The Broom Boy accepts some too and chews proudly, although the taste clearly disgusts him. This time it is John Mark they find outside Philo's gate, carrying a man whose back resembles an improperly plowed field of clay. John Mark is panting and crying.

"No," says Salome. She does not have time for either his emotions or the body he carries.

"He's alive," says John Mark.

"He won't be for long. We have no place for a dead body."

John Mark is not beautiful when he cries. Somehow his eyes seem even closer together and his lashes, clumped with tears, weigh his eyelids down. He can't wipe his face and so his upper lip and chin are a mess of snot. It is abundantly clear to Salome that John Mark is the kind of person who is the first to die in a riot.

"Leave him here. Go back to my study and write down your stories. Leave this place while you still can. You are of no use here." *Go*, hears Salome from somewhere distant. *Go and build your house of stone.*

But John Mark pushes past her with surprising force and stumbles down the alley and through the back entrance of the house. The street rages around her, but Salome is suddenly ten years in the past, in the water of the River Jordan, moonlight boiling a path down its length, Yeshua's hard words pushing her away. Perhaps because she is exhausted—from lack of sleep, from telling the stories of Yeshua last night, from the wailing and violence around her—she lets herself return to that terrible moment: what if she had refused to listen to Yeshua? What if she had thrown away the thing she had trained her whole life to do and followed her son instead? Her heart clenches, and the stones below her feet tremble and give way.

She opens her eyes to piercing pains shivering up the insides of her nostrils; the Broom Boy's right hand cups her neck, and with the left he holds the open container of ammonia salts in front of her. "You did well," she says. He squats beside her and lets Salome use his shoulder to push herself upright again. A high-pitched scream from just around the corner quickens their movements; Salome and the Broom Boy choose two patients who can still walk on their own (a laboring woman and a man sweating with stomach pain), and together the four return to the upstairs room.

Dusk arrives, and on the other side of the city Asha brings in her cushion of pins. Each of the customers who has stopped today has mentioned the rioting in the New Jewish Quarter and then, in the next sentence, has turned the conversation elsewhere. In order to stave off pricks of fear, Asha lights the candles on the small altar in her room and then holds a tiny clay dish with frankincense over one of the flames. She remembers little of the caravan that was her home when she was young, mostly just a blazing fire, the sound of bells, and this sweet scent. And also the other young boys, given knives at the age of six, how during the long stretches of walking they would scout the sides of the road for dead creatures—voles, lizards, swallows, frogs, locusts, mice—and then impale each thing on their knives. The point of the game was to have your knife covered, hilt to tip, in dead things by the time the day was done. If you roasted them on the fire and ate them, you were brave and worthy of something that none of them could actually name.

This is not a story about unkindness; no one cared that Asha did not participate. But she remembers the heft of those knives, weighted down with animals and blood, lined up in the light of the fire, and the clean blade of her own, unused. How she knew then that she would never be a man.

And so Asha prays for Salome's safety. She asks Sekhmet to protect Salome's hands and brain and liver. But she does not pray for a change of heart; she does not pray for Salome to become anyone other than who she is.

When night comes, the pain in Philo's upstairs room becomes more acute. Nadjem has cleaned the boy's head wound three times, but it is not enough; in the morning they will need to remove a portion of the skull. It should be done now, but there is not enough light to see by. So the father with sunken cheeks cradles the head-wound boy in his lap, trying to stay upright but occasionally swaying into sleep. The man with the stomach pain, whom Nadjem has diagnosed with bladder stones, curls into himself and weeps beside the fever woman, who thrashes her ancient arms with surprising force. Carabbas wakes disoriented, and though they try to keep him still, he paces around the perimeter of the room. "You've done nothing," he says to no one in particular. "You've done nothing and they are angry." Salome offers Carabbas dried apricots, but he bats them away and they go scattering into the shadows.

The pregnant woman, ashamed to be leaking blood in the sight of strangers and men, makes for herself a nest in the corner, and Carabbas steps over her as he walks the walls, a wash of his scent drifting down upon her each time he passes. The mangled-arm man has been given tears of poppy, and Salome presses her fingers to his neck over and over to make sure the dose is correct. She refuses to look at John Mark, who blots at the Dragged Man's back with a rag soaked in comfrey water. The Dragged Man cannot manage the depth of a moan, only the high mewl of a kitten, each breath a thin note of pain.

Finally, John Mark says loudly, so that Salome cannot possibly ignore him: "A dose of poppy for him. Please."

"No."

"Or henbane."

"No."

"White mandrake?" John Mark does not try to keep the begging from his voice.

"You know your medicines well for someone who is not a physician."

"Please. He is suffering."

"He would not be suffering if you had left him in the street as I told you to."

"He would be dead."

"Yes. And he will be dead soon anyway." And John Mark sees the face of the woman who shoved her child's head into the ground, who laid her wrist across a flame to gather affection, who gave her only child to another woman.

"You have no compassion."

"And you have no sense. We have some medicine—not much. This is not a pharmacy. I have no idea how long we will be trapped inside this room. If I gave the medicine to everyone in this Quarter who was suffering, it would help no one."

"When Yeshua chose to divide the bread, there was enough for all."

"What did you say?"

John Mark is silent, but Salome has heard. "You think Yeshua would be of use here? Come with me." Salome pushes herself up from the floor beside the Mangled-Arm Man; it is late and she should be exhausted, but John Mark has injected her with fresh rage and purpose.

"Where is there to go?" John Mark asks without looking at her.

The father of the Head-Wound Boy shushes his son but looks at the two adults whose voices have risen.

"To the roof. The dirty bandages need to be washed and hung before morning. We won't be able to go to the fuller's. Come."

John Mark presses his rag gently to the man's back.

"Nadjem," says Salome, and Nadjem squats down beside John Mark and elbows him away.

"You're making a mess of it," says Nadjem.

And so John Mark truculently follows Salome to the roof with a load of dirtied bandages and rags and then fetches water from the cistern, and vinegar, and a lamp, and they begin. John Mark is sure that Salome will lash out immediately, tell him how he has gotten Yeshua all wrong, but she holds her tongue. Their eyes burn and the stains are stubborn; John Mark stirs at the sopping mess with a wooden washing stick, and then Salome wrings out each piece of fabric and hangs it on the washing line.

After an hour of work, three baskets still remain. "We will let them soak," says Salome. She sends the Broom Boy for food, and he returns with bread and garlic oil, a few dates. The scent of vinegar is too strong on her palms for Salome to taste the food, but she makes herself eat anyway.

Salome thinks of Asha, of her quick hands laying out the pieces of latrunculi or combing the hair of one of her Girls into a folded topknot. The easy way she twists hair into the net of a new wig. What comfort it would be, at the end of the day, to rest her fingers on Asha's belly, to feel Asha's breath in the palm of her hand.

Salome can also see, perfectly, the disdain Asha would find for her if she heard the stories of her past. Salome knows because she has seen it in John Mark. Even today she has caught him looking at her, and she knows he is seeing her past, is regarding her with disgust. And let him. She will stuff this man full of it, all of her wrongs, all of her misdeeds, and then she will go to Asha—lighter, ready.

John Mark rolls a bit of bread into a small ball, pops it into his mouth, and stands. "I will return when the rags are done soaking. I don't want that man to be alone."

"He is not alone. Nadjem is with him. And besides, if you don't eat more food, you will not be of any use to him. I have told you too much about Yeshua's childhood. What you wanted to hear was his ministry. Sit down."

John Mark does so slowly. He thinks he can hear the cries of the Dragged Man, but it could be the wailing of almost any person in the Quarter. He wants to be beside the man and also he wants to be here, in the clear air, eating and listening. What would Peter the First say? That the Messiah calls us to feed the hungry, to take care of those who are injured and ailing? Yes, but also to tell the story, for the story is salvation. *The story is the help we offer beyond measure.* John Mark's first job is to know the story, to get it firm as a ball of bread inside his mouth so that he can physician the word to others. "Go on," he says, tearing off another hunk of the loaf.

"I am skipping ahead, now," says Salome. "Yeshua is a grown man."

28 CE

Yeshua's hands were clumsy in the dark. Not in the finding of the wound. That came easily, better than me, even. His fingers went intuitively to the ache, the growth, the break, the rash, the unsound place. His diagnoses were brilliant, but his treatment was often flawed because he tracked not just the wound but the pain around the wound. He patted when he should have applied forceful pressure, held his breath when he used the needle to bind puckered skin, closed his eyes just as he began a cut with a scalpel.

We were treating Asaph that night, and luckily he didn't need surgery; he only had an aching tooth. He needed only a rag packed with comfrey and chamomile, some whispered words of distraction, and an escort back to his crumbling home. His breath was sour; his teeth darkened from the wine he'd already drunk to ease the pain.

Yeshua had never liked the feel of the stool, so he squatted next to Asaph's form, tilted Asaph's jaw toward the light of one of the lamps. Above us, clouds prickled with twitches of lightning, brief flashes in which I could clearly see the spittle trailing from the corner of Asaph's mouth, the prickle of beard growth on Yeshua's neck.

"Open further," said Yeshua, and Asaph obeyed. While Yeshua pressed below Asaph's ear lobe and worked his way down the throat to make certain there was no spreading infection, I mixed the herbs in my mortar with a little olive oil, then wrapped the mixture in linen I'd beaten until it was thin, almost sheer—until I had a tiny package perfectly sized for the space behind a back tooth. I gave it to Yeshua, supervised his placement, and when he placed it too cautiously, I reached my finger in over his, causing Asaph to gasp and choke. But I ignored the sounds and focused on pressing my finger down directly over Yeshua's, hoping that he would feel the necessary firmness in his own body. If he didn't get the medicine to rest on the back ridge of the tooth, it wouldn't be effective, and Asaph's pain would increase. But I could see, as we removed our hands, as Asaph coughed and spit and the tiny crease appeared between Yeshua's eyes, that my son thought I'd been unduly aggressive.

"Remove the medicine before you eat or drink," I said. "Let us know if the pain is not better in two days." But Asaph was already sitting up, swinging his body toward Yeshua, gripping Yeshua's forearm, proclaiming his muffled thanks to him. Then I watched him press a few prutot into Yeshua's palm.

"Come," said Yeshua, and they made their way up the hill, leaving me with the leftover scent of lamp oil and the seizing sky. I could hear Yeshua whispering—a prayer or a song. He always did this, smoothed on words of comfort, the blessings of Yahweh, as though these things were simply an extra bandage, as though adhering the promises of a god to those in pain was not dangerous in the least. But then, at that moment, I thought it was a thing that could be fixed, just like his uncertainty, his overly tentative handling of Asaph's pain. I thought, if we could just leave Nazareth, all of this could be remedied.

I had spent the last twenty-two years teaching my son medicine but also saving what we had earned at the clinic. I had enough money to take both of us to Alexandria. And I still had the scroll that promised me entrance to the library, a job at a clinic of my choosing. I will explain how the scroll came into my possession later. The point is that I still hadn't found a way to peel Yeshua from this place—from Mari. Until this day.

By the time I made my way from the makeshift clinic back to the cluster of houses, the storm clouds with their white tics of lightning had moved off to the west. The sun rose and the gauzed world appeared: the cistern, Caleb's olive oil press, the mustard bush where the birds ate the seeds and, fattened, stayed in the same place to shit them out again. The familiar road that gave way to meandering tracks drifting up and down the hillside, the walled courtyards shielding two-room houses. The only difference was the figure of Yeshua, waiting outside my courtyard.

"Auntie," he said. Though his speech difficulty had diminished, he still often drew out the first sound of a word, just slightly, and then often rushed headlong into the next sound so that his voice hitched up suddenly louder, stronger.

"Peace to you," I said.

"Here." He pressed the coins Asaph had given him into my hand.

I nodded in thanks.

"There is a prophet," he said.

I nodded again. There were prophets and magicians and doomsayers who traveled all over the countryside. There was always a prophet.

Yeshua looked in my eyes, took both my hands. "No, Auntie. A real prophet. He's rumored to be at the Jordan, a four-day walk. I am going to see him tomorrow. Will you come?"

My hands in his hands were suddenly wet with sweat. "Does Mari know?"

"Mari knows that I am going. She is glad for me to go. I did not ask her to come along, if that's what you mean."

"And you want me to come?"

"You always talk about all there is to learn elsewhere. You've told me about Rome, Auntie. I know you like to see new places, and you are always worried about the medicines in your case, that we are running low on tears of poppy. We will likely meet merchants along the way."

I began nodding vigorously, too vigorously. I knew if I spoke, I would not be able to keep the trembling out of my voice.

"Good," he said. "I will come for you tomorrow morning." Then he turned into his courtyard and left me to turn into mine.

I walked directly to the wall, pressed my forehead to the stone, found crevices for the tips of my fingers. I clung to the wall as though I were on a cliffside, as though below me were bottomless space. This was my chance. A four-day walk was ample time to convince Yeshua that once we reached the Jordan, once we glimpsed his prophet, we should continue to Alexandria. I had enough money for us to travel there, to begin a life. We would get work in no time. We would take one another's arm as we climbed the library steps. I had seen enough of Alexandria, remember, to still recall its taste faintly on the back of my tongue.

I clung to the wall and watched Mari move to Yeshua through the dawn light. Watched him bend to her so she could touch his face, rubbing her thumbs over the bridge of his nose, his cheeks, his eyelids as though she were blind, as though she hadn't seen him hours ago, as though night had been intent on stealing him. Then she took his hand and led him below the oak tree, where a single stool sat in a tumble of leaves. She began to squat beside it, but he squatted instead, rested his hand on the stool so she was the one who sat, and then they both bent their heads and began to pray.

Meanwhile, Josef coaxed the fire in the brazier, added the barley to the water, a pinch of salt. Meanwhile, Josef brought clean hay to the underground stable, lead the goat and donkey to the small back pasture, fetched three bowls from the inside shelves. Smoke rose from their courtyard and Mari and Yeshua's voices rose with it, their heads bent together, their fingers laced. Josef tapped errant sparks with his sandal, scooped the finished porridge into bowls, and rested the bowls on the table, on top of the faint outline of Greek letters Yeshua and I had carved into the wood when he was small. Josef ate his porridge standing, his back to me, and then returned to the house with his own empty bowl.

Still I gripped the wall. Still, their prayers continued. Until the porridge stopped steaming, until Mari opened her eyes and looked at me directly, though the crack was small enough and the distance far enough there was no way she could have known for certain I was there. But I promise you she held my gaze, John Mark. Over thirty years had passed since Yeshua's birth, and nothing between us had changed.

Nothing except that I was finally ready to take my son back from her.

I helped Nathan with the sheep that day but returned early to prepare my house for departure. There was little to do. I made sure the food was secure and the goat had clean straw. I unpacked my medicine case to calm myself, refilled the wine and olive oil, checked each limewood box to see which herbs were low, set out the probes and blades and hooks, rerolled each of the four cloth bandages into a tighter spiral. I divided the money I had and placed some at the bottom of the medicine kit and some in my traveling bag. Then, with a needle and thread, I sewed the remaining coins into my traveling cloak.

When I was finished, I took down a small package wrapped in simple linen cloth; inside was the letter, sealed with wax, and two stolas, one silver-gray and the other blue. I slid out of my own tunic and let the gray silk swim over my skin, surprised by the tightness of the fitted band below my breasts, how naked my shoulders felt, bared between the thin straps. The tunics we wore in the Galilee were long and mostly unfitted, though some women wove belts to decorate their waists. But mostly it was wool that we hemmed and then rehemmed when the bottom began to fray. It was so strange to see that my legs were hidden in the stola but to have them feel free, easier.

"What's this, Salome?"

Josef, who never came to my house unannounced, stood in my doorway, milking pot hanging heavy from his hand. His eyes brushed the unpacked medicine vials, the sealed letter, the places where my aureoles pressed dark against the bust of the stola, and his easy smile was completely absent. He looked like he'd been bitten.

"Josef," I said. "Peace be with you."

But he turned his whole head away from me, offered me only his profile.

"What is this?" he said again.

Instead of explaining, I turned to the shelf that still held bread from the morning. I put some in a bowl, spooned olive oil over the top, and offered it to him. After more than thirty years of spurning the rituals of the place, I suddenly wanted to show him that I had learned something, that I was capable of obedience, too.

He shook his head, batted the offering away. "Salome," he said.

"This is a stola. From my time in Rome."

"I know what a stola is. Why are you wearing it?"

"How do you know I don't wear it every night?" I tried to chide, but my voice came out flat. Josef was the one who usually joked; it was usually his warmth that was contagious, that loosened my tongue.

"You're going with Yeshua," he said.

"He invited me."

"Mari knows that you're going."

I kept my voice brusque when I said: "We'll only be gone eight days or so. Four there and four back again."

Josef squatted down and touched the money hemmed into the edge of my traveling cloak. Then he stood and looked at me.

"Bandits," I said defensively. "Yeshua should do the same."

"Mari will follow him," he said. "If he doesn't return, she will find him."

"Why would we not return?" I looked at him directly then. We were the same height. Creases fanned his eyes, and though he had wiggles of gray in his beard, his hair, his eyebrows were still perfectly dark.

He reached out his hand and cupped my neck. "Salome," he said again, his voice a half groan. A thicket of bees between us. Though his hand didn't move, its warmth trickled from my neck to my shoulder, to my breast, my ribs, my belly. I wanted to lean forward, into him. To see if his body could take on my weight. I wanted the scent of his collar, his neck, wanted a body against my body inch for inch. I closed my eyes; in that darkness I was ready to give myself over to him. To let him do with me as he wished, not out of obedience or fear or desire but something else I couldn't name. My body became the look patients offered on the examining couch before the tears of poppy or henbane was given, when they knew they were being offered a sleep from which they might never return. Josef's hand remained—but he didn't move it higher to smooth my cheek or lower to feel the rounding of my hip.

I opened my eyes and stepped away from him. His hand fell away and the buzzing between us dimmed. The light the lamps threw was no longer erotic in the way it fingered the walls. From the room next door, the goat scraped her hoof on a fieldstone.

"We are going," I said.

The next morning I watched for the last time as Mari and Yeshua huddled together under the oak, this time passing back and forth the words of the prophet Nehemiah while Josef mixed oil and flour and water and salt to make a simple dough, while he pressed rolled balls of it between his palms and laid the circles on the heated baking stone. When they were done cooking, he dolloped on a bit of yogurt from Eden, the goat, and brought the bread to them below the tree, a serving in each hand.

They didn't reach for the food but continued the recitation, and I watched Josef's hands fall slowly, as though the bread grew heavier with each passing moment, and I thought of the way he dug his tongue into the inside of his lower lip as he worked the stone of the wall, the way he rested his chin on Eden's back while he milked, pulling the liquid out of her based on touch alone. And I thought, of course, of his hand on my neck the night before, the way he said my name as if it were a net holding all he wanted. I already felt his absence.

Finally Mari and Yeshua finished their recitation and took the bread from Josef. They walked closer to the fire to eat, letting the soft heat warm their calves. Now they were only a few feet away from the wall, so I could see where dust had collected in the folds of Yeshua's traveling cloak and see the flush gathering like a noose around Mari's neck. She recited the contents of the bag she had packed for him, like one final prayer, and then took his face between her hands.

"You will return in eight days' time," she said.

"I will return," he said.

"I will pray for you every moment, every moment until I see your face again." She took hold of his ears then, as if he were a pitcher, and though Yeshua's back was to me I could see his neck tighten and pull, just slightly, away from her grip.

"I will return," he said.

Mari released her hands but the flush continued crawling, up her neck and over her cheeks and into her eyes so that she wept, silently but continuously, as Yeshua slung the bag over his shoulder, kissed the top of her head, embraced Josef, and left.

Perhaps I should have felt guilt then, but I did not. Empathy perhaps, for the grief that would overtake Mari when she realized Yeshua wasn't returning. But I didn't dwell on her pain. I focused on the tightening of Yeshua's neck instead. Bodies don't lie. He wanted away from her; he needed a life without Mari in it. I just had to make certain that we were far enough away in eight days' time that when Yeshua didn't return, she wouldn't be able to follow.

Every story needs comic relief. Josef taught me that, laughing when I wiped shit across his face as we held a dying infant between us. I have never been good at humor myself, but I appreciate it in others. I imagine you will not put humor in your story, John Mark. You will suppose your audience will not take the story of your savior seriously if they grin while reading it. Perhaps you're right. And it is true that the next part of this story I did not find funny while it happened—but it does seem funny now, because remember, I had waited for years and years to leave Nazareth with my son. Months and months I'd plotted and longed to be on the road with him, Alexandria ahead of us. For years I had made do with the plants I could collect in Galilee and the offerings of the occasional traveling caravan. But I had no cauterizing irons, no trephines, no tradesman nearby who knew how to craft leg braces. Our secret nighttime clinic had kept me fed with enough practice to satiate me, but I longed for the pace of an actual clinic, the training that awaited both of us in the library, beside the best surgeons of Alexandria. I needed only to convince Yeshua of the absolute necessity of the plan. And I would have four days to do this, I thought. Four days to quell his doubts and tempt him with all that we could do and learn.

After Yeshua left Mari and Josef, he found me standing at the entrance of my courtyard and greeted me with a smile. And we began our journey in companionable silence.

For two minutes. Until he stopped at another courtyard fifty paces down the road. The sound of Asa's coughing appeared before Asa did. It was not a consistent sound, that cough, but varied depending on Asa's mood. Sometimes it was a continual throat clearing, other times it was puffs of air that he panted, open-mouthed. When he truly wanted to make a show of it, he'd bend over with his hands on his knees and let his whole belly jiggle with the sound and let the blood run to his face, just to show how awful his affliction was. His cough was the animal bell that let you know where he was in the village, always.

You know, John Mark, that ailments are not hard to come by in the Galilee. So many of the prohibitive techniques I learned in Rome— diet, exercise, the rocking cure—these were useless there. Diet was determined almost entirely by season and harvest, labor was the only exercise anyone bothered with, and the rocking cure required horses and carriages, of which there were none. So people suffered, John Mark, and after years and years of treating them and standing beside the shrouded forms of those whom my treatments failed, I knew the common complaints: withered limbs from poor eating, fevers that came with the mosquitoes in the springtime, broken teeth from the stones no one could be bothered to pick from the lentils, frail bowels that refused to hold any sort of food. Women died because their babies wouldn't turn, or because their husbands put another baby inside them too soon after the first. One woman died because her labor lasted for four days, and because she was unclean in her laboring, she wasn't allowed to eat. When it came time to push the baby out, she didn't have the strength.

In Rome those with faux illnesses had irritated me, but they were easily seen and dismissed. Here, Asa's perpetual and entirely invented cough was an affront that enraged me every time I heard it. And I knew it was invented because he had come to Yeshua and me on numerous occasions. We had tried horehound in wine, charcoaled figs, a lavender paste—"Ah yes!" Asa would say every time, speaking to us in a clear and unfettered voice. "Now that's lovely." But by the following day the cough would return.

Why didn't I confront him about this? Perhaps I should have, but Asa had the cheese. You understand. Delicacies were basically nonexistent besides on feast days and trips to Sepphoris and traveling caravans. The rest of our lives was made up of porridge and bread, stews of lentils or chickpeas, rarely spiced, sometimes dolloped with yogurt or honey. There were olives, but most of those were pressed. There were grapes, but most were small and bitter and turned into wine. But Asa had three cows. And with their milk he made cheese. I have lived in Greece and Rome and here, in Alexandria, and this was the best cheese I have ever tasted. It was thick and sweet. You could add it to almost any other food and it made that dish creamier, richer. Suddenly, eating was an act you wanted rather than needed to do. And the village story was that the cows loved Asa's cough. It sounds absurd, but it wasn't entirely unfounded. When he stood near one of the cows and coughed, the beast would approach him and reach out with its tongue to lick his face. Probably it was the saltiness of the phlegm that collected around his lips, but regardless, the cows did love him. And even when heat thinned the harvest, those cows were fat and happy.

Ach. This has been a long side story. But I wanted you to know exactly how far my heart dropped when I saw that Asa and his cough would be joining us. How would I talk to Yeshua? How would I convince him to come to Alexandria with Asa coughing at our heels?

Asa slapped Yeshua's back in time to his coughs and then held up a bag that dripped slightly with moisture. "For the journey," he said. "The freshest we had." I wanted to snatch that bag and press my face into it immediately. But Asa, of course, did not acknowledge me at all. I fell into step behind them.

Then we stopped again. This time it was Caleb who emerged, holding his withered arm with his strong hand. Behind him, in the courtyard, I glimpsed his wife. She did not appear sad about his departure. Caleb's affliction was certainly more real than Asa's, but Caleb used it as an excuse to do absolutely nothing. Sometimes I saw Caleb and his wife out at their small plot of land, Caleb standing with a stick in his hand, pointing at what needed to be done while his wife labored on her knees. I didn't even know the wife's name, but I admired her; sadly, the other women did not. They mocked her skin, browned and stretched from hours in the sun, and said that doing all of the men's work had thinned her breasts, stripped the fat from her hips.

Now it was Yeshua, Asa, Caleb, and I. In Nazareth, four people traveling together was a procession, and people came to the entrances of their courtyards to watch, spooning the last of breakfast into their mouths. Then the jeers began:

"Are you off to see the p-p-p-prophet, Yeshua?"

"Will you return with two good hands, Caleb?"

"Will you be strong enough to give your wife a child?"

"Better ask the prophet to bless your seed as well."

"Maybe you'll find a wife in the Jordan, Yeshua."

No one mocked Asa—there was the cheese to consider—but I noticed a few people coughing quietly.

I have not made clear, perhaps, who Mari and Josef were in this community. Mari's father, Abraham, was a rabbi who taught only two students and kept synagogue in their home once a week. People thought Abraham was eccentric, but he was also respected—they did not bear the same patience for his daughter. They had seen Mari sitting at his feet when she should have been learning to weave or cooking or fetching water from the cistern. They saw the way her moods careened, the way Abe permitted her to stay in the house for days doing nothing if she simply wet her face with a few tears. And Josef was the failed son-in-law. The builder who took too much time at each task, who cared about beauty and rightness when only efficiency was needed. After Abraham died, the village story went, Josef coddled Mari in the same way Abraham had. And then there was Yeshua, a strange child who went around mouthing prayers, whose words still sometimes got stuck between his tongue and the roof of his mouth. Yeshua, who, no matter how much he ate, retained the thin ribcage of his actual father. He possessed my height and dark coloring but his father's lighter, thin hair, small teeth, round eyes. Mari and Josef were both people of solid bearing, but diminished height. Yeshua's body didn't seem to fit the family, but his eccentricities did.

People still clutched his arm in our clinic. Wept into his shoulder. Told him he was blessed, a miracle, a favored descendent. The mending of pain made them enormously grateful for a day or two. But as days went on, health offered them the ability to tell different stories to themselves about their suffering as obstacles they themselves had conquered, parables about their own virility and strength.

Though I was not entirely surprised by the content of the taunts, it was the first time I'd heard any of this spoken aloud.

"Tell the prophet I'd like a better grape harvest."

"How nice you're leaving your families to tend the fields."

"An eight-day Sabbath. What a brilliant idea. Why didn't I think of that?"

We walked on, Yeshua bending his head slightly to Caleb, who was gesturing with his healthy hand, Asa coughing to cover the ridicule. And we had almost made it, only three houses left, when a boy of about five ran at us and grabbed hold of Yeshua's traveling cloak. Yeshua tried to pull the cloak free, but the boy laughed and flapped the cloak with his arms, making a galloping motion with his legs and clicking his tongue the way men do to order animals forward.

The jeers turned into chuckles.

"Get off," said Yeshua under his breath. He gripped one of the boy's hands with both of his and peeled the fingers apart. But Mari had fastened the cloak securely so he couldn't remove the boy's other hand without turning the other way, which he did, at which point the boy grabbed the cloak again with the hand Yeshua had just undone.

Finally, Caleb wiggled his withered hand in the boy's face, and the boy recoiled enough for Yeshua to take back the cloak and wrap it more securely around his form. We hurried on, looking at the ground, and I am not proud to say that when I heard a splattering sound and more laughter I did turn, one more time, to see the boy with his robes hitched over his hips, arcing a perfect stream of piss at our retreating bodies.

That was my last sight of Nazareth: the malicious glee on the boy's face, the Nazarenes gathered along the edges of the road, and far off, on the other side of the laughter, Mari and Josef, leaning into one another. Josef raised his arm, but I turned away without raising mine. I focused instead on the steady drops of moisture from Asa's bag of cheese, marks that would exist only until the sun arrived. Then our trail would evaporate, swept clean.

Travel was tedious and slow. My own legs were muscled from tending the sheep with Nathan, and Yeshua was in good health since he and Josef often traveled to and from Sepphoris for day-labor jobs. But Caleb and Asa were slow and peppered Yeshua with questions about the prophet he couldn't possibly answer: would the prophet bless each person individually? Was there a record of his healing? Had anyone suffered bad fortune as a result of meeting with him? Would he try magic on people, or only prayer?

Instead of simply saying yes or no, Yeshua offered stories in return. Usually a small story, about animals or the way houses were put together, or how some crops withered while others thrived. I found the stories annoying; if a patient comes to a physician, you do not tell them their pain is like a wealthy landowner, and it would be insulting to offer the changing of seasons as a balm to their continued infertility. But Asa and Caleb leaned closer when he responded this way. Asa ceased his coughing and Caleb let go of his withered hand, let it move along with the rhythm of the rest of his body. I didn't speak. My calves took on a deeper shade of brown from the dust the men kicked up.

When we stopped to rest, which was often, Yeshua blessed all of the food before we ate it, even if he'd already blessed it previously. I kept my eyes open while the men prayed; I refused to even move my lips along with them, but I studied Yeshua's face, how his eyelashes did not flutter but lay heavy on his cheeks. The way the fine lines around his mouth and at his forehead eased, the way he smiled, just slightly, in a way that reminded me of Josef. But whereas Josef's smiles were always offered to another person, Yeshua's smile seemed to travel inward, toward himself. Though Asa and Caleb were transfixed by Yeshua's stories, they often grew distracted during the prayers, picking at flaking skin or scratching their noses. If Yeshua felt their impatience, he didn't let on.

We spent the first night in the courtyard of a rich Gentile's home. We rolled up as best we could in our sleeping cloaks, my body a good ten feet from the bodies of the men. In the morning I woke to dew on my face and the sounds of the slave readying the outdoor fire for breakfast. Yeshua was gone—likely to relieve himself outside the courtyard wall—but the other men still slept, so I turned my head slightly and watched. The slave had a droopy face and thick limbs. She didn't wear a headscarf, and her thin brown hair was secured back with a band of fabric dulled to a color that was no longer any color at all. Her tunic was too short and revealed legs covered with bites—insect or rat, I couldn't be sure, only that a few looked swollen and infected.

She used dough for the morning bread that had been mixed the night before and risen, puffy and white; the home's brazier was far more complicated than the ones in Nazareth and contained a small oven into which she placed a series of small loaves. Then she stood, staring at the fire, absentmindedly scratching at her legs.

"Peace be with you," said Yeshua, startling both of us.

"This food is not for you," she said. "If you want water, the cistern is there." She nodded toward the corner of the large courtyard.

"I brought these"—Yeshua showed her a handful of plants—"to help with your bites."

The slave looked at him suspiciously. "Are you a witch doctor?"

"No," said Yeshua, "I am a physician. My training comes from Rome."

My heart began to beat furiously in my chest. I inched my body forward, hands clenched together beneath me.

The slave did not invite him closer, nor did she shoo him away.

"Do you have a small bowl I could use to boil water?" Yeshua continued.

The girl narrowed her eyes. "I have to get breakfast. They'll be awake soon." She went back into the house and returned with a serving platter but also with a small bowl already filled with water. She put it on the brazier.

"This is plantain," Yeshua said, showing her the leaves. "It grows all around this house. It's good for many things. You can make a tea with it or add oil and wait a few weeks to make an ointment. But today"—here he used his cloak to remove the already warmed bowl—"we'll just boil a lot of leaves in a very small amount of water." He dumped some of the water out and then shredded the leaves apart with his hands, adding all of the bits to the bowl. Then he put the bowl back on the fire and waited.

"Do you have a long rag for wrapping? That would help, too."

The girl shrugged. She looked as if she'd spent her life learning how to keep her face disinterested at all times.

She took the loaves out of the small oven; they were golden and steaming, and my stomach growled below me. After heaving the serving platter onto her shoulder, she slipped back inside the house, returning seconds later with a few clean rags.

"Be quick," she said haughtily, in a tone she must have borrowed from her mistress. "They're going to discover in a minute that I forgot something they don't even really need."

Yeshua nodded. He gestured for her to sit on a low stool and then knelt in front of her. The slave girl straightened her shoulders and raised her chin slightly; she'd never had another person bend at her feet, and certainly not a man. Using the end of a serving spoon from the table, Yeshua pressed and mixed the leaves until a thick paste presented. Then he used his fingers to smear the concoction over the most inflamed bites.

"That's hot," said the girl, accusatorily.

Yeshua pulled away his hand and sat back on his heels. "I can wait."

I pressed my lips together to keep from ordering him forward, but the girl did so for me.

"You'd better do it now, otherwise they'll call me off and it won't be done at all."

I watched as Yeshua finished with the paste, as he wrapped the bandage correctly: first around the bridge of the foot, then the ankle, then higher, around the bites. The order was correct, but he didn't pull the fabric tight enough; within an hour it would be sloughing off her. But mostly I was proud: of his ingenuity, of his use of plants found within the vicinity, of his easy teaching so the girl could continue the healing on her own. And those words: "I am a physician."

He knew who he was, he knew what he wanted; I just needed to figure out a way to talk to him privately. I just needed to convince him that it was good and right to pursue medicine, to leave Nazareth behind.

I sat up on my knees and only then noticed that he had not finished with the girl. He held her calf with both of his hands, the length of her foot pressed against his chest, and though I couldn't hear all of his words (he spoke quietly and his back was turned), I knew from the rise and fall of the tone that it was a prayer. I could see the slave girl's expression, though. She'd tipped her chin downward and her face contained the softening light of a woman gazing on a week-old infant once the birthing pain has passed but the strange miracle of birth remains. Though I never cared for the laws of the Nazarenes, I could see this moment through their eyes: a Jew praying over a Gentile, a man at the feet of a woman, a landowner (however impoverished) bending before a slave. And though I didn't feel their disapproval, I did feel a strange dark uncertainty in my chest. Perhaps that's not the correct way to describe it. It was like seeing chaos, like dark thunderheads moving toward you and the sudden strange stillness when the animal sounds fall off and the solid stones of your home seem flimsy against the power of the clouds. Softness turned into hurting fury.

I took a breath and rid myself of that vision. We were leaving the customs of Nazareth behind. My son was a doctor treating a patient. Nothing more. Nothing more.

A cough rose up beside me, and then there was Caleb's voice saying, "Salome. Salome. What have you made us to eat?"

On the fourth day of travel the landscape changed. We moved from the rise and fall of rocky hills and wide plains and simple plots of subsistence farming into the green choke of the land near the river. The dirt track we followed was narrower, less traveled, and we passed through the open vowels of frog song and shadowed tunnels of shade. Gnats flurried around our heads, and there was the deep, thick scent of new growth.

Each day I was certain there would be a time when Asa and Caleb would fall back far enough that I could talk privately with Yeshua, but he coaxed them along with stories and questions. Each night after dinner the three of them bundled themselves an ample distance away from me, and I had only the rocks beneath my shoulders as talking companions. I wasn't worried exactly. "I am a physician," he'd said. And there had been his neck, tightening away from Mari's grip.

"Acknowledge the possible negative outcomes but don't dwell on them," Rufus had said during my training in Rome. "Know the wrong roads only enough that you take the right one." It wasn't that I didn't consider what might go wrong: that Yeshua could refuse my suggestion, that we might grudgingly trudge back to Nazareth, that life might continue as it had for the last thirty-two years—or that we might arrive in Alexandria to find that after this much time, my sealed scrolls held no sway. I acknowledged these possibilities on our walk, and I dismissed them. I focused on the necessary treatment, not the roads that led to further illness.

What I did not consider much at all was exactly where we were headed. I suppose when Yeshua first asked me to go, I conjured the image of a devout man standing knee-deep in a stream, trickling water over the heads of figures who waited their turn patiently along the bank. I figured a neat beard, a wet hem, the summoning of the strength of Elijah. Perhaps a few ragged tents off to the side. When we arrived, I assumed there would be a version of synagogue: a scroll opened and a chair brought for the man who read the scroll, songs about crossing from one place to another, prayers of yearning for a land and a destiny that had been swept away, the men huddled together and the women pushed to the far outskirts of hearing.

But then, near noon on the fourth day, we arrived. The place was no version of a synagogue; it was a swarm, a press, a fervor, a froth. It was part carnival, part marketplace, part traveling camp. Vendors sold spiced nuts and yogurt, figs halved and honeyed, crickets crackling with oil and heat. Stalls and tables and blankets lined the river but not in the orderly way of the Roman agora. This space was haphazard, crammed: wooden stalls pressed so close to the water that the front stilts were halfway sunk in mud, the blankets of the token-sellers stained with the footprints of people who refused to divert their paths, the scents of body sweat mingling with the bitter char of offerings and the sweet rot of fruit dropped and trampled. Behind poorly hung curtains, hoarse men whispered about how from their altars the smoke would rise directly to some god's mouth. In dry dirt farther up from the bank, a magician drew a circle in the dirt and stood inside it, pressing a hot coal to his forehead. Beside him, inside a different circle, a dwarf dangled a toad over his open throat. We passed a man with a makeshift kiln and a block of red clay who would carve you an amulet in an instant, your face on one side and the face of any savior god you pleased on the other. We had arrived not at the place of the prophet but at the place of *all* the prophets.

The chaos delighted me, but Caleb cradled his withered hand close and Asa held on to Yeshua's upper arm, forgetting to cough. Yeshua's face was pale, waxy, but he was alert; his head swung from side to side. You could see the effort it took him to take all of it in.

Off to our right, a vendor held a scroll above his head. "Prophets! Prophets!" he said in Greek, in Latin, in Aramaic—the three parts of my life unfolding in quick succession on his tongue. When he noticed our attention, he switched entirely to Aramaic: "Elijah's own words. Right here. Take this home for your own synagogue. Show your people you have come to the place of clean water. Of the pure word. One denarius only."

Yeshua's face relaxed into his inward-facing smile, and he stepped forward with both of his palms open in a gesture of shared intimacy. "Then Elijah said to Ahab"—his words were smooth, glinting—"as Adonai lives, whom I serve, there will be neither dew nor rain in the next few years except at my word."

The vendor's face remained impassive. "One denarius," he said again, poking at Yeshua's empty right palm. "No coin, no scroll." He transferred his attention beyond us to the prospect of more willing customers. "Elijah! Micah! Nehemiah!"

"Let me see," I said, stepping forward.

"One denarius," he said again without actually looking at me.

I held out the appropriate coin, but when he reached for it, I pulled my hand away. "I want to see it first."

"I can't break it," he said, pointing to the waxy seal.

"Unroll it," I said again, holding up the coin.

The vendor's eyes flicked to the men, but none of them corrected me. The vendor scanned the crowd again for an easier target and, finding none, sighed dramatically. "I suppose there's one in here that's already undone," he said. And then he made a great show of groaning while digging through his crate of looped papyrus, finally emerging with one that was crumpled at one edge, only the residue of wax remaining. "Here," he said.

"You can't let a woman touch that!" said Caleb, suddenly springing self-righteously to life. Asa started up an indignant coughing fit, spraying flecks of mucus across the scroll and the vendor's forearms.

I put my hands behind my back. "I won't touch it. Unroll it."

He did. And I could see from the way his eyes flicked uneasily between the papyrus and my face that he couldn't read.

"There's no Elijah there," I said. "Those are the accounts of a baker, from the looks of it. Measures of wheat and salt. Records of loaves sold, names of fellow merchants. The cost of a new oven—there."

Before the vendor could pull the scroll away, Yeshua reached out, quick as a snake, and grabbed it. Without hesitation, without tenderness, he ripped the scroll in two. This took effort; the fibers were thick, but his rage managed it. Then he dropped the pieces on the ground and made a show of twisting them into the dirt with his sandal. Asa spit on the ground emphatically and Caleb shook his withered hand at the man as though the vendor's false scrolls had caused his ailment.

"I get them from a man in Alexandria," the vendor said weakly. "I know some letters. That's all. Move off if you're not going to buy."

We did move off, Yeshua's knuckles white around the strap of his traveling bag, and soon came to a grouping of tables that held baskets of herbs and small, poorly fashioned clay cups. Behind the table a huge fire burned over a large, makeshift brazier where at least twenty different cups balanced precariously. Three men squatted in the dirt near the fire, working furiously with their mortars and pestles, occasionally pulling clumps of plants from the baskets or pouring drams of olive oil or water or milk into their mixtures. Standing just behind the table, a dark-skinned man wearing a robe etched with gold thread called out to people, asking for what ailed their bodies, their minds. When someone lingered and offered an answer, he made a show of springing into action, finding just the right clay cup on the brazier or ordering the squatting workers to pour their sweat into the best medicine they'd ever made. By then the passerby, intrigued, had pulled out a coin, and eventually paid for the medicine, crafted right before his eyes, just for him.

Yeshua and I stepped closer to the tables to gauge the quality of the medicinal plants; I thought perhaps I could buy some to refill my supplies. "This is only thistle and mulberry," said Yeshua. He turned to the vendor. "Are those willow leaves?"

The vendor shrugged.

"These are useless," said Yeshua loudly.

"Ah!" said the vendor, stepping closer, completely unperturbed. "Here is a man whose ailment is suspicion!"

The few people who had gathered to wait for their medicines shook their heads.

The vendor reached out his arms to the crowd. "Is this not a place for belief? Can healing ever come to us if we are filled with doubt?"

When he turned his head, I could see the skin of his neck marbled pink and white and brown from a bad burn, likely not so long ago. Even though I despised what he was doing, I longed to treat the injury; Yeshua noticed the burn as well—and perhaps something in the man's eyes, which were rather like Josef's, a shared mirth. *We understand*, said his eyes, *but these fools do not*. I nodded slightly, but Yeshua shook his head and walked swiftly away.

Let me be honest: I felt such a profound sense of satisfaction then. Such deep joy. There was Yeshua, finally seeing these prophets, these vestiges of gods and religions, for the false props they were, for the stupid, flimsy hope they presented to those who were suffering. Yeshua had grabbed the scroll decisively, and the way he spoke to the medicine vendor was aggressive, precise, demanding. These characteristics had lain fallow in Yeshua for so long that I had despaired whether they existed at all, but being away from Mari had changed him—I was sure of this. No longer was he simply a vessel for tenderness and prayer; the Yeshua beside the Jordan appraised and judged and acted. It was then that I knew, truly knew, that my son could be not just a good physician but a great one.

We moved on through the crowd—and I began to enjoy myself. After years in a crumbling town, I was in a place of both action and anonymity. We trudged through the smoke of bloodied entrails and sale calls in multiple languages, between chorused chants and the clay figurines of Egyptian gods, pressed into rows in the soft earth. We passed men with hair slicked to curls on their foreheads and women with darkly kohled eyes, their hair knotted and pinned; we wove through tunics splashed with color—scarlet and indigo, green and orange—and the glint of bracelets and hair pins, buckles and breastplates and the metal collars of slaves. Roman soldiers ate beside traders from Lebanon; a group of widows, faces streaked with ash, begged together up and down the bank. And it wasn't just people. I saw animals again: a burst of yellow birds in a cage, a snake curled in a bowl, a dog with long legs and regal bearing howling at a trail of incense.

As the afternoon wore on, I watched Asa and Caleb slump under the cacophony of this new world. Even Yeshua's rage ebbed toward exhaustion. But I felt only a coursing energy under my skin. I knew how to shift my hips through the crowd, knew to avoid the men with watery, bloodshot eyes, knew how to tsk-tsk at the beggars and refuse to touch their hands. When Asa wanted to buy a bowl of grapes, I used Greek instead of Aramaic to fetch a lower price; I checked the scale (and found it weighted) when the vendor proclaimed Caleb's sack of olives to cost far more than it was worth.

We shared the olives and grapes and the last of Asa's cheese near a clump of hawthorn bushes far enough away from the river that we could hear one another speak. The men nestled together in what little shade the shrub provided while I sat, shading my eyes in the spring sun. Even the sweat running down my back, between my breasts, felt good, as though the past was pouring off me. When the men determined that it was time to continue to search for the prophet, I let them go on without me, told them I'd find a group of women near the tent site with whom to settle. "I need some rest," I told them.

And, finally, I did. The energy coursing through me had turned into the kind of exhaustion, the kind of need for sleep that can come only when you know things are well. Yeshua and I were beginning our new life, he was letting his true self emerge, and I was finally back in a world I knew how to navigate. Though this place still retained the vestiges of Jewish law (there were no women selling wares or making charms as there would have been in Rome), this part of the Jordan was not far from the Dead Sea, from Jerusalem, and only a half day's walk from the Ridge Route (a road unpaved by Romans but beaten smooth and wide, the people claimed, by the feet of their ancient forebears). So although this strange place certainly wouldn't have had me as a physician, I was no longer the strange Gentile who dirtied the water in the well, who touched a man's shit-covered feet, who barked after sheep like a boy, and whose Aramaic still sounded sloppy and slurred.

I walked up the low rise and found a group of women and a patch of shade, and I slept the sleep of one who was finally at ease with her life.

I woke to a girl's hand upon my skull, moving my head back and forth slightly to sluice the dreaming off me. The screaming followed close behind, far off but insistent, a singular, animal sound. "Something's happened at the river," said the girl. Miriam was her name, I thought. Or Hannah? She had introduced herself before I drifted off. By the time I rose to my forearms the girl had run away, following the other women of her family who were chasing down the scream.

Then I fit the sound into a body. *Yeshua.* In seconds I was on my feet, medicine case in hand, feet slapping at the earth, calves cramping. It didn't take me long to reach the crowd. I pinched and elbowed, buried headfirst between hips that swayed together. I shoved and slithered. The sound grew louder and I thinned myself, a sliver, a knife, until I made it to the river. Until I saw my son.

I was wrong. He was not screaming but kneeling beside the man who was, whose body drew upward with pain. This must be the prophet, I thought: soaked cloak, bare feet, matted beard. Even in his agony the man's hands groped across the sand as though to bless. My son's hands, meanwhile, skimmed the air, reaching toward the prophet and then away as through his skin might scald. Yeshua's lower jaw worked too, circling around words his lips refused to form.

The crowd had gathered close but not too close, an audience for a two-person play.

The prophet screamed and screamed and screamed, his midsection moving up and down in tandem to the sound.

Minutes passed and the crowd's unified pant of panic turned into the slow, even breath of spectacle. Those nearest the event sat down; children began to move stealthily along the edges of the crowd like cats to find a better view. Beside me two men shared a bowl of curried nuts, pleased that the prophet's pain did not belong to them.

The prophet screamed.

Then murmuring began inside cupped hands, behind the raised curtains of headscarves. A squatting child pointed and yelled, "What's inside that man?" and then looked up expectantly. "A demon, perhaps," said a man with a halo of red skin around his neck, and I could feel the crowd pull back. Straighten. Then the voices began in earnest: "If not demon then / but who he's touched / if sin gets out / he'll make it worse / sink us all / in Syria they say / didn't come all this way / devil reek / the way he clicks his teeth / noticed before / fine words, but evil tempts / he wasn't right / dung promises / he'll kill us shaking / he'll get us all / he'll be on us / what's in him." Asa and Caleb were nowhere to be seen, and farther down the river I saw a man with heron limbs leading the newly baptized up the bank, away. The man with the red neck picked up a stone. Another dug his staff into the sand, right-left-right; the grinding bored into my head.

The flutter of Yeshua's hands. Parchment caught by wind. My son's thin ears, his tender skull. The whorl of hair behind his ear. I willed my son to be a coward. To get up and walk away.

The prophet screamed a scream that could mean so many things: bowel infection, bladder stone, twisted spine. My son remained.

The crowd grew louder. Boys dug rocks and handed them out to men who rolled their shoulders, loosened up their jaws. Two charlatans, tzitzits unraveling, held bowls of water and consulted about how best to turn this scene to their advantage. The man with the inflamed neck spit. A boy flicked a pebble off his palm. Yeshua flinched when the pebble hit his cheek, but he did not turn.

The prophet's howls were almost covered now by the excitement of the crowd. They had put all of their fear into the stones they were holding, and I knew they would throw them at the prophet. A fair share would hit my son. His hands, his ears, the whorl of hair behind his ear.

I was not willing to watch him die. I stepped forward, knelt on the other side of the prophet, and leaned forward so Yeshua could hear my voice, calm and steady and clear: "Ask the patient for his symptoms."

Yeshua did not look at me but tilted his head upward instead. He raised his hands, lower jaw searching for words, and grabbed two bunches of air inside his fists. As he pulled his arms toward the ground he leaned over the prophet. "Where?" he said in a steady, unhitched voice.

The prophet managed to float one hand up and over his abdomen, then the hand flopped back and clutched at the sand; he dug his heels into the bank, the holes now so deep they'd filled with river water. Yeshua closed his eyes, ran his hand gently from the man's collarbone to groin. He cocked his chin upward, said to the clouds: "It's distended. Here."

"Pull his cloak taut so I can see."

Yeshua did. The lump was the size of a child's fist.

The prophet howled louder, sand in his hair, blood on his chin from where he'd bitten through his lip.

I wanted to ask Yeshua for the possible causes. Wanted to hear his diagnosis. Wanted to watch him raise his slender fingers as he described our possible methods of treatment. But of course, there was no time. The crowd snapped their jaws. A boy held a stone to his eye, measuring distance.

"It's likely an internal organ. You must push it back in place." I could have pushed it back in place, but I knew this crowd. Though more worldly than the Nazarenes, they still would have christened me a witch. They wanted their anger, and a woman was the best cavity they could have stuffed it in. "Use your palm. A slow but steady pressure. Keep pushing until you cannot feel distention. You must be fast now. Open up your eyes."

He kept them closed. Chin up, he slid his fingers over the prophet until he found the knob of bulging skin again. He laid his palm flat, and when he rose up onto his knees to press I threw my own weight over the prophet's shoulders so he would not twist and mar the healing.

Then there was the prophet's burnt-cedar scream into my ear. Yeshua's voice so loud I could feel it at the base of my own lungs: "Be gone!" And then a distant sound like thunder passed overhead, the timbre of my own son's voice galloping across the arc of blue. Then the prophet became soft dough beneath me, panting, eyelids quivering.

I peeled my own body upright again and looked at Yeshua. His hands were not against the torso of the prophet but raised, thrown back into the air as though to show he meant no harm. The crowd was silent, deciding what kind of creature to become. A boy brought the river stone he meant to throw into his mouth to taste it. The red-necked man covered his mouth with two broad hands. The begging widows shook their heads so hard their wrinkled jowls quivered.

Yeshua stood in the quiet and helped the prophet to his feet. They walked together, without speaking, to the center of the river until the water curved brown and thick around their waists. On the other side of the bank, more had gathered. Most stood slack-armed, waiting.

The prophet raised his right forearm and Yeshua wrapped both his hands around it. Then my son leaned backward, letting his feet rise off the bottom, until his whole body skimmed the surface. For a few moments they stayed like this, the prophet moving his mouth around words none of us could hear until upon some impulse or instruction Yeshua let go. His body sank, feet then waist then torso, and then finally his head into the river until only his two hands remained, white wings that spasmed twice and then were gone.

At that moment I was a child again, thrashing below the surface of the sea, my father's hands upon me.

"Remember, you can stand," I said into the quiet.

Ten yards farther down, he appeared. And then the crowd knew what it wanted to see. Cheers swept down both sides of the bank. The widows raised their wrists into the air; people kissed the stones they thought they'd throw and placed them into pockets, satchels, even inside the warm corners of their cheeks. Children pressed their hands into the places where the prophet's heels had made divots in the bank, and strangers gripped forearms, barked laughs of pure delight. Already I could hear them retelling what they'd seen. I knew how stories changed, how they could slither or sprout wings.

I knew who my son was. But I knew they would tell it otherwise.

And judging by the way his eyes refused to open, Yeshua already believed the story they would tell. I pressed the heels of both my hands, grainy with river sand, into my eyes. There would be no Alexandria for us.

38 CE

Salome stares at her hands. She is wringing out a rag soaked in vinegar, but she is also scouring blood from wool. The wind that smooths this rooftop in Alexandria is also the wind that heckled a small promontory in Greece. It is dark here. A lamp flickers, illuminating a plate of bread, a man with close-set eyes who looks at her expectantly, and a youth with long limbs and a harelip who has fallen asleep sitting up, an amphora wedged between his knees. There is the sound of crying; the sound is not coming from her. Perhaps it comes from the dovecote in the corner of the roof? Do doves make that sound?

"And that was it? You just gave up?" The man with close-set eyes speaks from his position on the floor of the rooftop. He seems excitable but not dangerous. Salome shifts her weight to her left leg to ease some of the pain in her hip. "After all that time," the man continues, "after all of that effort, you just never bothered to ask him to go with you? You just let that be the end?"

Salome wrings out the rag she holds and then plunges her hands into the basin for another, but she does so too aggressively, and water splashes into her face. And it is then that she remembers Asha's face, similarly doused, the splash and her recoiling. Then she remembers the clinic and Philo's house, John Mark and Nadjem, the riots and her patients: the Mangled-Arm Man and the Fever Woman and all the rest. She should check on them, but she is very tired.

"Come and wring out the rags," she says to John Mark, who in turn nudges the sleeping Broom Boy awake. For a few minutes there is only the sound of the excess water splashing on the roof, the long strips of cloth they hang like the green fingers of branches over the Jordan.

Then from the far side of the roof comes the creaking of the stairs and then a gentle panting, and then there is Philo himself, stepping into the lamplight. The shadows hollow all their faces, but Philo's looks particularly gaunt and haunted, as though he has lived three different lives since the last time Salome saw him in his study.

"How are your cherubim?" Salome asks, not unkindly, rising to her feet.

Philo gives a gentle tug at his beard. "I came to say that you should go. Now, while things are quiet."

"We have patients downstairs."

"I know. The elders will care for them as best we can."

"I thought you wanted a clinic."

"I do. But the Greeks will return again tomorrow. Things will be worse, and I am not certain they will honor your physician's robes; I am not even certain they will see you. Return to your quarter of the city, Salome. And you, John Mark, find a ship that will take you anywhere but here, and then, whatever shore you arrive on, tell them our story."

Although Philo is speaking to them, he gazes into the darkness between them, and when he finishes his small speech, he doesn't wait for their responses but turns and descends the stairs.

Salome waits until his footsteps have retreated to speak: "He's right, John Mark. You should go. These aren't your people; this is not the place for you to die."

"Did you give up? Did you walk away?"

"What?"

"After Yeshua's miraculous healing of the prophet. You simply left? Decided that it was not your story?"

"Yes, I did," says Salome. "Something like that."

28 CE

I sat on the bank for a long time. Listened to the leftover questions about the quaking prophet and the man who'd taken power from the air and pressed it to the prophet's gut and cured him. How the river ate the healer and then gave him back. One woman whispered loudly that she'd heard the prophet entertained women in his tent at night. "Since my husband's member is a little bent and hard to rouse, I wouldn't mind a turn on him."

"It's the other one I'd want," whispered her companion, hoarse with mystery or desire or the incense now smoking in four bowls lined up where the prophet's body had lain. "If he put his hands upon my womb. What then?"

"You'll never get near him now," replied her friend. "At least not today. Though it depends on what he wants and what he likes. Did you bring earrings? Ocher for your lips?"

"I left all that at home. Cyrus said this place would be all Jews. My blond hair was decoration enough."

"Anyway he'll probably be a one-trick wonder. He'll stuff his magic hands inside his armpits, and we'll never hear of him again."

"Still, he did have slender hands."

"He does," her friend corrected.

"He does."

It's embarrassing to admit, John Mark, but it was a tiny puff of pride I felt for the way they wanted him. So different than two days earlier when the splatter of a child's piss chased us out of town. But in both cases the dumb people saw in Yeshua what they wanted to see: tongue-tied coward or spiritual healer. Never just the person that he was.

A hawk wavered on the air, made a sudden plunge into the river, then lifted with empty talons. Crows jostled over a dead fish, the scales dispersed and only pulp and bone remaining.

The day dragged on. The sun sank slowly behind the tallest trees.

Finally, cloak soaked and muddy, I picked up my case and wandered back toward the lazy splay of tents.

They'd made a place for Yeshua already. He stood on an overturned cart, a large fire just before him and rings of people fanning out around the flames. Asa and Caleb, suddenly his good friends again, stood a few feet from the edges of the cart, keeping the infirm at bay, the ones who were already begging to be touched, pleading their cases with tears or open wounds. Most of the audience consisted of men, but I could see the two Gentile women from the river, a few of the begging widows, and the willowy form of one of the women I had met earlier, hugging an amphora to her hip.

Yeshua looked out above the sea of faces toward the stalls that lined the river, occasionally casting his eyes down to a figure who stood at the right edge of the cart. The wind pulled Yeshua's voice and the edges of the fire toward me and then pushed both away, so I caught only a few phrases: "Whoever seeks," and "the realm compares," and "how a widow longs." And I thought of Anna, the only real widow he knew, who provided food for Nathan and charged the Nazarenes a fistful of barley each to see their own reflection in a piece of beaten metal her father had brought back from Syria ages ago.

I admit I was proud of the richness of his voice, the way it coated the faces around the fire. The way they leaned closer to him, even into that heat, so that their cheeks and foreheads shone and glistened. Everyone infected by the fever of my son, I thought, absorbing every croak of his throat. Sea sponges.

I moved around the circle of bodies to the left to see if I could catch his eye or more of what he was saying, at least. Finally, I was close enough to see the straight length of his nose, the slight swell of bone along his forehead. He gestured with his empty fingers, the heels of his palms, rather than the closed fist and thumb most Galilean men use to carve a story in the air.

I saw Yeshua the man before me but also Yeshua before he had a name. Yeshua when he was red stick limbs, fine black hair on his shoulder blades, indigo eyes, and screaming.

Yeshua's face half-hidden in Mari's cloak, white flakes of skin above his eyebrows. The rock of the boat from Alexandria to Joppa, thunderlight across his eyelids. The stench of his shit familiar, orange and buttery.

Yeshua on his back, raising his toes to his mouth. Yeshua fattening on Mari's milk.

Yeshua learning to walk, hand against the side of the house, around and around, refusing to stop, tiny fingertips raw from the stone. The bowl of lavender water I made for him to splash in.

Mari carrying Yeshua until his legs dangled to her knees. Mari lying on her pallet, windows stopped with rags, moaning low. Yeshua curled at her feet, matching his voice to hers.

Yeshua shaking me awake in the middle of the night. *I'm hungry, Auntie. I'm hungry.* The roll of his eyes, side to side, when I pushed him to the floor.

Yeshua touching his tongue like it did not belong to him. Yeshua massaging his face to make the sounds come cleaner, then clapping his hands in our faces, frustrated from trying.

Yeshua making a place for sick worms: wet bark and comfrey leaves pressed into the space between two tree roots. Yeshua weeping when no worms arrived.

Yeshua sick with fever. The purple murmur he made in the back of his throat. Josef and I, carrying Yeshua between us to the mikveh. Entering the coolness together. Cupping water up and over his forehead, cradling his head against my neck, Josef holding Yeshua's feet like oars. Thinking, *We will bring you alive into tomorrow.*

Yeshua carving Greek letters into the courtyard table with Josef's chisel.

Yeshua with eyes squeezed shut, guessing the identity of my medicinal herbs by smell, by taste.

All of these Yeshuas were in the grown Yeshua before me, the Yeshua who kept glancing down at the figure at his right. Yeshua who stared like a lamb at the woman who silently repeated every phrase he uttered, who nodded encouragingly each time he placed his eyes upon her.

Mari. Who had promised not to come and had come anyway. Who knew. There Mari stood beside her son, pouring everything she was up and into him.

When I reached the point directly opposite her, she noticed me. Her mouth stopped moving, and then Yeshua noticed me, too. His mouth hung open, and I could see the red tip of his tongue touch his top lip, testing a tiny sore. Mari's face was not filled with rage or disdain; instead there was softness around her eyes, her mouth. She smiled, and I could tell she didn't want to hold this moment above me: she wanted to share it with me. All of her training, all of those hours in the courtyard, moving backward and forward through the stories of the prophets, through the litanies of armies vanquished and subdued, led to this moment. Proof that all of it was necessary, important.

Yeshua finally pulled his eyes away from the two of us and back toward the crowd of people. "Let me tell you a story," he said to them, "a story that belongs to all of us. A story of a people chased away from the land of their ancestors. A people who sang beauty out of suffering. A people who still live in darkness."

I watched his hands. Hands that had held cutting knife, hook, clamp, vise, poultice, enema, letting cup. His fingers dangled. The heels of his palms, ridged with veins, pressed into space in front of him. Useless space. These people leaned toward him and into the fire. I knew they would get sparks spit into their eyes, flecks of ash in their lashes for five sentences they wouldn't remember in the morning. Tomorrow they would go home with their ulcers and their diarrhea, their goiters and warts and unset bones. And they'd be no better for it.

Mari nodded and nodded, the corners of her lips pressing her cheeks so wide I thought she would split like a melon. She and I were holding our son between us again, as we had done three days after he was born, only this time we were letting Yeshua choose. And he did. In the middle of the next sentence, halfway through a metaphor about a landowner and a grape harvest, Yeshua cast his eyes down to Mari again, searching.

And Mari opened her mouth and, just as she had when he was a squalling infant, Mari gave him everything he needed.

I knew what Yeshua had chosen but still, after all this time, I had to ask him. I had to offer him the choice, at least. If he wanted to become some sort of prophet, he had to understand the life he was *not* taking up, that there were other choices besides Nazareth and swindling bewitched faces around a fire.

After most of his new followers had fallen asleep, after the fire was only embers and the vendors had pulled tarps down over their goods, my son walked back to the river, and I followed. He went to the place where the prophet had lain, a space now filled with amulets and almond blossoms and figs and bread. A small fire lit the face of a charlatan who balanced a stone bowl over the fire for sacrifices. "One prutah," he said to Yeshua, "but you have to buy your own pigeon, farther up the bank." Yeshua turned from him abruptly and walked another quarter mile down the river, away from the lingering noises of carousing and over-zealous prayer, before finally removing his sandals and wading up to his calves in the water.

"Who's there?" he asked without turning.

"Salome," I said.

I took off my sandals and joined him. I looked down at the darkness, felt the light skim of fish or river grass over the tops of my feet. Upriver someone howled.

"It was good what you did today. How you helped the prophet."

"That." He didn't look at me but instead waded farther out into the river, until he could rest his palms against the moving surface like a tabletop. I followed him. The water against my thighs was insistent, more powerful than I'd expected. I ground my left heel into the river bottom so my body would not be cajoled downstream by the current.

"Mari came," I continued, watching his face for a reaction. He gave none.

His long nose, bulge of bone at his brow, whorl of hair behind his ear. "Come to Alexandria," I said all in a rush. "Come and be a physician. There is training there. A library with thousands of scrolls. You could learn what you wanted. And I have a letter that will get us in—to the library, to a clinic. Work and another life. There would be enough money to send back to Mari, to Josef. They could live comfortably." Yeshua nodded slightly while I spoke as though he had heard these words, this argument, a million times before. But I pushed onward. "There would be all kinds of medicines and always enough. You could learn to roll pills, to amputate. I have heard they have ways of examining the inner workings of the skull without killing the patient."

He submerged his hands and then brought them a few inches above the water. We both watched droplets tick off his fingertips. Long moments passed. Then he did it again. I wanted to grab his hands and shake them as I had when he was a child and he played too long in the washing bowl. But I held still.

"They need me," he said finally.

"Who? These people? They need you more than those in Alexandria? There are plenty of sick people to go around." The water pushed my hips, insistent. The cold climbed my ribs until I felt it in my armpits, my shoulders. I tried a different tactic: "The city is beside the sea. The main boulevard is big enough for six carts to pass along, side by side."

"Sepphoris will be a new city soon."

"Sepphoris?" I said blankly.

"Abraham, Mari's—"

"—father," I supplied. He didn't like it when I completed his sentences, but I was impatient. I didn't want talk of Mari in the middle of this conversation.

"Died." He puffed out the last word.

"Yes," I said, unwilling to listen to him plod through the history. "There was a religious uprising. Many years ago. Abraham died while Mari and Josef were in Alexandria with me. I know. I remember when Mari received the news." I wanted to say, "I remember how she gripped the running board, how she forgot she held you in her arms. I remember how I had to grab your body before she let you tumble." But I did not.

"I have seen the stone they are using to rebuild Sepphoris."

"I have seen it, too."

"There are rounded gateways—entrances to squares and walkways and royal quarters—made of arches that fly into the heavens. The delicate swoop of a bird wing, Auntie, but made of stone." He made circles with his hands under the water.

"You want miracles of architecture? Come with me to Alexandria. Or we could even go to Rome. There are aqueducts, sculptures. Figures cut from marble that you would swear were filled with breath."

And that was when he turned to me, took my shoulders and adjusted me so that I faced him directly, so that the current pressed squarely against the front of my thighs. His voice took on the patient cadence I used when correcting his suturing techniques or explaining how to insert a clyster properly: "Listen to what I am saying. Two men were given stone to work with. One built a home, snug and secure. The stone was cut perfectly. No wind rattled into his bedclothes in the winter, no hot air drew sweat down his spine in summer. But the other man took his stone and made a flying arch, thin and useless for anything besides drawing the gaze up and into the sky. Which man honored Adonai more?"

I disliked his one-line sage speak and his stories, but I dislike this riddling even more. He was offering me a question with a single correct answer, a moral that was supposed to be a bell. Once rung, it would become a sound that defined your life. Not like Rufus's stories. "A man comes in bleeding from the mouth. What do you do first? Do you check for a laceration on his tongue or do you ask him where the pain began? Do you offer him wine to cleanse the blood or do you ask him to hang his head between his legs? You must make a decision quickly." But in Rufus's story there was no wrong or right: there were better and worse choices, but they led to different consequences. "While you are checking for a laceration on his tongue his eyes roll back in his skull. What do you do now?"

I knew the answer Yeshua desired, but I wanted to say instead: maybe the man who built the stone house could not conceive of arches. Maybe the man who built thin arches to Yahweh let his family freeze, surrounded by bricks of straw and dung.

"A physician is a worthy occupation," I said instead, the words thick in my throat. I hated that I needed to defend what we had done together all these years.

Then Yeshua moved his hands from my shoulders to under my armpits and he lifted me, so that my feet were no longer on the riverbed. I am ashamed to admit the sensation terrified me, John Mark. The water pressing against my legs, pushing, all that darkness and no purchase—it was chaos swirling around, and in that fear he said to me, "You are worthy," and he shook me slightly, for emphasis, as I had done to his small body when he came crawling to me to nurse so many years ago, except his shaking was gentle, except my head reared back not against the earth but against the soft swath of sky behind me. It is difficult to find the words, John Mark, for that sensation, that moment. I was lifted into the middle of swirling chaos, and I was held there in a grip that was gentle and firm. It was what I imagined death might be. I wanted my mother so badly in that moment. And Rufus.

And then I ruined it. Because you should know enough about me by now, John Mark, to know that I am not a woman who wants to be held in the middle of chaos. I am not a woman who trusts anyone's arms in the darkness but my own.

"Put me down," I said, "and then come with me."

He returned me to the ground and released his grip. "They are worthy, too," he said.

"Please come," I said again. And this time I let desperation edge my voice.

His tone shifted, and the next words contained the stiffness of law: "Go," he said, "and build your house of stone."

Those are the words my son used to dismiss me from his life. I took a wavering step toward him, into that current, but he stepped backward.

You asked if I gave up on him, John Mark. I did.

I made my way to the bank. By then the clouds had thinned so that when I looked back, one last time, Yeshua was standing in a long path of boiling moonlight.

"What do you do with the patient who refuses treatment?" I asked Rufus a few weeks into my training. "What do you do with the patient who believes he knows how to save himself?" And Rufus shrugged and blew his nose and said, "You let him die. Because there are a hundred other people who would do anything to be saved. Find them instead."

Then he finished unlacing his sandals and lay down on the cot in the medicine room, settling himself for a nap. I wiped down the mortar and pestle, the small table we used for mixing poultices. With eyes still closed he held up his index finger and said, "But then again, you never know. Sometimes the person does know best. Sometimes he lives. But," he said, resting his finger again, "it's not your job to decide."

Then he opened his eyes and raised himself up onto his elbow. "Unless, of course, the patient is Julia, Little Julia, Agrippina, Gaius, Lucius, Little Agrippa, Livia, or Augustus. Then you figure out how to make them believe the treatment they don't want is actually their idea. Or you slip the medicine into their wine. You do whatever is necessary to save them. Because if they die, you die. And probably you die unpleasantly."

He lay back down and closed his eyes. I began to carefully return the materials to the cabinet, one item at a time: scale, weights, marble palette, tub of beeswax. I was terrified of breaking something and losing the opportunity to learn.

"By unpleasantly, I mean," Rufus continued with eyes closed, "having your legs broken and being thrown in the Tiber. Or fifty lashes followed by a drowning in vinegar. Perhaps honey poured in your mouth and then the boars set upon you."

"I understand," I said.

"Maybe an elephant tusk used to disembowel you while you watch. Or, for the less creatively inclined, there's always the pit of vipers."

He was murmuring then, all of my possible deaths a lullaby. I closed the cabinet and pulled the blanket over his feet, since his toes always grew cold while he slept.

"Pulled behind a team of horses across the—" he whispered as I made my way out the door.

But all of that was long ago, when I lived in Rome. At the Jordan, as I walked away from Yeshua, I wiped the river silt off me as best I could and began the walk back to the sprawl of tents. I needed to decide what to do next. No, that is not true. I already knew what I was going to do next, but I needed to make a clean, logical path in my mind to that place. I couldn't have lived with a choice that felt hasty or lazy. The path I took to my decision went something like this:

Whatever certainty Yeshua had found in the last few days, he did not want to put it toward holding a scalpel steady, toward learning to press dislocated shoulders into place. He might, I thought, do these things in service of his stories, in service of all these people listening, in service of the stupid arches of stone he wanted to build below the heavens, going nowhere. So I could follow him. I could do exactly what I had done earlier in the day, assisting him so that his reputation as a healer expanded, multiplied. I would have done this, gladly, if he promised not to wash the healing in his blessings and prayers, in his stories about new kinds of kingdoms, delivered. A good physician fails the patient if he promises the presence of a god. To promise the presence of Yahweh to these people was a kind of harm I refused to watch.

And certainly, my reasoning went, this could not last for long. He'd botch a healing, lose their trust. His stutter would return in the middle of a fervent proclamation. He'd turn away the woman with the loudest mouth or get thrown out of a synagogue for reading without his tzitzit knotted. I remembered the hand upon my head all those years ago, the sharp yank of my hair when I bent over Nathan's feet at the cistern. The Jewish people had made so many rules, there was no way a prophet could abide by them for long. And should the people fan his flame into a blaze, the authorities in Sepphoris or in Jerusalem would snuff the chaos out.

And then, I was certain, he'd see. He'd know. Best to get all of Mari's teaching out of him before he came with me anyway. Let him see where that road went. Nowhere. Then he'd come. And by then I'd have a place for us to live, to work. When he finally made his way to Alexandria, I would know where to barter for the freshest sea urchin, where to buy a belt to hold his blotting rags. I'd fill a bedroll with the softest wool, scent a hanging cloth with shavings from cedars like the ones that lined the stream I took him to when he was five years old.

It was best, I concluded, to let this whirlpool of prayers and prophecies, stories and tender touch drain out of him. It was best to get Mari out of him. I thought of her wide-open lamb face staring up at him. I did not want to fight it anymore. Yeshua would come to Alexandria eventually, of his own accord. And I would be waiting.

As the choice became real, a strange fuzzing started up in my limbs, like puffs of cotton-thistle bobbing through the pneuma in my veins. For thirty-two years I had given my life to Yeshua. But somehow I'd raised a son who thought his story was the only one. "I was born in Greece," I wanted to say to him. "I was a slave in Rome. I was a hermit on a hill outside of Alexandria. We're all the savior god of our own story."

I left for Alexandria at dawn.

38 CE

John Mark's cheeks are wet. Even the Broom Boy presses the heels of his palms to his eyes.

Salome takes John Mark's shoulder in her hand. Her grip is surprisingly firm. "We're all the savior god of our own story. Find a ship, John Mark. Save yourself." Then Salome squeezes firmly, her thumb digging below his collarbone.

John Mark wants to protest, wants to be brave and courageous, wants to be the one who builds the arch with the delicate stone that swoops toward the mouth of Yahweh, whatever that would mean. But he thinks of the Dragged Man, back flesh torn to pieces, and the Tortured Man, urinating on himself with a burlap sack thrown over his head. He nods until Salome releases her hand.

They walk back down the stairs to the clinic together, the Broom Boy trailing behind with their plates and the amphora of wine. Neither Salome nor John Mark is sure how much time has passed. An hour? Two? The floor of the clinic is a strangely beautiful mosaic of bodies: Nadjem sleeps curled on her side, fingers wrapped around the forearm of Carabbas—to comfort or keep him in place, Salome cannot tell. The Fever Woman has nestled her head into Carabbas's underarm, and her feet touch, gently, the back of the Pregnant Woman, who still faces the wall. The boy drowses in the V of his father's legs, and the bladder-stone man lies like a lintel above the father's head.

Only the Dragged Man is still awake, apart from the others, making his strange mewling sound.

"Death is not the end," John Mark wants to whisper to the man. "The Messiah has come and washed away your sin." But when he lies down beside the man, he finds that those words will not come. Instead, what arrives is his father's favorite bedtime psalm:

"The trees of the Lord are watered abundantly, the cedars of Lebanon that he planted. In them the birds build their nests."

John Mark knows he should say his goodbyes, should slip through the darkened streets and fetch his satchel from Salome's study so that he can be at the harbor by dawn, but instead John Mark moves his face even closer to the Dragged Man's so that one breath moves between them, in and out, in and out, as his father did with John Mark when he was small.

"You have made the moon to mark the seasons; the sun knows its time for setting. You make darkness, and it is night, when all the animals of the forest come creeping out."

The man's eyes open, just enough that John Mark can see the dark brown of his irises, like a leviathan cresting the waters of the deep. John Mark puts his hand gently on the man's head.

"I will sing to the Lord as long as I live; I will sing praise to my God while I have being."

And then the high note comes from the man again, a mewl of pain inching toward song.

"John Mark," says Salome sharply once, and only once, to remind him.

But John Mark thumbs the curve of the man's cheek. A moment ago, all John Mark wanted was to escape from death, but now that he is here with this man, inside of death, John Mark finds it to be a holy place, known and without knowing.

"The trees of the Lord are watered abundantly," he whispers again.

Salome curls her body against the door and falls asleep.

DAY FIVE

38 CE

In the morning the Dragged Man is dead. John Mark fetches the elders from downstairs, and they all make a slow procession with the body to the rooftop. There is nowhere else to lay the Dragged Man, so they wrap him and nestle the shrouded body in the shadow of the dovecote. Secretly, the elders are glad to have a thing to do; it is refreshing to bicker over which herbs should be included in the wrap, who will read the burial prayer, who will do the wailing on behalf of the family. It is a relief to lower themselves into Philo's mikveh to cleanse themselves afterward. After the ritual bath they rub unguents into their skin, and each receives the ministrations of the barber. They begin their waiting again in the lower room, but this waiting is resigned. The mob will enter soon enough. It's only a matter of time.

Salome and Nadjem know this, too. And this is why, as soon as the day is bright enough, they ask the father to move his now-unconscious son to the examining couch, ask him to crouch over the child, keeping the boy's arms pressed to his sides, his feet from kicking upward. The blood around the boy's wound is thick and clotted and needs to be made to run freely so that any fragments of bone can be released. Salome places the end of a trephine over the wound so that the sharp teeth of the instrument will dig a perfect circle around it. She clamps the handle to the top and begins to turn it to and fro. The work takes precision and strength—too little force and the teeth will take too long to cut the bone, too much force and the trephine will cut the membrane below the bone and death will follow.

After a few minutes Salome pauses, and she and Nadjem inspect the skull with their probes; then Nadjem takes a turn with the handle. They go back and forth this way until Nadjem feels the tiny lift of the bone from the membrane. The cut is sharp, and though Nadjem's eyes are cloudy, Salome's are good enough to remove the one remaining chip of bone with her smallest forceps.

The boy opens his eyes at that moment, the soft red disk of his head open to the light. He does not fight his father's body. He simply says, "Papa, I was dreaming of stew, the kind with red lentils all the way from Jerusalem."

"What goodness Adonai gives," says the father.

It is 38 CE in Alexandria, and fathers still love their sons and boys still dream of hot food and physicians still smile with satisfaction when they have done good work. But it is also true that the Greeks are entering the Quarter, that there are more of them today, that four men use straps to carry a battering ram between them. The men swing the end against the first door they come to, once, twice, and the inside bar breaks and the door swings open. From the small altar inside the home they use a candle to light the hair of each member of the family on fire.

In the next home they press the face of the father into the bowl for foot washing until he has drowned.

There are too many homes, even in the shrunken version of the Quarter, for the mob to be able to enter every one, so they are haphazard about where they bring their terror. The only possible defense is silence, to make the self disappear so the self cannot be harmed. The people of the New Jewish Quarter cower and pray and wait.

38 CE

In Philo's house the elders sit, Judah and Elisha and Benjamin and Zeloph and Eleazar and Levi and Philo himself, washed and quiet, murmuring prayers together.

But above them the patients are feeling well enough to be terrified. From the street comes the sound of the hammering of the battering ram against the doors, the screams, the smell of burning hair.

"They are within me," says Carabbas, "and these walls are not sound." Most of the scratch marks have scabbed over, but his buttocks and thighs are still pink and inflamed with the burns. He taps lightly on the walls as he makes his rounds of the room. Meanwhile the Pregnant Woman has gone into labor; the pain grips her back, and she rocks on all fours in the corner. The Mangled-Arm Man has come out of his poppy stupor and into a field of pain, and he talks to distract himself while the boy begins to whine and push at his father's face because he feels better and does not want to wear the bandage. Only the Fever Woman is quiet. Forehead cool, she sits by the window hemming her headscarf. No one notices that she holds a needle but no thread.

Salome feels helpless, a sensation she despises and avoids. There is little else she can do for these patients; they are low on medicine and cannot risk a trip to the pharmacy. What procedures she is able to do, she has done. The Pregnant Woman is progressing slowly and Nadjem is already tending to her, warm compresses for her back and olive oil to widen the birthing space. The air in the room has grown thick with the scent of full excrement pots and clotted bandages and sweat and the milk-rot breath of the ill.

"I will get the bandages," she says to no one in particular, and then she climbs the stairs to the roof. The sun is a trinket in the lash of blue and bakes the timbers so they give off the scent of a dusty forest. Pulling the bandages from the washing line takes only minutes; they are stiff and tinted orange and brown, but they will have to do. One basket filled and then another. Salome makes herself walk to the roof edge.

There is less to see than she imagined. The real violence is still a few streets away; she cannot see the Greeks or their battering ram, only hear the thud and the splintering. A man runs down the street, trying each door, finding all of them locked. Thin dogs nose at the blackened ash of abandoned fires. A woman with a headscarf stands in one doorway, nosing her way into the crack, tapping her head against it softly. A cart, overturned, hides a small body curled inside what flimsy protection it permits. And everywhere, shards of broken pottery like flowers thrown before an emperor.

Why did she stay? It is clear to her today, in a way it was not yesterday, that her ministrations to these patients are likely worthless; the Greek mob will feast on Philo's rich house, on the bodies of the elders. This place will not be passed over. She thinks of Mari telling Yeshua the story of Moses, freedom as easy as the smear of blood across a doorpost. "What will you pack in your sack? What will you bring with you?"

"And so you left Yeshua," says a voice, and for a moment Salome is certain that it is the Jewish god come to have a conversation, so perfectly has he slipped into the braid of her thoughts.

But then she turns and sees that it is John Mark, sitting in the one piece of shade by the dovecote, his legs parallel to the shrouded legs of the Dragged Man.

"What?" says Salome.

"You left Yeshua," prompts John Mark.

"I thought it was unclean to sit so near a dead man," says Salome.

"I haven't touched him. The only shade is here. Come." John Mark moves over slightly so that there is a shadowed space into which Salome can wedge her aching hip and stained tunic and sweating brow.

The smell in the corner of the roof is terrible—bird shit and the new rot of this body and no breeze to lift it away. "You didn't leave last night," she states, and John Mark nods.

"Soon we will have our own burial shrouds, you know."

"I want the story of the Messiah," says John Mark. "I want all of it, and look, there is time. This is a simple thing you can give me. You left Yeshua," he prompts again.

"I have said so," sighs Salome. If she raises her chin and closes her eyes the air smells slightly cleaner. And there is comfort in the murmuring of the doves.

"And then what?"

"I went to Alexandria and waited for him to join me. And while I waited, I found a clinic. I immersed myself in the library. That was no easy task. Women weren't allowed—"

"But eventually you went back, to Jerusalem. You were there at his death."

"Yes," she says simply.

"Why did you return?" John Mark pulls his knees up and holds them to his chest, rests his chin on top of them.

"I returned because of Josef."

John Mark turns and assesses Salome's face directly. "Because of your feelings for him? That bee-hum?"

Salome cannot keep the irritation out of her voice. "You are thinking with the stick between your legs. I returned because he asked me to, because he'd come all the way to Alexandria, because he'd lost one of his front teeth and his nose was crooked."

"He'd been beaten."

Salome stands and pulls the basket of bandages into the shade. "If you're going to sit there, the least you could do is help me roll these." She puts a handful of the stiff linen strips into John Mark's lap and shows him how to wrap the linen around two outstretched fingers. After they have filled the bottom of the basket she says, "Josef had been beaten, yes. His whole face was shadowed with green and yellow bruises. His beard was worn away in patches from where he'd worried it with his fingers. I could not say no when he told me what had happened."

"Who had hurt Josef? Why did he come to you?"

Salome closes her eyes momentarily. The words fall like pebbles and ripple for a while, and then stillness returns and she can't remember what John Mark has asked. But she sees Josef clearly. "Josef told me the parts about Yeshua you already know: the cures, the teaching, the crowds. The tossing out of demons and the hour-long prayers over nets that somehow swelled with fish the following day. Josef told me how Yeshua would divide a few loaves of bread into a million crumbs and convince each peasant that Yahweh would do the work of expanding the speck to a meal inside their bellies. How hundreds of people walked around a hillside, each boasting a swollen gut." Salome's eyes are still closed, but she moves her hands to show the gestures: the prayer, the swelling, the breaking of bread, until the bandage she holds has completely unrolled.

"And some blamed Josef for Yeshua's actions?"

Salome opens her eyes and rerolls the bandage. Her motions are perfect, precise, the fabric catching around her fingers so that the roll stays fastened but loose enough she can slide it off her fingers. "Yes, Yeshua's actions were a toe in the ribs of so many: the Pharisees, the Sadducees, the Roman prefect. The people were divided; some followed him doggedly, of course, but others claimed he was false. The Nazarenes despised him."

"Why would the Nazarenes despise him?"

Salome waves his question away. "Tighter," she says, pointing toward the basket where John Mark's bandages slouch and unravel. "Remember, while Mari and Yeshua were traveling the countryside, Josef was back in Nazareth. He kept to himself, kept his head down, tended their plot, worked the occasional job in Sepphoris, fed the animals. But then arrived a season of flooding rains and then intense heat. Insects rose up in clouds and devoured the crops; what shoots remained shriveled in the sun."

"And the Nazarenes wanted a scapegoat?"

"Yes. Josef came home one day from Sepphoris and found Eden—the goat, you remember?—slaughtered. Her blood had been smeared across the lintel of their home and also—he followed a smear of blood to the back—also across the figures on his wall."

"The carvings?"

Salome nods.

"It would wash away, though, the blood. If they hadn't done anything to mar the stone."

Salome offers that short bark of laughter. "You are thinking like me, John Mark. It had not been marred, but it had been desecrated. Remember, Josef had shown no one his carvings, besides me—and Ezra, all those years ago. He was certain no one knew, though that was a foolish assumption. All of it was intensely private to him, but it was against the law. He'd created graven images."

"You shall not make for yourself a graven image, or any likeness of anything that is in heaven above, or that is in the earth beneath, or that is in the water under the earth," John Mark recites, thinking of how proud his father would be of his memory.

"Yes. And they beat him, too. But he would not tell me that part. Who or with what. Only that he understood the blood as a sign to him, to Mari and Yeshua, to pass by, pass on. To leave. And so he did."

"And instead of going to Mari and Yeshua, Josef came to you instead."

"Yes."

"Why?"

"Because he thought I could fix it."

"Fix it?"

"Josef knew if the Nazarenes, people they had known all their lives, were capable of this cruelty to him and to Mari—well, in that moment, Josef said, when he studied the blood on the wall, coating the faces of the people he loved—he knew the end of the story."

"I thought you didn't believe in premonitions."

"I don't. But I saw Josef's face, John Mark, and Yeshua's death was there—I could see it. I knew. I knew my son would die. But Josef and I also knew that there might be a way to prevent it."

"How?"

"I have not told you everything."

"Please tell me."

"I will have to begin at the other beginning."

"Which beginning is that?"

"We make a mistake when we believe the thread of one story can be teased out and understood without seeing the rug from which it was torn. Physicians make this error all the time."

Then a spilling of sound interrupts them, as if a dam has burst. John Mark and Salome rise to their feet in time to see at least a dozen Jewish men running down the street in front of Philo's house, pushing at one another's backs, holding hands and pulling like schoolchildren. And then four Greeks on horseback, with clubs and torches and swords. John Mark turns his back, but Salome makes herself watch until the Greeks have turned their horses down another street, until the bodies of the Jewish men have stopped moving. Then, from just a few houses farther down comes the thud of the battering ram and the splintering.

"We should return," says Salome, and they each take a basket of bandages.

In the upstairs room, the restlessness has turned to panic. The patients know what is coming but cannot watch it come; they only hear the sounds of it growing closer.

Carabbas shrieks suddenly "Be gone!" and pounds the wall sharply. The Pregnant Woman jolts away from the sound, and the boy cries out. The Mangled-Arm Man paces in front of the window, and the boy's father tries to sing his child a song too loudly and out of tune. And because the room is already filled with sound, the Bladder-Stone Man lets himself moan freely. There is no shame in his pain if others cannot decipher it.

Nadjem stands beside their depleted medicine supply, her arms hanging limply at her sides. It is only then that fear rises up in Salome's throat; she has never seen her friend be still, never seen her stop her movements. Both women know how to minister to fear, but only in small doses: the scent of mint or a series of questions to distract a patient from her pain, steady words and steady hands, clear diagnosis and clear treatment. None of this is sufficient for the anxiety galloping through the room.

Nadjem covers her face, and Salome realizes she never urged her friend to leave; she has been so overwhelmed with Yeshua and Asha, with John Mark and the treatment of the patients, that she has forgotten to dismiss her friend, to urge Nadjem to return to the Egyptian Quarter, to the niece she loves like a daughter. The patients will die and John Mark will die and Nadjem will die. Salome herself will die, and Asha will be left with the memory of Salome's dumb tokens of affection, generic and unformed and insubstantial. What has she done? Shame wheels through Salome; pain from her hip rises to her back, her ribs. Her knees buckle and she sinks to the floor.

John Mark catches her hand in time to ease her fall. "Tell them," says John Mark.

"Tell them what?"

"Begin at the other beginning."

"This is not a story to tell by the fire," she says roughly. She has to say the sentence twice before John Mark can hear it over the banging of Carabbas on the walls, over the crying of the boy and the wailing of the Bladder-Stone Man and the broken song of the father. "Do you see where we are?"

"I see where we are," says John Mark steadily. "Tell them."

And so Salome begins with the story of her home in Greece, her mother's cough, the seed pearl.

The room quiets a little. Nadjem takes her hands from her face, and Salome's voice becomes stronger. She tells them about her mother's death and the dwindling flock, about her father's gambling and the laborer who attacked her by the creek.

The boy stops pulling at his father's beard and the Pregnant Woman looks over her shoulder; the Mangled-Arm Man stops his pacing to sit at her feet, and the Bladder-Stone Man quiets his moaning, curls into the fetal position, and raises his chin slightly so he can see Salome's face. Nadjem lies down on the examining couch and closes her eyes, and Carabbas stops pounding the walls and taps gently at his belly instead.

The Fever Woman continues to push her threadless needle through the fabric. But she, too, is listening.

Salome tells them about pulling the rough, stained wool around her, about her home erupting in flames, about how the laborers first regarded her with awe and then as a body to sell in the marketplace. She tells them about the slave traders, the ship, the endless rocking. She tells them how she survived.

9 BCE

Inside the slave ship I was numb. I didn't try to see into the darkness; the grief of other faces would have made my own unbearable. Instead I tried to sort the sound of human groans from the aching sound the ship made. A day passed, maybe two, and the strong scent of char upon my skin gave way to other scents, piss and shit and menstrual blood, the fear of every slave who'd ridden the ship before ground deep into the fibers of the hull. And flaked below those scents, the dry-sunned whiff of wheat from days when bodies weren't the only cargo. I slept. And slept again. Someone placed bread into my hands; I tried to eat, but the barley wasn't ground up fine enough, so chewing felt like whip cracks on my teeth. The watered wine was passed in a bowl so big that, had the light been stronger, I could have seen my own face while I drank. Instead I saw that the surface wasn't flat but flecked with insects and hairs and the spittled mucus of everyone who'd sipped before me. Still, I drank.

We were herded into light that raked our eyes, then down a plank and into carts, each no bigger than a market stall, with crosshatched sides and roof. My cart held twenty-two of us—until two died, at which point the driver left their bodies in the ditch so that, he said, their limbs wouldn't hinder other carts. We took turns sitting, standing, sleeping, shitting, pissing. One girl vomited stomach bile while pressed into the center of our mass, and each of us quite close to her received a clinging baptism our saliva wouldn't wash. And then we had no saliva left—the sun robbed us of that, though we wove our wraps through the wooden slats to block the glare.

The second day, we sized up one another more profoundly. The other girls had come from Macedonia, proof of Rome's success, the gorgeous spoils of war: one with eyes that leaked pus like a springtime maple, one with a hand hanging strangely from her wrist, one with good-sized breasts who sucked her thumb continually, one with liquid burn marks down the insides of her thighs. One girl, not more than eight and lacking the bottom half of her two front teeth, sang a song, over and over again, until she arrived at the chorus, and then it curdled somehow and she began the melody again. The smallest two were six-year-old twins who decided I was their mother. I didn't mind; I knew their bodies needed me. They curled and recurled in my lap, tied and retied my stola's belt, counted and re-counted the spots upon my face. They were identical except for the way one's breath held the lazy sweet of rotting fruit and the way the other had a few soft, dark hairs that grew along her jawbone. I also knew I couldn't get attached, let my story tangle up in theirs. I didn't ask their names.

The older slave trader was rough but practical; we were income, after all. It did no good to him to have us further bruised or bloody. Beauty sells, and that will never change. The younger one, his son, still lived below his father's roof and could afford for us to break. When they stopped to eat or water the horses, the young one made a habit of stretching his arms between the bars to grab what flesh he could. And then, when we figured out a way to move as one large body, a school of fish that knew the sea monster was near, he took to aiming his piss at us instead. Most times he couldn't get his stream quite high enough, but if half a day had passed since last we stopped, he managed to wet us down and laughed.

Each night we stayed beside a *mansio*, a way station with an inn, a bar, some stables, and often a separate shed for fixing broken saddles, wheel hubs, and brake chains. The male slaves ate beside their masters, no ropes or manacles in sight, but I could tell these men were bound by the way they kept their gazes down, by the way they kept their mouths sealed shut when the other men slapped thighs and roared. When the masters pushed inside the mansio for stronger wine, their slaves bedded down below the stars, not far from where the horses stamped their hooves and snorted smoke into the air. But they never ran, never slipped off into a copse of beech or scrambled up a shale-scaled hill. It wouldn't have been difficult to leave; many days, we traveled by a river they could have waded through to mask their trail. In my exhaustion, in the atrophy of my once-strong limbs, in the midst of my despair, I always kept a store of strength. I knew if given half a chance I would run until I died. But these slaves stayed. They didn't even walk the edges of the light. They slept where a misplaced hoof could crush them. They stayed.

Day rocked into day. Sometimes the landscape was scorched and dry, the taste of wheat blistering blond across the backs of our throats, olive trees reaching crone hands towards the sky. Sometimes bridges arched into the winding streets of unfamiliar towns where little boys scraped sticks across the bars of our cart and feral dogs came out to nip at the wheels. Fertile farms gave way to craggy stones acned with lichen, green hills rolled down to a sea where white sails flecked the blue. Sometimes there came the scent of mint and thyme and other times the acrid stench of a field burning to stubble, and once, the smell of sulfur from a thick black pond. We passed carts with high wooden sides, the flash of fabric inside them; along the edges of the road travelers ambled: farmers and peasants, soldiers and women clutching the hands of ragged children.

Always the clatter of the wheels over perfectly orchestrated stones, cut to the perfect embrace; it gave me strange comfort that we were on our way to a place where someone cared deeply about how a thing was made. If only someone had cared as deeply about the construction of the cart; the left rear wheel, slightly larger than the others, jolted my body continually. Boys who stood at the edge of the road with amphoras of water called out the names of their towns. The words had the same rocking sea-sickness inside them: Brundisium, Venusia, Beneventum, Casilinum.

It was on the tenth day or the twelfth that I started doing hair. I'd been picking nits from the scalp of the one with broken teeth when I noticed that the touch kept her hum from turning sour. So I kept at it, combing my fingers through the brown tangle, so much more slippery than wool. First a braid, then a low ponytail. Then I parted the ponytail above the tie and somersaulted the end through the open section. As the day went on, I tried twisting the hair into rolls behind her ears and then mussing it at the crown so the front pieces could be pulled over the mussed section in a wave.

It didn't take long for the other girls to take interest. One stopped sucking her thumb long enough to pull threads from the hems of the cloaks to make better ties; in one marketplace, the one with the broken wrist talked softly with a skinny girl until she scampered off and returned with pins wrapped in fragrant petals of hibiscus. I remember how the color had gotten on her palm a bit, just a gentle smudge of pink right where you'd rest the spindle rod. I used the pins to sculpt the Broken Wrist Girl's hair into two floating rivers of black that hung just below her earlobes. The other pins I worked into the thin hair of the twins, matching poufs that made the most of little.

But then the younger slaver saw the pins and convinced his father they'd be worth something. The father looked on, feedbag held up below a horse's muzzle, while his son pulled the Broken Wrist Girl from the cart and then ripped the pins from where they lodged against her scalp.

"This one bites," the slaver said; a slap, and then his croaking laugh.

His father's voice: "Hurry it along."

The younger slaver held up the pins triumphantly, tufts of brown hair still clinging, then turned back to the cart. "Who else, then?" he said. While he'd been busy, I'd removed the pins from the terrified twins as quickly as I could. Now I held my hands between my knees, settled my gaze on a lone pink cloud that had captured all of the sun's setting rays on the horizon.

"The spotted face is hiding some," the father said. And then, to me, "Give them to me now and we'll be done." I should have given them. Now I want to tell that girl I was, "Save your stubborn rage for when it matters most," but then I didn't know. I kept my fist closed.

And so the younger slaver dragged me from the cart and squeezed my breast as though pressure there would open up my hand. When that didn't work he tried my fingers—but the muscles there were strong from carding wool and weaving. Then he grabbed my neck, but there his father intervened. "Stop. She'll bruise and fetch an even lower price. Like this," he said, and he came to me, his face impatient. "When you say stop, I will," he said, "and then you'll open up your hand." Then he wrapped two large paws around my knotted fist and squeezed. His finger hair was red; dry skin floured all his knuckles. The pins broke through my skin. The pain was not my mother's body at the bottom of the ocean, it was the worker's mallets making sense of stone it was the moon's bright fury at the water it was the eyetooth of Apollo it was—"Say stop now," the slaver said—and I did not and then the world was gone.

I woke to tenderness. It was dusk and we were stopped beside a mansio. My injured hand, thrust through the cart bars, was being dabbed at by a woman with kohled eyes and rouged cheeks. A swollen lip showed a sliver of her teeth, and one eye hung slightly lower than the other. Her shoulders gleamed as white as sheep's milk, with no freckles or scars to blemish them. Her stola possessed threads of silver to catch the light, but as I rose onto my knees I could see that the bottom hem was frayed and dusty. I stared with interest at my palm: two puncture sites from where the pin points had made their way into the fleshy pad below my thumb and the divot between ring finger and pinky. There was some pain but also a different sensation I hadn't felt before—it was both warmth and chill at once, and it radiated out from the two bloody holes down my other fingers and across my wrist.

The woman dipped her rag into a bowl and applied the salve again. Beside her on the ground lay an opened case filled with vials and ceramic pots. She slid a wooden tray aside to reveal a neat row of rolled bandages and a number of metal instruments. From a smaller section of the lower tray she pulled a needle, thread, and tiny scissors. Because my hand was numbed by whatever concoction she'd applied, I could watch without distraction as she pushed the needle through my skin and sewed two neat stitches to bind up each small wound. When she was done, she mixed some other herb with olive oil and soaked one end of a long bandage into this new salve before winding it three times around my palm.

"Keep it as clean as you can," she said. "Wash the bandage if they let you wash and lay it out to dry. Then wrap again. The thread will come out on its own."

"What was that salve?"

"Clove and henbane."

"Who are you?"

She touched her swollen lip tenderly with her pinky. Then she turned to the case, putting the needle and thread neatly back into their sections, sliding the tray back into place. "My father was a physician. I took his case." She shrugged. "That's all."

I pulled my hand back through the bars and pressed the bandage slightly. The pain was there, but she'd softened all the edges.

A broader woman near the entrance of the mansio made a clucking sound and the kohl-eyed woman's eyes pricked to attention. She closed the case and stood. "I have to go," she said. The way we plug in what is obvious to fill the spaces of goodbyes.

"Thank you," I said. And she was gone.

The next night we spent at a mansio beside a stream near the outskirts of Rome; the trader and his son herded us, a few at a time, into the water to bathe. When I saw the way the son watched, squatting on his haunches and splitting grass between his teeth, I refused to remove my tunic, but I did unwrap the bandage, wash it carefully, and lay it out to dry. We were each given a full bowl of lentils, as well as cheap olive oil to rub into our skin. I rubbed mine into my belly and thighs, where no buyer would notice the softness or shimmer. After the traders went to bed I did the hair of all the girls, though my right hand still ached and wouldn't open fully. My own hair I pulled into a braid, and then I stretched out on my back to sleep. The other girls slept sitting up, as though their futures depended on keeping each and every hair in place.

The road flattened and straightened as it approached Rome. We passed more and more grave markers etched with figures that I assumed must have been names or the last gasps of hope or humor or prayer. Rome was nothing like Elis; the towns near my home in Greece had buildings, but the buildings were fathomable, the height of four or five men stacked on top of one another. In Rome the buildings rose until the sky was only a narrow lane of blue. Even the heavens were proscribed.

We passed through an arch dripping with water, beggars contorted at the foot. Once we were inside the gates the whole city seemed made of arches: doorways rounded into the dark interiors of shops, elongated arches reached up to hold bridges and (I would later learn) aqueducts. And the streets were not simply filled with people transporting themselves and their belongings from one place to another. Storefronts and stalls shouldered their way forward, men calling out the wares in case passersby couldn't see them for themselves. When the cart paused to let a small caravan of three veiled litters pass, I watched a woman with rings on every finger bend and whisper into the ear of a man sitting at a rickety table. He nodded as she spoke and pressed his stylus into the wax tablet in front of him.

When the cart began to move again, a child leaped out of nowhere and grabbed two of the bars of the cage, wedging his bare feet into two of the square holes. His face was inches from mine, so close I could see the flea bites along his hairline, smell the garlic on his breath. He opened his mouth and wagged his tongue at me just as the trader noticed and flicked his whip in the boy's general direction. The boy released himself just as quickly, sending a glob of slimy mucus through the narrow gap between his two front teeth.

A little farther on, steam rose from a few buildings partially obscured by a wall. Etched over one doorway, a snake curled around a staff, just like at the physician's house in Elis. Outside the doorway, a line of five or six people, a few with obvious gashes, one pale-skinned man holding his belly, and a woman asleep on the ground holding an infant in her lap. Farther on we passed a man brushing flour off a bread paddle, a crippled woman who walked on her fists, a man with skin the color of soot behind a table piled with silk and peacock feathers. When there was a break in the press of bodies, I could see that the walls were covered with graffiti, scratched letters and images edging their way into every visual space that remained.

Rolling through the streets reminded me of my mother's breath: first a narrow press between rickety buildings, small altars with offerings, the choke of hissing meat—then the sudden gulp of a wide-open square of space, bounded by columned buildings and presided over by a statue, half naked, chest lifted. The slave market was in one of these wider spaces, near a pond hazed with gnats and flies. A few stalls sold tools and pottery, but the main focus was a crumbling wall at the south end. On it, a slave girl like us stood or tried to stand. Every ounce of her body—her shoulders and her elbows, her chest and hips and buttocks—sagged as if she'd had iron stitched into her tunic. But her chin, her chin, she had it cocked up toward the sky. Her hands were tethered; the sunlight fought and died trying to break through the halo of her tangled hair. I turned to our lot, sitting quietly, hair bound, and I was strangely proud.

A man who could have sold eight rolls of his own flesh and still had enough to live on stood on the wall beside the girl and barked out words and numbers in a tongue I didn't understand. Other men who stood before the wall punctuated his river of noise with occasional shouts and sometimes a hand, raised high and snapping. The girl and her marvelous chin were finally given to the hand that had snapped for longest. I strained but couldn't see the man who'd bought her fate.

As soon as she'd been sold, another took her place. And then another. Some girls on the wall made attempts to smile. Others wept. One spit at the crowd and received a cuff so hard from the fat-rolled man that she had to be sold unconscious. When one emaciated girl pissed out her fear, the heat of the wall sent the liquid steaming.

Our cart inched forward. The slave drivers brought us stale water and a rag to wipe ourselves, even a bottle of cheap perfume we were supposed to pour between our breasts and legs to season our own flesh. The Broken Teeth Girl sang again that curdled urgent song; one girl rattled at the cart latch; one simply stuck her hand out through the bars, fingers outstretched. I don't know what she hoped for: a sweet, a knife, some touch of comfort, or maybe a magic that could turn her into a dove and send her home to wrap her feet around the soft arm of her mother.

On and on. The booming voice, the snapping men. I tried to guess which one would snap at me: the one with hair gone white with plaster dust or the one with three trussed chickens hanging from a pole. The one who wiped his forehead with the inside of his wrist or the one who had white, toughened scar skin covering the right side of his face. And then, parting all of them, came the darkest man I'd ever seen. The tallest, too. He walked like he was out of practice; there was a sway and flex inside his limbs, like sea kelp drifting to the ocean's pull. But he was trying to be pillar-stiff like all the rest, and so he looked half regal, half enchanted. Around his neck a collar hung, but he supported his walk with a cane, dark wood dotted with the golden press of circles carved with some insignia I couldn't see, and his tunic was unwrinkled, made of clean, good linen.

Beginning at the end of the line, the Tall Man browsed the girls waiting for their turns upon the wall. He arrived at our cart last. I know there was tenderness or sympathy at least when he first peered inside, but when he met my eyes, his expression turned. Retreated. Went inside himself, I mean. What was left was bare room. Swept floors. He made his way to the elder slaver and offered him a purse, and then a simple map he drew with the tip of his cane into the muddy ground. The slaver shrugged and nodded and then we were off again, out of the market and through the winding streets. This time we followed a track along the green river, past two bridges and an island with a listing structure in the center. And then there was the Tall Man once again, still as a signpost on the right side of the road, his cane outstretched to point the way toward a small dirt track that wove up the hill on the south side of the river. It seemed impossible he could have made it there before us without a horse—perhaps, I thought, he was a priest or in possession of immortal blood.

At the top of the hill the track opened to a villa shaded by pines that draped their branches out instead of down. The slavers parked us in the shade and then herded us out, made us urinate and walk around the courtyard so that our legs would hold our weight again. We lined up in a row, and then we waited in the center of the outer courtyard, each girl given her own square of marble to stand upon. We waited and I counted the pillars (six) that stood between us and the covered breezeway. We waited and I tried, with the corner of my sandal, to scrape the dead leaves and insects from the crease between the stones. Helios creaked his wheels above us, and we waited. The elder slaver fell asleep on the driving bed; the younger stretched out below a yew, his cloak curled to make a pillow. Some of the girls sat. Others retreated to the shaded edges of the courtyard. The cicadas thrummed from the trees until their song became a bruise that made our hearing tender. One household slave emerged and pulled a few potted plants into the shade. A black-and-white cat stepped tenderly into the sun and made its way from girl to girl, licking at our feet, our palms. The Tall Man did not appear. Nor did the owner of the villa.

After an hour or two, another slave appeared with a broom and a girl of about four who followed with a smaller broom. The girl still had the rounded cheeks of babyhood and wispy blond curls cropped so that they floated like a halo. The two began to sweep the courtyard, the slave methodical and the girl completely haphazard, pushing the straw of the broom harshly against the ground and then riding the handle of the broom up and down the length of our line.

Soon the girl gave up the broom altogether and moved closer to examine us; I could tell by the authoritative way she ran her fingers over the woven tie of one girl's belt and squatted to examine the sores on another's feet that she'd seen adults gauge the quality of human bodies before. Still, whomever we were waiting for, to buy us or dismiss us, did not appear. The expressions we'd so carefully prepared when we lined up began to sag again.

The child finally chose to settle herself in front of the singing girl, likely because she offered a large, open smile.

"Maia," said the Singing Girl, touching the front of her stola. The child did not offer her name in return but instead reached out her finger and touched the Singing Girl's broken teeth. "Odous" said Maia softly.

"Odous," repeated the girl. Then she bared her own teeth and touched one. "Dens," she said.

"Dens," repeated Maia.

They repeated the process for eyes and nose and mouth. Then suddenly the girl reached forward with surprising quickness and pinched one of Maia's cheeks. "Gena!" she shrieked and then laughed high and cold.

Maia grabbed the pinching hand with equal quickness and folded it between her two hands. She smiled as she shook her head back and forth. The girl tried to pull her hand from Maia's grip, but Maia held it firmly, her smile unforced but firm. Tears began to roll down the girl's cheeks, and she let her arm go limp. Then she looked into Maia's open face and kissed her on the place where her skin had reddened from the pinch. Maia kissed the girl's hand before she let it go.

I was so busy watching this exchange that I didn't notice a woman standing in the shadows just beyond one of the six arches. But after the smack of Maia's kiss I heard a clucking sound, and the girl whipped her head around and ran to bury her head in the woman's long blue stola. The woman stepped into the sun for only a moment before cupping her hand over her eyes and gesturing all of us out of the setting sun and into the shelter of the portico.

The trader followed, speaking a version of Latin that sounded like clattering dice. The woman responded to him while winding her way through the line of bodies, and her Latin sounded like the road stones, known edges effortlessly fitting together. She didn't touch us except to lay an index finger to the side of a chin or cheek to turn a head to the right, the left. When she arrived in front of me, she stood for a long time. I could see her counting each of the spots on my face and noting the bandage around my hand. She finally settled on my eyes, and I took the chance to examine her as well. Her face reminded me of the inside of a shell, not just the smoothness of the skin but the way it seemed to hold and reflect light simultaneously. Her hair was pulled loosely to the nape of her neck; when she'd stepped into the sunlight, I'd noticed threads of auburn and gold, but in the shadows the color flattened into brown. Her hazel eyes sat atop gray-purple pouches of skin; I wondered how long it had been since she'd slept. She asked the trader some question while still staring. He shrugged, then remembered his manners, returned some stilted politeness.

When she'd examined everyone she returned to Maia and spoke in Greek: "I would like you to care for the children. You were right with her." She handled the words like a mother with a new baby, tenderness and awkward strangeness both at once.

Then the woman turned to the trader. "The hair is good," she said in Greek. "I need a person who makes hair."

The thumb-sucking girl smiled a tiny smile. I had spent the most time on her hair; it was the thickest and longest of the bunch, and I'd woven twenty small braids into what looked very much like a basket around her skull. The woman moved back to her and, using only her index finger, traced one of the braids from where it began on the right side of the ear over the curve of the skull.

Then she walked back down the line to me and turned to the trader to ask him something in Latin, the words clicking back together perfectly; he gave her a muddy response. She turned back to me and switched to

Greek: "Your hair is the only hair not beautiful. I think you did this." She pointed to the others. "You made these hairs."

I nodded.

"You also, then."

I followed her into the villa without looking back. I couldn't stand to say goodbye to the others, even with my eyes.

The only way to freedom, I decided that first week, was to learn everything I could. Not just Latin or how to heat the curling tongs but how to win the favor of those whom you despised. Where to plant the rosemary and how the sewage system worked. The only hope I had was my own curiosity. Here is what I learned:

I.

I worked for Julia. She was the daughter of Augustus, the man who'd chosen the word "emperor" to wear around his throat. Even I knew that. He'd let go of Octavian, a former self. Though I begrudged the Romans for the way they crushed us from afar, I understood his choice to change how he was known. When I changed my own name, four years later, from Lyra into Salome, I tried to wear the change like a choice instead of a necessity. Augustus lived with Julia's stepmother, Livia, on Palatine Hill, a "long enough" carriage ride away, according to Julia. Longer, she said, if we stopped for persimmons.

Julia had five children with a former husband, named Marcus Vipsanius Agrippa, who'd left her for a spear that pierced the left side of his throat. Three children lived inside the villa: Agrippina, the wispy blond four-year-old; Agrippa Postumus, a screeching two-year-old boy, and Little Julia, who at age nine had a dark demeanor and was trying to shrug off all vestiges of the word "little." These were the ones Maia cared for, for the most part happily. The two elder boys, Gaius and Lucius, stayed with their grandfather on the hill, learning whatever knowledge makes men think they might be competent to rule. Julia was now conveniently married to Tiberius, Livia's stepson, who, when I arrived, was off asserting Roman huff and polish into a backward countryside to make way for those stones, the ones we'd rolled across, that paved the whole world in one direction: Rome.

II.

A villa is a cold and garish place. I loved the atrium, which opened to the sky, and the dirt-floored courtyard just outside the kitchen, too, where you could hear the sound of horses being curried in the stables and the chatter of the slaves who tended to the grounds. But the villa's rooms were cold. Plaster and marble. Terra-cotta pots for a few unsuspecting plants that had to be smuggled into sunshine every morning. The cots and couches all had iron legs; the lamps were clay or stone. Most of the time I saw Julia's face as hardened too, reflected in the polished metal mirror that hung above her cosmetic stand. And then to balance all the hardness, all the light and growth they kept out of the space, they painted every wall in purple, scarlet, gold. Flowers that repeated in perfect patterns, vines that wove the way that they desired. One wall even contained an entire picture of a different place, including a parrot in a cage, all the breath and roundness pressed flat into their plaster. I hated it. And despised the way the hardness of the surfaces redoubled every sound. Every fallen plate and footstep on the floor was magnified.

III.

Julia's body. Hair and cosmetics didn't interest me too much. It didn't take me long to familiarize myself with Julia's hair. It was slippery and thick. It took half the day to dry, and any style needed to be half placed when the hair was half dry; otherwise, it all slid out of pins and combs. On days when we didn't have the time, there were the wigs, a red one and a black one. The black one's hair was short and rarely needed styling. The red hair was the longest and required hours of work to shape it into a new coquettish style, but I could do that work while she slept or rode or wove or took her litter into the city limits to do whatever rich women did. Her skin was smooth enough that it required little work.

Mostly I needed to cover the purple spots below her eyes and darken her brows and lips. I bathed her, too. And so I also knew the scar on her right shoulder blade, the rough skin at her elbows that no amount of lanolin would smooth. I knew the thin white marks like spiderwebs on the insides of her thighs. The way her scent changed right before her bleeding started, how too much wine made her phlegmy in the morning and too little had her walking the halls with tingling feet in the middle of the night.

IV.
Then there were the people. Nona, who ran the kitchen, was warm and steady, the epicenter of the house. The Tall Man, called Juba after a former client king of Numidia (though no one actually knew where he was from), was cold, mysterious, and unyielding. Abel, the head gardener, was quiet and smart; Pulco, the stable lead, sly and lazy; Cassia, the laundress, beautiful and flighty; Luca, sweeper and refuse collector, shy and gentle. And Julia, my mistress, fierce and just.

The main way I'd known people up until that time, remember, was from the bodies I'd watched moving through the streets of Elis. Also, of course, the workers with their muscle and their striking and their harm, and more recently the slave girls whose scent had become my own these last two weeks. So I knew something about the way a muscle moves along the back like a pulley when a man lifts up a mallet or how a man with pockmarks on his face also often carried weakness in his legs. I knew the kind of ache that housed itself inside my womb before my bleeding started, how long it took a burn to peel after the touch of fire.

But why humans did what they did was mostly mystery to me. I understood hunger and fear and thirst and grief and desire for affection, of course. And I had my mother's stories of the gods, who almost always acted out single spasms, jealousy or rage or lust or pride. Like the prophets in the stories of the Jews, the Greek and Roman gods each carried a simple badge of who they were and didn't stray. I thought these people would work the same way.

To slap a few words beside a name as though this were enough to explain a person is daft, I know. But please, imagine. I was in a new country, trying to learn Latin. But also I was trying to learn the language of how people related to one another: when to bow and when to cast the eyes down at the floor; when to speak and when to wake; how to hold your hands as you waited for your mistress to undress. Whom I could eat beside and what pitch of voice to use to ask for something I wanted. So I had shortcuts for how I understood each person.

By the time six months had passed, I thought I had a good grip on the place. I was close to fluent in Latin and had endeared myself to Julia. I had collected information that would serve me well when I escaped, because escape I would. Of this I was certain.

Then Tiberius came home.

His eyes were set wide on his face and pushed deeply into his skull. His large nose cowed his small mouth into an expression of permanent disdain. He had no beard, just a smattering of small red welts from ingrown hairs along his jaw and chin. I went to the atrium to greet him, and when Julia didn't appear immediately, he told me to fetch him a chamber pot and then had me hold it while he relieved himself below the awning of griffins and lotus flowers. He didn't look at me or ask my name. He let his tunic fall too quickly afterward and then cursed when he saw the wet spot darkening the fabric.

"Tiberius." I'd only ever heard Julia's voice come out as a single note—witty or kind, commanding or apathetic—but the way she said his name was a din of competing desires: sadness and frustration and tenderness and hope.

When Julia came to meet him, he gripped her shoulders and kissed her right temple, so close to the roots of her hair that I wondered if he tasted the lanolin.

"How was your journey?" she asked.

"You made it yourself a month ago," he said. "I doubt the route has changed much."

"I meant whether you were comfortable."

"One rarely speaks of a horse as comfortable. Is my mother here yet?"

"Yes," said Julia, voice even as the paving stones, "she's hiding just over there."

Sarcasm was not a tone Tiberius embraced. He looked at her face, sharply, then briefly at her breasts, her belly, before turning away again.

"Aren't you going to ask about the children?"

"I need my feet washed, if that's what you mean."

Julia did not respond. She tilted her chin toward the ceiling and blinked a few times. Seeing the vulnerable spread of her throat made me want to kill the man on her behalf. A minute passed. Then two. "Fine," he said, waving a hand in the air dramatically, "bring forth your children."

Maia must have heard the words but not read the tone because she emerged from around the corner, Agrippa Postumus on her hip, Agrippina's hand clutched in hers. Little Julia appeared behind them, but she stood in the doorway and didn't enter the room.

From another doorway, Juba entered with a bowl of water and knelt at Tiberius's feet. Tiberius bent to untie his sandals. "They look well," he said, without raising his gaze to meet the children's faces.

Agrippina broke free from Maia's grasp and skipped over to Tiberius, her blond curls quivering around her head. She thrust a terra-cotta doll in front of him. "Mama brought me this," she said, happily.

He took it from her and pretended to examine it carefully, swinging the hinged arms and legs with his index finger. "Does she like to swim?" he asked, dangling her towards the bowl of water.

"No!" shrieked Agrippina, grabbing for the doll. For a second I wasn't sure whether he was going to let her have it again or let it break between them, but finally he released it. Agrippina went scampering back to Maia.

"You should be careful," said Tiberius, still speaking to Agrippina but staring at the bowl of water at his feet. "You mother has a tendency to bestow gifts that don't last."

Julia raised her chin again slightly, but this time she couldn't keep tears from sliding out the corners of her eyes, though I don't think Tiberius noticed. She opened her mouth to speak, but instead of her words there was the shuffling and muted voices of further arrival outside. Juba left his kneeling position and soon came back trailing an older woman.

"Livia," he said, bowing his head. Agrippa Postumus promptly burst into tears.

"Quite a welcome," said Livia, smiling thinly.

"Where are Gaius and Lucius?" asked Julia.

"Oh, I thought we might have a quiet *cena* without them. Tiberius has had a long journey. He needn't be bothered with fuss." She looked pointedly at Agrippa Postumus. Maia was making shushing sounds and bouncing him, but he continued to wail.

"Oh, that's too bad," said Julia, raising her voice so she could be heard over the sobbing. "Seeing my boys always reminds me of the bright future of the empire. I'm so glad my father has taken such a personal interest in them."

"Yes. Well. I'm afraid they've been quite bored as of late. Felix does their lessons because your father is home so rarely, you know. And when he is home. Well." She made a knowing smile, though I had no idea what sort of knowledge it contained.

Julia finally turned and nodded at Maia, who herded the children away. Juba and two of the outdoor slaves brought in washing bowls for Livia and Julia. Agrippa Postumus's screams echoed down the scarlet hallway.

"He has a strong pair of lungs on him at least, your Agrippa," said Livia.

"He does," said Julia. "Those are from his father. May the gods preserve his memory."

"May the gods preserve his memory," mumbled Livia and Tiberius, almost inaudibly.

"You look better," said Livia to Julia. "Recovered."

"I'm hungry, if that's what you mean." Julia made a vague gesture toward Juba and me. "We'll have the cena now." She stood, and without letting me dry her feet or replace her sandals she headed down the hall. "The triclinium is this way," she said with false gaiety over her shoulder.

"I remember where my dining room is located," said Tiberius loudly, but Julia was already too far away to hear him. Juba finished with Tiberius's feet, and I laced Livia's sandals. Then they followed the trail of Julia's damp footsteps across the black and white marble tiles of the floor.

In the kitchen, I poured the chamber pot into the toilet beside the oven and used a pail of dirty water to flush the remains of Tiberius's piss down to the bowels of Rome.

The kitchen itself was filled with slaves, but Nona was at the center of the fray, handing out platters of pickled fruits and vegetables, snails and clams, cabbage soaked in vinegar. Clean utensils, pitchers of wine. Nona didn't trust me to serve yet, so I was relegated to scraping the bones and bits and uneaten scraps into the waste bin. The kitchen filled with the scent of smoke and vinegar and overripe fruit, bruised and broken open into sticky trails. There was a second course of boar and chicken, cubes of meat slathered in sauce, and then finally smaller plates of fresh fruit and nuts and bread soaked in honey.

When the bin was full, I was glad to retreat into the fresh air to empty it. I threw a handful of nuts into a terra-cotta pen and watched the dormice climb on top of one another, claws scraping skulls, to get to their sustenance.

When I returned from dumping the bin, Nona looked at me with disdain. "They're almost finished. You'd better get to the bedroom. And change your own stola first," she added, nodding at the fish scales and drops of oil just below the twist of my belt.

When she arrived in the bedchamber, Julia had me take down her hair and brush it over and over again until it gleamed. I picked up the cloth to remove the cosmetics, and she shook her head. Sounds from the dining area filtered down the hall: Tiberius's low grumble pierced occasionally by Livia's reedy whine. Finally, the sounds became more distant, and Julia sighed and then stood. "Unpin me," she said, and I removed the clasps at the tops of her shoulders, lowering the fabric gently so that it wouldn't touch the floor.

"Perfume," she said, and I used a tiny brush to paint the oil onto the tops of her breasts, behind her earlobes, on the tips of her hipbones. She turned and looked at herself in the mirror, touching the soft purple shadows below her eyes and the dimpled sag of her belly. Her skin took in the gold glow of the lamps so that she became another source of light.

"You are beautiful." My Latin sounded like Nona stabbing the tines of a fork through a crisped chicken skin. Stupid little gasps.

"Yes," she said, as if it was a known but unimportant fact. Then she climbed under the coverlet, and I turned to go.

"No, Lyra," she said. "You stay."

I stood next to the one small window, my hands gripping the curtain behind my back. The next morning, I had to take the curtains down and wash and iron them because my sweaty, oily palms had wrinkled them so badly during the night.

Tiberius was a controlled drunk. He didn't stumble or yell, but I could tell he'd been drinking by the length of time he took between each movement or gesture. He undid his own belt, took off his own tunic, then tossed them in my direction. He pulled the coverlet entirely off the bed and stared at Julia for a moment; his concave chest and the fur of hair across his shoulder blades somehow made his body unworthy of touching hers. But he did.

He climbed on top of her and placed her hand on his cock until he was hard enough to enter her, to make her face pinch up with pain. He moved quickly and precisely, and when she tried to lower his chin so he would meet her eyes, he closed his lids instead. After he finished, he climbed off her, never having touched her face, her breasts, her shoulders—all of the beautiful soft glowing places.

"There," he said, "now you can't say—" But then he shook his head, leaving the rest of his thought in the ether.

Julia raised herself up onto her elbows. "Did your mother tell you to do that?" Her voice was calm and certain. "Because it certainly felt like your mother."

"Cunt," he said, and then he took his clothing from my arms and spat directly into my face. The phlegmy mass landed just below my right eye, and I wondered briefly if the poison inside him might have the power to erase my spots. He threw his cloak around his shoulders and left.

I used a rag to wipe my face and then brought another to Julia to use between her legs. When she handed it back to me, it was tinged pink. Then she motioned at the bed. "Lie here beside me."

I lay on my back next to her, but she turned me so that I faced away from her and then wrapped one arm around my waist, curving the rest of her body against my spine. We lay that way for a long time before she spoke.

"He died on the sixth day after his birth. Three days before the naming ceremony."

She wove her fingers through mine and rested her cheek against the nape of my neck. I didn't know if I was supposed to be a replacement for Tiberius or her dead baby, or both. It was nice to be touched, to feel the residue of affection, but it made me feel uneasy not to know what it meant.

"A name is a thread between the dead and the living," she said quietly. "But I have no thread. So each day, he floats further away from me, and there is no way to draw him back."

I could feel her shaking as she cried, but when I tried to turn to comfort her, she held me firmly where I was. She wouldn't let me see her face.

We didn't hear Tiberius go out into the night with a dozen slaves, didn't see him on his litter surrounded by an aura of torches. From the villa we couldn't hear the carousing in Rome, couldn't stay his hand from further drink.

But by the noon the next day we knew that he'd eventually stood vigil across the street from his old house. We learned, because the slaves had no allegiance to Tiberius, the way his face contorted when his former wife, Vipsania, emerged, the way he asked two of the slaves to hold him back so that he wouldn't go to her.

Julia heard the story without betraying a trace of emotion. When the slave was done telling it, she simply said, "Go to my father. Tell him we'll dine with him this afternoon."

38 CE

When Salome stops speaking the room is very still.

Then comes a banging on the door below, not the banging of terrified fists longing to be let in but the banging of a log swung by straps.

The boy's eyes grow wide, and Carabbas digs his fingers into his own skin.

The Pregnant Woman stands and moves toward the door, but Nadjem intercepts her, then leads her back to the gathered circle. A wail starts up in the back of the Pregnant Woman's throat, but Nadjem manages to shush her down.

Downstairs, the pounding continues. The Bladder-Stone Man curls around his abdomen and starts to weep.

"What happened when you went for dinner?" John Mark prompts. "Tell us about the home of Augustus." He rises to help the patients closer, so that Salome's voice will be its own room, so that maybe their silence will keep them safe.

9-8 BCE

It wasn't uncommon for Julia to dine with Livia and Augustus; her sons, Gaius and Lucius, lived on Palatine Hill with their grandfather and his wife, and she liked to check in on them, to make sure Livia hadn't somehow relegated them to the stables. But I had never gone with her, perhaps because I wasn't yet trustworthy enough, perhaps because after departing the house Julia didn't have much need for a hairdresser.

But her whole demeanor towards me had changed slightly since the night before. That morning, as we heard the report from the slave, she had me kneel beside her chair and proceeded to pet my head like a cat. When I'd finished dressing her for the cena and turned to leave, she asked me to stay in the room but didn't offer me a task. I began to feel like the wispy shadow of her dead son, a not-quite-fully-human being she could hold close.

When Augustus came to greet us at the door, I gawked slightly. I was fourteen years old, John Mark, and only half a year before, I was washing the blood out of wool on a cliff beside the sea. What would my father have said if he'd known I would dine in the house of the emperor? I think he would have believed I'd be rutted by Zeus before I'd duck my head in Augustus's atrium. So I stared: he wasn't much taller than me, with a narrow chest and shoulders that looked thin and pointed, even under his tunic. His hair was blond, a few shades darker than Agrippina's, and his face was cleanly shaven. He looked like the kind of man who would have trouble growing thick whiskers at all. His blue eyes were bright and intelligent, but his gaze darted and moved constantly (my face, Julia's face, Julia's outfit, Julia's hair, my feet, the space behind us).

"This is my Lyra," Julia said brightly to her father. "I bought her a few months ago, and truly my hair has never looked better." She raised her arms and pivoted side to side so Augustus could receive the full effect.

"Truly," he said drily, though the edge of his lip curled up slightly. "What happened to her face?" he asked, staring at me but addressing Julia. "Is she diseased?"

Julia smeared her thumb across my cheek. "No, no, just birth spots," she said.

Augustus narrowed his eyes slightly and then nodded.

"Where are Lucius and Gaius?" Julia asked.

"Likely raising hell in the gardens. Livia found them practicing sword maneuvers on her favorite sapling yesterday." Again, the dry tone and curving lip.

"Is Tiberius here yet?"

"He didn't come with you?"

"He did not."

Augustus studied her but said nothing. Julia kept a light smile pasted on her lips.

"Your slave can go to the courtyard. We can eat."

"Oh, Lyra will stay with me. We'll go and find the boys and say hello."

Augustus furrowed his brow but didn't say anything. I caught him staring at my face again. Then my breasts. But not like the men in the market; there was hunger, but it was tempered by a sense of steady appraisal. He sighed, and his brow relaxed.

"Fine. I have a few accounts to straighten up while we wait for Tiberius." He turned and left the room.

Gaius and Lucius weren't all that much younger than me (ten and seven, respectively), but they immediately felt like a different species. Whatever intelligence they might have possessed was covered by a wildness that bordered on aggression. They embraced their mother until she had to tell them to stop squeezing, twice. Then they demanded to be told how strong they were. They lined up their calf muscles side by side for inspection and then dragged their mother over to where they'd tied a short rope around a rather frail-looking branch on a mastic tree. The hack marks in the trunk suggested that this was Livia's favorite.

We had to stand in the hot sun for what felt like a long time while each of them stood behind a line in the dirt, gripped the rope, swung forward, and released himself into more dirt just a few paces from where he'd begun. Each swing was accompanied by the throaty exultation, "Look, Mama, look!" although Julia was staring directly at them. I was tasked with marking their landing points in the dirt. They weren't afraid to correct me when my mark wasn't deep enough or accurate enough.

When Julia sighed, finally, and turned back toward the house I was glad she was so insistent about my company. The boys wanted me to stay to keep marking them.

Tiberius finally arrived. He hadn't been to a barber, and the red welts on his jaw were hedged with black shadow. I thought of the dark hair on his shoulder blades and his saliva running down my cheek.

During the first course of the cena, Livia explained in precise detail which festivals Tiberius had missed while he was fighting in Pannonia. The second course was mostly the sound of eating. Finally, Julia gestured to a slave and said loudly, using her voice of false gaiety: "I think Tiberius would like more wine." When the slave appeared at Tiberius's elbow, Tiberius motioned him away.

"You were out late," stated Augustus. Tiberius did not offer a response. "Moderation is necessary to an empire." Still, Tiberius did not respond.

"Julia is still not well," supplied Livia. She seemed to have only a single expression, and it was one of supreme control.

"I'm perfectly fine," Julia retorted.

"She no longer has a doctor on her staff," Livia added.

"Is that true?" asked Augustus.

"She freed him back in Aquileia. Along with all the other slaves who were with her."

"Why would you do that?" Augustus looked at Julia squarely.

"Moderation in all things," Julia replied. Then she raised her glass. "To new gates!"

"What?" Augustus narrowed his eyes at his daughter.

"Tell me, Tiberius," continued Julia, "do you find the new gate pleasing?"

Tiberius didn't take the bait.

"Which new gate?" asked Augustus.

"Vipsania has put in a new gate. The old one was rotten, I heard." She clicked her fingernails against her wine cup. "Tiberius paid her a little visit last night. More wine."

Augustus stayed the hand of the servant who moved toward Julia. "No more wine. But you shall have a doctor. I will see to that."

Within a week, Tiberius had been sent to Germania. A week after that, Julia entertained a lover. This time she didn't want me in the room while he lay with her, but she did want me to clean her after he left and to curl against her belly until she fell asleep.

Two weeks later, Augustus, true to his word, sent a physician. He wasn't entirely wrong to do so. Julia bled for a long time each month, and from time to time sores erupted inside her lower lip. During those times I watched her smile as she ate the salted meat at cena, wincing around the pain she thought might help her. Her scalp was scabbed in two places from where she picked it, and sometimes she bathed two or three times a day because of pain inside her wrists and knees. Julia, however, was not pleased about the physician. Across her lower back snaked a scar from a failed attempt at healing when she was young; she didn't trust physicians, and the one Augustus had sent did not exactly inspire confidence.

Short and round, with thick yellow toenails that matched in color the stringy hair that fell from a bald spot at the top of his head, Rufus leaked fluid: rheumy eyes, phlegm-filled nose, and sweat everywhere else, constant and abundant sweat, no matter the temperature, which he wiped using a rag that dangled limply from his belt. Julia refused to let him touch her.

Rufus didn't seem to mind. He kept busy around the villa. I saw him examining other slaves and even the horses, good-naturedly accompanying Nona to the market, even washing the outdoor stucco with a sponged stick.

A few days after he arrived, I caught Julia studying me carefully in the mirror; usually she closed her eyes and hummed or let her eyes ride invisible drafts in the air as she unspooled her thoughts about Livia's porcelain perfection or her father's uptight dress code or her most recent lover's tiny penis (but perfect tongue!). She liked to shock me, and though I tried to keep my face composed like Livia, I often failed. Then she would take one of my hands and kiss it and say, "I'm giving you an education, my Lyra. Appreciate it." But on this particular day she was serious and steady, watching the way I rolled the hair forward over her brow, the precision with which I parted it so that the split of the hair would not reveal the scabbed places or the large wart over her left ear.

I tried to avoid my own face in the mirror as I worked, but sometimes that was difficult. My face was different than the one I'd found in the polished metal in the marketplace at Elis. I had cheekbones now, on which my golden eyes balanced. The spots were still there, but unlike both my mother and Julia, who had wide eyes with small mouths and chins tucked underneath, my face was an oval and my mouth didn't hide. My skin was a few shades darker than Julia's and my hair was as close to black as hair could go without turning kohl, although most of the time it was hidden under my headscarf.

When I finished with her hair, she took my hand, though I hadn't yet begun to work on her eyes or lips. "Come," she said.

She guided me out to the portico and asked Juba to find Rufus. He arrived, sweating, a minute later.

"I want you to make her into a physician," Julia declared. "She's smart with her hands and a quick study. I want her to know everything you know. To be honest, I'd rather have her hands on me than yours."

Rufus started to lift his hands in opposition, but he saw Julia's glare and bowed his head instead.

"You'll start tomorrow. During the cena. I don't need her then."

The following day while Julia and a few of her friends lay prostrate in front of dishes of mashed nettle and sows' udders, Rufus guided me to the back of the villa to a small bedroom that faced the hills instead of the Tiber River. In the room stood a simple bed, a desk and stool, and a large ornate cabinet. Inside the cabinet were scrolls, jars of varying sizes made of glass and copper and clay, a few bowls, a pestle and mortar, a delicate-looking scale, a smooth piece of marble, and a collection of utensils that ranged from familiar spoons and scoops to tiny knives and pincers. None of it was organized, and all of it was covered with a smattering of mouse shit.

"We'll begin with this," said Rufus. "Remove everything. Scrolls here," he said, pointing to the desk. "Instruments on the bed. Line up the jars along the wall."

"You're supposed to train me," I said.

"This is training," he replied.

I spent the afternoon doing as he asked, and though I resented that I was still doing the work of a slave, I took pleasure in the feel of tools and instruments I'd never touched before. By the time Julia called for me, the cabinet was bare and the shelves had been wiped with water and vinegar. I'd arranged both the instruments and the jars by size, and Rufus had divided the scrolls into two piles based on some aspect of their contents he didn't reveal to me.

"Dispose of these," he said, filling my arms with one of the piles of scrolls. They felt damp from his sweat and the sprays of snot he'd bestowed on them as he worked.

I did as I was told, dumping them in the heap of broken shards and food waste at the edge of the property near where the freed slaves lived. But that night after I'd wiped the chalk from Julia's face and hung her silk stola and drawn her curtains, after I'd recited the tale of Andromeda and hummed her into sleep, I rose from my place on the floor beside her bed and walked back out to the pile. I squatted, one hand holding my tunic over my nose to deflate the smell, the other unrolling the scroll soaked with the least amount of refuse.

I couldn't read, but I knew that the letters were Greek from the figures my mother had drawn on the dirt floor of our home. Delta, psi, omega, and sigma were the only four letters I knew, but they winked back at me from the scroll like old friends. I carved a whole line of letters in the dirt by my feet. Light from one of the shacks illuminated my scrawling just enough for me to see how shaky and ill-formed my own letters were. Outside the shack on a line hung laundry, the smaller length of the child-size tunics beside the longer billow of the adult fabric. A woman stepped from the house with a baby who was coughing dryly. She bounced the child and sang until the coughing ceased.

I stood and pulled the night air into my lungs, trying to find the scent of pine or sea salt, but I got the sick rot of garbage instead. The moon, a chalked thumbprint in the sky, seemed to grow smaller, like Julia's baby, untethered without his name.

The letters on the scrolls made me want so desperately my mother's fingers combing through my hair, her scent of fire smoke and wet wool, her voice rising and falling, even the troubled sea-suck breath of her last years. Julia touched me all the time, but inside the touch was her own desire for comfort or possession. Meanwhile, I had to mother her constantly: helping her to dress, combing her hair, massaging her aching wrists, tipping water over her skull. I have always known how to mother with tenderness, John Mark. I could have been that kind of mother to Yeshua. But with Julia, tenderness became a duty, and my affection for her a thing she could wield against me.

I woke the next morning in the room with the medical cabinet. My head pounded.

"Here," said Rufus, handing me a hunk of bread and cup of diluted wine.

I touched my fingers to my forehead.

"You know the best cure for a headache?" he asked.

I shook my head.

"To learn to cure a headache!" he replied cheerily. He blew his nose on his rag, tucked it back into his belt, and held out his hand to me. "Pharmacology," he said, nodding in the direction of the jars lined up against the wall.

I declined his hand but stood up and slowly inched my way over to the far wall.

"Open each jar. Smell it. If you don't know what it is, stick your finger in and taste it."

And so it began. A few I knew by scent alone, but many I had to taste. After we identified each jar, Rufus would set it on the desk, picking each up from time to time to quiz me again. Ginger, fenugreek, vanilla; hyssop, aloe, carrot. When all the jars were on the desk he began moving them into groups.

"Dysentery," he said, moving three jars together.

"Ginger, fenugreek, wine," I replied.

He nodded.

"Toothache." He grouped together two other jars.

"Tears of poppy and milk," I said.

"Good."

"Pain in the spleen," he announced. But this time he didn't move any of the jars himself. I looked at him woodenly. "Give it a try," he said.

I hesitantly moved henbane and mandrake until they touched.

He sighed and wiped the sleeve of his tunic across his forehead. "That, Lyra, is likely murder."

I remembered all of it. I made a cabinet in my brain and stored the information on shelves inside, shelves wiped with vinegar and water, free from mouse shit and dust. But I made sure to keep henbane and mandrake bound together in my brain, like Artemis and Apollo or Romulus and Remus. By the end of the day my headache had disappeared, and for the first time in a long while I felt something close to contentment. Though the knowledge was ostensibly part of my future service to Julia, it felt separate from her, an object I could take with me away from the villa, a means to buy my way to freedom.

The more I learned, the more I resented Julia. It wasn't that she was unkind to me: it was the severity of her need for me. She was two people: witty, confident, and brassy in the public realm, and a puddle of sadness, a pit of emptiness within the confines of her quarters. On the day she finally let me accompany her to the baths in town, I had to walk beside her litter, holding her hand through the drape of the curtain. I had to sit beside her as she urinated, I had to be the one to scrape the dirt and oil from her skin, I had to be the one to massage her in the humid steam of the hottest bathing room. I'd never been given a lesson in massage (Rufus and I hadn't made it to that point in my training), so I pretended her limbs were linens needing to be wrung.

Julia didn't want me in the pools themselves, but my tunic and stola were so saturated from the steam by the end of the day that I looked as though I'd gone bathing. The linen clung to my body on the walk home, raising goose bumps on the backs of my arms and thighs. Julia's hand slowly relaxed in mine—she must have fallen asleep—and I stepped carefully, trying to avoid a pile of dung, a tipped piss pot, the slithery insides of a butchered animal coated in dust. Near the bridge to the island of Asclepius we paused to let a few other carriages cross our path from the other direction. At the edge of the river a man in a toga grabbed a handful of his slave's hair and pulled back his head, opening the man's jaw with his other hand to examine his throat. The slave's eyes rolled back in his head and his body went heavy. The master let him crumple to the ground. "If you're going to Asclepius to be healed, you'd better have a real injury to take with you," he said. Then he kicked the slave twice in the back and climbed back into his litter.

I must have squeezed Julia's hand as I watched because her voice wafted through the veil of the curtain, "Lyra, what is it? What's happened?"

"Nothing," I said tightly. "Just a man beating his slave."

"Oh," she said, "that's good." And her hand relaxed in mine again.

When we returned to the villa, she didn't order me to change out of my wet clothing. She wanted a hairpiece that added length, she wanted the stola with the gold rosettes around the neckline, she wanted wine lees used to color her lips instead of ocher, she wanted the thinnest palla, the one that showed her white shoulders through its wide knit. She watched as I applied the cosmetics and affixed the hairpiece with combs, but she didn't search out my face in the mirror, not once.

"How do you think the body is made?" asked Rufus. He was rooting around in the cabinet, unrolling the scrolls on the second shelf and placing them in different containers.

As soon as Julia's guests had arrived for cena I'd scooted away, and now I sat on the stool in the medical room, arms wrapped around myself, shivering.

"Well?" Rufus finally turned from the cabinet and looked at me with his watery blue eyes. "Why are you wet?"

221

"The baths," I said.

"Go change. I can't hear myself think over the sound of your chattering teeth."

When I returned, finally dry, I asked him whether he thought the baths were useful.

He sighed and held up his right hand, using his left to point to each finger as he recited: "Massage, exercise, eating, rocking, bathing." He waggled the thumb that represented bathing for emphasis. "Antonius Musa cured the emperor with baths when everyone was certain he would die." He raised his eyebrows at me. "But too many cold baths should be avoided."

"How many is too many?" I asked.

"These methods are used for prevention as well as treatment," he continued. "The body. The human body," he corrected, "is made up of particles moving freely. Think of the streets of Rome. When a carriage tips or a man stops to beat his slave, the people get blocked up. They push up against each other and turn irate. These blockages happen in the body, too. But what happens on a festival day?"

"I have never been in the city on a festival day."

Rufus pulled the rag from his belt and wiped his face as though just the thought of a festival day made him perspire. "On a festival day the streets are too full. It's a mess of piss and prostitutes, and it's hot and unbearable. Everyone cheering. Half the people don't even know why. That's a flood. When there's a blockage or a flood in the body, that's when you have a sickness. That's when we turn to pharmacology or surgery. But if we keep the body balanced, then we don't need drugs or knives."

"So we should just get rid of festivals and litters and slaves," I mumbled sarcastically.

"If Julia had wanted a political revolutionary, she would have told me so." He held his hand in front of my face and wiggled his fingers.

"Bathing, massage, exercise, diet," I recited somewhat blandly. He wiggled the final finger at me. I shrugged. "I don't remember."

"Rocking," he said. "Carriage rides and horse rides. For an infant, a cradle." I must have looked skeptical because, after tucking a strand of stringy blond hair behind his ear, he said, "You are welcome to invent a new system for treating the human body, Lyra, but until then we will use this one, which has brought health to many."

Then he untied his belt and removed his tunic so that he stood before me entirely naked except for his sandals. Bile filled the back of my throat, and I backed toward the door. I longed for Dite's wool to curl through my fingers or my shears to raise before me. If Rufus noted my fear, he didn't show it. "We'll begin with massage. Have you touched a man before?"

I stared at the floor and shook my head, tears stunning my eyes.

"Well, I'm a good man to start with. Exactly like those statues in the forum." Then he raised his right arm forward and put his left foot on the edge of the bed, freezing his face into a look of passive conquest. But his sagging, hairy belly touched his raised thigh, and his tiny, pale nipples hung onto pads of flesh almost as large as my own breasts. I giggled.

"That's better," he said. He lay on the bed and closed his eyes, which made staring at him considerably easier. "Start with my feet," he said.

I removed the sandals slowly. His toenails curled around the edges of his toes, thick and waxy. Around a shrubby knot of hair on the top of each foot, walking sores opened their pink, sorrowful mouths. The bottoms of the feet were almost black with dirt, and the smell was vinegar and yeast, swirled together at the back of the throat.

Rufus propped himself up on his elbows and noted my distaste. "You'll likely have to wash them first." Then he settled himself back contentedly and closed his eyes.

Washing feet was nothing new; I scrubbed Julia's every afternoon before the cena and usually at least one or two other times a day—at a bath or for another meal. But when Julia left the grounds it was always inside a litter or carriage; her feet simply didn't have time to collect the scent or the muck of Rufus's. I grudgingly fetched a bowl of water, rags, and a few unguents to cover the smell.

"No perfumes," he said when I opened the jar lid. He hadn't even opened his eyes.

"Why not?"

"Sometimes the body tells a story with a smell. If you cover it up, you can't hear the story."

"I wish I didn't have to hear the story of your feet any longer."

Rufus just smiled. "More pressure on the bottom of the foot. Good. Now pay strict attention to each toe. This is massage, but this is also anatomy. A foot is not simply a foot; it is part of a larger body. Pay attention to how mine works. Where does it end? How does the ankle move? Are any of the joints swollen? Are any of the sores infected? Are the particles moving freely between the foot and the leg?"

And despite the smell, despite spending the afternoon washing another slave's feet, I began to give myself over to the body, to this particular body before me. I'd known there were bones in the foot but I'd never tried to count them, never tested to see how far feet could splay outward or inward, never compared the thickness of the skin on the heel to the thickness on the bridge, never tried to track a vein all the way from beginning to end.

We repeated the procedure over the next four days: legs, torso, arms, head. Each day, Rufus instructed me on massage but also called out the names of parts below the skin (spleen, liver, bladder) and asked me what I felt, what I noticed.

And I told him:

His pulse was stronger at his throat than at his wrist. He gasped when I pressed below his bottom left rib but not his right. His stomach felt hard (he prescribed himself wild celery and plantain, and on the next day it felt softer, more malleable). The bone on his knee could be moved back and forth slightly. He had a rotten molar and horrible breath, a white coating on the back of his tongue. On the palm of his right hand, a thick, callused ridge from carrying the handle of his medical box. My fingers had a knowledge I didn't know they possessed. They knew how to touch and press so that I could see below the skin; they were my eyes into a new world.

Unlike the villa worker's, his penis didn't seem interested in me. It drooped to the right, against his thigh. Below it, his testicles retreated at my touch, initially, though he showed me how to coax them downward by warming my hands together.

And the more closely I examined him, the less his body was a representative of Rufus and the more it became one version of the human form, a creation worthy of study. Later, Julia snapped at me while I did her hair, so intent was I on counting the bones in her spine, in testing the cartilage of her ears to see how they differed from Rufus's. "I hope he's teaching you something useful," she said curtly. But that night she dangled her hand over the edge of the bed and didn't complain as I massaged each of her fingers; even with my eyes closed I could see the stretch of each bone, the buzz of particles moving from her fingertips to her wrist, elbow to shoulder to breastbone, up her throat and past tonsils, teeth, and tongue.

The day that I first went with Rufus on a house call was the day my life fully opened and then snapped shut again. It was six months since I'd started my training, since Tiberius had left for Germania and Julia had begun entertaining lovers. I'd been in Rome for a full year and my Latin was close to fluent. Rufus had taught me everything he could about pharmacology, anatomy, and preventive medicine within the walls of the villa. We'd treated, in addition to Julia's minor illnesses, the slave baby with the dry cough and countless cases of diarrhea and lung ache; I'd learned how to administer an enema and splint a wrist; Rufus had even grudgingly taught me to read and write, ostensibly so I could decipher the labels on medicine jars and the pharmacology recipes in our collection. But sometimes he made me translate a line from Cicero into Greek, and one interminable afternoon, he ground herbs with a mortar and pestle while I wrestled with some poetry he'd pilfered from Augustus's study. For all that he did know, Rufus was also adamant about all that he didn't know. He waxed dreamily about Egyptian medicine, spoke in reverent words about the library in Alexandria and all the knowledge it still contained (even though Julius Caesar had done his best to burn it down a few decades before).

But now that I knew the basics, I was hungry to learn more, and our household wasn't getting ill often enough. Luckily, my desire for more knowledge coincided with a new lover who Julia truly seemed to care about. His name was Iullus, and they spent hours in her bed, sometimes talking, sometimes staring at each other fondly while Rufus and I massaged them, sometimes drinking too much wine and playing a game of trying to see who could balance the most fruit upon the other's tilted face. This game I hated because it resulted in stains on the sheets that took repeated washings to expel. But her late nights meant that she often didn't need me until late in the mornings; on this day I convinced Nona to look in on Julia if she woke before I returned.

Rufus had a colleague named Phillipos who had a small surgery in the south of town, near Aventine Hill. This man was also a slave from Greece, but he didn't have to pay taxes; Rome paid him a tidy sum each month to saw off limbs and stitch up wounds.

But that first day, we didn't even make it to the surgery. We walked through the streets, sun just beginning to sift through the mists, the last few carts edging their way out of town. The city felt completely different at this time of day; I could see the crude drawings on the walls, hear the trickling of water into the corner fountains. It was early enough that a few candles still burned on one of the street shrines, and the woman who knelt before it looked holy instead of ragged or desperate.

Then out of the quiet came the caw of a woman shouting, "The gods have sent you! Come!" and dragging Rufus through an archway and into a smaller courtyard from which wooden steps snaked their way toward dozens of sleepy doors. She pulled us up one stairway to the second story and then the third, and then down a narrow wooden walkway that hugged the side of the building.

I could feel the shaking of the man before we crossed the threshold. He had fallen in the middle of the room, likely trying to dress for the day. He wore a loose tunic; a thicker brown one lay puddled on the floor beside him. His chin tilted up, up, up, jagging for the ceiling. Hands curled, frothing mouth stained pink. Two young girls were bent over the household altar, backs to the shaking man, while other family members and neighbors had gathered in the doorway, pallas and stolas pulled up to cover their noses and mouths.

"His legs," said Rufus, and I went immediately to where they twitched like water thrown on a hot pan.

Rufus went to his head and knelt, placing his knees gently over the man's shoulders. I copied the gesture, my hands over his shins, trying to press them into stillness, but there was a life in him that did not want to obey.

"That spoon. The wooden one," said Rufus, nodding at the wife. When she didn't move he said it again, loudly and authoritatively, all of his rheumy passivity gone. The wife brought it quickly and gingerly, dangling it between forefinger and thumb as though it might cause her to start quaking, too.

Rufus placed the handle of the spoon between the man's teeth and then took the man's head between his palms to keep his skull from banging against the floor.

I expected his shaking to stop then, as though the spoon was some kind of medicine. But he kept moving and we kept holding, on and on, though it couldn't have been more time than it takes the iron to twist a single curl of hair. His seizing worked its way up my forearms, and I imagined it shaking his internal parts, too: spleen, liver, lungs, heart. I held and held until the shaking was inside me, and then I tried to still the shaking in myself, to send that stillness back out to him: heart, lungs, liver, spleen; arms, wrists, elbow, tongue. Finally, the man stilled into sleep.

Rufus and I both leaned back, and he nodded at me. Rufus, who through his bent posture and physical exertion should have rained sweat and snot and saliva all over the poor man, was completely dry-faced and calm. He didn't reach for his rag. Instead he reached for the medical box. He slid off the lid. "Better to do what we can before he wakes." And then I saw that Rufus's hands were covered with the man's blood. "Seizing usually means a fall." I nodded. "Find a needle and thread and a small pair of scissors." Then he turned to the wife: "Clean rags and water."

My hands remembered which compartment to open for the needle and thread, which to open for the scissors. I removed vinegar to clean the wound and Rufus nodded approvingly.

With the small scissors he cut away at the bloody hair until we could see the wound clearly. He used the wet rags and vinegar to smear away the rest of the blood. Inside the wound was a sliver of white. The bone of the head, I knew, but it looked like something secret and private. Pressing the edges of the wound together with one hand, Rufus pushed the needle through to join the flesh together again. Back and forth, making the tiny bit of moon disappear.

He handed the needle to me and I took it, the thread tethering me to this particular body. "Once through," he said, and I did it. Skin was tougher than fabric, but the give when the needle pushed through was the same. I pulled the thread taut and handed the needle back to him.

"No tears in the wound," he clucked. I hadn't realized I was crying. I wiped my sleeve across my eyes. "Find the tweezers," he continued. "Check for splinters in his heels and elbows." It wasn't a necessary task, but I was glad to have something to do to stop the shaking that was starting up in my own arms.

When Rufus finished, we helped the wife move the man to the bed. Rufus left a jar of ointment with her and promised to return the next day.

"Shouldn't we stay until he wakes?" I asked as we clattered down the wooden steps.

Rufus shook his head. "He doesn't need us now. He needs comfort and healing. The wife will go to Phillipos if he needs something before tomorrow. Besides, we need to return you to the villa."

The sun had sucked the misty wetness from the streets while we'd been inside. Cutlers and bakers lined up their wares; fullers collected linens and dumped piss pots into their tubs. When we stepped off the paved road onto the dirt track, Rufus cleared his throat. "You can't behave like a woman when you're a physician," he said. "Tears don't belong in a surgery."

I nodded to avoid displaying the emotions beginning to constrict my throat again. How could I explain that my tears were for that white sliver of bone disappearing? For the way the body held a perfect innocence below its skin, a radiance that rendered a body simply a body. Stripped of skin, we were unrecognizable as slave or master, Roman or Greek. The body argued for an equality I had never thought the world might possess.

The curiosity and love I'd had for the human body as a young girl now had a purpose: the deftness of my fingers, the swiftness of my memory. I felt no hesitation in that room. No doubt about who I was or who I would become.

38 CE

Salome pauses to look at the boy then, absently sucking his thumb in his father's lap, not at his face but at his head, at the place where hours earlier she'd pulled out a perfect circle of bone. "Perhaps it seems obvious to all of you, because men grow with the knowledge that they will work, that they will do something for the world besides pushing babies out between their thighs, but it was a revelation for me. When I practiced medicine—and still, now, when I practice medicine—I am the girl cloaked in wool who walked through fire. John Mark, when I practice medicine, it's then I believe Yeshua's words to me in the river, all those years later: *you are worthy*.

"And so, filled with that first spasm of power and certainty, I did the stupid thing, the rash thing. When we returned to the villa, I went directly to Julia and asked her for my freedom."

But before Salome can say another word there is a horrible splintering sound and then a cheer, and then the battering ram again. This time each patient in the upper room feels the trembling, and all of them close their mouths and inch closer together. Every bit of their attention is cast toward the sounds downstairs.

The leader of this particular contingent of the mob is a willowy man with swollen tonsils who swallows often, whose Adam's apple, moving up and down the ridge of his throat, somehow inspires a kind of awe among the other Greeks. This leader sits down next to Levi on the dining couch and palms the man's knee with too much force. He bends down and sniffs at Eleazar's neck like a dog. "Sandalwood!" he proclaims, and the other Greek men laugh. The rest happens quickly: Benjamin is shoved off a low stool so that he topples against a blue bowl of oil resting on an iron stand. Zeloph is pulled up by his hair; a heavy sandal is kicked into his crotch. Some of the Greek men sweep the pantry shelves with their palms, pull open the bedroom trunks and steal the sweet-smelling burial unguents. Later they will present these oils to their wives as perfume.

Two men corner the servant girl in the courtyard, the one who washes so faithfully with vinegar. One places a mantle over her face so they will not have to look at her while they do what they do.

Ten feet away the Broom Boy has buried himself in the refuse pile. Gelatinous seeds slide down the side of his cheek and into his ear. Near his right hip are a few of the bandages from the upper room, the ones deemed too filthy to be washed, carrying the scent of rust and some spice like myrrh. Most of his covering is broken shards of pottery, those bowls used for animal fat that cannot be cleaned and so are broken instead. It feels as if the earth has cracked open and he is nestled in its entrails.

Before the Greeks can kill any of the Jews in Philo's house, the leader stops them. "Bind them together with thongs," he says. The bone slides up his throat and retreats again. "Tomorrow is a festival day. Let them be a spectacle."

And so they are led out of the house: Judah and Elisha and Benjamin and Zeloph and Eleazar and Levi. But their names do not go with them.

And Philo? Just before the Greeks entered, Philo ascended to the roof, ostensibly to pray. But his arms are filled with his manuscripts. While his friends are being bound, Philo is opening the door of the dovecote, is nudging aside some of the roosting birds with his knuckles so that he can nestle his scrolls into the stone niches. When he is finished, he moves toward the stairs, knows that he must walk toward his fate and finds that he cannot. Philo falls to his knees and shows his pecked and bleeding hands to Yahweh, asks if this small pain might be suffering enough.

Across the city, Asha brings honeyed water to quench the thirst of a woman who has tried on three different wigs, who leans close to the sheet of polished metal and asks if the blond color makes the tone of her skin too sallow.

Though most of the Greeks leave Philo's house with the elders, proud to walk the streets of Alexandria to show off their catch, a few men remain. Some splash in the mikveh, others pour the consecrated wine. One of the men creaks up the side steps to see who hides in the upstairs room. When the knock comes, it's Nadjem who stands, who tells the others to cover their faces as much as they are able.

Before the Greek has time to shove the door open, Nadjem has opened it a crack. She shows him only her eyes and the color of her physician's tunic. The man who stands on the landing possesses irises that shudder in the whites of his eyes. He is eager to make a discovery that will erase, momentarily, his own strangeness.

"Open this and show yourself," he says to Nadjem, pushing at the door.

"They are lepers," she says through the fabric, and moves away from the crack so that the Greek can see the group huddled in the center of the space, feel the pulse of their stench, hear Carabbas, who chooses to rise up at that moment, baring the wounds of his naked belly and shouting, "Disease!"

This showing is enough for the jittery-eyed man to retrace his steps, to lie to the others that the room is empty, that the mouse shit and broken furniture is not worth their trouble. He does not tell the truth because even to say the word *leprosy* is to associate himself with the disease, with the ones who are cast out and dirty. Instead he finds a beautiful red glass bowl and fills it with wine, reclines on one of the couches and balances the liquid on his belly. He closes his eyes so that the others will forget his strangeness, will believe he is one of them, his body untroubled, his vision still.

"We cannot let them hear us," says Nadjem.

"They will come eventually," says the Fever Woman. "You have no tunic," she says to Carabbas, and he looks down, as if remembering his own nakedness for the first time. There is grief in his eyes when he looks up again. "Let me make you one," she says. He brings the basket of bandages and she kneels close to him, pushing the needle into one linen strip and then another, leaving no trace of her work but the man's quiet supplication.

The boy cries quietly into his father's shoulder, and Mangled-Arm Man rocks quietly back and forth, eyes closed. Nadjem makes each of the patients drink water and then helps the Pregnant Woman to the pot in the corner, spreads her own legs wide so that the Pregnant Woman can use Nadjem's thighs to brace herself. As they move back to the group, the Mangled-Arm Man winces each time the floorboards creak. "They will come eventually," the Fever Woman repeats.

"Tell us, Salome," says John Mark quietly, "what did Julia do when you asked her for your freedom?"

8-6 BCE

"Come here," she said.

I walked to her bed. The room was dim, stale with sex and wine. As I drew closer, I saw a deep red scratch across her collarbone. She moved a few limp strands of hair to cover it.

"Kneel." I obeyed. The mosaic tiles bit into my knees. She grabbed my cheeks in her hands, the heels of her palms pushing my lips apart, nails digging into my jaw. She pressed her face so close to mine that I could see the shudder in her left eyelid, the crust of dried sleep at the inside of her right. "I have been to a soothsayer. Everyone else will be taken from me. But not you. You are the one I get to keep. The gods sent you to be mine."

She was crying, and she paused and brought my head forward, wiping her tears on the crown of my head. "I have treated you well. But if you ever, ever ask for your freedom again I will have your feet burnt, little by little, until they are stubs of charcoal, until they are unsalvageable. And you will sit in this room by that potted fern over there in a little iron chair." She clenched my face more tightly. "Tell me you understand."

I raised my hands and wrapped them around her wrists; below my thumbs I could feel the beating of her heart. I closed my eyes and saw the skull of the shaking man, the flesh eclipsing the tiny sliver of moon.

"I understand," I said.

She released my face and drew a deep breath. "Now, a bath."

And so began my double life. I was a slave until the moment I began caring for another body. Then my hands and mind forgot to be subservient, forgot that I belonged to someone else. Then my body belonged only to the work and to my allegiance to the innocence of bone and tissue and blood. My ability to do that work, to slip my slave-girl skin, hinged on my ability to be the perfect slave girl at every other moment. Nurturing was the work I belonged to, and medicine was the work that belonged to me.

It took months after that first house call before Julia trusted me to leave with Rufus again. For a few weeks, she wouldn't even let me visit the medical room or accompany Rufus as he treated freedman and slaves at the villa. But then she developed pains, and when the pessaries of olive oil I prescribed didn't work, she sent me to Rufus again. He suggested fumigation, so I lit herbs in a ceramic pot and spent an afternoon holding a lead tube between her legs so the smoke could waft into her uterus and heal her. When it worked, Julia unraveled my leash slightly.

This went on for two years, until I was almost eighteen. It might have gone on for the rest of my life if Rufus hadn't gotten sick.

8-6 BCE

Both of us did our best to ignore the illness for months. A growth below Rufus's rib cage had grown so large it had begun to put pressure on his other organs. His stomach and bladder could barely hold any food or drink, so he grew thinner, dehydrated. I'd felt the growth that very first time I examined him, when I was only fourteen years old, but then I hadn't known to worry; I was learning to see with my fingers, and though I reported what I saw to Rufus, neither of us knew it was cause for concern. Even if we had known, we never would have considered removing it, since surgery was always the last resort.

Until it was clear that we had arrived at the place of last resort, that not removing the growth would certainly kill him. I had seen Phillipos perform more than a hundred surgeries, and only around half the patients survived. My main function at those surgeries was as a glorified assistant: to mop blood, fetch instruments, to resecure the ties that bound the patient's wrists and ankles if they fought the pain too aggressively. But Rufus almost always made room for me to see the doctor's hands at work, so I knew the brown sheen of the liver, the pink coils of intestine, the knob of stomach. I knew the sound the saw made against bone and how far beyond the evidence of gangrene to cut to make sure the sickness didn't spread to healthy tissue. My eyes knew the insides of the body, but my fingers did not. Sometimes I had to curl my fingers to my palm and secure them with my thumbs just to make sure I didn't reach out and touch all of that writhing life.

"You will remove the growth," said Rufus to me one day when we were refilling the pots in the medicine room. His face was drawn in pain and his tunic reeked of urine; he tended to dribble little bits throughout the day, his squeezed bladder forcing it from his system before he could prevent it.

"Absolutely not," I replied. "Eat this." I offered him bread soaked in diluted wine.

He took a few nibbles for my sake and then walked briskly out of the room; his retching sounded like the earth opening, and I remembered my mother's story of Persephone and Hades, thought of the useless globs of wax on her household altar. Rufus retched again, and I was ready to bargain with the gods I didn't believe in. I would give up my hope of freedom forever if things could carry on just as they were, if Rufus could live. The future was a place I did not want to enter.

"Lyra, listen to me," said Rufus when he returned. "Chances are I'll die on the table no matter who holds the scalpel. The only good thing I've done with my life is to teach you. Well, that and the time I wrestled my mother's third husband to the ground and stuffed his face in pig shit. I served the world well then, too. The point is I'd rather die teaching you." He took out his rag and wiped his forehead, his underarms. Then he took hold of my shoulders and stared at me with his watery blue eyes. "We'll do it in three days' time. Because of the festival, Julia will be in the city. I'll make sure you have leave to stay. And you'll open me here."

I shook my head vehemently. "We have none of the—"

"I'll get you the supplies you'll need. I'll make sure we have a few slaves for fetching and mopping. If we do it at the surgery, Phillipos will grab the scalpel out of your hands as soon as my wrists are bound."

Still, I adamantly refused. Two days later he could barely walk to the pot to piss; when he didn't think I was listening I heard him moaning gently. It was my mother all over again, except this time I knew enough to save the person I cared most about in the world. And I was certain, in spite of my lack of experience, that I could do the surgery at least as well as Phillipos and probably better. I understood that this was hubris. It was for this kind of thinking my father had pulled me off the log at the beach, had thrust me into the churning sea. How can I explain to you, if you have never had the feeling, how certain I was of my own abilities? Rufus was my friend, and his body was mine to save. I was the one who could make him well again.

We had one day before the festival to prepare. We went through the surgery plan over and over before I attempted it. I scratched it on a wax tablet; I moved my fingers over the ridges and swells of Rufus's torso and recited the anatomy I understood by heart. He listed possible complications, and I offered solutions. We lined up together on the table every ointment or salve I might need, then scooted the table close to the bed so that they were each within the reach of my outstretched arm. We taught Luca and Pulco the names of the instruments and instructed them on how to stanch the flow of blood. The plan was to give Rufus just enough of the tears of poppy to drowse him and dull the pain. The rest of the suffering he would endure so that if I had questions, he could answer them through the veil of his twilight half-sleep. On this, Rufus was insistent. He was certain he could offer me wisdom with his body split open. So we practiced the dosing of poppy until we thought we had it just right.

Finally the day arrived. Julia left on her litter, but not before thanking Rufus for his service and promising to carve whatever he would like on his tombstone. She was trying to be kind.

All that I had wanted for the last four years was to perform a surgery myself, but now the body before me was my friend, my teacher and mentor, and I could not still my shaking hands. I mixed the poppy into milk, and he propped himself on one elbow on the bed to drink it.

"Three things, Lyra. No, four." He wagged his fingers in front of my eyes the way he had at the very beginning of our time together.

"One. If I die, it is the will of the gods. If you blame yourself, you will lead a miserable life. Two. Do not lead a miserable life. Three. If I die, I want you to examine every inch of my body. I want you to cut me apart. I want you to learn."

"But—"

"The Romans can fuck themselves. The Egyptians did it. Do it. It's the only way you'll really learn."

"I can't—"

"Hush up, the poppy's coming on. The fourth thing. Yes." He looked at me, squinting a bit as if he couldn't quite see my face. "The fourth thing is no tears in the wound." He wiped mine away with his thumb. Then he kissed each of my hands and lay back down, eyes closed. I looked at the mark we'd drawn together on his skin in charcoal. I picked up the knife.

"One more thing." His voice was quiet and wavy. "The rocking cure is as useful as a horse's ass." He smiled a little, and then the smile floated away.

I cut precisely, perfectly, down the length of the line we'd drawn.

I was prepared for what I found inside Rufus's body. And I was prepared for the way a patient's body reacts to pain: the straining against the ties, soiling the clothing, grinding the skull into the table, the terror in the eyes. I was prepared for the kinds of sounds that can emerge: deep howls, high-pitched shrieks, repeated requests to the gods, to mothers, demands for death. But I was not prepared to see pain occupying the body of someone I loved, for the way Rufus bit his lip until it bled, for the way, chin thrown back, he emitted a single, excruciating note of pain.

Faced with his suffering I could not do my work, and so I gave him more poppy. At first he fought me—he clenched his lips and continued to make that sound—but Pulco was strong, and he forced Rufus's jaws open enough that I could pour more liquid down his throat. I poured until Rufus's whole body relaxed and he fell into complete unconsciousness.

Once the sound of his pain was gone, I could do my work. I did every step perfectly. There were no complications. My closing stitches were as neat as the marching formation of the Thirteenth Legion. It was done. Luca held the bowl with the mass inside it, the exact color Rufus had predicted. I let myself fully exhale.

And then I rested my fingers against his neck to feel the beating of his heart, but the speed of the blood beneath his skin, the irregular race of too much poppy in the blood, made me cry out. Even as I did so, I recognized the rhythm. It was the furious flutter of wings before a bird takes flight, the vicious wriggle of a fish freeing itself from a net, the horse quickening its pace before the jump over the ravine.

His heart leaped. And he was gone.

Luca handed me the bowl, and he and Pulco gathered up some of the rags and exited to give me time with the body. Or perhaps because they couldn't bear to watch me desecrate it the way Rufus had desired.

I stared at the mass in the bowl. Quiet seeped out of it like its own sound and coated every surface in that room until I felt like I had wool stuffed inside my ears.

I knew that my own weakness, my own inability to watch my friend suffer, had caused his death. This was a far worse fault than botching the surgery itself or failing to treat for infection afterward. And even so, I knew Rufus would want me to snip the stitches across his abdomen, to test the weight and malleability of organs, to locate pockets of blood and bile, to learn from his body what I could. He understood what my future would be if he died: I would become fully a slave again, a slave who knew to administer lint plugs and groin cups when Julia's monthly bleeding grew too heavy or a poultice of balsam and centaury when a rotting tooth needed to be removed. But mostly my hands would go back to knowing hair. The curl and part and swoop, the braid and roll and bun. I would have no mentor, and my other chances to practice medicine would come haphazardly, occasionally. I would live my whole life hoping for the illness of those I worked beside. Rufus's body was my last chance to learn. Julia and the other slaves wouldn't be back from the festival for another few hours. I could take Rufus apart and put him back together again, sew him up and clothe him so that they'd never know what I'd done. Not that anyone would look that closely at the body of a dead slave.

I studied the body of my friend. Then I put away my cutting knives, the empty poppy vial and the ointment jars, the smaller amphoras of wine and milk. I rerolled the few blotting rags I hadn't used and closed the lid of my medicine case. I sat down beside Rufus and laid my cheek against his chest. I let myself sob against him for a long time.

I draped a sheet over his body and gently closed his eyelids. Then from the folds of my headscarf I took one of the few coins I'd managed to save since I had arrived in Rome, and I put it below his tongue.

38 CE

For a minute the room is entirely quiet, and Rufus's body feels almost tangible between them. But then the Fever Woman coughs and the Bladder-Stone Man begins a kind of panting weep; Nadjem rises and brings him St. John's wort, but he takes her hand and says, "Please give me poppy. Like she gave to Rufus." He nods toward Salome. "Let me go."

Salome nods, opens her medicine case, and takes out the poppy; she gives him less than he desires but enough to take the sharpness off his pain. After Nadjem checks the Pregnant Woman and says she feels the heels of the baby but not the head, Salome offers poppy to her as well. But now the vial of poppy is empty. In the morning when they wake there will be nothing to muffle the knife edge of pain. The patients will cry out, and all of them will be discovered. Or they will die because Salome does not have the tools or the light to cut for stone here, and a baby pulled out by the ankle almost always destroys the womb of the mother.

In the room below it is the hour of boasting. There was enough wine in the amphoras that now the Greeks slosh their words. One of them remembers a game from childhood in which a blindfolded person tried to guess the identity of his friends by touching their faces. If the blindfolded one guessed incorrectly, he was punched on the arm by the friend he had offended. So they burn the last of the lamp oil and take turns shoving their fingers into the mouths and nostrils and ears of one another, and it is true that in the dark, almost no one recognizes the features of the other.

Meanwhile, the Broom Boy crawls out of the refuse pile and helps the servant girl to her feet. Together they slink down the darkness of the side hall, past the roars of laughter and thumps of fists hitting muscle and up the creaking stairs, where Nadjem receives them after a series of quiet knocks upon the door. The stench of the Broom Boy is almost unnoticeable, so dank is the reek of the upstairs room; Salome washes the girl with soft rags and rubs balm of narcissus into her bruises. The girl chooses a place next to the Pregnant Woman and places a hand gently on her calf.

The boy sleeps in his father's arms, and strangely, the Fever Woman has fallen asleep in Carabbas's lap. He gently uncurls her fingers so the needle will not poke her palm while she rests.

Finally, it is only John Mark and Salome who are awake.

"That wasn't the end," says John Mark.

"What?" says Salome.

"Rufus's death. They might have heard it as the end, but I know you left Rome eventually. And I'm still not certain why you thought you could help Yeshua."

"Tomorrow we will probably die," says Salome. "Does it matter?"

John Mark realizes it probably does not. He was plagued with questions, he remembers, not so long ago. Those questions were his biggest concern. But they have been wiped away—by exhaustion and fear, yes, but also by tending to the bodies of others. He has been so busy paying attention to these bodies, to Salome's story, that his own doubts have fallen away. And he feels it, he does, that beautiful space Peter baptized him into: knowing and known. Somehow he has arrived here, but not because of answers.

"Your voice is a comfort to me," he says. "I would be grateful for your voice."

Salome smiles in the dark, a wry smile that no one can see. The death of her mind will likely be eclipsed by the death of her body. And her instinct, like the patient near death who pushes breath and urine and feces out all at once, is to excavate all of it, the rest.

And she feels tenderly toward this man, she realizes suddenly. Downstairs, a roar of laughter, a broken bowl. "It is good the rest are not awake for this," she says.

6 BCE

Different griefs set us to different tasks. The loss of my mother set me to obsessive work, carding and spinning and sweeping and hulling as a way to right the tiny ship of sorrow at the back of my throat. The loss of my father and my home turned me numb. In the slave cart I was simply a body among bodies, my heart wrapped in bandages so many times it was unrecognizable. But Rufus's death did not set me to work or silence; I was not filled with domestic determination or the ooze of sorrow. Once his body was washed and buried, once his remembrance was carved, I waited for guilt and sadness to overwhelm me, but desire and rage found me instead.

Where had it been, desire, all those years before? It should have fluttered at my wrists when I saw the forms of naked men at the baths. It should have listed up the sides of my ribs as I waved a fan to cool the man who probed inside Julia's mouth with his cock. It should have filled my cheeks when I heard the grain man talking out of the side of his mouth about an orgy he'd seen, how he could barely tell who was in what, how the women crowed like roosters. But I hadn't felt a thing.

Maybe it was because once I was sold, my body never felt entirely like my own anymore. Maybe it was because for the first year as I learned Latin and the rhythms of the house and the physical demands of my role, my body was so sapped of energy that there was none left for desire. Maybe it was because after I adjusted to those labors, I was so caught up in learning how to be a doctor that my brain was constantly circling around new pharmacological concoctions or a procedure I'd seen in Phillipos's surgery. Perhaps neither my body nor my mind had room for desire.

After Rufus's death, though, I was left with so much empty space. I no longer had to think to style Julia's hair or to choose the right stola (low neckline, thin shoulder ties for lovers; high neckline, thick shoulder straps for cenas with her father). I knew where her muscles rounded themselves into knots, and I knew the glaze of her eyes when she wanted to be left alone. When slaves and freedman came to me for remedies, sometimes I could see what they needed before they spoke, sometimes by sight, sometimes by scent. I kept supplies of horehound, wild celery, and frankincense at the ready.

I no longer had to think about my jobs, and so all I could think about was my body and the bodies that moved around me. My entire gaze was focused on the human form, not as a doctor who wanted to discover how the parts worked but as a woman who wanted to know what it felt like to have her breast rubbed raw by a man's unshaven cheek or whether the scrotum had the same texture as dried figs on the tongue.

When Julia's newest lover, Cornelius Scipio, visited, I stood near the door, listening to the sounds their bodies made; I took the plate of apricots and pears out of Nona's hands and delivered it to them myself so I could catch Cornelius running his hand down the length of Julia's thigh or pinching her belly affectionately. In the night I dreamed, again and again, that a star had burst between my legs; when I woke, I was slick and tender with pleasure.

All of this transformation in a single week. And racing along beside the desire was rage: my only real friend was dead, and I would never be a surgeon; the girl on the beach, waving her hands as she acted out the story of Arachne, was just a girl, and my hands were now just as useless as hers. Perhaps my imagination was not wide enough. But I knew that unless Julia died and freed me in her will, I would be yoked to her forever; she had promised me that. And unless I poisoned her or failed her as a doctor in some other way, she would likely live to a ripe old age.

I was a woman consumed by anger and desire who had no fear of recompense.

The next day we were invited to Palatine Hill for cena.

※

Julia and Tiberius reclined on opposite sides of the litter, a line of pillows between. I held Julia's hand through the scrim of curtain as we walked, and Tiberius, mocking her, insisted that Pulco hold his hand in case he fell asleep and dreamed of a barbarian Gaul. He'd returned from the north two days earlier and fiddled frequently with a scab on his forehead. He didn't touch Julia at all.

As much as I detested Tiberius for his behavior toward his wife, I couldn't stop myself from observing his body whenever a breeze shifted the curtain: the red welts along his jawline, toga bunched up to reveal the splay of his open legs, the dark hair that ran from his knees to the hem of the tunic, the sharpness of his Adam's apple in contrast to the gentle droops of his eyelids. The one time I'd seen them together in bed he'd been loveless, perfunctory. Had he been this way with Vipsania too? Or with the prostitutes he surely bedded in Germania? Were men the same kind of lover with each body they encountered, or did certain women (or men) unlock tenderness while others provoked gray distance?

Augustus and Livia greeted us in the atrium, the emperor's eyes crusted green at the corners and bloodshot with infection.

"Father," said Julia, using the croon of concern she usually reserved for Agrippina. She reached her thumb toward his face.

Livia caught her wrist. "You don't want to do that. Might be contagious."

Julia shook her arm free. "Fine. Where are Gaius and Lucius?"

"I'll take you," said Livia. She folded her hands tightly in front of her as she walked but held out her arm and slim fingers gracefully when it was time to direct our attention to the boys. They sat at a table near the garden; a screen divided their study area from the grass as though to prevent them from remembering spring. Hunched over scrolls and wax tablets, they looked more like boulders than scholars. Their father, Agrippa, had been Augustus's best friend, possessed of an acute military mind, but these boys always seemed most useful as objects to hurl at an approaching enemy.

Julia turned to me suddenly. "See if you can do something about my father's eyes, Lyra. I'm going to try to convince Gaius to recite Livy before we eat."

"We'll certainly be famished by the time he finishes," Livia remarked, though her lips barely moved as she spoke.

Trailing a couple of house slaves I'd rounded up in the kitchen, I found Augustus in his study at the top of the house. The room was painted to resemble a temple: scarlet, with white pillars at intervals and a golden rectangle meant to mark a door that wasn't there, or a window to some imagined future. On the left side of the room was a couch with a simple wool blanket. Augustus sat at a desk littered with scrolls. He wore only his tunic, his toga folded neatly over the back of his chair. His hand hung poised over a blank tablet, stylus quivering in the air above it.

"Julia sent you," he said, without looking away from the blank surface.

"She did," I said.

"Hold." He shooed the other two house slaves away and then made a series of dots on the tablet; it wasn't until he held it up for me to see that I realized it was my face with my eyes and nose and cheeks removed, just a constellation of my wrongness. He was clearly trying to provoke a response, so I didn't speak, tried to press the emotion from my face like Livia.

"So," he said finally, "what do you propose for this?" He gestured toward his eyes.

I held up one bowl. "Centaury and fenugreek, dried and crushed. I'll wrap this in rags and then soak the bundles in warm water. Then I'll place them on your eyes."

"Worst case scenario?" He narrowed his rheumy eyes at me and then blinked back excess moisture.

"I'm not sure what you mean."

"Best case is that I'm healed. Worst case? Blindness? Scalded eyelids?"

"The worst case is that it doesn't work."

"Fine. If anything worse happens, you will be beaten. I don't care what Julia says."

I nodded. Hated that I had to nod.

"Maybe the couch is best," I said, gesturing toward the far side of the room. "You'll need to keep your head tilted."

"If I desire."

"If you desire for the medicine to work."

He whipped his head back to face me but didn't say anything before settling himself on the couch, head tilted against the raised end.

I divided the herbs and placed them in the centers of two rags. I bundled them, dipped the bundles into the hot water, and quickly moved to the couch. He raised one of his arms, offering the wrist, and I touched the bag there first so he could approve the temperature. "Fine," he said. "Proceed." His eyelids were closed but wrinkled with his inability to relax. I set a rag over each eye and then blotted at the drops of liquid that ran down his temples, his jaw. When I moved to leave, he stretched out, quick as a snake, and grabbed my thigh.

I held very still. He didn't loosen his grip, so I studied him. His feet were cleaner than Rufus's, the toenails rounded into perfect crests. On his calves were smooth bald patches where sandal ties had worn the hair permanently away. His prone position and the fact that he was blinded by the bundles decreased his authority. Wrinkles fanned out from the corners of his eyes, and the sandy blond hair on his head was ghosting gray at the temples. He showed his age in other places too: the skin around his knees sagged, and his shoulders curved up slightly from the plane of the mattress. Here was a body like any other body, and yet this body could break my body. This body could tax my father so heavily that he would sacrifice his daughter, hurl his own body into the maw of the sea.

Still, Augustus did not loosen his grip.

"You're watching me," he said finally.

"Yes," I said simply.

"You are assessing me."

"I am assessing you."

He barked sharply, baring his small yellow teeth. "And what does a slave find?"

At any other time in my life I would not have answered his question honestly. Before that moment my life had been a thing I had striven to protect. After that moment there were other lives that required my existence. But at that moment I was ready to die, so I said: "I see a man who calls himself an emperor."

Then I grabbed his thigh, below his tunic, and he startled so violently that the bundles of rags almost tipped from his eyes. "But really," I whispered, bending so close that I could see the tiny white hairs along the rim of his ear, "he is a man. He is a body like any other body."

"Like any other body?" His voice had narrowed to a thin thread of steel; his grip tightened until his knuckles turned so white I could see the blockage of blood in his hand.

I squeezed back just as tightly, then peeled back his tunic with my other hand to reveal the cock that had begun to press against it. It was of him and not of him. It was a part of his body that I could possess. I took him in my hand and his midsection bucked upward. I climbed on top of him, and he didn't move except to grip my other thigh. I hitched up my stola and arranged myself over him so that the rest of his body couldn't touch me, and then I lowered myself onto him.

In my memory there is no pain; I did it slowly enough that I could watch the way my body made this part of him disappear.

I erased him over and over again.

When it was finished, I climbed off him and folded his tunic back over his midsection. Then I rinsed my hands in the bowl of cooling water, spread passivity across my face, and removed the rags from his eyes.

His breathing was still hitched, and a red flush covered his neck. His eyes fluttered open.

"Well?" he said.

"Better," I said. And though it was true that the crusted pus had disappeared and the inflammation had tempered, what was better was the eyes themselves. There was something troubled in them, and this satisfied me deeply.

"A new tunic," he said loudly, for the benefit of the slave surely dawdling just outside the room. We heard footsteps retreating. I placed the rags back in the bowl and turned to go.

"No," said Augustus, "I want you to see this." Then he untied his belt and disrobed. I don't remember his thighs or hips, the stretch of his belly or the swirl of hair at his groin; I don't know if his nipples were small or dark or if his arms boasted muscle or sinew. All I saw were the twelve brown spots: eight on the left side of his torso and four on the right. His chest was my face's mirror image.

Once, before he died, Rufus and I were on our way to Phillipos's surgery when we passed an apartment complex that had collapsed the night before. Sitting at the edge of the pile of rubble was a boy covered in plaster dust holding a clay lamp. We paused for a moment so that Rufus could inquire about the boy's condition, but the child ignored Rufus's questions, shrugged off the gentle hand Rufus placed on his shoulder. Scattered near the boy's feet were a few plums and apricots, a small bowl of olives, and a couple loaves of bread. While we stood there a woman approached, refilled the boy's lamp, and then departed again. An older child brought a small platter with sauced meat and set it next to the bread.

When we told Phillipos what we'd seen, he explained that everyone inside the apartment had been killed, including the boy's family, but although he'd been on the third floor and crumbled to the earth alongside them, he'd walked away unscathed. In the three days since the disaster the boy had refused all offerings. "If he keeps on like this," said Phillipos, "he'll join the rest of his family in a few days anyway."

"Don't you think that's what he wants?" I said.

"Doesn't matter what he wants," said Phillipos. "The gods saved him. Now he's spitting right in their faces. That can't be good for any of us."

By the time I left Augustus's room, the thrill of possessing him had been shattered. Instead of feeling invincible, I felt entirely vulnerable. I left his room acutely aware of the bruising on my thighs, the shaking in my calves, the dryness in my mouth—and I thanked the gods for each of these sensations, for the cloak of my own skin, for the way my body could move, of its own volition, from the study to the kitchen to the triclinium.

I was certain he would have me killed. As I watched him eat with Julia and Livia and Tiberius and the boys, I considered whether I could swim the Tiber with broken legs or pry a nail out of my own palm or apply the necessary ointments to whip marks on my own back. I wondered if I'd have a chance to say goodbye to Maia or Nona, considered whether the scrolls and medicine jars would be subsumed by dust and mouse shit once again. All the while I sat beside Julia's couch while she ate with one hand and idly twirled the hairs at the base of my neck with the other.

I was so focused on imagining my own death and trying to conceive of my own survival that I wasn't listening to the conversation. But at some point, I noticed a shift in tone, and then I watched as they collapsed a building on top of themselves:

How Augustus declared he'd take Gaius to Gaul, how important it was to prepare him to be ready to take over the empire.

How Julia glowed and preened and popped dates into her mouth with little sucking sounds.

How Livia kept clearing her throat and glancing at Tiberius but saying nothing to Augustus, how she sent back three different plates for not being clean.

How Tiberius swirled his finger through the oil on his plate and said that in that case, given that he was not needed, he would retire to Rhodes.

How when Julia declared she wasn't moving to Rhodes, Tiberius said, "exactly."

How Julia removed the palla that I'd draped artfully over a particularly revealing stola and said that if Tiberius retired to Rhodes, she would retire to the forum to seek new friends.

How Augustus stared at her breasts as he said, "You'll not behave like a whore, Julia."

How Julia said, "I won't behave like a whore, Father. I'll simply behave like a man."

How Julia stood, my hand in hers, and said, "Come, Lyra."

How Augustus stood and said, "Whores don't need slaves."

How Augustus looked at me and said, "Slave, you are free."

How it took Augustus and Tiberius together to extract my hand from Julia's grasp.

How Julia wailed and shrieked loudly enough I thought she might call her dead baby back.

How Augustus held her head still and Tiberius forced her jaws open so I could still her raging with tears of poppy.

How when Augustus said, "Slave, where would you like to go?" the word slipped from my lips before I could understand what it meant:

"Alexandria."

I was the boy covered in plaster dust, the one unscathed. Only unlike the boy, I stood up with my lamp and I walked away.

38 CE

Salome lies on her back, her right hand held by John Mark's left, the Broom Boy tucked around her ankles like a cat. She feels through her shoulder blades and her tailbone that the men downstairs have quieted. Occasional sounds waft up from the street: the slam of a door, the calling of a name, the patter of a single pair of feet. Most of the Greek mob has gone home to eat from their own bowls, to have the blood of other men scraped from under their fingernails.

"Emperor Augustus was Yeshua's father," says John Mark. The John Mark of three days ago or even ten hours ago would have risen to his knees with excitement. But this John Mark stays still and accepts this truth like an iron blanket.

"Yes," says Salome.

"And this was how you thought you could save Yeshua, by revealing his parentage? You were going to undermine his spiritual authority by revealing his political authority."

"Well, he was a bastard. Augustus's seed granted him no political authority."

"But it would have been enough to subvert his pronouncements against Rome."

"Perhaps."

A week ago, John Mark might have believed this, that in the face of evil there might be a thing to say, a string of words that would stop terror in its tracks. But now he is convinced that even if every Jew in every synagogue had bent down and proclaimed Gaius Caligula their god above all other gods, even if they had said exactly what they were supposed to say, the Greeks would have found another way to hate them.

"And Josef knew, all this time, that Augustus was the father?"

"No, but Josef knew I had been a physician in a wealthy household in Rome. He guessed that Yeshua might be the offspring of a wealthy

Roman. I was a slave." Salome slides her hand out of John Mark's grip and places it on her belly. Feels the good breath there rise and fall.

"And did you?" John Mark asks. "Did you tell his followers this truth?"

Salome knows she has a retort for this, but now she cannot remember. Salome has been awake for twenty-one hours, and in spite of all she has seen that day, in spite of the fact that the room stinks of urine and shit and blood, when she closes her eyes it is periwinkles that come to her, floating down from a gray sky. They cover her lips and the spots on her face, her aching hip and the callus in the middle of her right hand. Salome sleeps.

"And did you take his body down?" asks John Mark quietly. "And was he truly resurrected?" But like the dream flowers that fall on Salome, these questions feel strange and soft, beautiful but unnecessary.

Only the Broom Boy hears John Mark's words as he rises out of one dream to swallow a moment of consciousness and then sinks down into another.

DAY SIX

38 CE

Salome wakes with a start a few hours later, her mind sharp again. The others still sleep. The sky is knuckled with stars.

In two or three hours the poppy will shed its protective skin from the Pregnant Woman and the Bladder-Stone Man, and they will cry out and the Greek brutes will come clattering up the stairs to investigate. Or one of the Greeks, rising to relieve himself on the refuse pile, will hear the murmur of the doves and raise his eyes upward, will climb the stairs to investigate. Or the patients will not be found but will wallow in the airless room until by evening, two of them are dead.

Salome stands and threads her way through the slumbering bodies; the pain in her hip is sharp and she is grateful for it. The needling will keep her awake. She takes her medicine case and tiptoes down the stairs and along the side hall, past the slumbering bodies of the Greeks who drool against the fabric of the dining couches, out the rear door and into the alley. In the darkness, Salome removes a cutting knife and carries it in her right hand, the medicine case in her left, down the streets of the New Jewish Quarter, past whimpering bodies and between the shards of broken glass and broken pottery, until she crosses the sandbags and toppled stones at the border. Past the alabaster dove, past the empty homes, the lighthouse riding on her left shoulder, Salome walks until she reaches the lamps that have been lit, the streets that have been swept, the tidiness of a city that has not been desecrated. She puts even more weight than necessary on her right leg to keep the pain flashing, quick and steady, through her body. When she hears a man whistling behind the door of a bakeshop and smells the oven being roused, she quickens her pace. At the crossroads fountain she washes quickly, as best she can, cupping the cold water and running it over her calves, her forearms, her neck. She takes dried lavender between her fingers, wets it so that it releases more of its scent, rubs it on her breastbone and under her arms, then chews a pinch of licorice root to take the rot off her breath.

Then she crosses to the clinic and bangs on the door until her wrist tingles and Alexander pulls the door open, wiping grains of sleep from his eyes.

"You're early," he says without affect.

Salome follows Alexander over the perfectly scrubbed white mosaic tile of the examining room, past the cups on the side boards, laid largest to smallest, past the closed cabinets that hold washed instruments in neat rows, full pots of calendula ointment and decoctions of henbane and barley paste. The scent of vinegar rids the air of impurities and, nearer the windows, the scent of the herb garden is sharp and musky and sweet. All of this feels like absurd abundance—the quiet and space, the cleanliness and order—after the last days in the Quarter. In the side room Alexander lies down on one of the couches and throws an arm over his eyes. On his ankle he wears a bracelet, a gold snake wound around a silver band.

"Are you here to take the bandages to the fuller? To copy the patient notes from yesterday? To do a little weeding in the herb garden to make up for all of your absences?"

Salome pulls a stool up beside the couch and removes Alexander's arm from his eyes. "First thing this morning, I need you to send a group of physicians—five or six at least—to the New Jewish Quarter with a wagon. They will escort a group of patients here, and a man called John Mark who wears a physician's tunic, and they will do so safely. Nadjem is there and will help them. I need you to send for Castor, the one who has the clinic near the Sun Gate, who is said to open and dig for stones faster than a man can pass his lunch. And I need Albion to tend the woman. Her baby needs to be turned, and I could not do it. She will be coming down from the poppy soon, so it needs to happen quickly." Salome bores her gaze into Alexander.

"You are not serious."

"I am serious." She squeezes his arm, and he pulls it sharply away.

"The New Jewish Quarter is a bloody, violent mess. I wouldn't send my physicians there even if I thought the cause was good."

"I have been there, these last days."

"I wouldn't send physicians I care about."

Salome folds her hand in her lap. "You don't want me here," she says evenly.

"I was sleeping," says Alexander, closing his eyes not to sleep but against the dark cloud of intensity she's pulled into the clinic.

"I will be done."

Now Alexander lets his arm fall to the floor and squints at her.

"If you do this today, right now, as I have asked, I will be done practicing medicine here."

"How do I know you'll keep your word? There's no one here to mark this."

Salome shakes her head at him once, in disgust, and then lifts her tunic over her head and drops it on the ground between them. For good measure she undoes her headscarf and shakes her unruly gray hair loose from its plaits. She stands before him in her thin linen undertunic; Alexander studies the darker stains below her arms, the dark splotches of her nipples, the texture of crotch hair pressing against the fabric. There is a burn scar he has never noticed before on the inside of one forearm, round and pink and vulnerable. And on the outside of the other forearm, a purple scar in the shape of a circle. Without her tunic and her severe head covering, she looks like any other old woman grinding barley in a courtyard or rocking an infant in a cradle.

Alexander pushes himself to a seated position. "I could have done without the theatrics," he says. He toes the fabric of her fallen tunic in a slow circle on the floor. "Draw me a map that shows how to find the place. But find a blanket to cover yourself first."

Salome turns to fetch papyrus from the small library.

"And then you'll go home," says Alexander.

"I will stay to make sure that they arrive, that they are cared for appropriately. Then I will—"

"No," says Alexander. "You will draw me a map, and then you will go home."

And it is then that Salome feels sharply the sag of her breasts, the looseness of her skin, the darkened color of her teeth. If she is not a physician, what is she? Salome knows the answer: an old woman of no real use to anyone.

Salome finds a brown tunic in the small triclinium and pulls it over her stained undertunic. It does not smell of horehound or lavender or calendula: it smells of bread and sweat, like a regular human life. Salome does not braid her hair or bind it with the headscarf. The loose strands feel strange against her neck, her cheeks. With an ill-fitting tunic and her hair wild and unkempt, Salome leaves the clinic.

The sky is pinking itself awake. On the Water Way, the hair of the wigs flutters, blowing across the dowels as though they had faces to hide. Asha makes the porridge and resents that she is the one making the porridge. She adds rosemary to the water and dried figs on top. She straightens the coverlet on Salome's cot and touches the sheet that holds the cedar shavings, just to be sure they still release their scent.

Then Asha sits in her own room before a polished rectangle of metal, patting a powder of white lead to the dark spots below her eyes, to the yellow sallow below her cheekbones. If Salome were here, Asha would have her do a Livia knot: two parts in the wig hair, sides rolled under just above the ears, middle section teased upward, and front piece lifted over the teased section to create a wave that draws the eye up the length of the face. But Salome is not here, and so Asha does all of these things to the wig herself. Her fingers are agile and tender and she takes extra time with the front piece, using a bit of beeswax from the jar by her bedside to encourage each hair to its place.

But when Asha places it on her head, she already wants it off. The inner netting chafes her scalp; already she can feel the place on her neck where a scab will be scraped off today. All day she will have to think about whether the sensation on her neck is the wind or blood from the scab. No one wants to buy a wig from a woman whose head is bleeding.

To give up a thing you love just before you would have lost it anyway should not feel like a sacrifice. But to Salome, it does. She should go home and sleep. She knows this, her body needs it, and she has promised Alexander. But she cannot leave until she knows the patients and John Mark and Nadjem are safe, and she cannot yet return to Asha, not when she has one foot in the Jewish Quarter and one foot in the past. Besides, she is almost done with the telling. John Mark will be here soon. Then Salome will finish the story and go home. "Asha," she will say, "here I am."

Salome finds a bench near the crossroads fountain to sit. She massages her right hip ceaselessly to keep herself awake. Time has grown strange this week, bloating and constricting, racing itself and twisting in on itself, doubling back and over and under, around and through. Time is the knot the Greeks tied around the Dragged Man's feet and the bergamot peel unraveling in her mother's hand; time is the swift rush of the Jordan River and the steady drips of moisture from Asa's bag of cheese. Time is slave and physician, martyr and mother, Salome thinks. Time is a psalm exhaled from the mouths of the living into the mouths of the dying. Salome watches the clinic and presses her thumb deep into the nestled ball of pain.

The sun lofts its orange light now, and in the Jewish Quarter Nadjem is praising every god she can think of. From the window she watches six physicians, clad in indigo tunics with red thread at the throats, emerge from the covered wagon the clinic uses for carting bandages and hauling water.

Alexander, a man who cannot speak without sounding like an ill reed, stays downstairs to talk to the Greeks while the other physicians climb the stairs and usher the patients down.

There is no mob streaming into the Quarter this morning because today is the day of the festival. One of the Greek men downstairs attended the gymnasium with Alexander when they were young. They remember together, fondly, one teacher who passed air constantly, uncontrollably, and another who stopped every hour to apply ointment to his eyes. The Greek with the shuddering irises watches the patients for signs of leprosy and, seeing none, does not mention Nadjem's diagnosis to the other Greeks, but instead recedes to the back courtyard where contamination cannot find him.

And so the physicians turn the wagon back toward the center of the city, and the Greek men who spent the night in Philo's house, who yesterday beat the elders, splintered the gate, drowned a man in his own mikveh—these men chat amicably with Alexander, as though this street were any other street, as if they did not have the blood of yesterday still upon their hands.

Behind her closed eyes, Salome's mind slips and returns, slips and returns. But she does not let herself drift into sleep. She can feel Alexander's dismissal in her bones, and the muscle below her right eye twitches with exhaustion and rage, but she keeps her gaze set on the clinic. True to his word, Alexander has not unrolled the awning, has not opened the clinic doors. A few people stand against the wall anyway, but Salome can see even from this distance that if they are well enough to shift and cross their arms, their need for care is far from urgent.

When the cart pulls up, guided by the physicians, Salome does not make herself known. She watches as John Mark and Nadjem, the Broom Boy and the physicians each escort a different patient into the clinic: the Fever Woman and Carabbas, the boy and his father, the Mangled-Arm Man and the Pregnant Woman, the servant girl and the Bladder-Stone Man.

Salome is sixty years old. She has been a Greek, a slave, a Nazarene, and a physician of Alexandria; no one will tell her any longer to what or to whom she belongs. She is determined to finish her story so that she can return home. Salome will bring the latrunculi board to the front of the shop, and she and Asha will drink barley beer and warm their ankles in the sun. Below the table she will rest her hand on Asha's knee, warm and easy.

When John Mark leaves the clinic an hour later, when he spots Salome at the fountain, he almost doesn't recognize the woman in the ill-fitting tunic whose hair is losing a battle with the wind. But then she fills a cup with water and gestures him over and begins peppering him with questions about the patients and then, yes, she is Salome again. He answers as best he can. The stones have been removed, the body closed, and the man is not dead. Not yet, at least. The baby was successfully turned and delivered, and the woman's womb was ripped at least a little in the process, but the bleeding has been stopped. Nadjem was with the new mother when John Mark left. The others are well and no longer need much care. But John Mark is worried about the clinic being closed, worried that when word spreads about the patients inside it will be mobbed. And to be relatively safe here, in this tunic, it feels like sickness on his skin. He covers his face with his hands. Bends over his knees.

"I am going to tell you the next part of the story now," says Salome. "I need to go back and tell you something I forgot, about when Yeshua was young. So that you will understand what I did later on in Jerusalem."

John Mark does not want to hear the next part of the story. He wants to rip every one of those statues out of the synagogues, wants to wrap a bandage around the entire Jewish Quarter, wants to find those who were taken for the festival, wants to break every chain, wants the Greek mob and Herod Agrippa and Flaccus and Caligula flogged until they are mere smears of blood on the street.

Salome nods at him and takes his hand and then begins her story anyway. And John Mark listens, not because he wants to know what she will say any longer but because he needs to rest and her voice has become a dwelling place for him. Soon the day will push forward and the festival will begin and he will have to decide what to do next. But for now, the morning is still fresh, and no one is out but those who need to be: vendors lining up wares, boys drawing water and sweeping the streets, and the Egyptian men climbing the lamps and extinguishing the light.

1 BCE-3 CE

The year Yeshua turned four, Mari and Josef left him with me for three nights so that they could make a pilgrimage to the village where Mari had birthed and lost her baby four years earlier, on the way to Alexandria. They had wrapped the baby in a rug, then, and been allowed to lay his tiny body in one of the tombs; they promised themselves they would return to collect the remains, to bring his bird bones back and place them in an ossuary in the tombs outside of Nazareth as soon as they could. But then there had been Abraham's death and the loss of Simon, Mari's mistrust of me and her unwillingness to bring a small child along on the journey: so many reasons to delay the journey. Finally, though, they went. This was the sweet spot of time after I had first begun to introduce Yeshua to medicine but before Mari chastised me for it, before I placed my wrist into the flame.

What matters, John Mark, is that for the first time in my life, I was alone with Yeshua. The day they left, I took him to a thin stream that snaked its way through a knot of cedars just a ten-minute walk from Nazareth. In the summer the stream disappeared entirely, but in the spring it was a thick enough thread for a small boy to wade in. You could almost hear the trees pulling the water up into themselves. I was collecting periwinkle, which spread itself in thick vines in the shade near the stream bed. I offered Yeshua the plucked heads of the flowers, and he'd take them to a linen cloth we'd laid over a rock in the sun so they could immediately begin to dry. I believed in collecting the roots as well, though Rufus had thought there wasn't any good to be found there. But I dug and selected those carefully so as not to kill the web of flowers.

"Wash these," I said, handing Yeshua a handful of curling tendrils. He took them diligently into the stream, pulling up his tunic as he squatted so as not to get it wet. His fine, thin hair fell over his ears all the way to his neck, curling up slightly at the ends; I wanted to smooth those hairs, to splash some of the cool water on his neck, but I did neither.

"What are the uses of periwinkle?" I asked.

He pulled the roots from the stream and held them to his chin. "As a beard. See, I'm like Papa."

"A good likeness," I said, though of course I had a different man in mind. "What else?"

"Fever?"

"No."

"Toothache?" He wandered over to the rock and laid the roots out precisely.

"No."

"Now it looks like the foot of a pigeon or a dove."

"Yeshua."

"Anna let me touch a dove. Did I tell you?"

"You did. But not the uses of periwinkle. Come."

He walked back to me slowly, pausing to study objects on the ground and tip his head to the sky. He was at the age where each gesture was a war between obedience and independence. "Look now," I said, "I'm clipping even some of the shoots that haven't flowered. They will be useful to us, too."

He squatted next to me but gazed at my face instead of at the flowers. He reached up then and rested his palm upon my cheek. "Could the flowers make your spots go away, Auntie?"

I stopped what I was doing. His hand, still plump with baby fat, was warm and tender. I let myself put my own hand over his. "I am afraid not."

"That's good. I wouldn't want them to go away. You would look naked. Like the bald patch on Asaph's head." Then he slipped his hand away and I was left with my hand on my own cheek, the hard ridge of my jaw.

He plucked a few blooms then, waddling on his haunches between the soft pops of purple. "Tell me where Mama and Papa went," he said without looking at me.

I hated the sound of that word, Mama, a snake thrown into my lap. I stood and stretched my back. "Tell me the uses of periwinkle."

With his right fingers he began to roll the petals he'd collected in his left palm. He moved his fingers back and forth, faster and faster, until the petals had darkened and shriveled, until they'd torn and become nothing more than a dark smudge in the middle of his hand. "These aren't good for anything," he said. Then he sat on his bottom with his legs out straight in front of him, cradling his hand as though it were injured.

I went to my medicine case and got out a rag and the tiny pot of licorice root. "A taste?" I said.

He put out his tongue in response and I put a tiny pinch of the sweet, dried root upon it. Then I took the hand with the periwinkle wound and began to wipe it clean. "Have I ever told you about Rufus?" I asked.

He shook his head, moving his mouth thoughtfully around the taste he loved. "Is he here?" he asked finally, looking around as though there might be a man hidden in the white willow.

"He's not here. No. He lived in Rome. He was my teacher."

"Did he teach you prophets or letters?"

"Letters some. But mostly medicine."

"Rome is where the soldiers live."

"Yes."

"Do people there have to wear sandals?" At that age Yeshua looked for every excuse he could find to go barefoot.

"Yes, they do. Lots of fancy sandals."

"Did your friend die?"

"I want to tell you the story of someone he saved."

"Who?"

"A man with a spear in his thigh."

"A real spear? From war?"

"A real spear but not from war. The man was in an argument with his brother."

"Tell me."

And so I did. I told Yeshua about the man with the spear and then another story of a man who cried tears of blood. While I did so he let me wipe his hand, and then he began to pick the flowers again, of his own accord, handling them gently, bringing them to the warm rock to dry. You asked me, John Mark, days ago, about my tender memories. This is one. The scent of cedar, the color of the periwinkle, Yeshua's small feet, white and cold from the stream. The gentleness of that work.

After that day he didn't ask me anything else about Rufus. Until the next year, when Mari and Josef made their pilgrimage again because they had been unable to locate the bones on that first trip. This time we were weeding the plot of land when Yeshua said, "Remember your friend? That Rufus? Tell me another story about him." And I did. Rufus became the story I told to fill the space of the story I couldn't tell: the story of Mari's lost baby and Yeshua's birth. How I gave him up. Who I was. One story pregnant with another story. The truth of our relationship spinning in the birthing waters of Rufus the hero.

The next year, the year of Yeshua's fever, the year I put up my medicine case and turned away from him, Yeshua was sent to the widow Anna while Mari and Josef went away; that year contained no stories of Rufus. But the year after that, our pattern resumed. "Tell me another story about Rufus."

"Which ones have I already told?"

"The Spear Man, the Man Who Cried Blood, the Leper, the Woman with the Wandering Womb, the Croaking Boy, the Grandmother with Too Many Teeth."

"Have I told you about the Seizing Man?"

"No."

And I began again. But I put off, for a long time, telling him about Rufus's death.

8 CE

When Yeshua turned twelve, Mari and Josef took him to Jerusalem for the Passover feast. They let him believe that this was where they had gone every other year and that now he was of age to join them. He puffed with anticipatory pride. I watched them make their preparations for three days; one entire afternoon I spent gazing on them through the wall, eating a melon from Egypt. I can taste that melon now, John Mark! Traders had come through, a caravan on the road, and some of us had gone down the dusty slope and haggled. Most of the Nazarenes bought practical things: lentils or salt or new blades for their pruning hooks. I bought a sweet green melon from Egypt, split it in half, scooped out the slimy seeds and laid them on the straw for Eden the goat, and then stood with a spoon at the wall, scooping the wet flesh into my mouth.

On the other side of the wall, Mari and Josef and Yeshua bustled around with great purpose. Shaking out bedding, comparing the weight of blankets against their predictions of cold, measuring out the right amount of barley flour, legumes, dried fruits. In a burst of unaccustomed glee, Mari even sent Yeshua for a hunk of Asa's cheese. He came back with a handful, licking the running threads of white off his wrist.

"What next?" Yeshua said, over and over, never so helpful in his entire life.

"Bring the stools in from the yard, child," Mari would say, or "Test this satchel to see if you can shoulder it for the journey." Then Yeshua would scamper like a puppy, banging the stool legs against the door frame as he tried to wrestle all three in at once or strut around the house over and over again, looking down slightly at his own chest to see the way it flared open more widely as it supported the weight of the bag. Josef mostly busied himself in the small plot of land they tended, gathering what he could before they departed. When Mari and Yeshua weren't packing, they were gathered beneath the oak tree, passing the stories of the prophets back and forth as though when they arrived in Jerusalem there might be a test of knowledge.

That day, with the melon, I remember because Yeshua came to my courtyard and I had to step away from the wall quickly, spoon halfway to my mouth.

"Auntie," he said joyfully, "Mama wants to know if you have a decoction or salve we might take to treat the road dust and the city smoke. I told her we use horehound or yarrow for lung ache. Right?"

I offered him the pleased smile he desired. I was tempted to say there was no need for medicine: they would be there such a short time, no smoke would cloud their lungs. But offering him medicine was a way of sending part of me along with them. "Come, why don't you see what we have? You take what you think you might need."

"Is your case here or at the clearing?"

"Here. I brought it back last night."

He fetched the case and laid it open in the light of the yard.

"Not in front of the courtyard doorway," I hissed.

"Auntie, everyone knows about the clinic."

"They know but they don't want it known."

He widened his eyes at me to show he thought the gesture stupid but then moved the case to a part of the courtyard a passerby would not easily see. He found the horehound and yarrow, and he took a small vial of olive oil and two bandages as well. He touched the vials of henbane and poppy. "I could take these. In case there is an emergency?" he asked.

I shook my head. "You know why not."

"Because an overdose kills a patient faster than a surgeon's knife," he recalled dejectedly.

I recalled Rufus, of course. The fluttering of his heart and the way, cheek pressed to his chest, I felt the heat drain out of him. There would be no story of Rufus this year. Instead of having our three days together, alone, while Mari and Josef went on their pilgrimage, they would have him and Jerusalem, and I would have the plot of land, a few ill Nazarenes, and Eden's swollen udder.

"No poppy or henbane, but take that melon." I nodded to my small outdoor table, where the other melon half sat. Yeshua tucked the medicines under one arm and grabbed the melon against his hip with the other. "Careful not to drop it in the dust."

"I know, Auntie," he said, his back already turned.

"And Yeshua," I said sharply. This was the first time he would truly be away from me. Though I'd lived with a space between us for twelve years, his body had always been close enough for me to see, to touch if I desired. Yeshua turned at the tone of my voice to look at me.

"Yes, Auntie?"

But I couldn't think of what to say. Instead I stuttered: "Don't try to pack the melon. Eat it now, before you go."

"I will not hoard it to myself, Salome. I will share it." I could hear in his voice how proud he was to try my name on his tongue the way a man would, to jump ahead of me to the lesson he already knew.

I didn't want a single bite of that sweet melon in Mari's throat. But I nodded at him and forced a smile. "Good," I said. "Peace go with you."

The mood, when they returned a few weeks later, was greatly changed. All three of them were quiet, though I could not tell at first whether their quiet masked exhaustion or rage or fear or grief. Mari immediately confined herself to the house, let whatever mood it was devour her. Josef made a quick meal of porridge the second they returned, though it was midday, and set the bowls on the outdoor table. He ate without calling either Yeshua or Mari to the table and then headed for the fields. When Yeshua found the porridge, he took one of the full bowls and set it at the entry to the house. He bent over the other bowl so far that his chin almost touched the rim and shoveled it in without sprinkling salt or adding dates.

I thought perhaps he'd miss our clinic hours that night, but Yeshua arrived before I did. He'd already lit the lamps, wiped the leaves and dust from the examining couch, and brought water from the cistern. I knew better than to ask, "How was your journey?" so I busied myself with a small fire in a brazier we'd built nearby for making decoctions and, in the winter months, for a way to warm our hands. Yeshua was twelve then; he'd been with me at the clinic only a few months and usually he was eager, bright. That night some anger or grief cloaked him like a birthing caul. I didn't ask.

Soon Asaph stumbled down the hill, this time with his walking pains. On the examining couch he pulled up his tunic so his legs were fully revealed, thin, veined sticks covered in scabs and scratches from all of his itching.

"I will get the calendula," Yeshua said quietly.

"Very good." I raised my voice slightly so he could hear my approval. "Get the lanolin as well, and a mixing pot. We need enough for both legs. And check the calendula for mold." We'd gathered the calendula at the end of the summer and mixed it with a small amount of oil, but if the jar lid wasn't tight enough, black mold could form, and the flower would do more harm than good.

"It still looks orange, Auntie."

"Good."

I mixed the thick, petaled oil with the lanolin to make a salve. Then I began the massage, beginning at the bottom of the foot and working my way up the leg. I showed Yeshua, as Rufus had shown me, how to work my thumb between the ridges of muscle, how to use the salve to gently soften the scabs and skin before digging into the deeper tissue. I worked all the way up his thigh and around to the muscles that connected his buttocks to his hip. Then I wiped my hands on a cloth and handed Yeshua the salve. "Now the left."

While Yeshua worked, I busied myself at the fire, breaking up mint and lavender for the tea that would help Asaph sleep. This gave Yeshua time to begin his own work without my eyes over his shoulder; he needed to find his own way into the body of the patient. But once the leaves and stems were boiling, I did return.

Yeshua's eyes were closed. He ran his fingers softly up and down Asaph's leg, finding the scabs with his fingertips; then he returned to certain places and pressed in with his thumb, but he didn't move it along the tissue as I had shown him. He pressed in a singular space, like checking a fruit for ripeness. Each time he did so, Asaph groaned—but it wasn't the sound he had offered at my touch, the protest of pain. It was as though the pressure of Yeshua's thumb opened Asaph's mouth and allowed the pain to come streaming out. Yeshua's thumb was still so small, the scabs dark islands in the golden light of the lamps. He went on this way for a long time, the tea bubbling behind us, the occasional bark of a wild fox cracking the night, until the tea had thickened to syrup and my own legs were weary from standing. When Yeshua was done with the pressing, he ran his hands along the tops of Asaph's legs in even, parallel strokes, not deep enough to alter the flow of pneuma at all—but I did not correct him.

We gave Asaph the tea and he sipped it quietly, all the words drained out of him. He pulled two prutot from a pocket inside his cloak and offered them to Yeshua. Then he stood and began to walk back toward town. For just a second I could see his retreating form in the lamplight, how his legs and arms moved together smoothly, how age seemed to have slipped from his skin.

When Asaph dissolved into the night, the strange golden richness of the moments of Yeshua's tending dissolved too, and irritation overtook me.

"Because your touching worked that way once, it doesn't mean it would work that way again."

"It's what he needed."

"Perhaps it felt that way to him in the moment. But the pain and itching come from the stifled flow of spirit in his veins. You have to use deep pressure in between those muscles, as I showed you, to get it flowing again."

Yeshua took out the rag and vinegar and began to clean the examining couch.

"Do you hear what I'm saying? It's dangerous to try an unproven treatment on a patient. Don't think because he walked away happily tonight that your way was right."

"Should we keep the lanolin and calendula?" He held up the bowl.

"You think that because your pressure was similar, was almost the same as mine, that the difference was negligible. The point of training is that you must do exactly as I say and exactly as I do so that when the difference is not negligible, the patient survives."

He bent over to sniff the bowl, dipped his finger in and ran a little of the salve over the top of his own hand. I wanted so badly to grab him by the ears and shake him senseless. But I remembered the look of terror in his eyes when he was little and had come to me in search of milk, when I'd thrown him back against the dirt floor. So I chose barbed words instead.

"Do you want to know how Rufus died?"

"Rufus?" He looked surprised, holding out the bowl of lanolin still. The sky was lightening, and somewhere behind us a warbler was taking up the dawn song.

"Rufus died because I thought that I knew everything. Because I hadn't prepared myself correctly. Because my tender feelings took over my physician's training."

"Rufus is dead?" Yeshua's eyes were glassy; he looked almost comatose. I ignored his absurd question because I was angry and I wanted to force this story down his throat. I wanted to push humility into him. So I told him about Rufus's death. How I couldn't stand my friend's pain, how I overdosed the body, how I refused to desecrate his remains. I offered him every excruciating detail: the welling up of blood, the shit that stained the operating table, the way, in the end, Rufus's eyes rolled up and only white emptiness stared back at me.

When I finished, he was quiet. We were quiet together in the light. Then I got up to tamp down the coals of the fire, rage replaced with exhaustion.

"I told them I was going to die," he said to the thin white light.

"What?"

"That's why Mama and Papa are so mad, why they won't speak to me."

"You told Mari and Josef you would die, and they are angry? Death is a fact of human life."

"I told the priests. In the temple. That I would die and that my death would mean something. Most of them turned away and laughed. But there was one who saw me, and he knew me, Auntie. He blessed me and wanted to keep me there."

I couldn't hear him, John Mark. Not the real words he spoke. All I heard was self-righteousness, all I heard was confidence beyond measure. And do you know what I said?

"Yeshua, you will die like the rest of us."

And he said, "Auntie, Rufus offered you a gift, and you did not receive it. There are other kinds of death."

38 CE

When she finishes, Salome looks at John Mark expectantly. Salome knows he will exclaim, with spittle flying, about Yeshua's foretelling, about the way he treated Asaph's injuries; most of all she expects John Mark to pepper her with questions about Yeshua's death.

But John Mark is not even looking at her. He is watching the plaza fill with bodies—most pressing into the theater. A man in an extravagant helmet sings a song on one corner, and vendors from other parts of the city have pulled their carts here today so that the whole area is thick with smoke and scent.

How did this happen? Salome wonders. Only seconds ago the plaza was sedate, ordinary.

John Mark hands her the drinking cup. "What are we going to do?" he asks.

"What?" asks Salome.

"The festival," says John Mark. "In the Quarter, they say over one hundred were taken yesterday to be tortured for entertainment today."

She sees the urgency in his face, but somehow that fear feels very far away from her. Her body will be used up soon anyway. It is not so precious to her. But Yeshua is precious, and she needs John Mark to be a receptacle, to take the ending of the story from her so that she can be free of that story and let Asha press her cheek against her own cheek, so that she can give herself to Asha without regret or shame. But this means she no longer has room in her mind for this present unfolding.

"Come to my study where it is quiet and hear the rest," she says. "Ask me your questions."

"You can do something," says John Mark. "You saved the ones in the room."

"I'm done being a physician now," says Salome. She lifts the fabric of her brown tunic as proof. "Didn't I tell you that?"

John Mark looks wounded. He has a kind of sadness in his eyes that looks dredged up from some unfathomable abyss, and Salome does not have the energy to look at his sadness or tend to it.

"Come and hear the story," she says, standing.

"I cannot," says John Mark.

Salome sighs. "Then I will write it down for you. I will have it delivered."

"What am I to do? If I cannot save them."

Salome regards him steadily. "Go and see."

Salome returns to her study and moves the flourishing basil from the windowsill. She waters the other plants and moves the marjoram into the sunshine, removes a few of the thumb-sized leaves that have gone yellow. She smooths one of the pages of the pharmacopeia that has come loose from the wall. She folds up the bedroll and moves John Mark's traveling cloak and bag into the cabinet; both, for some reason, smell of cardamom. She takes out parchment and ink well and begins to write:

Greetings to you, John Mark, from across the city in the Greek Quarter, greetings from the sight of the harbor, from the steps of the great library—ach. John Mark, you know I have no time for pleasantries. Here is the rest of it. I fear that without your questions steering my narrative it might swing off course. I do not, by my nature, always know what things to include. I see how your questions put skin and muscle around my tellings. I am grateful for that. I hope, in short, that you will know that however annoyed I was by your questioning, I was grateful for it. Questions are an indication of a sound mind. Rufus told me that. Or perhaps I told you that. Or maybe you told me that Peter the First bestowed that knowledge on you. The longer I live, John Mark, the more I think that wisdom has a way of snaking through us at the strangest moments, of letting itself be spoken and then slithering away again, leaving us as dumb as before. Maybe this is as close as I will ever come to a belief in gods. Maybe there is wisdom in this story. Maybe I can give it to you. I will try.

Josef had come to me in Alexandria, remember, beaten and torn and asking for me to fix things, to save Yeshua. And I, either out of stupidity or overconfidence or hope (I'm not sure which of those is the worst character flaw), said that I would do my best to help.

On the boat ride from Alexandria to Joppa, Josef and I practiced what we would say and how we would say it and before whom we would utter the words. Saving Yeshua, we determined, hinged on turning a substantial number of his followers away from him at a public moment. We imagined him standing on a wall, on a stage, on an overturned cart, and we imagined ourselves speaking the truth (valiantly!) beside him, and then we imagined everyone turning away. We imagined an emptying—of a plaza or a street corner or a marketplace or a hillside. Then he would be left, a sweating sage shaking pronouncements at the dry air. The Sadducees and Pharisees would cover their smiles; the Romans wouldn't think he was worth the exertion of a spear thrust in his direction.

Sometimes on that boat ride Josef would offer me a piece of food, a date or an almond, and he would place it in the center of my palm and wrap my fingers around the offering. As he had done that day beside the wall all those years ago. And sometimes, as we practiced, as we recited our words, he would take my wrist and press his thumb beside my vein there until he could find my heartbeat, and he would keep it there while I spoke and my voice became sure and calm. You are young, John Mark, and though we have not spoken of it, I assume a part of you hopes for passion. I wanted it, too, I did. Even then—but Josef gave me tenderness instead. And I let myself be tender.

It was also on the boat ride that we decided I should lie. Augustus's words on the scroll said I was free, said I was a renowned physician, granted me entrance to the library and a clinic of my choosing. But all the words were Latin, and Yeshua's followers could likely read Aramaic if they were lucky, a few Greek words if they were blessed. We decided I would say the scroll was a declaration of parentage, then Josef would confirm my claim, how I gave Yeshua to him and to Mari on a hill outside of Alexandria. We knew that in speaking these things we might save Yeshua—but in doing so the real certainty would be that each of us would lose the person we loved most. Neither Mari nor Yeshua would forgive us this betrayal. The more we practiced, the heavier the words became until they were nets we scraped along the bottom of the sea.

I had never been to Jerusalem. It did not possess Rome's high bearing or magnificence of architecture, nor did it imitate Alexandria's wide boulevards and even grid of streets or her airy sense of learning. In Jerusalem the whole city leaned toward the Temple Mount, a magnetic heart. A wall surrounded the Court of the Gentiles, and inside that was the Court of the Women and beyond that the Court of the Priests, and beyond that the Holy Place, and inside that a curtain, and on the other side of the curtain dwelt Yahweh, the god of the Jewish people. And though I did not believe in this god, I could feel in this city the belief of the people pressing toward the place. Or maybe I was still seasick and that was the lean I felt; truly, everything I say about my time in the city should be considered carefully, John Mark. I was in pain, and when a patient is in pain, as I have said, their understanding of the world is never trustworthy.

Yeshua was not in the temple or the marketplace. We did not find him on a plaza or preaching on one of the bald hills outside the city walls. It took us a whole day of walking and inquiry to find him; finally, as the sun retreated, we found him in the home of a wealthy widow. The room he occupied was pressed with followers, and many others filled the widow's small courtyard, sitting in clusters on traveling cloaks, eating or sleeping or muttering quietly. Some women worked hand looms on their knees, and others worked pestles around in large stone troughs of barley.

Josef and I elbowed our way into the room.

John Mark lets himself be pressed and carried by the bodies of the crowd into the theater. He sits at the end of one of the benches, one leg still on the ground, half his body ready to watch and the other half ready to bolt. Within minutes the theater is full and the entertainment begins. From an entrance on the other side of the theater comes first the insistent chirp of flutes and then the bodies of the six players, men who have wrapped their thighs in animal skins and strapped goat horns to their skulls. This band of satyrs quickly steps the perimeter of the theater; when they pass John Mark, he can see their lined eyes and the way their lungs pump to press air through the narrow hole of the instrument even as they dance. After one rotation the satyrs exit the theater and return with three Jewish men bound together with chains and three Greeks dressed only in loincloths, heroes of a local gymnasium. The Jewish men are affixed to a ring in the center of the theater, and the Greeks are led to a small stage on which sit three large baskets.

John Mark watches the stoning that follows. He keeps himself in the theater by leaning his upper body on his right thigh to prevent himself from sliding off the bench. He pays attention to the way at first the victims try to free themselves, to unfasten the chains, but how once the first Greek throws a stone they huddle together, covering their heads, pulling them low. One of the Jewish men begins to claw at the stones of the theater, as though he might be able to lift one up and use it as a shield. John Mark notes the oiled skin of the men on the stage, how they take their time, extending their left arms to mark their targets before throwing with their rights. How their hips swivel with each throw, how they pause momentarily after each release, arm outstretched, to follow the arc of the stone, how they form their living bodies into statues, how they stop themselves in this moment in time so the audience can rest their eyes on the beauty of their flesh. And they are beautiful. As the statues of Caligula are beautiful. And he watches the bodies of the Jewish men, how they quake like dry earth pelted with rain. John Mark watches the way two of the men try to get under the body of the third, like burrowing animals. He sees the way the third man lets them, the way he widens his own body to protect theirs.

When the men are finally dead the satyrs prance out again, the flutes replaced by drums so small the sounds pop inside John Mark's ear instead of thumping at his heart. The satyrs lift the gymnasia men onto their shoulders. The crowd roars. Meanwhile three buffoons enter, faces painted and donkey tails strapped to their asses, to remove the executed bodies.

"It is done," says John Mark.

The man next to him turns with a wide smile and slaps him on the shoulder. "No, no," he says, "it is only just beginning!"

Salome writes: The room Josef and I entered was divided into two parts. At one end, beautiful silk linens in rich colors had been laid over piles of straw to create stations for reclining. About ten men lay on the blankets, dining on trays piled high with figs and nuts and cheese. Yeshua was not among these men. I caught sight of Caleb propped up on his withered arm and then heard Asa's raspy cough. In the shadowed part of the room other followers sat and stood, facing the blanketed area as though observing a work of theater. The men on the blanket spoke loud enough for the others to listen. They talked about the prophecy being fulfilled, about whether the authorities would come, about who knew their whereabouts, about whether the governor would risk killing a Jewish prophet. Their faces wore cloaks of urgency and fear around their self-importance, and it is necessary, John Mark, to say that for these men, these first disciples, Yeshua's chosen ones, there had been nothing in their lives to prepare them for this moment of importance, for how to wield it. They were not eloquent or humble, but they should not be judged for that.

It wasn't until my eyes adjusted to the dark that I saw Yeshua, foot-washing bowl between his knees, lowering a follower's heel into the water. He did the washing quickly and moved on to the next person, never looking up into the face of the person he touched but staring at each foot as though it were a face—that is, a thing about the person worth seeing. As he worked his way through the dim portion of the room, I understood that these people weren't listening reverently to the men heaving predictions across silk blankets: they were waiting for Yeshua's touch. He made his way to me and somehow, John Mark, I thought he would know me instantly, the way I knew the whorl of hair behind his ear, the way he sat on his left leg and pulled his right thigh up against his chest when he squatted, the cluster of three pink spots on the back of his neck. But he did not look up at me or say my name or pay me more attention than anyone else. And though he washed my feet gently, I felt in that touch his dismissal in the Jordan.

In a few moments he would finally know I was his mother, and saying so would sever him from me for good. We say "a mother gives a child life" as though it happens once. But John Mark, a mother pushes her child into life again and again and again. Yeshua would not love me, but he would live. He had his calling, yes, but I had mine.

John Mark's eyes ache, though he cannot tell whether the pain is from exhaustion or from what he has seen. A poet enters the theater next and recites a long work that those who can hear find quite funny. On the other side of the theater, where John Mark sits, the crowd can make out only an occasional phrase and the waving of the man's arms. Many people leave to buy food from the vendors outside. By the time the satyrs escort the poet off the stage, the air around John Mark is curried with coriander and garlic and the tang of fish sauce. He hopes he will not vomit.

A group of six Jewish women are led out next. They avert their faces from the crowd, and though they are still clothed, their head coverings have been removed, their long dark hair undone. John Mark can feel their shame. With the women come a troupe of dancers; it is impossible to say how many. Some wear the horns of deer on their heads and others carry quivers of arrows strapped to their chests and grip bows one-handed. All of them bound and twirl and fly through the air, and then the hunter dancers begin to release arrows (ones that must be weighted and dulled at the tips—John Mark cannot tell, seeing only that they fly slowly in graceful arcs over the heads of the chained women) and the dancers dressed as deer catch these arrows, somehow, impossibly, and the crowd gasps and applauds, gasps and applauds. The oiled bodies of the dancers gleam and pulse with life. John Mark is so busy watching them that he doesn't notice the man in the bloodied apron until he is almost upon the women. He holds a piece of meat the length of his forearm, pink and marbled with fat. For a split second John Mark thinks it must be venison, so intent has he been on the leaping of the deer, but when the crowd takes up the chant, "Eat it, eat it," he understands that it is pork.

The butcher approaches the first woman in line, holds up the piece of flesh and jiggles it. The crowd roars, "Eat it, eat it," and the dancers continue to leap, to waft arrows over the line of women. The butcher grabs hold of the woman's hair, pulls her face up to that the crowd can see her lips pressed into a tight line, the shake of her head. John Mark expects the butcher to shove the meat into her mouth anyway, but he steps away from the woman, and instantly an arrow whistles into her chest and she folds over it. John Mark feels as though a fist has been pounded into his diaphragm, all of his air gone; the spectator beside John Mark sets his meat pie on his knee to pound John Mark on the back.

"I've seen this before. The real archer is below us."

John Mark nods.

"Are you ill?" asks the man. "The vendor just down the Water Way uses better cuts for his pies. Maybe you had a pie from the stand by the clinic? My cousin had one there a week ago and had the runs for three days. I've heard the man there just grinds everything together: entrails, eyes, bones, all of it." John Mark just shakes his head.

The second woman refuses to eat and is executed.

The man beside John Mark whistles. "I went to gymnasium with a fellow who had that kind of aim. It was something to see."

But John Mark is watching the third woman, who opens her mouth slightly, has the raw meat thrust between her teeth, receives the roaring benediction of the crowd, and is unchained by one of the satyrs and led past the entrance where John Mark sits, and is released. Free.

The woman stumbles to the crossroads fountain and cups handfuls of water into her mouth and spits it out again. Then she sinks to her knees and huddles there. Men standing in line to buy cups of barley beer elbow one another, raise eyebrows, and nod. But before they can pay their money and approach her, John Mark is there, lifting her up, escorting her toward the door of the clinic. But the caller will not let him in, and the patients in line under the turquoise awning revive enough to call the woman the words Caligula and Flaccus have given them: alien, foreigner. "Away," they say. "You are dirt, you are chaff, you are the redsweat of the water horse, the tainted clay that explodes inside the kiln."

And so John Mark forces the woman to walk, as quickly as she can, down the Water Way, away from the crowd. He does not know where they are going, where to go. "It is better to let me die," says the woman. "It is better to let me die."

Nadjem, who is not a Jew or a Greek, who has not slept for twenty-eight hours, who is leaving the clinic finally to return to her own quarter, to her own family, sees John Mark half carrying a woman who scrapes with her fingers at her tongue as if it were on fire.

When you are a physician, the line of patients is endless. Each day, when the awning is rolled up and the doors of the clinic are closed, Nadjem returns home, and while she eats her food and sweeps her floor, while she wrings out her indigo tunic in the water, her own people come to her with tooth rot and backaches, with the cough of linen fibers that clog their lungs, with infected cuts in their feet from stones in the bottom of the Nile, with fingers severed by the sharp knives they use to slice the papyrus. Salome once told Nadjem about a question she had asked her mentor, Rufus: "What do you do with a patient who refuses treatment?" How Rufus had explained that you find the hundreds of others who still need to be treated. Nadjem nodded appreciatively then, did not say, "This is a question and an answer rich people make." The question that follows Nadjem is: When do you stop treating patients? How do you close a door or close your eyes? There are patients in the Egyptian Quarter she should check on, and she would like to sleep and then eat honeyed sweets with her niece. But John Mark's face is twisted up with horror, and she knows that Salome would want her to help. Nadjem also knows her old friend will not make demands of her for much longer.

"John Mark!" she calls, and when he turns: "I know a place where you can go."

When Nadjem catches up to her the woman turns. "I think I would prefer to die," she says to Nadjem and looks her fully in the eye, and Nadjem understands what she means and what has happened. When they arrive at the wig shop, Asha understands, too. And the two women brush John Mark away and take the Jewish woman to the courtyard in the back. They warm water and they add lavender oil. "I need a mikveh," says the woman. Asha and Nadjem do not reply, but just as Asha did for Salome, they wash her hair, they sponge her neck, they apply unguents to her skin.

And John Mark knows that his job is to return.

After he finished washing Josef's feet, Yeshua took the bowl to the courtyard to empty it. When he returned, he took the lavish food tray and went outside again, although whether Yeshua offered the food to the followers sitting outside or threw it to the dogs, I can't be certain. He returned with bread and wine. A darkened loaf, a small amphora of posca—not the rich wine of celebration but the tart drink of poor Romans.

Yeshua squatted in the middle of the silk blankets and stared at the bread and wine for a long time. Everyone was quiet and still. After a while I thought perhaps he had fallen asleep. It was then that Josef took my hand, his thumb against my wrist, and together we took one step and then another until we came to the edge of the blanket, until our features were revealed in the light. Asa began to cough loudly, and Caleb simply said, "Not you." But I held my ground. And the disciples turned their attention to Josef's bruises and nodded amongst themselves as though his injury earned us the right to speak.

And finally Yeshua looked up from his position on the floor and saw me. And saw Josef. And he stood, still holding the bread, and stepped toward us and gazed at us.

And I opened my mouth. "I am—" I said. "I am—"

"This," he said, tearing off a piece of the loaf, "this is my body, and I give it to you." His words were so strange and the gesture so unexpected that I stilled my tongue. Josef let go of my wrist and I felt, again, how alone I was in the world. Yeshua fastened his eyes to mine. "This is my body," he said again, and I knew he was putting not just food but also Rufus's death, my greatest mistake, into the air between us. He held the bread not in front of my hands but in front of my lips, even though to place food directly into the mouth of a woman in front of all of these people was akin, in the world of Nazareth, to touching a naked breast. But he held it steady between us. "This is my body," he said. "Please receive this gift."

And that same hand that had grabbed me around the ribs in Alexandria, that same force opened my mouth and let him put the bread inside it. That same hand squeezed the tears out of me, like a weak woman, as I chewed, as I swallowed all of the words I had prepared to use to save him. "Do not be afraid, Auntie," he said to me then. "There are other kinds of death."

Then he offered a piece of bread to Josef, and Josef fell to his knees to receive it.

John Mark returns to the stadium, where the Greek spectator has been kind enough to reserve a sitting space with his meaty hand. John Mark watches a man burned with green wood. He watches a man crucified on a pole, both hands nailed together above his head, legs broken and then nails pounded through his anklebones. John Mark watches a battle in which a handful of Jewish men are given the leg bones of pigs to defend themselves against young Greek boys who are proud to wield swords almost half their height. "That one's mine. He's mine," says the Greek man beside John Mark. "The redhead." And John Mark watches the red-haired boy push back the helmet that falls into his eye and runs toward three of his friends, who have managed to get one of the Jewish men on the ground. He raises his sword with considerable awkwardness and brings the blade down onto the man's ankle just as one of his friends stabs the man's neck. The Greek man leans forward, squeezing his own knees as his son swings; he claps when the son manages to bring a gush of blood. The Greek man grips John Mark's shoulder and asks, "He will be tired later, won't he?"

And John Mark lets the Greek man see his face.

The man draws his hand away and looks at John Mark with disgust. "Well," he says, "you are a physician."

The stones are swabbed clean and the crucified man is lowered and the burnt wood is swept away and then the satyrs return, this time playing horns that curl, each in a half spiral, and they make a procession, a mock announcement of royalty. And in this way the elders are led in.

I left the room before I had even finished swallowing the bread. Outside, night had fallen and some of the followers had built small fires in the courtyard. There was scarcely room to step between the bodies, and I realized then that I was in a strange city where I knew no one; there was nowhere for me to go. On the other side of the courtyard I watched women exit through a small gate, and I followed them into the courtyard of the house next door. There were fewer people here, mostly women and children, and the windows of this house radiated light and song.

I walked into that house, that neighboring house of song and light, completely numb. It was much warmer in the room than outside and the air was thick with a scent I didn't recognize at first; there was myrrh and sandalwood, but also it was, I realized, the scent of gathered women. Not since the cart in Rome had I been this close to a group of women. And then, the scent of us gathered together had been horrible. This was something different, rising dough and coals wet down with water and hair oil and wild oregano.

A woman embraced me when I entered, and she did so without stopping the song she sang; I felt the vibrations in her chest when she pressed her breasts against mine. She offered me a bowl and a fist-sized rock and nodded toward a table in the center of the room piled with a variety of herbs, with bowls of lanolin and beeswax and an amphora of olive oil. Along one wall a group of women sat with a linen sheet between them, each bent over a different section with needle and thread. And it was then that I recognized the song: the one Mari had sung to Yeshua when he was small, the one that asked the listener what he would bring on the journey to the promised land. And I understood, then, that we were making the preparations for Yeshua's death: the shroud to wrap him in, the unguents and musks and ointments for his lifeless skin. And there, on the other side of the room, was Mari in a chair (I had never, in all our life together in Nazareth, seen her in a chair), and on her lap was a bowl. And I watched as the women came and poured what they had ground in their small bowls into Mari's larger one while Mari stirred, seasoning the burial balm with her stupid, ceaseless tears.

Feeling found me then, John Mark. Rage. Rage at Josef, for not saying anything in that room when it became clear that I could not, for dropping my wrist as Yeshua held up the bread, for lowering himself to the floor after being offered the bread, for his stupid submission. Rage at Yeshua, for using Rufus, for putting Rufus's body, my memory of that shame, into that bread. Rage at Mari, for her utter lack of resistance, for making herself the queen of motherly grief. But mostly I felt rage at myself, the same rage I had felt in Alexandria when I turned around, when I followed my infant son to Nazareth, rage at my own weakness.

And so I walked directly to Mari, and when I stood before her she raised her face to me, and John Mark, she wept and smiled at once, both emotions so hard and bright that it was like someone slamming two rocks together, sparks flying. "Salome," she said, "it is good and right that you should be here." And she reached out her hand.

I put my empty bowl into it, and I said, "You did this. These trappings of the grave belong to you. His death belongs to you."

And then I went back to the courtyard, and I found a corner and I threw my traveling cloak around myself and pulled up my knees like a petulant child until I became the smallest version of myself. And once the rage bled away and my breathing returned, I saw the truth that remained: All these years I had worked, trying to claim Yeshua as my own, trying to be the better mother. And what had I done? I had taught him some useful things about medicine, perhaps, but also I had brought injury and fever upon him, tried to tempt him away from what he loved, and then failed to save him from death when I could. The truth was that the only good thing I had really ever done as a mother was to give my son to Mari.

The elders are stripped before the crowd. No longer are they Judah and Levi and Elisha and Benjamin and Eleazar and Zeloph. Now they are the one with the bowed legs, the one with the concave chest, the one whose wisps of gray hair cover his shoulder blades like wings. They are the one who falls to his knees after the first blow, the one who covers his face with his hands, the one who dies after the seventh blow because the scourger strikes too close to his head. They are the ones whose flesh, unearthed by the pieces of metal wound into the leather strips, becomes airborne, they are the ones whose screams become prayers and then grunts and then mewls and then nothing. They are the ones who are ground into nothing.

The Greek man leans toward John Mark. "This was supposed to be the best part of the festival, but they're so old." And then he reaches with his index finger and thumb into a pouch of spiced nuts, moves them side to side until he finds a choice one, coated more fully in cumin. He pops it into his mouth. "It doesn't take as long as you'd hope."

John Mark leaves the theater. It turns out he is not a person who can watch. Or at least, he cannot watch it all. He doesn't know if this makes him sane or makes him a coward, or both.

I watched as much of Yeshua's crucifixion as I could. I will tell this part matter-of-factly. It is the only way I can tell it.

I woke in the courtyard the following morning still certain I had failed to be a mother to my son. I found out he had been arrested while I slept, but I followed the others to the trial. Stood inside a crowd that roared for his death. Saw the way the Jewish governor wore his robes in the Roman style. I saw Yeshua scourged. I saw him heft that beam onto his shoulder. Then for a long time he was lost in the crowd. But I followed him and watched, as I walked, for stones marked with his blood. I made myself look.

Where was Mari? Where was Josef? At the front of the crowd, buoyed by Yeshua's followers. I was a woman without a people, without a family. Many people fell away when we reached the gates of the city; curiosity pulled them only so far. They had meals to make, jobs to return to, children to tend. Perhaps a hundred people went onward.

When we reached the hill where they would raise the crosses, the crowd was even smaller. I saw Mari and Josef and the handful of men they called Yeshua's disciples nestled together at the base of the slope, and I found a place near to them. We could not see Yeshua then. He was above us; he was being forced to press his back to the beam, but this we could only imagine. We heard the sharp ring of the first nail pounded into his wrist and his scream, and Mari's scream followed his, answered his, and she fell to the ground. I know this because the rest of them fell away from her, stepped back, even Josef. To let her have her grief, I suppose. I suppose it was reverence. I suppose they meant respect. The second nail rang out and there was his howl and hers, and she took up dirt and pressed it into her face, her mouth, and then she began climbing the hill, like an animal, on all fours, and they watched. They could not see Yeshua, and so everyone watched her and did nothing.

She did not know, John Mark. She did not know until that moment that he would die. And suddenly she knew. And her grief was wild in her limbs.

And so I went to her. I got down on my knees and I draped myself over her, I pressed my breasts to her back, and I wrapped my hands around her hands and lifted them from the earth. I pulled her back until she was resting against me and wrapped our left arms around her belly and our right arms across her chest, and when the final pounding came (it took three swings of the hammer to drive the nail through his feet), she opened her mouth and took the flesh of my forearm into her and she bit and screamed her grief into my skin.

Then they pulled the ropes and raised the cross so we could see him. The twitching of his hands. The lolling of his head side to side to see, trying to clear the blood from his eyes. The way he tried to stand on his wounded feet so he could pull air into his lungs. The thin skin of his chest. His sweet, beautiful ribs.

And then the followers went to him, edged themselves farther up the hill, tried to place themselves in his gaze. And I saw him, dying, and finding them with his eyes, each person who came, though I could see what it cost him to look. He had nothing left to give them and still he gave them this intimacy. And the followers turned away from the cross carrying what he had given them. I saw that, too. And I saw him bestow words on his disciples, though I could not hear what he said.

Then he closed his eyes and he was dying but he was not dead and time lolled onward. And many left, satisfied that they had seen his death. I understood. I did not fault these people. I wanted to leave every minute I was there. By early afternoon there were perhaps twenty of us left. Some people shared bread, talked in low tones. I could see them begin to lose themselves in conversation and then look up and remember where they stood. Mari moved off my lap, but we stayed there, in that place, sometimes squatting, sometimes sitting, sometimes kneeling. Sometimes one of us fell asleep upright and woke with the weight of her own head pulling her to earth. I saw Josef with the others, but even he did not come near.

And then the wind came. It stirred the tops of the trees and then sank lower, pulling up the dust and tiny rocks of that hillside and throwing all of it into our mouths, our noses, the tender corners of our eyes. And then the rest of them left, to seek shelter near the face of rock where the tomb was hewed that we would lay him in. They held out their arms and the wind caught their cloaks and pushed them like ships toward a harbor.

Mari and I stayed. We pulled each other up until we huddled at the base of the cross. We heard the Romans curse as the wind overturned their jug of wine, as it sent their dice scattering, as it pushed the beams of each of the three crosses together so that they screeched. There was a gust of wind then, so big that Mari and I stood and used our own bodies to keep the cross from toppling. And after this gust the Romans soldiers gave in—it would be bad for the crosses to topple in the night. They took them down to save face; they took them down to avoid another trip to Golgotha in the morning.

But just before that final gust that made them change their minds there was a moment of stillness. The wind hushed and lay down. The soldiers wiped their eyes; one scrambled toward the back of the hill where the wind had blown Yeshua's cloak around a shrub. In this quiet Mari and I looked up at him, at his eyes, bruised in their sockets, at the crust of blood caked on his left cheek, at the yellow swelling at his jaw. He opened his eyes as much as they allowed and he drew in enough breath, thin little pants, to say to us: "This is your son." And then he gave his gaze to each of us in turn. And when he looked at me it was the moment in the Jordan, not when he dismissed me, but the moment just before, when he had held me in the chaos, when he had told me I was worthy. But this time, in the stillness at the base of the cross, he said instead, to Mari and to me: "Look. This is your mother."

*

And then came the final gust of wind that made us press our faces to the wood and wrap our arms around each other and the beam that held him. And after that the soldiers undid from the cross a body they were certain was dead and offered Yeshua to us.

*

John Mark leaves the theater and washes himself at the fountain. The water tastes impossibly good on his tongue. It seems a miracle that he can swallow, that he can feel coolness against his neck, that he can walk on two good legs. No one pays him any mind. Men slurp the foam off barley beer and fan the vendor's cooking smoke away from their faces. Boys fill amphoras at the spigot and flick the water at one another. Though the plaza is busier with festival goers, there are still servants lifting loaves of bread in the bakeshop to see which bottoms are scalded, there are still women fingering necklaces that hang from nails on the jeweler's open door. Men exiting the baths touch their clean-shaven faces, and a small crowd gathers around a juggler who throws eggs high and higher into the air. From the theater a roar goes up and almost no one turns toward the sound. What is happening inside the theater is not happening here, less than a hundred feet away, just as what is happening in the New Jewish Quarter does not touch the Royal Quarter, the Egyptian Quarter, the Greek Quarter. How many times in his life before this moment has he been steps away from agony and terror and simply not known? Or heard the roar but chosen to ignore it?

John Mark's traveling bag, safe in Salome's study, contains enough money for his return to Jerusalem. The First Followers would welcome him back and he could stay in the city, living in their community, occasionally sent to proclaim a story he cannot seem to keep fastened on his tongue. But the questions, the ones that hounded him and haunted him—they have disappeared.

Or he could go to the harbor and he could find a boat going almost anywhere. It is the beginning of the month of Tishrei, and sailing weather will be good for at least a few weeks longer. He could go to Rome or to Tarsus, Troy or Ephesus.

Instead he walks back to the New Jewish Quarter. Past the abandoned homes, the half-opened doors, the alabaster dove. Inside the Quarter everything is quieter. People move slowly, cautiously, bringing small things to help one another: rags, oil, water. In the synagogue where John Mark preached five days earlier, some men sleep on the benches while others talk in groups in hushed tones. Wavery light drifts down from the round hole in the ceiling. The rabbi sits in his chair, and it seems strange that neither he nor the chair are damaged, though that of course is not entirely true. A scroll rests in the rabbi's lap, and he stares at it, the tip of his index finger stroking his lips.

"Peace to you," says John Mark.

The rabbi looks up. "You are the one who preached to us. About the messiah from Jerusalem."

"Yes," says John Mark. And he sits down then, beside the rabbi, and he does what he has never done before, even to his father: he lets his head fall gently against the rabbi's knee.

"Are you here to preach again? It is a difficult crowd today." The rabbi makes a hollow laugh, but he places his hand tenderly on John Mark's head. "Your savior banished death itself. Isn't that right?"

"Perhaps."

"Perhaps?"

"I don't know," says John Mark, and it is then that he begins to weep. He clings to the robes of the rabbi who is not his father but somehow smells of his father. And he sobs for all that he has done and left undone, all the bodies he has seen in the last days: broken and beaten, healed and bandaged, wailing and singing. And the rabbi strokes his head.

"We are lucky then," the rabbi says, "that Adonai takes on the knowing for us. Maybe today you do not need resurrection. Maybe you need the God who lifted up the curtains of the Red Sea with His mighty hands, who makes a way, who is always making a path for us to freedom."

"Tell me that story, please," says John Mark.

The rabbi lifts his hand away. He points a single finger toward a few men who have entered bearing straps and rope and a small cart to move the statue of Caligula. He points toward a woman who has just begun to wash a scorch mark from the wall. He points toward men in the corner who divide up provisions to deliver. "Let us clean our house and help our people," says the rabbi, "and then we'll have a story." John Mark takes the scroll tenderly from the rabbi's lap and places it onto the shelf below the seat of the chair. Then he stands and helps the rabbi to his feet.

※

Salome writes: I have rested a little, John Mark, and put a little mint on my tongue. I have an illness in my mind, John Mark. A forgetting. I think you know this by now, but it is important to write it here, to have it known. I do not want my story doubted, but I am still physician enough to want to offer you all of the facts. Right now I can hold your face in my mind, your close-set eyes, your little encouraging head nods while I speak. I have put your traveling cloak into my lap because the smell reminds me of you; I realize you have had the scent caught on you all along but muffled by other things. My mother still is lavender, and Yeshua is cedar, Asha is water lily, Nadjem is sandalwood, and now you are cardamom. I have known you for only five days and you have a scent. I do not know what this means.

I know I left you in some kind of darkness, but I do not remember what. And I am sorry if my leaving caused you trouble. I am sorry if my future leaving causes you trouble or these pages cause you trouble. There is a boy here who sits on the landing and fetches me things. I am grateful for him but do not remember him. He says he is from Philo's house and promises he will help me home. He says he knows you and will deliver these pages. I hope this boy will find you and you will know how to use them.

This was not a story I wanted to tell. And I will not lie and say that I needed to tell it. Humans need food and water and pneuma coursing through their veins. Occasionally help from other people, I suppose. Although I did not want or need to tell you this story, John Mark, I will also say that five days ago I could not look my future in the face, and now I can. Whatever that means. Ach. I have told you I am not good with the curled words of stories.

Maybe all I mean to say is that I am ready, now, to go home.

I have only one more thing to tell you if you will hear it.

The disciples carried Yeshua's body to the grave. They brought supplies so Mari and I could wash him and anoint him, could wrap his body in the shroud. Josef and a few of the disciples made a makeshift tent and slept outside. They didn't know he still lived, didn't think to check. But as soon as she touched him, Mari knew. His body did not stiffen, his wounds still oozed blood, and when she pressed her hand against his chest, she felt his heart.

She held her hand there, John Mark, on his body and she looked at me. "Save him," she said.

How can I explain the tone of those words? Not a command. Not desperation. It was the voice of a mother stating her most basic desire. She bent and found my medicine case in my bag and handed it to me. "Save him."

I was his mother, too; of course I wanted Yeshua to live. And I wanted to be the one to save him, to vex the Fates, to thrust clean breath into his lungs and bind his broken legs and knit torn skin. Ever since I'd sat upon that rocky ridge outside of Alexandria, squeezing my milk uselessly into that clay-made drinking cup, ever since my body had failed to sustain him, I had been waiting, wanting him to need me. And now, finally, he did. The process of healing would be difficult, I knew, but occasionally there were those who survived a crucifixion. All of my training, everything I'd learned in Rome, in Nazareth, in Alexandria had readied me for this. I opened my medicine case.

And when I did, a brief, hard glint of brightness struck my eye. Reflected, surely, off a blade or hinge or glass ointment jar. And in that dumb, strange flash of light, what I remembered was the small white bit of bone I had glimpsed when I crouched with Rufus above the Seizing Man: how in that moment I knew my purpose, how I had bathed that wound with tears because all the wayward things about me suddenly felt right and good. John Mark, although it sounds like a story as thin as any myth, I tell you truly: when that light pierced my eye, I understood my son. Not his god love, not his parable riddles, not his vision of a kingdom of righteousness, but his singularity of purpose. Because I know what it feels like to make a home inside a calling, John Mark. I know how it feels to be certain you will disturb the world.

I loved my son before, but in that moment I knew him, and I knew that if I stood in the way of who he was meant to be, I would deliver an injury worse than death.

So I gave Mari the task of washing the blood from the wounds on his feet. And while she did so I took from my medicine case the henbane and mandrake. ("That's murder," I heard Rufus saying, and I nodded to his memory and continued on with steady hands.) I poured a little of each medicine into the mortar and ground them into dust. I added milk. And because Yeshua was not strong enough to drink, I dipped my fingers in that bowl and let the liquid dribble into his mouth. Again and again, I fed my son. Thirty-four years after his birth, Yeshua finally took the milk I offered him.

Mari thought that I was doing my best to save him, and I did not tell her otherwise.

When I was done, I helped her wash the rest of his body. I bandaged the wounds. And we waited.

I waited for him to die and she waited for him to live, and at some point we slept, holding our son between us.

38 CE

The Broom Boy walks close enough to Salome that if she falls, he will catch her. Without her indigo tunic and tight headscarf she looks softer, he thinks. He was a little afraid of her in the upstairs room of Philo's house, of her spotted face and her quick tongue, but also he could tell she was one of those adults who saw the world in a very clear way and expected others to follow suit.

But he can see now, as they walk, that Salome is missing one tooth and the others are yellow in color. She is the same woman, but all of her points are dulled somehow. Gray hair sways around her head and she limps, one hand cupping her right hip. The skin of her face sags instead of stretches, and her mouth hangs open slightly. Spittle gathers at the right corner of her lips. Moments ago, just outside the study, Salome had been sharp again, placing papers into a satchel and asking him to describe John Mark three times so she could be certain that he would deliver the papers to the right person. But now, moments later, this other version of Salome is not certain about where she lives. And so he has to ask her to describe the house, the smells of the street. He asks whether it is near the East Gate or the West Gate, the library and harbor, or the gymnasia and small theaters?

They walk down one street and then another, stopping for water at small fountains, and he sees that she is growing more tired. This makes him uncomfortable. She has promised to give him money and food when they arrive, but until then they are lost and hungry.

It is a man pushing a wheelbarrow of half-dead fish who finally rescues them. "Salome!" he exclaims, "look at my perch! From the Nile this very morning, destined to be your dinner tonight." He wipes his brow and wiggles the cart slightly, ostensibly to make it look as though the fish are swimming, although they are most certainly not. Salome looks at him blankly and then at the fish, and the man bends closer to her, pushes his sweating face into hers until she takes a step backward. "Those fish are diseased," she says.

"Ah!" says the man. "That's the spirit."

"Nicodemus," Salome says, her voice like a bird alighting on the branch.

"Let's take you home so that you can put my fish directly into sauce."

"I will not buy your fish," she says, but now she is smiling a little in recognition. Nicodemus leads them gently home, chiding her a little as they go, until she falls into perfect step beside him.

The sound of Nicodemus's voice brings Salome back to herself and she remembers: the story is complete, it has been expelled from her body and stuffed into the satchel the Broom Boy carries. It will sail away with John Mark on a ship to elsewhere. How her words are used is none of her concern. Her only concern now is Asha, who appears like magic before her, bent over her blanket of pins and clasps. The hair of the Girls sparkles today with combs: emerald, pearl, lapis lazuli. Salome does not hear Nicodemus say, "I'm off then," doesn't notice as he sloshes his way onward, humming an off-key tune.

Asha looks up then and half smiles, as though Salome is neither a strange nor an unwelcome sight. "There you are," she says, and after she casts her eyes back to an errant pin, "Have you finished in the New Jewish Quarter, then?"

This is the time, Salome knows, to say, "I have chosen you. I am ready to be with you completely." It is time to tell Asha what happened in the New Jewish Quarter. It is time to collapse inside Asha's embrace. Time to rest her hand on Asha's warm belly, to run her fingers along the crease of Asha's thigh, time to let her breath warm the back of Asha's neck. Salome has scrubbed herself raw for this moment, but she has never actually considered what it is that she will do or say that will convey her new intentions to Asha.

She stutters toward Asha and stops on the other side of the bench, the spread of pins and clasps between them. Her hands suddenly feel absurd; she cannot remember how a regular person holds their hands. Folded in front? Clenching the sides of the tunic? And her tongue feels like one of Nicodemus's dead perch. She forces herself to lift it, to touch the ridge of her teeth.

Asha inclines her head slightly toward Salome and looks at her with concern. "What is it?" she asks. Her wig is made of coarse black hair rolled up into a high Livia knot at the top of her head. Two tendrils of hair frame her face, but the wind has tucked one of the strands behind her ear.

Salome raises her hand to bring the thin curl of hair forward, a gesture she repeated a dozen times a day for Julia: a simple thing, one small intimacy.

But it is so heavy, her hand. And trembling. It hangs over the dark blanket of pins like a dumb, naked branch. Why can't she move it farther? Why can't she say, simply, what she feels?

Asha becomes very still. She watches Salome's hand, too, with the same stupid hope she has carried for ten years. But when Salome's left hand reaches up and pulls the shaking right hand back to her chest, Asha doesn't wait; she folds the blanket and carries it back inside.

The Broom Boy is relieved when Salome finally drops her hand and the two women turn to go inside—though even he can feel the wake of sadness that trails them.

At the back of the house, in a sleeping room with a single cot, two stools, and a table, a different woman, much younger, hair in a soft plait down her back, studies a game board with black and white pieces and sips from a cup of barley beer.

"Who is this, Asha?" asks Salome, taking a step back into the hall. She looks at the Broom Boy and then at Asha with a guilty expression, as though she has forgotten something important.

"This is Sarah," Asha says gently. "John Mark brought her here today. I am teaching her our game. She is getting quite good. Come"—and even the Broom Boy can tell that the wig seller sounds much more exhausted than she did ten paces away, in the courtyard—"I will get you a drink and you will play with her next."

How is it, Salome wonders, that already I have been replaced? As though in the walk from the front courtyard to the sleeping rooms, Asha had time to conjure a new companion. But perhaps this Sarah is the companion Asha deserves. And so Salome offers Sarah something that approaches a smile. "You are welcome here." Then she turns to Asha. "Tonight I am going to rest. Perhaps tomorrow we will have the game." Then Salome says, slowly and carefully: "You should let this Sarah help you with your undressing."

Asha looks as though someone has punctured her, all of the pneuma coursing out of her. She sets a hand against the doorway to steady herself.

The Broom Boy is hungry. And he is tired of this strange adult pantomime. As Salome turns her back on Asha and Sarah he says loudly, "I am ready now," a phrase which he immediately regrets.

But Salome ignores him. Instead she crosses the hall into a room with two cots, one with a sheet hung above it. Salome sits on one cot and begins to unlace her sandal; the Broom Boy feels a severe pinch on his upper left arm.

"And who are you?" Asha's face is defensive and fierce, close enough that the Broom Boy can see a few stiff whiskers on her upper lip, the way the pores are wider at the edges of her nose.

"I helped her home," he says defensively. "I have papers to deliver on her behalf. But she promised me food and coins."

Asha lifts his chin to look more closely at his face. "Are you from the New Jewish Quarter?"

And the Broom Boy knows it is a dangerous question, but he thinks of Salome pulling his arm, forcing him into the street in the middle of the riot, telling him to be brave. Behind Asha he sees Sarah looking at him with interest and she reminds him; there is something in her face, like the servant girl, some kind of hurt that wants to be acknowledged. "Yes," says the Broom Boy.

Asha's face immediately softens. "I see," she says. "Then we will get you sorted."

Across the city, in the New Jewish Quarter, John Mark stands behind a small table in the synagogue where he spoke five days earlier. A line of people snakes around the perimeter of the room and as each person comes forward, John Mark pours a cup of grain into the proffered bowl or plate or cup. The rabbi dozes in a chair nearby.

John Mark has been standing at this table for three hours, but he does not feel tired. When the line abates, he has promised to help sweep the street and then to use his physician's tunic to fetch medicine from a different part of the city.

He knows that in her study in the great library, Salome is finishing the rest of the story that he was so hungry to hear. When the Broom Boy brings him the pages, John Mark decides, he will not read them. He is as hungry for the ending of a story as anyone, of course, and he has a strange affection for Salome. Part of him wants to know where she stood when Yeshua was crucified, what it felt like to wash the grave dust from the Messiah's limbs.

But he finds that he cannot believe that the telling of the Resurrection is the most important story to tell. It feels too much like swirling magic smoke into the air. For centuries his people have been telling the story of the Exodus, of how a whole people survived illness and violence, how they escaped the persecution of a vengeful leader. When he is very still it is not Peter the First who comes to him, not the image of Yeshua feeding the people with crumbs of bread or even Salome's story of fevered Yeshua in the mikveh; no, what arrives is the moment in the Red Sea, water washed up into walls, a group of people moving to safety together. It is within that story that John Mark feels a kind of thundering promise. And anyway, he is a better listener than a talker.

There is medicine to fetch and streets to clean and people to feed; he will tell the story with the actions of his life rather than the words of his tongue.

When's Salome's pages come, he will give them to someone who is ready.

Meanwhile, the Broom Boy stands in the doorway of Salome's room, bread and barley beer thickening his belly, waiting to be paid so that he can deliver the satchel of papers to the nervous man with the close-set eyes.

Salome has been fiddling with one of her sandal ties, trying to unknot it without actually looking at it. She stares at something in the center of the room. The Broom Boy is too tired to guess at what kind of vision she's having.

He cannot hear the lap of the sea or feel Salome's father's hand on her head, pushing her below the waves so the gods will not see her hubris. He doesn't feel the burn of salt on the inside of her nostrils, the gag at the back of her throat.

Maybe her father did understand, thinks Salome. Not her hubris in imitating the gods, not her belief that she might change the world—Salome regrets none of that—but her arrogance in thinking she could armor herself against the world and then understand anything about tenderness or intimacy. Salome is certain that she loved Yeshua as best she could, but loving Asha seems to require a softness, a vulnerable underbelly she does not possess or that she has forgotten how to reveal.

There is a gentle tug on her foot, and Salome lets the boy take it. The knots are tight and her fingers are tired. Her wrists are tired. The muscles around her mouth are tired. Her hip aches. She gives herself over to the memory of the sea.

In the doorway, the Broom Boy lets the satchel scrape against the doorframe. The sound startles Salome into seeing that it is Asha on the floor before her, loosening the tie, unwrapping the bands of leather from her ankle. Still, Salome cannot raise her tongue to say the necessary words, cannot remember what those words might be.

The Broom Boy clears his throat. "Am I to go then?" he asks. And he shakes the satchel for emphasis.

And then Salome knows what to do. Such a simple thing, really. Like realizing in the middle of drowning that the water is shallow enough for you to stand.

Salome does stand then, one foot bare and one foot with sandal tie flapping, and walks to the Broom Boy, slips the satchel off his shoulder, and presses three coins into his palm. "Go in peace," she says in Aramaic, the words coming to her quickly, easily, although the Broom Boy knits his brow quizzically. "It means 'Go with Adonai,'" Salome explains, and the Broom Boy shrugs, flashes them both a smile, and is gone, tightening his grip around the coins, the most money he has ever held at once.

Salome eases through the pain in her hip to a seated position next to Asha. She takes the pages from the satchel and with shaking hands places them in Asha's lap.

Salome studies Asha's thin fingers, the bridge of her nose, the arch of her perfectly plucked brows, the shadow of her long lashes in the sweet shallows below her eyes. It is Asha before her and also Yeshua; this is a room in Alexandria and also a room in Jerusalem, tender hands on her feet and tender hands on her feet. She has spent so much time keeping these moments apart from one another when, she realizes now, they were always meant to live together, side by side.

Asha studies the flurry of black scrawl across the parchment. She knows this gesture means something to Salome, but she cannot read Greek, doesn't understand why Salome's breath comes so heavily.

"This is my story," Salome explains, and the words are quiet, barely a breath. Asha has to lean close to Salome to hear them.

"I am—" says Salome, and she looks at Asha and all of her veils and guards and hardness are gone. "I am—" she says again, and emotion closes her throat, pours out of her eyes.

Asha puts her hands on either side of Salome's face. "Oh beloved," she says, "I know who you are."

Then Asha rests her body on the floor, her head on Salome's thigh, her hand cupping Salome's knee. And Salome eases the wig off Asha's head, uses the tips of her fingers to trace the almost invisible divots in Asha's skull.

"I know you," says Asha again, "but tell me your story anyway."

And Salome begins: "I was born on a cliff overlooking the Ionian Sea …"

It is the first day of the festival, the third day of the riots. In a few weeks, Flaccus will be ousted from his governor's seat. He will be the one to run and hide and cower. A few months after that, Philo will travel in a delegation to Rome to argue for the freedom of his people. Two years later, when Caligula tries to insert a statue of himself in the Temple in Jerusalem, Herod Agrippa will intervene on behalf of the Jews, imperiling his own life. The scent of bergamot will return to Agrippa, and the image of a green rind, unwinding, but he will not remember where the memory comes from; he will know only that it is his turn to do what is right.

Now Egyptian boys climb the high lamps, torches between their teeth. Day and night declare a truce, soften toward one another, and touch heads. The sky is dark enough that the lighthouse flame is visible, but not so dark that it steals the light from everything else.

In the Jewish Quarter, John Mark sweeps together shards of pottery and glass; the whole street is filled with these teetering mounds. It is a strange thing, he thinks, to find hope in a pile of dust.

In the Egyptian Quarter, Nadjem lets her niece choose which figure they will put at the center of their altar, lets the girl light the bundle of juniper and papyrus. They lie together on the cot and the niece tells Nadjem about cloaking herself in mud, how she survived the visit of an angry god.

The Broom Boy walks down the Canopic Way. He is twelve years old, and it does not occur to him that he could remain outside the Jewish Quarter, that he could make another life more safely elsewhere. His father died when he was young, and his mother made a small sum by selling him to Philo to be a servant in his house. Philo is a distant sort of man but never cruel. He has taught the Broom Boy to read and sometimes lets him organize the scrolls or press the metal seal into the melted wax. He gives the boy clean hay on which to sleep, enough food to eat, and on festival days the freedom to wander the streets of Alexandria with a coin to buy a sweet.

For the first time, the Broom Boy has three coins in his pocket, and so as he walks, although he does not consider going anywhere else, he does feel the weight of those three coins and he wonders what it would be like to have two more, or ten. What that weight would feel like, who he might become.

On the rooftop of his house, Philo chants the ceremony of the dead while pulling his scrolls from their roosts of pigeon shit. He lets himself weep continually, for his cowardice, for the man wrapped in a shroud beside him, for Judah and Levi and Elisha and Benjamin and Eleazar and Zeloph. It is impossible to think about returning to his essay about cherubim. To his musings on sacrificial postures or the tilt of the heavens or the life of Moses.

And then there is a boy beside him. Gently moving him aside. The sweet boy with the harelip, to whom he has been teaching Greek. The boy reaches into the dovecote and does not flinch as the birds peck at his wrists.

"What will you write now?" he asks Philo, as though Philo does not have tears running down his cheeks, the scent of bird shit all over him, blood speckling his tunic.

"What will I write?" he says, uncomprehendingly.

The Broom Boy hands Philo the scroll he has retrieved and then reaches his hand in again. One of the doves lets him touch, for a sweet second, the softness of her belly.

"You should write this story," says the Broom Boy. "The riots. Flaccus and the statues and how they dressed that beggar as Agrippa."

"I don't write histories," says Philo, exhaustion edging his words.

The Broom Boy shrugs and brushes some of the dried bird shit from the parchment before him. "How else does anyone remember?"

"Judah and Levi and Elisha and Benjamin and Eleazar and Zeloph," says Philo.

Now it is the Broom Boy's turn to be confused.

"Those were their names," says Philo. And he sees the way that grief and guilt and regret will rise up around him but how telling this story might be a way through.

The world darkens. Lamps are extinguished. Children are soothed into dreams. By the Nile the papyrus whispers its strange and shivering song. The wind swirls the hair of the wigs, Asha's Girls, into knots that will need to be undone in the morning.

Asha sleeps in the cot below the cedar shavings. Salome rests on her own cot, coverlet pulled to chin, the steady breath of her beloved beside her. If she raises her chin and closes her eyes, she can still find the scent of cedars. Finally, thinks Salome, it is done.

Salome closes her eyes.

EPILOGUE

It is morning when she wakes, the mist like a fabric in the process of being torn. Mari's hand still rests on Salome's hand, but the slab on which they laid Yeshua's body is cold beneath Salome's forearm.

Salome walks out into that woolly light. Periwinkles blanket the ground and hillside, the purple blooms stretching a path all the way back to the city gates. In the distance, Salome can see two, perhaps three, figures moving in the direction of the tomb. Although she has not eaten in hours, the sweet flavor of dates lingers at the back of Salome's tongue.

And here, crouched just before her, is Yeshua, filling his arms with the delicately flowering plants. When he stands, Salome can see that he is the same as he was the night before: the bruising at his eyes, the blood on his cheek. There are the bandages she wrapped around his hands and feet, there are his beautiful ribs, his paper-thin ears, the whorl of hair behind his ear, his large eyes, his curious stare. He is the same, except she knows with certainty that the man before her is no longer her son. He does not belong to her anymore.

Salome feels her bones weaken, feels her whole body sliding down to the earth, and the man before her, he drops his gathered blossoms and catches her up in his arms.

DISCUSSION GUIDE

1. Gospel means "good news." Discuss the title of the novel. Do you think Salome's story is ultimately "good news"? If so, for whom? If not, why not?

2. When Salome and Rufus are treating the seizing man in Rome, Salome has a moment of revelation about what she is called to do in her life. Have you ever had such a moment? If so, was it brought about by a moment of crisis or calm? Did you have a mentor like Rufus in your life at the time?

3. The political situation in 38 CE Alexandria features oppressive mandates, power-hungry leaders, and religious persecution. How does our current historical moment mirror Salome's? In what ways have we, as communities, nations, and individuals, changed for the better over the last 2000 years?

4. Just after Yeshua's birth and again on the banks of the Jordan river, Salome is forced to choose between motherhood and medicine. How and why does she choose differently in each moment? Have you ever had to sacrifice, downplay, or erase parts of your identity to pursue a calling or passion? What were the costs and benefits of doing so? What places or communities allow you to bring all the parts of yourself into them?

5. The *Gospel of Salome* offers portraits of Yeshua, Mari, and Joseph that are quite different from standard Christian interpretations. While you might not agree with Schwehn's imaginings, how did the novel invite you to question or reconsider the motivations, desires, and temperaments of these characters?

6. Mari is deeply engaged with spiritual concerns, Joseph finds solace in art, and Salome loves medicine. How does each character go about sharing their gifts with others? How open is each character to the other forms of knowing? How might staying siloed in a particular discipline or way of understanding create problems? When might it be necessary?

7. Salome knows that if she reveals her son's parentage publicly, Yeshua will likely sever her from his life for good. Sometimes, as parents, partners, and friends we love someone by doing something that might not, from the outside, look very much like love: stepping out of their lives, setting a difficult boundary, or stating a hard truth. Have you ever had to love someone in this way? What were the repercussions? Would you do the same thing again?

8. Salome ultimately helps Yeshua die. Do you think she was right to do so? Are there any circumstances in the modern era in which you believe it's morally acceptable to help someone die?

9. At the end of the novel, John Mark decides not to preach the Christian story of resurrection because the story of Exodus speaks to him more deeply. What teachings, stories, mantras, or bits of advice shape the way you live your life? Under what circumstances is it good to share these life-changing words with others and when can this sharing be problematic?

10. How did you understand the epilogue? Is it a dream? A vision of the afterlife? What does it mean that Salome knows in that moment that Yeshua is "no longer her son"?

AUTHOR'S NOTE

I have been a practicing Christian since birth, but I have always felt more comfortable asking questions than reciting creeds. However, throughout my life, whether I was a bored teenager or self-righteous young adult or distracted new parent, I loved the biblical stories: complicated, contradictory, difficult stories about women turning into pillars of salt and voices speaking from flaming bushes and angels gesturing in empty tombs.

The actual language of the Bible offers only faint outlines of the dramatic events; usually, we are not given motivations or intentions or regrets, the scents of synagogues or the dialogue spoken by minor characters. Part of my own faith has always been imagining my way into these stories, not because I think my own mind can fill in the truth of what happened, but because I long to live inside those moments in a way that the given language of the stories does not permit.

Writing this novel was not a quest for an alternate truth but a means to live inside questions: What relationships and intimacies did Jesus forsake to do his work as Messiah? What sacrifices does Christianity ask of us? How might religion steady us in times of crisis? Is it necessary to believe in the Resurrection to consider oneself a Christian? I don't think the Salome in this novel existed, but I hope that perhaps, like many of the noncanonical Gospels, her imagined story opens space for reengagement with the biblical stories.

Research was crucial to the writing. The only firsthand account of the Alexandrian riots of 38 CE comes from *In Flaccum* by Philo of Alexandria. While present-day historians still regard many of Philo's details as fact, many call aspects of his account into question (Sandra Gambetti's

The Alexandrian Riots of 38 CE and the Persecution of the Jews: A Historical Reconstruction is a great example). In general, I have remained faithful to much of Philo's account while taking some liberties with the order of events. It should also be noted that Roman Alexandria was divided into five districts (not four), each known by a letter of the Greek alphabet. Josephus claims the Jewish population was relegated to one district and other evidence points to Egyptians settling in the southwest part of the city and Romans occupying the palace district. That said, I have simplified the habitation of the districts as a way of clarifying the cultural tension that absolutely did exist between these communities.

Discovering the details of healing in ancient Rome was a true delight. I am indebted to many sources, perhaps most notably *Doctors and Diseases in the Roman Empire* by Ralph Jackson, *Ancient Medicine* by Vivian Nutton, "Rufus of Ephesus and the Patient's Perspective in Medicine" by Melinda Letts (British Journal for the History of Philosophy, Sept. 2014), and *Dioscorides: On Pharmacy and Medicine* by John M. Riddle.

For theological and historical insight on Jesus and Judaism, key sources included *Galilee in the Late Second Temple and Mishnaic Periods* by James Riley Strange and David A. Fiensy, *Excavating Jesus: Beneath the Stones, Behind the Texts* by John Dominic Crossan and Jonathan L. Reed, *Stone and Dung, Oil and Spit: Jewish Daily Life in the Time of Jesus* by Jodi Magness, *Documents for the Study of the Gospels* by David R. Cartlidge and David L. Dungan, *Jewish Women Philosophers of First-Century Alexandria: Philo's 'Therapeutae' Reconsidered* by Joan E. Taylor, *Early Judaism and its Modern Interpreters*, edited by Robert A. Kraft and George W. E. Nickelsburg, *Meals in Early Judaism: Social Formation at the Table*, edited by Susan Marks and Hal Taussig, and *Archaeology and the Galilean Jesus: A Re-examination of the Evidence* by Jonathan L. Reed.

I drew on a number of different sources to piece together the details of Salome's life in Rome, but perhaps most significantly *Augustus: The Life of Rome's First Emperor* by Anthony Everitt and *Peoples of the Roman*

World by Mary T. Boatwright. Mary Beard is, of course, always a font of wisdom and inspiration.

Midway through the writing of this book, I had a conversation with a Jewish friend who converted from Christianity. When I asked her about her decision, she explained that she's an Exodus person, not a Resurrection person; that is, the story that spoke to her most profoundly and that offered her the deepest sense of hope was the story of Moses, central to Jewish tradition, rather than the Easter story that resides at the center of Christian tradition. This conversation helped to shape John Mark's trajectory in the novel.

I don't think there's a right story or a right religion, but I do think that the stories we choose to tell and retell deeply affect who we become.

Reader, I hope you find stories, religious or secular, that challenge you and comfort you, that provoke brave action and invite quiet contemplation, stories that lift you up in the middle of chaos and remind you that you are worthy.

ACKNOWLEDGEMENTS

Thank you to Rebecca Makkai, author and literary community builder extraordinaire, for choosing this book for the Wildhouse Fiction Prize. I am so grateful for Wildhouse's mission and the folks who support it: Wesley Wildman (for vision), Ava O'Malley (for publicity magic), Melody Stanford Martin (for aesthetic genius), and, most of all, Rebecca Johns for her intuition, support, and sharp eye. Thank you for loving this book, Rebecca.

Thank you to Barbara Poelle, the best agent ever, whose belief in this book from the very beginning kept my own hope alive, even when the plot went horribly awry or the outside world encroached. Thank you to James Bock, for his kind support and astute suggestions.

Thank you to those who read drafts or portions of this book along the way and offered enthusiasm and honest critique: Anjali Sachdeva, Michael McGregor, and, of course, Supergroup (Jana Hiller, Kate Schultz, Sarah Hanley, Sean Beggs, Brian Rubin, Coralee Grebe, and Christine Brunkhorst).

Thank you to the Collegeville Institute for providing time and space to work on this novel at two critical junctures. Collegeville Dancing Writers: you brought the joy. Mary Potter: thank you for sharing your story.

Thank you to Hal Taussig for chatting about the Mareotic community and to my colleagues in the St. Olaf religion department for fielding random queries. Thank you to Emily Carroll for sending me medical papers on obscure subjects and responding to my absurd questions with thoughtful answers. Thank you to Cynthia Carau for writerly commiseration when I needed it most. Thank you to my colleagues and students in the St. Olaf English department. Thank you to Anne Groton and Clara Hardy for last minute help with Greek and Latin. Thank you to Jessica Peterson White and the incredible staff at Content Books for keeping our town stocked with good literature and Jellycats. Thank you to the myriad friends and family members who keep me sane and surround me with love and care—there are too many of you to name here, but I hope you know who you are.

I'm deeply grateful to the spiritual communities that have nurtured me, challenged me, and offered sanctuary for my questions: Bethel Lutheran Church, the Community of St. Martin, and Holden Village. Thank you to the many pastors in my life whose preaching and witness has consistently comforted the disturbed and disturbed the comfortable.

Most of all, deep love and gratitude to Peder Jothen. Thank you for exploring Rome and Jerusalem with me. Thank you for reading 432 drafts of this book, including the one in which Salome gives an enema to a hippo. Living with a writer isn't easy; you do so with unbelievable amounts of patience and grace.

Finally, Reader, I am filled with gratitude for you. Books wouldn't exist without you. Thank you for finding space in your busy life to imagine your way into this story.

ABOUT THE AUTHOR

Kaethe Schwehn's first book, *Tailings: A Memoir*, won the 2015 Minnesota Book Award for Creative Nonfiction and her chapbook of poems, *Tanka & Me*, was selected for the Mineral Point Chapbook Series. Her debut novel, *The Rending and the Nest* (Bloomsbury, 2018) received rave (and starred) reviews alike from outlets such as *Library Journal, Booklist, The Washington Post, Kirkus*, and more. She currently teaches at St. Olaf college in Minnesota, and is at work on her next novel.

www.ingramcontent.com/pod-product-compliance
Lightning Source LLC
LaVergne TN
LVHW040458111025
823270LV00042B/644